"Vampires, ancient evil, a centuries-[...] [f]orbidden romance? Montoya brings it all, and I am HER[E for] every second of it!" **Tracy Wolff, author of the Crave series**

+ + +

"Compelling, vivacious, and filled with heart. Montoya breathes fresh life into the vampire-and-vampire-hunter trope with a vivid world beautifully woven with Latinx lore and a romance both searing and tender." **Amélie Wen Zhao, author of the Song of the Last Kingdom duology**

+ + +

"A confident romp that is equal parts witty historical romance and captivating paranormal adventure. Montoya's signature blend of panache, humor, and heart makes *A Cruel Thirst* exactly the kind of Latinx vampire novel I wanted to read!" **Isabel Cañas, author of *Vampires of El Norte***

+ + +

"Angela Montoya has created a vampire myth that is inspired by Mexican lore but entirely her own. Readers will root for the fierce Carolina, who forges her own destiny and makes her own rules in this lush historical fantasy romance." **Zoraida Córdova, author of *The Inheritance of Orquídea Divina***

+ + +

"A magnificent take on vampire lore. Angela Montoya takes the classic trope of vampire × vampire hunter and breathes new life into it, in more ways than one. A must-read for fans of good books. Period." **Kamilah Cole, author of *So Let Them Burn* and *This Ends in Embers***

+ + +

"With action that will have you on the edge of your seat and banter that will leave you grinning, *A Cruel Thirst* has everything you could want in a paranormal romance." **Margie Fuston, author of *The Revenant Games***

A CRUEL THIRST

ANGELA MONTOYA

INK ROAD

First published in the UK in 2025 by Ink Road

INK ROAD is an imprint and trade mark of Black & White Publishing Ltd
Nautical House, 104 Commercial Street, Edinburgh EH6 6NF

A division of Bonnier Books UK
5th Floor, HYLO, 103–105 Bunhill Row, London, EC1Y 8LZ
Owned by Bonnier Books, Sveavägen 56, Stockholm, Sweden

Interior art used under license by shutterstock.com

This is a work of fiction. Names, places, events and incidents are either the products
of the author's imagination or used fictitiously. Any resemblance to actual persons,
living or dead, or actual events is purely coincidental.

A CIP catalogue record for this book is available from the British Library.

ISBN: 978 1 78530 801 7

1 3 5 7 9 10 8 6 4 2

Interior design by Michelle Gengaro and Ken Crossland
Printed and bound in Great Britain by Clays Ltd, Elcograf S.p.A.

FSC
www.fsc.org

MIX
Paper | Supporting
responsible forestry
FSC® C018072

www.blackandwhitepublishing.com

For wild-hearted daughters:
May you continue to give the world hell.

The FUENTES Family Tree

1562–Present

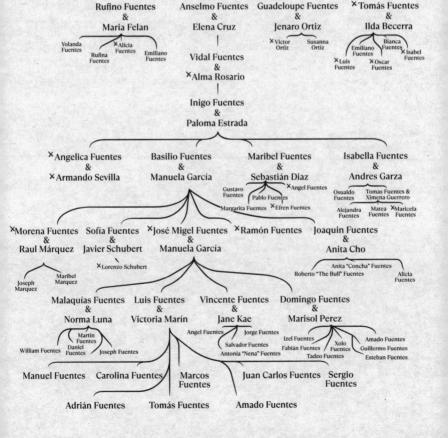

Basilio Fuentes & Catalina González

- **Rufino Fuentes & María Felan**
  - Yolanda Fuentes
  - Rufina Fuentes
  - ×Alicia Fuentes
  - Emiliano Fuentes
- **Anselmo Fuentes & Elena Cruz**
  - **Vidal Fuentes & ×Alma Rosario**
    - **Inigo Fuentes & Paloma Estrada**
- **Guadeloupe Fuentes & Jenaro Ortiz**
  - ×Victor Ortiz
  - Susanna Ortiz
- **×Tomás Fuentes & Ilda Becerra**
  - Emiliano Fuentes
  - Bianca Fuentes
  - ×Isabel Fuentes
  - ×Luis Fuentes
  - ×Oscar Fuentes

Inigo Fuentes & Paloma Estrada

- **×Angelica Fuentes & ×Armando Sevilla**
- **Basilio Fuentes & Manuela García**
- **Maribel Fuentes & Sebastián Diaz**
  - Gustavo Fuentes
  - Pablo Fuentes
  - ×Angel Fuentes
  - Margarita Fuentes
  - ×Efren Fuentes
- **Isabella Fuentes & Andres Garza**
  - Osualdo Fuentes
  - Tomas Fuentes & Ximena Guerrero
  - Alejandra Fuentes
  - Matea Fuentes
  - Maricela Fuentes

Basilio Fuentes & Manuela García

- **×Morena Fuentes & Raul Márquez**
  - Joseph Marquez
  - Maribel Marquez
- **Sofía Fuentes & Javier Schubert**
  - ×Lorenzo Schubert
- **×José Migel Fuentes & Manuela García**
- **×Ramón Fuentes**
- **Joaquin Fuentes & Anita Cho**
  - Roberto "The Bull" Fuentes
  - Anita "Concha" Fuentes
  - Alicia Fuentes

José Migel Fuentes & Manuela García

- **Malaquías Fuentes & Norma Luna**
  - William Fuentes
  - Daniel Fuentes
  - Martin Fuentes
  - Joseph Fuentes
- **Luis Fuentes & Victoria Marín**
- **Vincente Fuentes & Jane Kae**
  - Angel Fuentes
  - Jorge Fuentes
  - Salvador Fuentes
  - Antonia "Nena" Fuentes
- **Domingo Fuentes & Marisol Perez**
  - Izel Fuentes
  - Fabián Fuentes
  - Tadeo Fuentes
  - Xolo Fuentes
  - Amado Fuentes
  - Guillermo Fuentes
  - Esteban Fuentes

Manuel Fuentes   Carolina Fuentes   Marcos Fuentes   Juan Carlos Fuentes   Sergio Fuentes

Adrián Fuentes   Tomás Fuentes   Amado Fuentes

A CRUEL THIRST

Never trust the gods, for they do not wish us to live easily.

—Izel 6:13

CHAPTER 1

Lalo

LALO VILLALOBOS HATED MANY THINGS. LONG WALKS, CROWDED streets, unkempt suits, people. But one thing he hated above all else was his word not being taken seriously. Tonight, he would prove to everyone he was no fool.

The parchment in his hand shook like the remaining leaves on the trees rustling overhead. He stepped beneath the light of a lantern and eyed the paper once more to make certain he had read his handwriting correctly. He had, of course. He knew this location to be correct, but he couldn't quite let himself believe it. All this time, his parents' killer had been lurking close by.

He walked past this very building almost every day and never had a single suspicion that the monster dwelled within. Even in the moonlight, Lalo could see that the three-story structure was clean and well-kept with wrought-iron awnings and a black tiled roof. It looked perfectly ordinary within the bustling city of Los

Campos. Lalo and his sister, Fernanda, lived less than four streets away, in a townhouse constructed in a similar style.

In that very townhouse one year ago, he stood by his bedroom window and witnessed his parents being murdered under flickering streetlamps. He watched in paralyzing horror as a woman with auburn hair, pale skin, and delicate hands tore into their throats and left nothing but corpses behind.

Lalo shuddered and stuffed the paper into his pocket. As he did, his fingers grazed against the wooden stake he'd carved from the root of a willow tree. Vampiros couldn't stand the touch of tree roots. Lalo thought that fact extremely odd when he first learned it, until he understood the origins of their kind. They were born from a selfish human willing to make a deal with one of the gods of the underworld. Any person who had gone to religious instruction as a child would know these gods are tricksters. Deals with devils always came with a price.

Tecuani was the first god one met when they entered the Land of the Dead. He was the hunter of hearts. His lone purpose was to ensure a person was truly deceased before they moved past his domain and into their next trial in the Land of the Dead. Tecuani was there to make certain a person's heartbeat no longer thumped within their chest and that their soul was no longer connected to the Land of the Living. If he found someone with a pulse, he took on the form of a jaguar and chased them down. He clamped his fangs into their flesh and drained their blood until there was none left.

Tecuani was bound to the Forest of Souls, the initial stop for the newly departed. If he tried to move past the tree roots that stood as a barrier between the realm of the living and the dead without an invitation, they'd wrap around him in a tight grip.

Nor could he step foot inside the river that separated his domain and the Valley of Remembrances, or else risk being dragged down into the water's infinite depths by lost souls. It made sense that the vampiros he helped create would be weakened by the same elements, ones as harmless as wood and blessed water.

Lalo hoped that tale was true. Otherwise, he would be woefully helpless once he marched inside the building where he believed his parents' killer resided. Entering some place in search of a predator with no true plan of what to do after was a bad idea, but he needed to see the monster with his own eyes. Lalo needed to be sure she was the one he saw so clearly in his nightmares. Only then would he know for certain he hadn't gone mad like everyone in town seemed to believe.

In Lalo's nineteen years alive, he'd only been to a handful of balls. They were awkward and stuffy and every mother with an eligible daughter kept thrusting them at him as if he were a prince. He didn't like dancing, and he wasn't particularly fond of small talk, which made for an uncomfortable time. Lalo was happy to be alone, but Fernanda was like their parents. His younger sister enjoyed fun. Unfortunately, his going around Los Campos warning people about a woman with fangs and glowing eyes had put a damper on her invitations to events in the last year.

He chewed on his bottom lip as his eyes scoured over the building again. He would get revenge for Fernanda. And selfishly, Lalo wanted to prove everyone who laughed in his face wrong.

He stepped forward, hands shaking. According to the young man he overheard in the public library, the trick to obtaining entry into the secret cantina was to knock once, pause for four seconds, then knock three times in quick succession. He grabbed

3

the knocker and followed the instructions. His heart pounded as he waited. And waited. And waited.

Just when he thought he should try again, he heard the locks disengage. The door opened a crack. Thumping guitarróns and blaring trumpets poured out of the shadows but nothing more.

"Hello?" Lalo said, peering into the darkness. No one was there.

His brow furrowed, but he stepped through the threshold with caution. He slipped inside the doorway and jumped when the thick wood slammed shut behind him.

"Not the warmest of welcomes, I see," he whispered. Clearly, un vampiro didn't worry much over social norms like etiquette.

Slowly, he made his way down a dank corridor, following the music and laughter. He didn't dare brush against the walls because his jacket had only just come back from the cleaners and who knew what sort of messes monsters left behind. A few people littered the hallway, their arms wrapped around each other, their voices hushed as they whispered sweet nothings into their partner's ear.

He eased around them and entered a large room with wine-colored walls and an immense bar at the rear. It was a wonder he could see anything with so little candlelight and so much tobacco smoke in the air. His coat was doomed to go back to the cleaners now. The band played a riotous tune, and people writhed about. Lalo's eyes snapped back and forth. He prayed to whatever gods still listened that he didn't see anyone he knew. Though, he supposed they would have to explain their appearance in such a scandalous place too.

Lalo jolted. His breath caught in his throat. There, standing not twenty paces away from him, was the woman who terrorized his every nightmare and waking moment. Her long red hair was pulled into a chignon. A lacy gown stuck to her skin, showing off every sharp angle of her. And those eyes, her terrifying, horrible eyes were as red as before. He found himself frozen in place. He didn't even think he was breathing. *She was real.*

The woman slipped away, slithering toward a darkened corner. Lalo forced his legs to follow.

"Discúlpeme, por favor," he said as he bumped into a dancing couple.

"Excuse me," he offered as he attempted to pass a woman in a gown that had gone out of fashion long ago.

She turned to him, and Lalo had to hold in his gasp. Her pupils glowed in the low light like a cat's. But not with the golds or blues one might be accustomed to. This woman's eyes shone blood-red just like the killer he sought.

His already thundering heart tripled in speed.

Vampiro.

Lalo stumbled back, but the woman reached out and snatched him by the buttons of his shirt. She jerked his body toward hers.

"Your pulse is loud and strong, mi amor," she purred. One of her fingers slid up his neck. Lalo's innards coiled in disgust. "Are you here with someone?" she asked. "Are you claimed by one of my siblings?"

Siblings? There were more than two vampiros here?!

There hadn't been many police reports about attacks like his parents' that he could find. His research on humans who'd been murdered by people drinking their blood had brought him to findings from countries far from Abundancia and a single case from some tiny pueblo to the north two hundred years ago. Lalo had assumed his parents' killer was the only beast in the city

5

of Los Campos. And now, here he was, learning he'd walked into some sort of nest of them.

He needed to know more. He needed to understand what he was up against.

"I am here for the woman with red hair," he said.

The vampiro clutching him sniffed. "I do not smell Maricela on you."

She had a name. The beast who shattered his life had a name. For some reason, that made things worse. It made his nightmares feel real.

"I am going to her now," he said.

The woman hissed and released him. "You'll find Mother in her private room."

Mother?

Maricela was this creature's maker then.

Leave, the intelligent part of his brain urged. *Get away from this snake pit before it's too late.* And yet, his feet carried him on.

He had no clue where Maricela's private room was, but he didn't dare ask. He stumbled through the throng and winced when he noticed several other vampiros within the cantina. The eyes were a telltale sign, but there were other things too. They had an almost feline way of carrying themselves.

Two vampiros wearing matching suits danced with the guests. Another one was sitting at the bar, pretending to drink bourbon as the humans he was with knocked back shots with liquid the color of blood. Another vampiro was nuzzled up to a person's neck.

Horror roiled through Lalo. He understood why this place was called *The Den.* It was quite literally a lair for these beasts to feed upon innocent souls.

6

This was a job for officials, for the police, for the militia. Not one nineteen-year-old boy with a sensitive stomach. Alas, here he was, in the rear of the cantina, guided by resentment and curiosity.

He stepped into a hallway that smelled of spilled tequila. The music was still loud but grew muffled as the corridor cut to the right. Lalo stopped just before a door that was slightly ajar. Candles flickered from sconces on the papered walls.

Am I really going to do this? he asked himself.

What other choice did he have? Lalo hadn't known a moment of peace since that dreadful night. He was constantly peering over his shoulder. He didn't dare let his sister out of his sight if they had errands to run after sundown. Killing Maricela was the only way to end his suffering. He would not let another child become orphaned like him. He wanted to take down every vampiro in this cantina. Though, that sounded rather impossible, especially considering he'd never even been in a scuffle before. But if he had proof of at least one vampiro's existence, he could go back to the authorities. They would *have* to come to the cantina and exterminate the rest of the foul beasts themselves.

He stuck his hand into the inner pocket of his coat. His fingers wrapped around the wood he had painstakingly sharpened, and he tugged it free. *Time to end this now.*

"Searching for someone?" a sultry voice queried from behind.

Lalo spun around.

His eyes widened.

Maricela stood before him. Her posture was perfect. Her demeanor was refined. No one would believe such a poised woman capable of the terrors Lalo had seen her inflict. That was the way of un vampiro, he'd discovered. They disarmed their victims with false humanity. But there was nothing human about the woman before him. She was a predator, hunting for hearts to devour like Tecuani.

"Pray tell." She gestured toward the stake in Lalo's hand. "What do you plan on doing with that toothpick in your grasp?"

Lalo raised the weapon in question. He could only pray she didn't notice how much it quivered because of his shaking hand. "Do not come near me, fiend. This is willow root, and I know how to use it."

He didn't. Not in the slightest. The only semblance of a weapon he knew how to wield were the knives he used to slice through seasoned meat at the dinner table.

"What have I done to deserve such vitriol? To be called a *fiend* in my own home," she asked, smiling as if this were an amusing game to be played.

"You took my parents from me. You ruined my life."

"I've ruined many lives. That is how I stay so beautiful." She batted her lashes. "I'll offer you a bit of comfort, señor. If your parents looked anything like you, I'm certain they tasted divine."

Her tongue slithered over her front teeth, stopping at the fangs that had elongated to dangerously sharp points. His insides quaked. Why in the stars did he think coming here was a good idea? That had perhaps been the problem. He wasn't thinking and simply acted. He wasn't typically impulsive. Gods, if he died tonight, his sister would reach into his grave and throttle him.

That could not happen. He wouldn't allow Fernanda to live in this world with no family. With no one to care for her. She was only seventeen, and her prospects had stopped calling when he'd become the boy who cried vampiro.

Lalo lunged, thrusting his weapon toward Maricela's heart. The vampiro simply swatted his hand, and the stake thumped to the floor.

Maricela glared at him, a dangerous growl emanating from her throat.

He spun, trying to flee, realizing he'd made a grave mistake, but something hit him, and his back slammed against the wall. Bits of dust and plaster smattered over his hair and fell into his mouth. He coughed, but it was cut off by Maricela's palm, pressed into his chest. Her other hand shoved his head to the side, exposing his neck.

"No," he managed. He tried his best to fight her off, but she was like a statue, hard and unshakable. Vampiros were strongest after they drank human blood. Maricela must have had a feast because her skin was like marble.

She opened her maw.

"No," Lalo whispered. "No. No. No!"

Sharp fangs pierced into his flesh. The sudden shock of pain clogged the scream bubbling up his throat. Just as quickly as it came, the ache dissolved away, and Lalo couldn't feel anything from his shoulders to his toes.

Saliva, his mind screamed. *Her saliva is dulling your senses.*

Her teeth sank deeper, and his eyes rolled back.

Images of his life flashed before him. Holding his mother's hand as a boy. Clapping when his baby sister took her first steps. The joy of finding a good book. The heartache of being left to his own devices as his parents gallivanted about the city, bouncing to whichever gala or ball or exhibit was hosted by the most popular socialite that week. He saw the night they died. Saw Maricela's jaw clamping down upon his father's throat.

Lalo watched the memories of him trying to tell the officials what he had witnessed. They laughed him off. Told him to stay away from horror novels. He saw himself in the library day and night, searching for clues about what he had seen. Then he saw himself moments ago, speaking to the woman with the out-of-fashion gown. He heard his own thoughts, contemplating how he'd slay the vampiros within the cantina.

Maricela tore away from him. Her irises blazed molten red. "You came here to kill my children. You thought you'd harm my beloveds?"

"You took my family first!" he cried. "You are draining my life force as we speak! Shouldn't *I* be the one who's angry?"

She sneered. "I will make you pay for your insolence, Eduardo Villalobos."

Lalo's eyes widened. "How do you know my name?"

"Blood reveals all." She leaned forward, her lips brushing against his ear. "Now that I have tasted you, I know everything. I have seen your innermost thoughts. I know your dreams and nightmares. I could go on, but I won't because punishment awaits you. Perhaps I should start with that pretty sister of yours."

No. He had to get away. He had to get back to Fernanda. "If you let me go," he wheezed, "I'll never return. I promise."

A rumbling laugh emanated from Maricela. "You know too much. You have seen my home. My children. There must be consequences to your actions. You are a smart boy, you understand this, no?"

"Please . . . I cannot die."

She brushed a nail down his cheek. "You *will* die, Lalo. But fear not, your death won't come tonight. I want you to suffer first. I want you to feel what I feel."

"What? No ... please ..."

"We can be fiends together." She gripped him by the hair and dragged his body into the darkness. He screamed for help; he begged for mercy. Instead, he found agony.

Lalo stumbled down the cobblestone walkway in the middle of the night. Half tripping, half running home. He dug his trembling hand into his pocket, fumbling through lint and who-knew-what before he wrapped his blood-soaked fingers around the key. He tried to disengage the lock but winced.

Everything was so excruciatingly loud.

The key scraping against the metal mechanisms within the deadbolt. The babe crying five doors down. The damn moth bumping against the lantern glass above his head. Every sound burrowed into his skull and grated against his brain.

A rodent scuttled across the road to his right, and Lalo nearly jumped out of his skin.

"Shit," he whispered.

He rarely cursed, but he figured he was owed this vice after everything he'd just been through.

Closing his eyes, he forced his breathing to calm, his mind to stop racing. He needed to focus on one simple task: opening the door.

When he heard a soft click, he let loose a sigh. The familiar scents of his past and present kissed his senses. The tallow polishes his father used on his boots. The citrus soaps his sister loved but only because their mother loved them first. Lalo breathed in deep. He never thought he'd see home again.

He glanced over his shoulder, eyeing the empty road, before shutting the door behind him. He rested his head on the cool wood. His sticky fingers splayed over the frame etched with his and Fernanda's height measurements from a childhood that no longer seemed real. The room was blessedly dark, concealing his sins within the shadows.

"Get out of my house!" a familiar voice screamed.

Lalo had but a second to duck before a fire poker smashed into the wooden frame where his head had just been.

"Get out of my house, thief!" his sister shrieked, readying to clobber him.

"It's me!" Lalo yelled. "Fernanda, it's me!"

"Lalo?" She lowered her arms but kept a tight hold on the fire poker.

"Yes!" he replied.

Though there wasn't a single candle lit, Lalo could see his sister clearly. Her almond-shaped eyes, green like their mother's. Her small nose and angular face, similar to their father's. She and Lalo shared the same warm brown skin and slender builds but that was where their resemblances ended. She was always laughing and talking to anyone who passed by. He was rather moody and preferred the company of the characters in books over actual friends.

Surprise flickered over Fernanda's features. Then came relief. And next rage.

"Where have you been?" she asked, seething. "I haven't heard a single word from you in three days! I searched everywhere. The library. The courthouse. The church. Father's business. Nada. Where were you?"

Three days? Was that all? It had felt like a lifetime. Like *three* lifetimes.

"I have to tell you something, Fernanda, but promise to stay calm."

"That statement alone has my heart rate rising."

She wasn't lying. He could hear her pulse thumping against her neck. Could smell her blood rushing through her veins. His mouth watered.

"Oh gods," he said, feeling the bile climb up his throat. "I can't believe this is happening," he whispered.

"What, Lalo? What is happening? Tell me now, or I will thump you with this poker." She shook the metal bar in her hand for proof.

He didn't doubt she would. She once threw a boot at him when he didn't tell her who asked about her in the market fast enough.

"We must leave," he said. "Right now."

Her features twisted with confusion. "What?"

"I need you to pack whatever you can. Take our most valuable items. I'll send a note to Father's advisors that we are going on sabbatical, and I'll figure everything else out later. But right now, we must get out of Los Campos."

"Lalo, what happened? What did you do?"

His mouth went dry. "I went to the cantina I told you about," he admitted.

Fernanda's jaw dropped. "You cannot be serious."

"I wish I wasn't." Saints, what he wouldn't do to take the last few days back.

"Why are you so insistent on torturing yourself? Whoever or whatever killed Mother and Father is gone."

"She was there," he whispered. "I saw her with my own eyes. She was exactly the beast I remember. They are real, Fernanda. Fucking vampiros are *real*. And we need to get out of the city. Now."

Even though they were draped in darkness, Lalo could see his sister's face go pale. "Can't we go to the authorities? Perhaps the militia? Surely there is someone who will help us."

"There is no one who will save us now. Do you remember how I told you they need human life to survive? I was right. But it isn't solely the blood. It's the existence within it. The memories. The joy. The pain. The life. All of it. That monster bit me. She *saw* me through my blood. Every thought I've ever had. Every book and journal I've read. She knows everything. She saw my research. Our family. This house. She drank and drank, and I could do nothing to stop her until I was no more."

"What does that even mean?" Fernanda's voice was shrill.

"I am dead!" he yelled. "I died, Fernanda. That miserable beast killed me!"

"You aren't making any sense. You are alive, Lalo. I'm speaking with you right now."

"I have been turned, Fernanda. I'm a monster."

She shook her head. "That cannot be true. You seem fine."

Fernanda snatched up a matchbox from a nearby table.

"Don't!" he shouted. He couldn't let her see him like this.

His sister raised her brow and did as she wanted, like she always did. She struck the match and lit the candlewick. A small flame flickered to life. Lalo hissed at the sudden brightness and tucked his face behind his arm.

His sister gasped, and his heart sank.

"Your hands," she whispered. "Your clothes."

Lalo turned away from her and examined his arms. The

14

sleeves of his coat were torn to shreds. And his palms were still stained with blood and the mysterious inky gore that spilled from vampiros' veins.

"Whose blood is that?" Fernanda asked.

Hot tears filled his eyes. "Everyone's."

The horror of what had transpired filled his mind.

He woke with a start. He didn't know how or why or when he'd gotten there, but he was lying on an icy floor. His throat burned with this frantic sort of thirst. The desperation was like nothing he'd experienced before. He scrambled to his feet and ran up the stairs, only to be met by a barred door.

He wrapped his fingers around the metal bars and shook with his entire might.

"Help!" he had screamed.

A seductive laugh bounced off the stone walls and crashed into his skull. He grimaced at the sudden ringing in his ears.

"Can't you feel it?" Maricela asked. She stepped out of the shadows, her lean body draped in an emerald gown. "I still remember when I was turned by my maker." She breathed in deeply, as if the memory smelled of jasmine. "I was mad with need. My throat was on fire."

That was exactly how he felt. Like if he didn't douse himself with water, he would burst into flames.

She half grinned. "The only thing to quench that thirst was another's life."

He gripped his neck. "What have you done to me?"

"You should already know. You are an expert on my kind, are you not?"

Lalo's mind reeled. Maricela had bitten him. She'd drained the lifeblood right out of him and— His eyes bulged. He was going to be sick. "You forced me to drink your blood!"

But when he swallowed her blood, he saw bits and pieces of her memories, not her entire life like she had with him. He caught only small glimpses of her past. A mountain with jagged, spinelike ridges. A valley tucked away from the rest of the world. He saw other memories too. Thousands *of them. Other people's memories. Her victims, he realized. He was seeing her victims' lives. When un vampiro drank, they took their life force and time. Every ounce devoured counted for days stolen off their life. It seemed the more vibrant the life, the faster it was taken.*

She had turned him into the very thing he wanted to destroy.

"I will never drink a human's blood," he hissed.

"And I don't intend on letting you. Though, I suspect by the third day of being un sediento, you will be begging me to let you feed." The tip of Maricela's tongue toyed with one of her incisors. "I told you I wanted to see you suffer. And suffer you shall. Un vampiro who does not devour life suffers a fate worse than death."

His brows pinched.

"If we do not consume, our own bodies begin to turn on us. Your organs will devour you from the inside out. You will become a monster worse than I. I can assure you of that." She winked and turned her back to him.

"Where are you going?" he bellowed.

As she started to walk away, she said, "I have business to attend to. I'll come back in a few days just to listen to your screams."

She had been right. After the third day locked in the cantina's cellar, the thirst had become too great a burden for Lalo to bear. His veins, his intestines, his damn eye sockets felt as if they'd explode if he didn't consume life right then. And his screams continued to go unanswered. Everything was a blur after he gave in to his thirst. All he remembered was tearing the bars from the wall and sinking his teeth into the first body he saw.

Lalo gazed down at his bloodstained hands. "Maricela turned me. She made me un vampiro just to see me in pain. I couldn't stand the agony. I broke free, and I killed everyone in my path. Nothing could stop me."

Fernanda's eyes widened. "Holy shit."

"We have to leave," he said, starting for his room. "We've got to get away before Maricela returns and sees what I did to her children."

His pace quickened, but Fernanda didn't budge.

"Holy shit," she whispered.

Lalo slowed in the middle of the hall. "Come on, Fernanda. Hurry."

She shook her head slowly in disbelief. "Holy shit."

"Fernanda!"

Her gaze snapped to his and she gasped. "Your eyes are glowing in the light."

"Yes, I know. I'm a godsdamned vampiro, remember?"

She blinked. "And he cusses now, too! What has become of my poor, perfectly boring brother?"

"Now's not the time for jests. Let's go." He started forward but halted when his sister asked, "Can you fly?"

"What? No. Have you not listened to me talk about my research once during this entire year?"

She shuffled forward, the fire poker still in her grasp. "What about shape-shifting? I feel like I remember you saying something about that. Can you turn yourself into a bear or something?"

Lalo threw up his arms. "It's like you purposefully get the

facts wrong." He pinched the bridge of his nose. "Tecuani is the god of souls. He can be summoned to the Land of the Living and revive the deceased but at a great cost. I found the journals of a father in the southern country of Santemala who begged Tecuani to bring his young daughter back from the dead."

"That's so sad," Fernanda said.

"Indeed." But that wasn't the point his sister should be focusing on. "The girl rose to life, but she was different. She took on the traits of Tecuani. He is jaguar-like in every way. He is fast and strong and has exceptional hearing and sight during the night. The man's little girl no longer wished to play with toys but to hunt for human hearts. She wanted blood, specifically her father's blood because it was he who called forth Tecuani." Lalo turned to his sister. "Note that there was *no* mention of a bear in that explanation. I don't even know where you came up with such a thing."

A single brow raised on Fernanda's face. "You are telling me *you* are now like a jaguar?"

"Yes. To an extent. One that needs human blood to survive."

"So . . ." She crossed her arms. "No flying."

Lalo scoffed and stomped away.

"But where will we go?" his sister called after him. "We can run from that vampiress all we want, but what about you, Lalo? I might not listen much, but I do remember you saying when un vampiro feeds, it steals time from their victim. I know you. I know you'd never wish to do something like that."

She was right. He refused to steal another person's life.

So what was there to do? His eyes flicked to the small desk tucked away in the dining room. A year's worth of research on vampiros lay stacked inside the drawers.

There was one place he could go for help. One place that maybe, just maybe, might offer him a way to turn himself back. But it was a long shot.

"I found one case of vampiros in our country. It is from some two hundred years ago and there isn't much to go on, but traveling there to get more information is the best plan I have." He paced across the room and pulled open a drawer. Lalo riffled through parchment and articles he had copied word for word from the Los Campos library catacombs. Stealing the whole book would have been easier, but he had standards of decorum to uphold. A library was a sacred place, after all.

"There," he said, pointing at an old map.

Fernanda grabbed the candle and held it toward the parchment. She peered down. Her brow furrowed.

"Del Oro," she read out loud. "Where in the hells is that?"

"By my best calculations, it's three or four weeks' ride to the north."

Fernanda balked. "But you said she's seen your thoughts. Won't she know you might try and go there?"

A good point. "I'll tell Father's solicitor we are headed east for a long while. Surely word will get around town with us leaving so abruptly. And if Maricela knows my mind in the slightest, she'll assume I'd never be foolish enough to actually risk such an arduous journey north for something that might not even work."

"True. And you are, or *were*, quite averse to danger."

Something crashed just outside their window. Fernanda clamped a hand over her mouth to seal in her scream. They stood in stunned silence. Waiting. But Lalo could hear nothing over his sister's thundering heart. And he hated it. He hated himself for causing her even more distress. He'd been the one to hold Fernanda as she screamed for their parents. He had been the one to wipe her tears and braid her hair while she finished her final days of school. Lalo made a promise to himself that she'd never lose him.

And she wouldn't.

Nor would he let anything happen to her. He'd find a way to remedy this. To keep her safe.

He grabbed the map and the many notes he had taken since their parents' murders, then started stuffing them into his father's old satchel.

"Quickly, pack only what you can fit in one trunk," he ordered.

She nodded and turned for her room.

"Don't forget Mother's jewelry," he added. "And Father's pipe. We will have to barter them to pay for a coach on such short notice."

Fernanda stopped and glanced over her shoulder.

"What exactly is in Del Oro?" she asked.

Lalo sighed. "My only hope."

CHAPTER 2

Carolina

Del Oro

A CALLUSED HAND FASTENED OVER CAROLINA'S MOUTH. HER eyes shot open. The instincts she'd been honing since the age of ten flared to life. She slid her hand upward, reaching for the dagger hidden beneath her pillow, then stilled when she heard her nickname spoken in a feather-soft voice.

"Lina."

She squinted through the darkness. Blinked hard.

He was home. *Finally.*

Carolina's grandfather had been gone for over a week. Hunting the foul monster that had killed Señora Costas near the river that wove through the valley. La señora shouldn't have been out there. She shouldn't have left her home and family after the sun went down, but her husband was ill, and people believed she was desperate to bring him water from Orilla del Río.

The area was sacred, a long-retired cemetery from generations before that overlooked Del Oro. People still traversed the overgrown path to pray for their loved ones and, because of that, most believed the waters nearby were blessed by the dead. Going there had been a fatal decision.

Abuelo and his men had mounted their horses the moment her family said she was missing. Her body had been found, drained of blood. Carolina's abuelo and his men galloped toward the forest where the sedientos came from without hesitation. *Sedientos,* that was what the people of el pueblo had come to call them. The thirsty ones.

Since he was home, and waking her from sleep, that must mean they had found the vampiro and sliced into the fiend's heart as it deserved.

Carolina's eagerness could no longer be contained. She had to know about the hunt. Had to hear everything Abuelo did. *What did the sediento look like up close?* she wanted to ask. *Was it as frightening as the last one that had scaled over the thick walls surrounding el pueblo?*

There were varying kinds of monsters. Some looked perfectly human. Others slightly less so—their nails too long and sharp, their teeth too. But some sedientos looked like corpses escaped from the grave. They all shared two things in common, though: blood-red eyes that glowed in the dark when the light hit them just right and a wicked thirst for human life.

She started to speak, but Abuelo's hand was sealing her lips shut. Carolina raised a single dark brow. Her grandfather grinned. His graying mustache quirked upward like a second smile.

"Shh," he mouthed. He jerked his chin in the direction of

22

Carolina's slumbering cousin in the next bed over. Nena was rather unpleasant when roused too early from her beauty sleep. Even if that untimely awakening was due to their grandfather's return.

Abuelo's hand slipped away from Carolina's mouth, and he stepped back.

"Come," he whispered.

Eagerly, Carolina threw off her bedsheets, grabbed her boots, and tiptoed barefoot after him. Abuelo was a large man, tall and strapping, just like her papá. But Papá's footsteps could be heard from anywhere within the casa. He stomped about as if he carried the weight of the world on his shoulders and didn't care who took notice, whereas Abuelo moved here and there quiet as a tumbleweed. Carolina envied him for it. She wasn't so graceful. She'd often been likened to one of the newborn calves in their pastures. The ones that trampled over flowers and barreled through brambles just to get to their mothers. But she tried her best to move like her abuelo because she wanted to *be* like him. Patient. Nimble. Strong. Courageous. The best damn sediento hunter in Del Oro.

They slinked down the stairs and turned right, snaking their way through the long corridor toward the rear of the casa. The hand-painted tile was cool underfoot. All was quiet, save for the comforting sound of her great-uncle's snores coming from his bedroom nearby.

That was the thing when one lived in a great rancho with their family and their family's family—even in the silence, there was noise.

When they made it to the kitchen, Abuelo stopped before the exit.

"Boots on," he whispered.

She nodded, a smile burning her cheeks. She couldn't help it. Anytime Abuelo woke her up in the middle of the night, it was either to train or to teach her about weapons and how best to slay vampiros. This midnight meeting was something they started the day after Carolina turned ten.

Each of her five older brothers had started training to be hunters at that age. Carolina just assumed she would too. But when she ran outside into the courtyard to join her papá and hermanos, Papá had vehemently denied her.

"This is not your place," he had said simply and walked away. As if that was all the answer she needed.

Carolina had been destroyed. She idolized her father. She loved watching the people who guarded el pueblo ride and hunt for monsters. She pleaded with him to let her join the guard. But he silenced her with a stern look and sent her inside to help her mamá with the cooking. As she stomped through the hallway toward the kitchen, she decided she would prove him wrong.

Papá might have dismissed her, but Abuelo was never one to turn away his grandchildren.

"I have something for you," he whispered, breaking up her thoughts. "I'm sorry I missed your birthday."

She shook her head. "You had important work to do. And no one felt like celebrating when Señora Costas was taken so viciously and suddenly." El pueblo was small. Three hundred people lived within the town at most. Every loss was felt within the community because everyone knew and cared for each other as best they could.

"But you only turn eighteen once," Abuelo said. "I don't want you thinking I forgot about you, Lina."

24

Her heart warmed. "Did you bring me a new pistol?"

She used some old hunk of metal to practice her aim and only when storms came into the valley to conceal the blasts from her papá.

"Better than that," he said. "Now put your boots on before the rest of the house awakes."

Carolina squealed ever so slightly and shoved her feet into the worn-soft leathers.

He pushed open the back door and peeked outside. The sound of crickets chirping floated into the quiet kitchen. The cool autumn breeze caressed her cheeks, practically begging for her to step into the midnight air. She closed her eyes and sighed at the fresh scent of grass and earth. Of moisture still dripping from nearby leaves after yesterday's rain.

They weren't supposed to be outside the casa after sundown. No one in el pueblo usually risked stepping beyond the stuccoed walls of their homes for fear of exactly what had happened to Señora Costas. But Carolina was with her abuelo, who was the best vampiro hunter of the Fuenteses. And she could hold her own. She'd been throwing daggers into bullseyes and proficient with a rapier since she was twelve. Certainly better than her brothers Manuel and Sergio.

"The coast is clear." Abuelo winked. "Follow me."

They swept out of the great house and into the shadows. Warm light flickered from the torches that lined the fences. Carolina's home was an immense estate and the heart of Del Oro. If there was a funeral or fiesta to be had, it took place there. The Fuentes family had lived and worked the lands for generations, and they shared the fruits of their labor.

Every inch of the hacienda held memories for Carolina. There was the large marble fountain she and Nena sat in when the heat of summer became too great to bear. Next to the grain shed grew a scraggly bush, half-dead after she tumbled off the shed rooftop and fell onto it. The chicken coop, where she once hid for an entire day to avoid the wrath of her brothers and their friends after she had thrown rotten eggs at them, still stood. Each memory made her giggle or wince, but she loved them all equally, and she never wished to leave this place or let go of those feelings.

A cow mooed from one of the pastures beyond. Carolina's family's rancho spread for acres and acres on end. Stopping only at the stone walls that marked as a border between their lands and the forest. Raising cattle was their livelihood. No one in the entire country of Abundancia bred better steers than the Fuenteses. Even their family crest bore the image of a bull skull—a symbol of strength, determination, and honor.

She followed Abuelo through her mamá's prized garden and past the stables, which were large enough to hold an army's worth of horses. Not that an army would ever come so far north. The only guests Del Oro received were traders come to barter for leathers and the occasional drifter.

Carolina stopped suddenly when she rounded the back of the barn. Bales of hay had been set in various positions with wooden sticks jutting out of them at odd angles. A single box with a shiny bow practically gleamed from a wooden crate.

Abuelo grabbed it. "For my eldest granddaughter," he said, his voice full of pride. "Your abuela would be delighted to see the woman you've become. You have her same spunk, you know?"

She'd often been told how much she acted like her late grandmother, who she was named after. How they had a fierceness about them that was unrivaled, which made her immensely pleased. Because Carolina favored her grandfather's side, the Fuenteses, in every other way. She had their same stubborn nose and jaw. Their same pretty black hair and skin that browned in the sun. But she'd inherited their same temper too.

Smiling, Carolina took the gift her abuelo offered. Her brows pinched together. She tried to keep her expression neutral, but the box didn't hold the weight of a new pistol. Slowly, she removed the lid.

"A rope?" She met her grandfather's gaze.

He chuckled. "Do not look so offended, Lina. A reata is un vaquero's greatest ally."

"But I don't want to be a cowboy. I want to be a hunter. I want to elevate the Fuentes name in Abundancia." Mostly she wanted to show her papá how wrong he was for not believing in her. Being the best sediento hunter to live would surely do that.

"The kind of weapon doesn't bring us triumph, Lina. The ferocity of the person who wields it does. Believing in yourself and what you are capable of is sometimes enough on its own, no?"

She blinked down at the reata. "I don't think a rope is any match for a bullet regardless of who uses it. And it's far less fun."

"One does not kill sedientos for fun, Lina. We are here to protect humans, livestock, whatever lives and breathes within the great valley of Del Oro. We only pursue vampiros when those fiends pose a threat."

She laughed bitterly. "We just scattered Señora Costas's ashes! And last month four of Don Francisco's ranch hands were laid to waste. Two months before that, Lorenzo was taken from us. They weren't mere *threats*, Abuelito, they were assassinations. We should be going after those monsters, not waiting for them to come for us. We should find their home and burn it to the ground."

Abuelo's mustache twitched. "I used to think that too, but you will learn with age that some evil cannot be destroyed. Not without destroying some of the good we've built, too."

"What does that even mean?" she questioned.

He shifted his weight. "Do you want to learn how to use this lasso, or do you want to talk my head off all evening?"

Carolina smirked. "Can't I do both?"

"Not if you want to impress your papá and the other—" Abuelo's head snapped in the direction of the stables.

"What is it?" Carolina asked. She hadn't heard anything.

Abuelo held up a hand to silence her.

A horse whinnied. Her family's dogs began to bark from their shelter in the chicken yard.

Reaching for his rapier, Abuelo started forward. Carolina moved too.

"No," Abuelo said. "Go and get your papá. Hurry."

Carolina's pulse quickened. "What is it? A coyote? A skunk?"

"Go, Carolina," he hissed.

She flinched. Abuelo rarely, if ever, used her real name. Whatever it was, she had to tell her father quick. She started to run toward the main house, her gift still clutched tight to her chest. Something dashed through the shadows to the left of her. Carolina stumbled to a halt. She scrutinized the gardens but saw nothing.

A long howl rumbled through the air, and more dogs from el pueblo joined in. A warning that something terribly dangerous neared.

An icy gust tickled her skin. Her long hair fluttered ever so slightly. Chills rippled down her spine when she heard the crunch of dead leaves directly behind her. Slowly, Carolina turned toward the source of the noise. Standing before her in the shadows was a figure so disturbing her eyes prickled with tears.

The creature appeared almost human. But where there should be fingernails sat a bed of dagger-like claws. Where teeth should be sprouted elongated fangs. It was naked and slightly bent over as if it were in pain. In the moonlight, the monster's skin appeared ashen, practically blue. And the eyes. The pit in her stomach grew. Its eyes glowed blood-red.

Sediento, Carolina thought. One that has given in completely to its thirst, at that.

But how? How did un vampiro get through the hacienda walls?

Shit. She'd let her little brothers play in the chicken yard that afternoon. Had they left a side gate open?

The vampiro lunged forward so fast, she didn't have time to dive out of the way. Pointed claws dug into her shoulders. Carolina cried out. The agony was instant, the pain overwhelming. She tried to jerk herself free, but the sharp tips only dug deeper through her muscles and into bone. Carolina kicked out. Hitting the monster's shin with the point of her boot.

The sediento snarled. It opened its maw. Beads of inky saliva dripped down its chin.

Disgust roiled through her. And then rage took over.

This pinche prick won't best me on my own land!

She threw up her hands, smacking the vampiro in the jaw with the gift box that remained in her grasp. She swung again, landing another blow. The vampiro's claws burrowed deeper into her flesh. Carolina screamed in torment. But she did not stop hitting. She could not lose to the first beast she ever fought. Her father would never let her join the guard if she did. Most likely because she'd be dead.

A rope circled the sediento's neck. The monster flew back, hissing and snapping its teeth together, fighting against the leather braid holding it at bay.

Carolina's hands fell to her sides, horrible pain pulsed up and down her arms. Blood dripped onto the dirt. *Her* blood. And lots of it.

"Lina!" Abuelo roared. Her eyes snapped to just behind the vampiro, to where Abuelo stood, his prized reata wrapped tight around his right hand on one end and the sediento's throat on the other. Abuelo had saved her and not a moment too soon. He took out his rapier, made solely from obsidian, and pierced the snarling monster deep into its heart. The vampiro's eyes went wide, glowing a deep crimson, before the monster crumpled into a heap on the dirt.

Moonlight illuminated the sediento's face.

Carolina sucked in a breath as realization took hold. "Lorenzo?"

Her cousin had been only seventeen when he went missing months ago. His body had never been discovered. Carolina's great-aunt still held out hope that he would find his way home, but not like this. Not when bloodlust had completely overtaken him.

Abuelo raised his pistol, aiming right at Carolina's head.

Her eyes widened.

"Duck!" he yelled.

She dropped flat on her belly as a blast rung through the skies. Carolina whirled around in time to see a second sediento stumble. The monster grasped at its chest before toppling onto its back.

"Holy hells," she panted.

Abuelo knelt beside her. "We've got to cover your wounds.

The blood will draw more sanguijuelas in." He tore at the bottom of her nightdress. His fingers shook as he wrapped layers of cloth tightly around her limbs.

His focus shifted to something behind the barn.

"Lina." Abuelo's voice had gone stone-cold. He rose slowly. "Get ready."

Carolina turned her attention to where her grandfather stared. Five more monsters barreled toward them. She shoved herself to her feet as Abuelo fired his weapon. Hitting most of his marks but not all. He took down one. Two. Three.

The terrible click of an empty chamber sounded in her ears.

"You need to reload!" she shouted.

"Here!" he said. He threw his rapier toward her. She caught it by the hilt, gritting her teeth against the fiery pain pulsing in her shoulders.

"Two on the left," Abuelo said calmly as he pulled wooden bullets from his bandolier. "Four on our right."

Four?

Carolina spun to see. She wished she hadn't.

"Remember what I taught you, mija. You must pierce the blessed blade straight through its heart. It'll sever whatever ties the vampiro's spirit to the Land of the Living. If that won't do, cut off the head. But don't let those fangs touch you. Their bite dulls the senses."

Carolina nodded and readied her stance.

Abuelo pulled back the hammer and let the wooden bullets fly. One down. Two. Three.

He missed a shot as the fourth sediento leapt high into the air, dodging his fire.

Voices rang out from the hacienda. Footfalls pounded from

31

just beyond. Candlelight filled the windows. There were frantic shouts from men, someone yelling to get her papá, Don Luis. The alarm bells clanged in the tower. Papá would be furious. There hadn't been any sort of attack this close to their home in ages.

Abuelo pulled back the trigger. The monster that he'd missed let out a piercing screech when a bullet lodged into its chest.

But the other two vampiros had suddenly disappeared.

"Where are they?" she panted.

An icy draft slithered across the back of her neck. Without hesitation, Carolina wheeled around and slashed her rapier through the air. The blade slipped through stony flesh. Just enough to stun the vampiro. She thrust forward, as Abuelo had taught her, and found her mark deep within the monster's heart.

The blood-red eyes of the beast turned a dull brown. For a second, for a fraction of a moment, Carolina could swear she saw something human within. Sorrow. Relief. Regret. But then it fell to the earth flat on its face.

She grinned. She'd killed her very first sediento.

"I did it!" Carolina turned to see her grandfather's smiling face.

"Well done, Lina," he said.

Carolina's eyes widened. She screamed in horror as the last vampiro jumped onto Abuelo's back. Before she could gather her thoughts, before she could even act, the sediento sank its fangs deep into her abuelo's neck.

"No!" Carolina wailed.

Abuelo fell to his knees, his eyes rolling back into his head as the monster clamped down harder.

Carolina ran toward them. She thrashed her rapier over the monster's face. The vampiro jerked away from Abuelo with a bone-chilling hiss, tearing loose muscles and veins. She lunged forward and pierced the beast with her blade. A gargled cry escaped its gray lips before the sediento tumbled away.

Abuelo crumpled. Carolina slid in the dirt and caught him before his head hit the ground. His weight on her injured arms was too much, and she cradled him in her lap.

"Lina," he whispered, then coughed. "I . . ."

"Shh," she whispered, her shaking hand trying to stanch the heavy flow of blood. Her chin quivered. Hot tears pooled in her eyes.

"I'm sorry, Abuelito." Carolina tried to hold back her sobs. "I'm sorry."

"For what?" He coughed. "You had your first kill. And you are safe. That is what matters."

"No. *You* are what matters."

Abuelo groaned as he reached for something. "You must practice every day, Lina." He brought the reata, the reason they were outside, to his chest. "Show your papá what a great fighter you are."

Carolina shook her head. "*We* will show him, Abuelito. We will show him together."

Black dots filled Carolina's vision. Her fingers tingled with pinpricks like they'd fallen asleep. She had lost so much of her own blood. She could feel it caking over her skin, her nightdress. Her blood had spurred the other vampiros into a frenzy. Her mistake had brought them here in droves. She should have been better aware of her surroundings. She should have seen Lorenzo coming. No, not Lorenzo. She wouldn't let that thing have her cousin's name.

"Father!" Carolina's papá roared. "Father, no!"

Papá's large frame collapsed beside her. His dark eyes flicked from Carolina to his father, to Carolina again.

"Are you . . ?" His voice hitched.

"I'm fine." Her chin wobbled as she moved her hand to show her grandfather's gaping wound. "But he isn't."

Papá dropped his head. "Dammit," he whispered.

Wails of sorrow echoed around Carolina. Cries for her abuelo, Don José Miguel, rang through the growing dawn.

"What can we do, Apá?" Carolina asked her father. "Is there no way to save him?"

But she already knew the answer. Abuelo had lost too much blood. There was no way to mend the torn veins and flesh.

"You should not have been here!" Papá snapped. "What were you doing outside at this hour, Carolina?"

"I . . ." What right did he have to be furious with her? He had never believed in her abilities to fight, to hunt. But look what she had done. She'd killed a sediento. Two, actually. Abuelo believed in her. He was the only person that ever did. And now he was dying.

Abuelo's fingers wrapped around Carolina's wrist. "This isn't your fault."

"No," Papá whispered. He snatched the reata from Abuelo's chest and clenched it in his grasp. "It is yours, Father. May you find peace in the Land of the Dead knowing my Carolina might have joined you this day."

Papá pushed from the ground and shoved through their weeping family.

"Saddle your horses!" he roared to the men standing by. "We must secure the town!"

She watched him go. If she could at that moment, Carolina would have tackled her papá to the ground and boxed his ears for being so wretchedly heartless.

"Lina," Abuelo rasped.

34

Carolina's focus fell to his face. "I'm here."

A tear snaked down his temple. His lashes fluttered.

"Don't go," she whispered. "Please."

"I love you, mija."

Carolina sobbed. "I love you, too. I love you so very much, Abuelito."

A long exhale came from her grandfather. Carolina waited. Her gaze bore into him, begging for him to take another breath. But that inhale never came. His soul was no longer there. Carolina shut her eyes tight and said a prayer to the gods of the Land of the Dead as her family wailed to the heavens above.

"Be kind, Tecuani," she whispered. "Grant my abuelo passage through the Forest of Souls. Be gentle, Atzin. Grant my abuelo safe travels through the River of Sorrows. Be merciful, Itzmin. Grant my abuelo sure-footedness through the Valley of Remembrances. Be gracious, Tlali. Grant my abuelo steadfastness to move through the Desert of Iniquities. Be caring, Chipahua. Grant my abuelo strength to climb the Mountain of Retributions. Be understanding, Xipil. Grant my abuelo permission to enter the gates to el Cielo."

She saw her mother crying, her cousins, and the rest of her family that remained. She never wanted them to feel this pain again. And she knew Abuelo wouldn't either. Death would come for them all, but not at the hands of un vampiro.

"Don't you worry, Abuelito," Carolina said through her tears. "I will kill every last sediento if it is the last thing I do."

LOS CAMPOS PRESS

RENALDO ORTIZ   OCTOBER 8, 1646

WOMAN FOUND DRAINED OF BLOOD. SMALL PUEBLO PLAGUED BY FANGED BEASTS.

The quaint, desolate pueblo of Del Oro has been at the center of terrible tragedy as of late. A woman by the name of Alma Rosario ██████ was found drained of her blood after being missing for some time. Local priests detected brujería as the woman awoke from her grave and attacked mourners. One trustworthy source said she had fangs like a demon.

What do you think, dear readers?

Is she a demon? A witch? Or is some other sort of devilry at play?

CHAPTER 3

Lalo

Four Weeks Later

LALO AND FERNANDA HAD HURRIED ALONG BUMPY AND DESOLATE roads for one month and two days. It was a wonder he didn't have a crook in his neck from checking over his shoulder constantly, searching through the kicked-up dust for anything amiss. But so far, there was no sign of Maricela or any vampiros under her dominion.

The logistics of traveling so far northwest had been a nightmare. They had to hire cocheros that didn't mind driving their wagons hard through the night. And find carriages with thick curtains that didn't let in the sunlight.

There was no sun in the Land of the Dead. Souls moved easiest within cool shadows and so there was no need. Because of this, Tecuani, as powerful as he was, was weakened by the fierce rays of the sun. So too were the monsters he helped create. Lalo had read that vampiros who had recently been turned could withstand sunlight for a brief time because some of their humanity was still intact, but it wasn't a pleasant experience by any means.

On the fifth day of their voyage, Fernanda had stormed out of the inn they were tucked away in, itching and fuming over the bedbugs she'd found under the cot. Blaming Lalo for their misfortune, for everything bad in her life, as siblings who had to flee from vengeful vampiros sometimes did. He went after her, forgetting who and what he was, and found himself staring up at a cloudless sky. His flesh bubbled and burst with pus after mere minutes. His insides felt like they were being boiled. The pain was unspeakable. And the oozing blisters destroyed his perfectly pressed clothes.

From his research, Lalo knew he could heal himself quickly by feeding on human blood. But he refused. He couldn't stand the thought of seeing another person's intimate thoughts, of slithering through their memories as well as stealing away their life. So he tried his best to hunt whatever animals he could on the way—healing just took much longer. But not taking in the sustenance truly required made his skin feel clammy and his bones brittle.

"Why do you appear so miserable?" Fernanda had asked on a particularly long stretch of barren road. She sat up. "Are you still thirsty?"

Lalo rested his burning forehead on the cool windowpane. "Terribly. Wretchedly. Unbearably so."

"But you just caught a rabbit."

He winced. He would rather not be reminded.

"I need human blood to feel full, Fernanda. That is how this works. I've told you this a dozen times." Fernanda's attention span rarely lasted long. And where her brother was concerned, it seemed to be even shorter. Lalo sighed. "If sedientos don't consume human life eventually, we start truly dying. And dying hurts like hell."

"Then you must find a human who is willing to . . ."

"No," he said firmly. "When we consume human blood, we take time from their life, remember? Every ounce I drink could steal days or weeks from them, and I won't do it."

His ears still rang from the shrieks of those he had attacked in the cantina when the bloodlust grew too strong. He could taste the humans' fear and hear the hissing of vampiros as they tried to fend him off. It made him sick. And yet, he was desperate for more. The thirst coiling around his veins was like a parasite squirming inside him. Clawing at his senses. Burning his throat. Urging him to give in. He couldn't let that happen. He knew if he did, he might be lost to his sister forever.

But feeding on animals would not suffice for long. By Lalo's calculations and from the scribblings of another vampiro who resisted the thirst, he gave himself less than a month before his body gave out and he became the true monster Maricela had warned him of.

He turned away from Fernanda and glared out the small window. His spine straightened. Through the intermittent breaks between the trees, he could see a vast valley. Small adobe homes littered the open space, warm light glowing from their windows. At the center of the valley, sprouted un pueblo of squat buildings with a few larger structures. A church was one, most likely. The town hall. Perhaps a school. His brow furrowed. The entire pueblo was encircled by a tall barrier made of thick stone.

The carriage bumped over a rough patch, causing the siblings to jostle back and forth. Lalo was about to complain, but Fernanda gasped.

She jerked the curtain open farther. "Is that Del Oro?"

Del Oro, the town where Alma Rosario had been found dead centuries ago. Her murder was the first of its kind in Abundancia as far as Lalo could tell. It was by pure luck that he'd discovered her obituary in the library catacombs, since those records weren't often kept back then. And it was only there because the poor woman's death had been featured in a paper that highlighted conspiracy theories and tales of the macabre.

Woman found drained of blood, the article stated. *Small pueblo plagued by fanged beasts.*

The next editorial in the paper was about little creatures that stole away people's teeth. Lalo imagined not too many scholars read that sort of fluff. But he had been desperate to understand the monster who had taken his parents from him. He needed to prove to everyone that he hadn't simply been in shock, as the officials claimed.

Fernanda crossed her arms. "El pueblo is tiny. What do people even do here?"

"Sí. It is much quainter than what we are used to." Their home city of Los Campos was a lively place full of the very rich and the very poor. Lalo and his sister had grown up with anything a person could want—meat at every meal, the best private schools one could afford, new shoes the second the heels of the last got scuffed. Their parents may not have offered all the love a child needed, but they had tried their best to make up for it in possessions. Not that Lalo needed much. Books, tailored

40

suits, a trip to the barber once a week. Sometimes twice, if they hadn't trimmed his hair to his liking. He was a simple man, in his opinion.

Fernanda squinted. "Why is Del Oro so heavily guarded?"

Lalo peeked out the window. Along with the border wall, at one entrance, sat two people mounted on horses.

He scanned through his memories of the little information he had been able to glean about the town. Del Oro was founded in the late 1500s by the Fuentes family. They were haciendados mostly, running ranchos and trading with pueblos and marketers nearby.

"One article claimed that el pueblo was nearly decimated by fanged beasts. But that was generations in the past. Certainly that couldn't be why the wall around the main hub of the town was built. Perhaps it's meant to keep out bandidos," he offered. Since the current mayor, Señor Luis Fuentes, had taken office, reports of "animal" attacks had decreased. There was no official statement about vampiros in any article Lalo found, but he understood what an "animal" attack might mean. That had been exactly what the officers in Los Campos had called his parents' slayings.

The carriage shuddered as the wooden wheels moved from dirt to stone. The only home he could rent on such short notice with a hint of privacy was at the top of a hill that overlooked the town. At the edge of the forest, it had not been lived in for many years because the tenants had gone missing. But the woman who brokered the lease agreement assured Lalo it was still "livable." Whatever that meant.

Fernanda smirked as she entered Lalo's quarters. "You couldn't help yourself, could you?"

His new room was immaculate. Everything was in order. Just the way he preferred it.

"I was bored," he said in his preferred monotone fashion.

Fernanda snorted. "Only you would try to cure boredom by dusting books."

"They aren't just any books. They are the possible key to my salvation." He had snuck in a few of his favorite novels as well. Lalo knew he shouldn't waste any extra space inside the trunk he brought when they fled, but he couldn't help it. He didn't have the heart to leave everything he loved behind.

"Have you found anything new?" she asked, hope dancing in her eyes.

Fernanda had gone into town to purchase supplies and see if she could learn anything useful about the pueblo. She'd come back with some texts she said were about the town history from the tiny library that also stood as the courier office.

"Nope." He flicked one of the borrowed books shut. "There wasn't a single sentence about vampiros inside these."

She shrugged. "It was the best I could find. The woman at the counter kept making the sign of protection when I walked in. People are absolutely aghast that we're renting a home so far outside the walls. One asked if we had a death wish like the Alicantes who built the home."

He rubbed a hand over his face. "Did you ask why they have barriers surrounding el pueblo?"

"Unfortunately not. I was too busy making eyes at the most beautiful girl walking by." Fernanda swept past Lalo and plopped onto his perfectly made bed. She glanced around, her brows quirked with displeasure. "It is a tomb in here."

His intestines grumbled, desperate for blood. If he didn't feed soon, he might lose whatever control he had.

Everything was beginning to feel like the constant thrusting of penknives into him. Breathing. Walking. Thinking.

Fernanda truly observed him for the first time since she had entered his quarters. "You're going blue around the lips."

Consuming one's life force kept a sediento looking nearly identical to how they were before being turned. Not consuming made them appear as if they were living corpses. Their organs started failing. Their skin went ashen. Their bodies quite literally began feeding on themselves. But he'd rather shrivel into a worm than feed off another human.

"You need nourishment, brother. I'm sorry the butcher hasn't provided what we asked of him yet."

Lalo dropped his gaze to the floor, the shame and wretchedness of that truth overwhelming him.

"What will you do?" Fernanda asked.

"About finding clues on how to turn myself back into a human before it's too late?"

"No, you blockhead. About feeding. There will be nothing to turn back into if you don't eat."

Dread seeped into Lalo's body. He sighed heavily and turned away from his book.

"I will have to hunt down a deer or something." A small rabbit wouldn't suffice.

His life in the city had never given him cause to hunt. Even when the other menfolk went on holiday in the country, he preferred to stay back and read or review his father's business ledgers. He didn't even know how to properly ride a horse. Sure, he could dress the part well enough, but he never had the need to go faster than an unconcerned trot.

"Do you want company?" Fernanda asked.

"I'd rather hate myself in private, thank you very much."

Fernanda's gaze held his, and he hated the pity he read there. She'd give him that look whenever he declined an invitation to a ball or charity event. As if staying away from social activities because he didn't like them was the very sorriest of things. At least now her sympathetic glances had a good reason behind them, he supposed.

"The sun is setting," she said. "You should probably go."

He rose from his chair, grabbed his cloak, and pulled the hood over his head. "No need to wait up for me, sister. I have no idea how long I will be."

He was incredibly fast, due to the power of Tecuani thrumming inside him. And his senses were extravagantly heightened. But that didn't guarantee a kill. Half the time, he simply couldn't force himself to take the life of whatever creature he had caught. He'd eaten meat all his life but that didn't mean he wanted to be the one doing the butchering.

"Oh, I'm sure I'll be up," Fernanda said, suddenly smiling. "I'm going to go back in town tomorrow to make friends. Perhaps they can help us find more clues about this Alma woman you mentioned. If she truly is the first victim on record in Abundancia, surely these people should know something about her. I must pick out the perfect dress to wear for such an occasion. Do you think the young people here know the latest fashions?"

His fingers shook as he fastened the button on his cloak. "I'm certain they do."

"That is good at least." Fernanda stood. "Best of luck, brother."

Lalo grunted and watched his sister flutter away. He was glad Fernanda was here to help him. She really was a sociable sort, more than he'd ever been. But would they be safe here? Even so far from the city they fled. If he made the expedition to Del Oro, Maricela certainly could.

He shuddered before stuffing that thought away. Best to worry over one thing at a time. At present Lalo's insides were churning. He had to find some animal and feed, or he'd never have a chance to turn himself back like he so desperately wished he could.

Sighing, he left his room and started down the hallway. He could only pray he wouldn't get sick while feeding and ruin his clean boots. Again.

CHAPTER 4

Carolina

When the house had finally gone quiet and her cousin Nena was tucked deep into her blankets snoring gently, Carolina slinked out of her bed and crept to the loose floorboard under her vanity. She snuck a glance at her door, but it was shut; only the soft glow of the sconces could be seen from underneath. Biting her lip, she dug her nails into the panel and pried a slat of wood back.

There, in the dust and darkness, was the clothing she often used when training with her abuelo. A loose black blouse, thick gloves, and—she smirked—pants. She grabbed the obsidian throwing daggers she used in practice and set them beside her. The black stone was the only thing besides wood taken from the roots of trees that could make a death blow because of its natural wards against evil. Then she pulled out the reata Abuelo had given her and placed it on her lap. She'd found it in the trash bin after her papá had taken it away. Carolina rubbed her thumb over the braided strips of leather.

"I miss you, Abuelito," she whispered. "You were the only one to ever truly believe in me. I won't let your death be in vain." Carolina had not forgotten her promise to her grandfather the night he was slain. She'd never let her family hurt like that again. She would kill every sediento she could. And she'd do it with or without her papá's approval.

She took the garments and weapons and slid the floorboard back in place.

Carolina stripped off her nightgown and prepared in silence.

When her boots were laced, she stood and eyed herself in the looking glass. If Abuelo could see her now. Her mouth went dry at the thought. There was no one in the world who would be prouder of her. Certainly not her papá. But her actions tonight might change his mind and everyone else's in this pueblo. She'd find a sediento, slay it, and bring its fangs back as evidence of her kill. She'd show them she was as good a hunter as anyone in her father's guard.

Heart thundering, she placed a mask she'd cut from an old cape over her face. She didn't want to get caught and snitched on before she even made it out of the hacienda. She figured it'd be best to stay concealed until she wanted to make herself known.

She tugged on her flat-brimmed hat and grinned. In this outfit, she no longer looked like the prim and proper daughter of the mayor. She dressed like a monster hunter. Though she'd never seen a hunter with such temptingly round hips. She winked approvingly at her reflection.

"What in the stars?"

Carolina whirled around. Her cousin Nena had woken up, her mass of dark curls falling into her eyes. Nena shoved them back and scrambled onto her elbows. "Carolina?"

"Um . . ." Carolina tore the hat and mask from her head and attempted to conceal them behind her back.

Nena snorted. "There's no use trying to hide now. I already saw you done up like some masked vigilante." She cackled, the sound like a gun blast within the sleeping casa.

"Quiet!" Carolina grabbed a pillow from her bed and chucked it at Nena. It bounced off Nena's face and landed on her lap.

"Hey!" Nena protested.

Carolina rushed to Nena's bedside and knelt before her. "You must not tell a soul about this."

"About what? What *is* this?" Nena gestured toward Carolina. "Is the fiesta we're having tomorrow evening for Abuelo meant to be a costume party?"

"No. I . . ." Carolina chewed on her lip for a moment. "Nena, you must promise to keep a secret."

Now Nena's attention was truly sparked. "What sort of secret? Why are you dressed like this? Are you planning on sneaking out?" She gasped. "Is it about a boy? Or a girl?" Nena's thick brows wiggled. "Have you kissed yet?"

Carolina shook her head. "This isn't about kissing, Nena. *Saints.*"

Nena's jaw dropped in shock. "Did you do something *more* than kissing?"

Her cousin was thoroughly awake now and sitting up. Her hands rested on the pillow; her nightdress hung loose over one shoulder. Nena was the prettiest girl in el pueblo by far. She was curvy and had dark brown skin that always smelled of citrus and vanilla. She was only three months younger than Carolina, but they lived vastly different lives.

Antonina Fuentes was free to do whatever she pleased because the things she loved most—dancing, flirting, sewing, and donning beautiful dresses—fit into what her parents expected of her. Nena would happily marry a suitor of their family's choice because marriage meant she could finally travel away from Del Oro. That was perfectly wonderful for her, but it wasn't what Carolina wanted in life. She didn't care about shopping or capturing the attention of gentlemen. What Carolina wanted was to hunt. And not for this season's most coveted lace.

"What is the secret you wish me to keep?" Nena queried. "So long as it isn't something that will put you in danger, I am ready."

"Well ... about that ..."

Carolina slowed her stallion as they came to the entrance of the forest. The usual sounds of midnight greeted her—crickets, leaves shuffling in the breeze, water flowing from a stream nearby. But she would not let the normalcy trick her. Nor would she let the thrum of fear in her mind turn her away now. She had never been so far from el pueblo. Not once in all her eighteen years. She wouldn't let her own trepidation ruin this moment.

"This is the worst idea you've ever had," Nena said.

"Hush," Carolina whispered. "Do you want the entire world to hear us?"

She wouldn't let Nena ruin this moment either.

"What world?" Nena replied. She had put a mask over her face as well, but there was no denying who she was. Her figure alone would give her away to anyone from their town. And Nena had never been shy about that.

Nena searched left and right. "The only people I see are the two fools right here." She gestured at the two of them.

Carolina rolled her eyes. "No one asked you to come."

"What did you expect me to do when you told me what you were up to? Just nod my head and say *best of luck*? You're my cousin, I must look out for you."

"You're younger than me. *I'm* supposed to be looking after you." Nena fluffed her curls. "But I am far more mature."

Carolina scoffed. Nena scoffed in return.

After a moment, Nena said, "I think you forget sometimes that he was my abuelo, too."

This gave Carolina pause.

"Everyone is hurting, Carolina. Even your father. But is sneaking out to prove you're some warrior worth risking your life?"

Carolina took a deep breath. "I know you think I'm mad for wanting to stalk vampiros." She eyed her cousin. Waited for Nena to deny it, but in true Nena fashion, she pursed her lips and nodded. A small laugh escaped Carolina. "But Abuelo trained me well, Nena. I can shoot and ride better than any of my brothers. Yet, because I am the daughter of Luis Fuentes, I must sit quietly and look pretty."

"There is nothing wrong with looking pretty," Nena said.

"I know." Carolina certainly didn't mind when people complimented her appearance. She quite liked her high cheekbones and arching brows and the way her lips curved into a pout. But she didn't want to just be some person's dutiful wife. She wished for the wind to run through her hair. She wished for sedientos to see her and retreat in fear.

"You want to be beautiful and have dirt under your nails," Nena offered.

"I suppose I do."

"Then I shall get my hands dirty too. Unfortunately." She said that last part under her breath.

"You should go back, Nena. You've never wanted to fight." Carolina had asked Nena to join her with Abuelo once. Nena had laughed in her face and went back to her puzzle. "This will be dangerous, and you don't know how to wield a weapon."

"Then what is this?" Nena reached into the bag strapped to her horse's saddle. She pulled out a cast-iron pan.

Carolina sighed. "*That* is what you brought? Not any of the dozens of sharp knives in the kitchen?"

"This thing is heavy. I'll hit the monster. You stab it through. Piece of cake."

Carolina had half a mind to turn around and go home. She shouldn't have let Nena come. The forest wasn't a safe place for her. Nena hadn't exactly given her a choice, though. She threatened to tell their nanny the second Carolina left without her. A dirty threat. Something Carolina most certainly would have done if the roles were reversed. And if she wanted to bring back her kill and present it at the fiesta to show everyone what she had done, she might not be able to do it on her own.

"All right," she said. "Let's go. Stay right behind me."

Carolina slipped off her horse just outside the woods the sedientos always came from. She wanted to slither about like the monsters she'd come to slay, and it would be much easier on foot. She tied her stallion, Guapo, to a boulder and helped Nena do the same with her mare, Luna. Carolina adjusted her belt laden with her reata and daggers. She'd also stolen a machete from the barn. The time had come to prove her worth as a Fuentes and as a fighter.

She shoved a thorny branch out of her way and entered the woods. A dankness clung to the air. The branches above stretched like skeletal fingers, blocking out the moonlight. Even the vegetation felt menacing. She understood why, locally, the forest had been named Boca de la Muerte—Death's Mouth. It was like a flytrap. Everything within the woods seemed as lethal as the next. And with sunlight unable to seep in during the day, it was no wonder vampiros considered this place to be home.

She pulled the machete from its place on her hip and offered it to Nena. Her cousin shook her head and raised her pan. Carolina clamped her lips shut to hold back her laugh. Nena had a way of making her giggle during the worst of times. Whenever Carolina got in trouble, which was often, she could never risk meeting Nena's eyes. The last time she had, Carolina burst into a fit of hysterics, incensing her papá. Carolina had been forced to pull weeds and dried-up leaves from Mamá's garden until the entire plot was clean. Her back ached for days and Nena didn't even come outside to help. In fact, she made faces at Carolina from their bedroom window. The wretch.

The girls wove deeper into the trees. Taking slow, methodical steps forward, Carolina felt before her with her free hand. Her fingers slid against rough bark and thorny brush. Her boots treaded on a bed of pine needles until they came upon hard-packed earth.

"I've found a game trail," she whispered. All sorts of animals used it to get to the creek just east of where she stood.

"What's that?" Nena asked quietly. She pointed at something dangling from a branch ahead.

Carolina plucked it off and rubbed her thumb against what appeared to be a bit of torn cloth.

Nena grabbed the scrap of fabric and sniffed. "It smells like the citrus soap the merchants bring in from the ciudades. Saints, I can't wait to marry so I can travel all about Abundancia. I'll go to every dress shop I see."

"Why would this be here?" Carolina whispered to herself, ignoring her cousin. "And more importantly, why is the smell so fresh?" Her brow furrowed. "Perhaps it's from a bandito. Or . . . what if this fabric belongs to a vampiro's next meal? Have we had any traders come to town this week? A member of their party could have gone missing."

Nena shook her head. "They aren't expected to arrive for a few more days."

A muffled cry sounded through the brush ahead. Both girls stared at each other, mouths agape.

"What do we do?" Nena whispered.

"Someone's life is most likely in danger. Let's go."

She slipped the cloth and machete into her belt holster and ran up the path as fast as she could. Carolina kept her ears perked, her eyes wide.

Another strange noise stopped her in her tracks. Nena bumped hard into her back. She stumbled forward but caught herself before falling.

She heard slurping. Then a moan, followed by a gag.

Carolina's muscles tensed. Whatever it was, it was feeding on something.

She crept behind a thick oak and peered around the tree.

A figure sporting an elegant cloak hovered over some sort of body. The copper tang of blood tainted the air. Carolina squinted, hoping to get a better view through the darkness.

The figure shifted, and she could see the prone body on the forest floor was that of a buck. Two gaping holes lay open on the animal's neck and blood oozed out. Carolina's nails dug into the bark of the tree.

The monster let out a guttural groan.

Her hands itched to sink a stake into the fiend's heart.

"Stay here," she mouthed to Nena.

Nena gripped her cast-iron pan harder and nodded once.

Holding her breath to quiet her pounding heart, Carolina slithered around the trees. A twig snapped underfoot. *Shit.* The creature's head shot up, its spine going straight. It turned in her direction, slowly.

Carolina didn't waste a second. She sprinted forward, readying the machete. Her body slammed into the monster's. She used her entire weight and strength to tackle it to the ground. The sediento didn't fight back, didn't even lift a hand to protect itself. It simply huffed a dramatic breath as they crashed into the earth.

Carolina was on top of the sediento at once, her machete to its neck.

The hood of the cloak fell from its face, and she had to hold in her gasp of surprise. The sediento was a young man, maybe even the same age as her. And he was ... *handsome.* So much so, her heart gave in to a little flutter.

The wretch had a well-kept mustache, like the young men she'd seen in Nena's socialite papers. He was utterly human-looking and more beautiful than any boy she'd ever witnessed before. *A waste.*

With a growl, she dug her blade into the soft flesh of his throat. A tiny squeak escaped his lips. His fingers wrapped around her wrist with his beastly strength. He jerked her body off him, and she tumbled into the dirt.

"Oh no," he said. "I didn't mean to . . ."

Carolina smacked into the trunk of a tree, her teeth rattling in her skull. The sediento was to his feet in an instant, moving toward her. He was tall and slender but with wide shoulders that spoke of strength. *Well, she was strong too.*

She readied her weapon, ignoring the pulsing headache blurring her vision. "Enjoy these moments, bloodsucker," she spat. "For they will be your last."

The boy put his hands up in surrender.

"I—I didn't mean to throw you like that," he stuttered. His voice was smooth as silk. Shock ran through her. She'd never heard one of them speak. "I promise," he said, inching closer to her. "I mean you no . . ."

Nena ran from her hiding place, screeching like a mother hen. She raised the pan and cracked the vampiro hard across the face. The sediento staggered, his hands going to his cheek.

"Hells below!" he bellowed.

He was calling to the other devils, beckoning them to assist him. "Not on my watch," Carolina growled.

She scrambled to her feet and swung the machete at the sediento. His eyes went wide with disbelief, but he skittered away just in time.

"Wait!" he shouted.

She swung again and again. Each time, he dodged her

advances. She snarled with frustration. Her arms were already tiring. She hadn't fully healed from the attack a month ago, the attack where her abuelo had been viciously cut down.

Fiery rage burned within her at the thought.

"You will die this night," she snarled, grabbing her rope.

"But . . . I'm already dead."

"Do not mock me you . . . you . . ." *What word was worse than "life-sucking prick"?*

"Deplorable demon?" he suggested.

"Do not finish my sentences, you deplorable demon!"

"I will happily stop, when you cease trying to murder me!" He ducked, and her lasso missed its mark.

"Never!" She flicked her wrist and this time the reata found its home, wrapping around his waist. His mouth fell open. Digging her heels into the dirt, she yanked so hard, he lost his footing and dropped to all fours.

"Señorita, please . . . if you would just . . ."

Stars above, he was attractive. She'd never seen any magazines or weeklies with a face so fine. He wasn't a *he*. She had to remind herself. He was an *it*. An abomination. A thing to be destroyed. But it was rather hard when he was so striking.

"What are you waiting for?" Nena yelled. "Kill him already!"

"Shut up, Nena!" Carolina held her dagger to him. "Your death will be slow and vicious," she said to the sediento.

His eyes bulged. "These lands are free to hunt, are they not? I saw no signs saying otherwise. I have done nothing wrong."

She laughed bitterly. "Your very existence is wrong, devil."

A muscle in his strong jaw flexed. Her traitorous knees weakened at the sight. And in that moment, in that wretched second of distraction, the sediento spun around and ran. He pulled the rope out of her hand, sending her toppling into the dirt once more.

"Bastard!" she screamed.

Carolina flung the knife. The gleaming blade flipped through the air and sank into a tree just as the sediento dipped low.

She hit the ground with her palm. "Dammit!" Carolina climbed to her feet and gave chase. She burst through the brush but he wasn't there.

"What the hell?"

Fingers clenched her shoulders from seemingly out of nowhere, pushing her against a large tree. The sediento's hands were strong on her arms but not in a crushing way as she had felt once before. He towered over her, but she would not be intimidated.

"Why are you doing this?" he asked, his voice laced with panic.

She scowled, although he wouldn't see it, considering most of her face was covered with her makeshift mask.

She could hear Nena thrashing behind them. Carolina needed to keep him distracted long enough for her cousin to come with the frying pan in hand.

Carolina raised her chin and forced herself to meet his eyes. Eyes, she realized, that were honey brown. Not glowing blood-red. *How could that be?*

"What are you?" she asked. "Why do you not have the devil's eyes like the rest of your ilk?"

Alarm clouded his features. "Are there other vampiros here? What do they look like? Does one have red hair?"

How dare he ask her questions? *He* should be answering to *her*.

She kneed him hard in his groin. He hunched over with a startled moan.

"That really hurt!" he wheezed.

"That's the point, pendejo!"

She dug her fingers into her boot and pulled out another throwing dagger. Seeing what she was doing, the sediento bolted away. She flung the blade and watched as it found its target, sinking deep into his shoulder.

He cursed—more like screamed—but continued to run.

Carolina shoved a low-lying branch out of her way as she dashed after him. When she made it to a clearing in the woods, she jerked to a stop. She surveyed the area, spinning in circles.

"This can't be," she said. She peered into the trees above. "This cannot be!"

The sediento was gone.

She let out a frustrated growl and stomped her foot. There was nothing in the earth. Not even a single footprint. Though, the lack of light could easily be to blame for her not being able to see much. She wasn't a sediento. She did not thrive in darkness.

That boy was smarter than any vampiro she'd seen before. They were normally so lost in their bloodlust, they didn't think of fleeing. Lorenzo couldn't even communicate. But this one did. Had the sedientos somehow evolved? Were new kinds of monsters coming to hunt her people?

Nena suddenly came through the thicket, panting and sweaty. Leaves and branches clung to her curls.

"You ditched me!" she huffed.

"I was a bit distracted."

Nena's eyes flicked about. "Where is he? Did you slay him?"

"No, I . . ." A breeze fluttered through the trees, bringing with it the scent of smoke. Carolina tilted her head. "Why would there be a fire way out here?"

The nearest rancho was at least seven miles away. She wouldn't smell anything from here. She rushed forward.

"Carolina, wait!" Nena called after her.

But she was already slicing through the forest at a hound's pace.

Carolina's feet skittered to a halt when a lone hacienda popped into view. The rundown manor was the old Alicante estate. No one had lived there in years and yet the tiniest bit of smoke puffed from the chimney on the eastern end of the home. A single candle flickered past one of the windows on the second floor. Carolina's back stiffened. She couldn't be certain from such a distance, but it looked as though a lady had walked by. It happened again, and—yes—it was someone. The figure stopped before the window. The woman waited there for what felt like ages. She stuck her nose close to the glass as if she were trying to peer into the surrounding woods.

Was she waiting for him? The monster? Could she be one too?

"Dammit, Carolina." Nena grabbed Carolina and shoved her behind a tree. "Have you no self-preservation? Someone might see you."

"That's not just someone," Carolina said. "There is a sediento inside."

"*No*," Nena said slowly as if Carolina couldn't grasp that word. "The Alicante estate is being rented by a family from some port ciudad. Puerto Blanco, I think. I'll have to check the map and see where that is."

"What do you mean? How do you know this?"

"It's only been the talk of el pueblo for a week."

"I wouldn't know that because no one has spoken to me since . . ." She couldn't say it. She didn't want to bring up Abuelo now.

"*I* told you, days ago. But you were too busy not listening."

"Who are they?" Carolina asked.

"A brother and sister. I haven't seen the brother yet, but I did catch a glimpse of the sister in town this morning." Nena grinned. "She's . . . rather attractive, I won't deny that."

"You said you saw her in the morning? Was the sun out?"

"Sí. Very much so. And the girl didn't burn or even flinch. She's as human as you and me."

"But we don't know about the supposed brother. He could be the monster." She started forward, but Nena grasped her wrist.

"It would be rather rude and highly improper for the daughter of the mayor to suddenly show up on their doorstep at this hour," Nena said. "There will be too many questions to answer if the siblings tell people we came banging on their door at this time. And what if you're wrong? Also . . . you're in pants!" Nena waved her hand at Carolina's legs.

Nena had a point. Chewing on her bottom lip, Carolina made her decision. She would go home before her family caught on to their absence. She could stand getting in trouble, but she wouldn't let Nena be punished for her choices.

"Fine," she said. "But as soon as I can, I'm coming back here to see what is what."

Nena smiled. "I'll come with you."

"You're not tagging along just to flirt with some pretty girl."

"I know." Nena wrapped her arm around Carolina's shoulder. "That's a bonus."

From the journal of Friar Alejandro Ibarra

Throughout the seventy-six years I have served the church, I have learned of and witnessed for myself the various famines, obstacles, and maladies inflicted on us lowly humans by the gods. But perhaps the cruelest of these impediments is <u>the death curse</u>, or, as some would call it, vampirism. The creature holds the power of Tecuani in its heart but must consume human life to survive.

Vampiros aren't merely shells thriving on Tecuani's power alone. Their hearts still beat, their organs still work, but when one perishes, their blood turns to tar. Un vampiro must feed on fresh blood, on the essence of life to stay powerful and to keep their insides from failing.

It is my understanding that the gods wish us to retain valuable lessons through our sufferings, but I will never see why a god would raise a soul from the grave only to turn it into a monster.

CHAPTER 5

Lalo

OF ALL THE WRETCHED SITUATIONS LALO HAD BEEN THROUGH, this was perhaps the most inconvenient. He'd fallen, right through some foxhole or cave, and wedged his body into an uncomfortable knot. *And* he had a knife stuck in his back. But he was safe from *her*, at least. That vicious monster of a girl hidden behind a ridiculous mask. Not to mention her companion had had the audacity to hit him with a pan.

She'd mentioned dealing with his ilk before. Had she seen Maricela? He gulped. But then he thought about the wall barricading the main pueblo from the world beyond. Perhaps vampiros had really been here all along.

Hope flooded his chest.

"Luck might finally be on my side."

Del Oro was el pueblo where Alma Rosario's body had been found. As far as he could tell, she was the first sort of victim in

Abundancia to have died by being drained entirely of her blood. If she was truly the first, it could only mean Tecuani had been summoned somewhere nearby. The vampiro he created would still be here, for they were bound to the lands where they rose from the grave. If Lalo held any chance of turning himself back or at the very least ridding the world of monsters like him, he needed to find that vampiro.

According to the diary he discovered from one Friar Alejandro, a known expert on maladies inflicted by the gods, the only way to end the "death curse" was to find the firstborn monster and cut it down. That would sever the power of Tecuani from within all sedientos made from the original. Maricela would be no more, as would the threat of her wrath. And Lalo's thirst would dissolve.

Considering that terror of a young woman knew about his kind, she might know specifically about Alma Rosario and the beast that took her life. He had to speak to her. The only problem was, she wished to kill him. And she'd been rather cruel about it too.

With shaking fingers, he reached behind his back and gripped the hilt of the dagger currently wedged into his shoulder. He gritted his teeth and tried to pull the blade out. Lalo's stomach seized, and he almost vomited.

"Pathetic," he whispered. "You are absolutely pitiful."

Lalo felt as if he had waited long enough. From his estimations, he had been crammed inside this hole for over two hours. He was certain the women weren't on the prowl any longer. But now the birds were beginning to chatter, which made him nervous. Birds didn't often chirp until daybreak.

Grunting, he tried his best to squirm around so he could push himself up and out. His body hurt like bloody hell. Lalo would heal, of course. He had the blood of that buck flowing through him. The life he'd taken would mend what was broken. It would take much longer than if he'd drunk human blood, but there was nothing to be done about that. In his mind anyway.

His stomach pinched at the thought of what had transpired and how embarrassing this situation was. How appalling was it that anyone would come upon him while he fed?

At least they didn't see him hunt. That would've been a greater humiliation. Lalo hadn't even been going for the buck. He'd been chasing a raccoon but tripped and toppled right into the poor creature, fangs first. His only solace was that he had caught the buck so unaware that it didn't realize what was happening before it was too late.

The saliva of un vampiro stunned and numbed its victims. The buck did not know any pain. Lalo would have tasted it in his blood otherwise. Still, Lalo saw flashes of its memories. He saw it grazing in a meadow full of purple and yellow flowers, butting heads with another male, and spotting the loveliest doe.

Lalo inched toward the opening but stiffened. A shaft of glowing sunlight cut a line straight through the entrance.

"You cannot be serious," he groaned. He would have to stay here, inside a dingy den, for at least eight hours? Had he still wore his cloak, he could have tucked all his extremities inside and bolted home, but the cloak had somehow fallen off during his fight . . . and then humbling flight. His shirt and breeches wouldn't protect him enough from the sun. And if he *did* try and that masked vigilante was out there waiting, what then? He'd have no way to protect himself.

Sighing, Lalo nuzzled against the stone and curled into a

ball, making sure to keep the dagger lodged inside his shoulder from touching anything. He began to recite the alphabet backward. Something he'd done since he was a boy to pass the time. Lalo didn't want his brain to relax. For whenever it did, his thoughts found their way to one of two things: the night his parents were killed or when he was trapped inside the underbelly of the cantina.

Overthinking didn't work, and, unfortunately, he fell asleep.

His throat burned with need. His veins felt like they'd been dried to dust. His insides itched so terribly, he wished to claw into his skin. He thought he might go mad.

A giggle floated down the steps. From behind the barred door, Lalo could see two pairs of shiny boots. He heard hushed voices and soft kisses. The scent of warm bodies caressing slithered into his nostrils. He breathed in deeply. His mouth watered. Fangs he didn't even realize he had sunk into his bottom lip.

A desperate, all-consuming need exploded through his system. He couldn't think. Couldn't hold himself back. His own consciousness retreated and let the beast win.

With a strength he'd never known, Lalo tore the door from its hinges. He lunged forward before the couple could even turn their faces toward him. He jumped onto the first person he reached, piercing the man's neck without an ounce of grace. He drank and drank and devoured. Lalo saw the man's life flash before him. He had a wife and child. Lalo knew he should stop, but he couldn't. He drank until there was nothing left.

The woman screamed and bolted up the steps. Lalo jerked his fangs from the dead man's flesh and dove after her. He burrowed into her, tasting her soul. She wasn't this man's wife. She had memories of her own husband mixed in with this torrid affair.

Footsteps pounded through the cantina. Hisses mixed with screams. Lalo knew there were sedientos within the throng, but he didn't care. He had no fear. Only feverish thirst. And it was far more powerful than anything. He tore through a swarm of bodies trying to stop him. He bit and clawed and bathed in their screams until the noises ceased.

Lalo jerked awake with a gasp. He shot up, bumping his skull on the cool stone of the den. He rubbed his head as his brain frantically came to terms with where he was and how he'd gotten there. That masked girl. The scuffle. His cowardly retreat. His tumble into the cavern. This, the nightmares, the screams, the lives he had taken. They haunted him every time he closed his eyes.

He shifted and winced. The angrier woman's scent lingered on his clothing. And it was ironically pleasant, with hints of vanilla, leather, and the soft velvet of lavender. How could a person so quick to inflict pain smell so sweet?

Lalo rubbed his hands over his face. Everything was so complicated. This new normal was quite literally the very last thing he wanted for himself.

Boring. Dull. Safe. Quiet. Those had been the things Lalo longed for in his life. And now? Well, now he was stuck in a hole after fighting off some spiteful vampiro hunter and her pan-wielding sidekick.

"Lalo!" Fernanda's voice echoed from inside the woods. "Lalo!"

"Thank the gods," he sighed. His body tensed. *What if this was a trap?* That beast of a woman might have his sister at knifepoint. If that were the case, Lalo needed to save Fernanda at once. But that killer might best him again. And then he'd have to watch the disappointment play on his sister's features as he was slain. She'd think, *why was I cursed with such a miserable brother?*

He pulled himself up just enough to glance out. The light of day had subsided, and the deep blues of dusk peeked through the canopy.

"Lalo?" Fernanda's brows were raised, surprised. She was also unaccompanied by anyone trying to murder him. Her pinched face softened with relief, and she put her hand to her heart. "Praise the saints! You're all right."

He was dusty and grimy and stiff from head to toe, and it felt almost as bad as being knifed by that fiend. "I spent a whole day trapped in some foxhole. I have been stabbed and assaulted with cookware. I'm hardly all right."

Fernanda put her hands on her hips. "And I spent an entire day thinking my brother and only family was forever lost."

Lalo's stomach sank.

"But you aren't. Which is fantastic, because I have the most exciting news."

"Is that so?"

"Yes!" Fernanda rushed to his side, plucked a beetle from his coat, and flung it away.

Lalo gasped in horror.

"Look." She thrust out a letter. "It's a special invitation for a fiesta tonight. Two young women brought it. The party is being put on by their family."

"Two young women?" He eyed the scrawling letters written by a delicate hand.

To Señor and Señorita Montéz:

They had changed their surname from Villalobos to Montéz to be inconspicuous and planned to tell anyone who asked that they came from the farthest city they could find on a map, Puerto Blanco, instead of Los Campos. He didn't know how far-reaching vampiro communication lines could travel, and he would not make it any easier for Maricela to find them.

I have recently learned of your arrival to our glorious pueblo. It is not often I come into acquaintance with new people my age and thus would love to invite you to the fiesta my family is hosting. I would be honored if you would attend as my special guests.

Warmly,
Carolina Victoria Fuentes
del Rancho Fuentes

"Fuentes," he whispered to himself. *The* Fuenteses. As in the founders of Del Oro.

"Oh, Lalo. She was the loveliest girl! So polite and funny, too. I imagine she has dozens of suitors. And her cousin was quite fetching." Fernanda clapped her hands.

"When did you receive this?" He held the letter to his nose, sniffed it. His entire body went stiff. Lavender, vanilla, leather. His bones rattled. This . . . this was the scent still clinging to his clothing. She had visited his *home*.

"Carolina was certainly inquisitive," Fernanda said, a grin warming her entire face. "She's eighteen, you know. I suppose because she's the mayor's daughter, she asked so many questions about us."

He gulped. "Like what?"

"Where we hail from. Why we ventured here. She even requested to see a portrait of you."

The audacity. "What did you do?" he asked.

"I told her we had unfortunately lost most of our possessions in a fire. It was the first thing I could think of. I couldn't exactly say we stole away in the middle of the night to escape a vengeful vampiress."

That was sort of a relief. "But . . ."

Fernanda rolled her eyes. "Don't worry, brother. I was perfectly charming and convincing. As far as she and everyone I have spoken to thus far know, you are a scholar, and I am your younger sister and ward. Which is mostly true. Now that you are no longer operating father's boot business, you can dedicate all your time to research. And clearly, I take care of you, but we don't need to fuss over details." She quirked her lips into a grin. "She seemed so curious about you, though, which was odd seeing as I was standing right there. I am far more interesting. Perhaps she's determined to lay eyes on you before anyone else. I can't imagine there are too many unattached men in these parts."

"Indeed."

"She asked me at least three times where you were. I told her you had business to attend to in the next pueblo over."

The next pueblo over was at least a day's ride away and surrounded by a river. A sediento could never cross the flowing waters because of the curse. Perhaps that would at least convince the daughter of the mayor that he wasn't a monster.

"Saints, I wish you would have been there," Fernanda said. "They were so amiable. I think we will be the best of friends. Or more. I'm not sure yet."

"When did they come?" He suddenly had a horrified feeling she was lurking somewhere nearby, readying her blade, or her lasso.

"Perhaps an hour ago."

He recoiled. *Only an hour ago!* He'd just barely missed her. She could still be in the woods now, spying. Lalo took his sister by the arm. The movement brought on a fresh wave of pain. That wretched dagger was still lodged in his shoulder.

"Come on, let's get inside," he said. Trying his best to not sound as frightened as he was. "I need you to help me get this thing out of my back."

"What dress should I wear to the party?" Fernanda asked.

"We aren't going," he said. How could they? This young lady, this—he eyed the invitation—Carolina Victoria Fuentes, was playing with him. The fiesta was most likely a trap.

Fernanda walked beside him, nearing their casa. "You said we should speak to the locals and get information. Carolina is a good start. She seems more than knowledgeable. She said we should be careful. That the forest is full of deplorable demons."

Lalo let out a bitter laugh.

"Do you really think I can handle being in a room with so many people?" he asked.

Fernanda pursed her lips. "Maybe we can stick some goat dung into your nostrils. That way you won't take in everyone's scent and want to devour them?"

"Not funny."

His sister beamed. "I disagree."

They moved up the steps and into the house. Lalo wanted a bath and some quiet. But how could he possibly let his guard down when there was a killer on the loose? In fact, that killer had been inside his home. He could smell her everywhere.

"We are going to the fiesta," Fernanda said. "And that is final."

Lalo huffed, incredulous. "I am your guardian, little sister. I say what is absolute and what is not."

She raised her chin in defiance. "You are not the boss of me."

He wasn't. He knew that. He could never truly boss Fernanda around. He didn't think there was a soul in Abundancia who could. But he wasn't going to lose this battle.

If this Carolina was bold enough to go to his home, she was bold enough to do just about anything. They might show up to her fiesta and have stakes flung at them as soon as they entered the doorway.

No. He wouldn't risk it. He wouldn't put Fernanda in any more danger than she already was in. The possibility of Maricela hunting them down was terrible enough.

Carolina Fuentes might have tried to set a trap, but he was far too smart to walk into it.

CHAPTER 6

Carolina

To hold a fiesta when her abuelo had only recently been laid to rest was utterly preposterous. He should be here. With them. But this was tradition. They mourned, then spent weeks praying to the gods of the Land of the Dead for safe passage. After, in the darkest part of the night when the veils between this world and the next were thinnest and the souls could watch from el Cielo, they drank and danced and remembered all the good their loved ones had done.

Rather than imbibe wine, she would honor him tonight by killing a sediento.

Carolina could picture it. That boy would saunter into the foyer, thinking they'd never met before and she believed him to be human. She'd sweep through the crowded hall and stab him right in the heart.

But what if he used her invitation to strike first?

He might very well tear through the room and decimate her entire family. She laughed that thought away. Nearly every man in her family was part of the guard. A sediento would stand no chance. Especially one that ran from a fight as he had last night.

"There you are," Mamá's voice came from down the corridor. She was a vision in a flowing gown with flowers embroidered into plum-colored skirts. One hand rested on her round belly; the other was motioning for Carolina to come.

Carolina picked up her heavy skirts and swept forward. She'd been hiding behind the arches in the corridor. The guests hadn't even arrived and already she was tired of them. But as the only daughter of the mayor of Del Oro, she was expected to be the epitome of grace and poise. Neither of which she felt like being at that moment.

The entire hacienda had been draped in roses, poppies, and marigolds. Abuelo's favorite things like tamales, sweet squash empanadas, cured olives, tobacco, and mezcal were set on the ofrenda. Mamá had a block of ice carted down from el pueblo to the north and sculpted in Abuelo's likeness. Nena complained that the artist had gotten Abuelo's nose all wrong.

"Mija," Mamá said, grinning. "You look absolutely stunning."

The gold adorning Carolina's neck, wrists, and ears made her brown skin glow. Half of her dark hair had been pulled up and pinned into a tiara of wild lilies. The rest hung in long curls down her back. Her cheeks had been rouged and her lips painted the same color as her gown. She felt beautiful.

But underneath the beauty and refinement stirred a killer. And she needed to stay focused on whatever was to come. She had a mission. If this Eduardo Montéz was as foolish as she hoped, he would be in the mix of guests, soon to arrive. Which was why she had strapped two obsidian knives, a stake of birch-wood, and her reata to her thighs. Uncomfortable? Yes. Necessary? Also yes.

Mamá kissed Carolina's cheeks and squeezed her hands. "You will be the most stunning person in attendance tonight. Rafael won't be able to take his eyes from you."

"*Rafael?*" Carolina's eyes went wide. She hadn't heard that name in years. "Rafa is coming?"

Rafael Pico had been a pest when they were children. He was always pinching her and teasing her. He'd throw rocks at her head and call her vampiro bait anytime she scampered past his home. The day she finally had enough and popped him in the nose, Rafa cried to his madre like a baby. They were frosty to one another after that, but she always felt his gaze lingering over her when he came to play with her older brothers. He and his family moved away when he and Carolina were fifteen. She had been glad to be rid of him, but their parents remained close. Their families had once spoken of the fine match they would make once she was of age. Carolina could retch at the thought.

"Amá," she said slowly, facing her mother. "Why is Rafael coming to Abuelo's celebration of life? People from other pueblos don't often venture so far during the night."

"Well . . ." Mamá gulped. "Your father invited him."

"For what purpose?"

Her mamá's pale face grew a bit fairer. "I told your father it was too soon, but he insisted."

"What are you talking about?"

The *clip-clop* of horse hooves sounded from the cobbled road that led up to their casa. The mariachi, which was situated near the entrance, began to play. The horns blared. The vocalist sang.

The strum of el guitarrón matched the beat of her now racing heart.

"We'll speak about this later." Mamá donned her hostess's face, one of controlled ease and poise.

"But . . . why is Rafael coming?"

Mamá ignored her and plastered on a smile as friends and family from their pueblo started pooling through the doors. Through her teeth she said, "Wipe that scowl off your face."

As Carolina did what she was told, Don Salvador entered, sporting his signature white sombrero and matching charro. His wife, Doña Laura, wore a dress so wide she had to twist to the side to fit around the gargantuan melting ice sculpture. Next came the Cho family. Then the Schuberts. The Rodríguezes.

Carolina greeted each visitor with a delicate bow, a kind word, and a promise to dance with one of their sons or daughters later in the evening. The entire time, Carolina's eyes went to the entrance, waiting, watching. But no Montéz siblings came. Perhaps they had chickened out. Perhaps they were smarter than she thought.

Mamá elbowed her side. "Look, Carolina. It's Rafael's carriage." A sleek coach drawn with two horses as black as the night sky eased to a stop.

"Are his parents coming?" Carolina whispered.

"Rafael's papá is ill, and his mamá won't leave his side."

"Rafa should have stayed home too," she grumbled.

The crowd parted ever so slowly as a strapping man with wide shoulders, golden brown skin, and the prettiest smile Carolina had ever seen walked up the stairs and toward the arching doorway.

"*That's* Rafa?" Carolina asked. This *man* was not the gawky boy she remembered.

"Shh, Carolina," Mamá hissed. Her grin widened. "Rafael." She leaned up and let him kiss her on both cheeks. "Thank you for coming on such short notice."

Carolina's brow furrowed. Why had her parents sent for him?

"I should be thanking you, Señora Fuentes."

"Please, call me Doña Victoria."

Why would Mamá ask him to speak to her so informally?

"It would be my honor." Rafa bowed low with a sweep of his massive arm.

Mamá blushed, most irritatingly.

"You remember my daughter, Carolina." Both sets of eyes turned on Carolina. She was almost too stupefied by Rafa's size and chiseled chin to remember what she was supposed to do. But she saw the glint in his gaze. Clearly, he knew what a striking figure he was. That annoyed her beyond measure.

"Wonderful to see you again, Carolina. You have blossomed into quite a woman."

What a strange thing to say to a person. She crossed her arms, noticing his eyes traveling up and down her figure. "I hardly remember what you looked like back then so I cannot gauge whether you've improved or not. My apologies."

His smug smile faded a fraction. Carolina smirked. She had been around powerful men all her life. Thus, she understood they hated nothing more than a confident, sharp-tongued woman, which was exactly who she was. She wouldn't change that for anyone.

"How have you been, Rafael? I heard you have just returned from Los Campos," Mamá said, trying to lighten the conversation. "Will you be staying in these parts for long?"

"I have been well, Doña Victoria. I will be returning to the

76

ciudad once father is back on his feet. You and your family should visit sometime. The ciudad, I mean. You would love to see such a splendid place, I'm certain of it."

"Oh yes," Mamá said. "And so would Carolina. Wouldn't you, Carolina?"

Carolina nodded numbly, though she really couldn't care less. Her attention was focused on the door. That sediento was like nothing she'd seen before. Every monster to attack el pueblo, at least while she had been alive, was inhuman. They had claws and piercing fangs; their eyes glowed blood-red. Thirst controlled their every move. Eduardo Montéz had seemed—

Her mamá's heel dug into her toes. Carolina hissed.

Mamá glared at her before quickly masking her irritation with a polite laugh.

"The clothing boutiques in the capital city are divine," Rafa continued, oblivious to the silent argument between mother and daughter. "I am welcome at the finest places. There isn't a single retailer that would turn me away." He chuckled. "Or should I say, they wouldn't turn my pocketbook away?"

"Now you have piqued *my* interest," Nena said, scooting her way between Rafa and Carolina. She wore beautiful poppy-colored skirts and a lacy bodice cut low in the front. Her mass of curls hung in tight tendrils around her shoulders with a single sunset-orange rose tucked behind her ear.

Her rump bumped Carolina farther from Rafa. Nena glanced over her shoulder and winked. Carolina mouthed her thanks.

Rafa's eyes flicked to Nena's cleavage before snapping up to meet Carolina's gaze. He had the nerve to appear as unabashed as ever.

"When Carolina and I are . . ." He stopped when her mamá

shook her head. "*If* we become more acquainted, I shall take you and your cousin here to see whatever you like. I have been told I am a generous host."

Wait, Carolina thought. *What did he mean by "when Carolina and I"? When we what?*

Did her parents call upon him with an ulterior motive? Rafa's family owned one of the largest tanneries in Abundancia. A union between the two families would make for a profitable business opportunity. She'd heard such a thing said before growing up but paid the notion little mind. Carolina assumed everyone knew she'd never marry for anything other than love.

She turned toward her mamá, sneering.

"There are my girls," Papá's voice boomed. He gave Mamá a kiss on the cheek. He shook Rafa's hand. "Rafael."

"Señor Fuentes," Rafa said stiffly, as any caller would do to a potential father-in-law.

That had better not be the case. There would be hell to pay, if so.

"Mija, I have found your esteemed guest," Papá said to Carolina.

She balked.

He came.

And at the exactly right moment. Everyone was still milling about, drinking and gossiping. The true festivities had yet to begin. She wanted to let out a villainous laugh.

The absolute fool had fallen for her trap.

Her fingers inched toward her daggers. Her heart began to race. This was it. Time to show everyone how brilliant she was with a blade. Time to show them what Abuelo had trained her to do. Papá would get to see her in action. He wouldn't be able to deny her skill.

She beamed with glee.

Papá swept to the side.

Carolina's jaw dropped.

Fernanda stood smiling in an emerald gown. She bowed her head and dipped into a well-practiced curtsy. "Good evening."

Carolina peered around her. The young man with the devilishly handsome face wasn't with her.

"Where is your brother?" Carolina snapped. When everyone's eyes flicked toward her, she splashed on her sweetest smile. "I mean, Fernanda, how wonderful of you to join us," she said, trying to seem gracious rather than disappointed.

Where was the sediento?

"Thank you for inviting my brother and me to your beautiful casa," Fernanda said. "We were both so flattered that you would personally request our company, Carolina."

Something nibbled at the back of Carolina's mind. The way Fernanda had framed her sentences gave her pause. Fernanda had made sure to mention the summons to the Fuentes home. She had made sure to add that Carolina, in particular, had been the one to invite them in. Vampiros could only cross the threshold of a person's home if given permission. If anything went awry, was Fernanda letting everyone know Carolina would be to blame?

"A pleasure to see you again," Nena all but purred. She was too busy trying to flirt with the vampiro's sister to care about Carolina's hands balling into fists at her sides.

"Again?" Papá questioned.

Carolina jolted. Papá could not know anything about last night. Or their journey back to the Alicante estate to bring the invitation this afternoon.

"We met in passing when Fernanda came into town the other day," Nena said.

Fernanda's smile did not waver. "Ah sí. And what a lovely meeting indeed."

"Did you come to the fiesta by yourself?" Carolina blurted.

"I did. I hope that is not too improper, but my brother . . . he . . . he was rather tired after his trip yesterday." Her gaze flicked from Carolina to Nena.

Carolina pursed her lips and narrowed her eyes. Fernanda clearly knew it was them who had tried to kill her brother. So why exactly had she come?

Del Oro is un pueblo located in Monterey County, twenty-seven miles east of the Coast. Because of its great distance from Alta California's main ports and economical hubs, el pueblo is unincorporated. The picturesque pueblo of Del Oro was founded on October 9, 1584, by Basilio Fuentes.

The name Del Oro derives from the gold found in the riverbeds by early settlers. The local soil is rich in minerals, and the valley is known for its cattle and agriculture. The town sits below the small mountain range of Basilio's Point, which is best known for the controversial name given to its southernmost peak, Devil's Spine. According to the 1820 census, the town population was 276.

Sanchez. 1825. *Alta California, Abundancia: Pueblos, Cities, & Topography*. First Edition.

CHAPTER 7

Lalo

THE HEADACHE THUMPING THROUGH LALO'S SKULL WOULD NOT go away. Feeding on animals wasn't enough to keep the thirst at bay. The migraines were coming more frequently. The peppermint oil Fernanda picked up from the town apothecary could only do so much. Still, he'd take suffering over ruining another person's life any day.

Sighing, he turned on his back and stared up at the ceiling. His shoulder healed quick enough. Though, that had been an ordeal. It took his sister several attempts to yank the blade free. At least, that was what he had been told. He fainted after the first try.

Lalo pushed himself to a seated position. His brow furrowed. Everything was eerily quiet within the casa.

His senses roamed over the house. He couldn't hear a thing, and he could always hear Fernanda. She was either clacking away at the out-of-tune pianoforte left in the home, or humming some off-key operatic melody, or giggling while she read inappropriate magazines about love in the city.

Fernanda was noisy. Even in sleep. So where was she?

A spike of fear ran through him. *Did that huntress in the woods come back? Had Maricela found them?*

Lalo shot out of bed and bolted across his room, ignoring the stabs of agony piercing his brain. He jerked the door open. The knob slammed into the wall, leaving a large indent. He hissed. There went any hope of a stealthy ambush on his part.

"Fernanda!" he called. There was no point in being quiet. Not after the walls had just rattled because of his newfound strength.

He sniffed. Nothing smelled amiss. Just the normal scents of the house. Fernanda kept sprigs of rosemary and some extra lavender in every space to help mask all the human smells that were wretchedly alluring when one was a vampiro.

"Fernanda?"

Nothing.

Panic bloomed to life within him.

Lalo ran through the halls. His bare feet slapped over crooked planks.

"Fernanda!"

She was not in the small library. Or the den. Or the kitchen. He bolted across the casa to where her room was. He slammed another door open, sending it smacking into the plaster yet again. *He really should learn how to control his power.*

A lump lay under the covers of her bed. But he was not daft. There was no heart beating underneath the quilt. He knew her tricks. She had often rolled towels together and formed them into the shape of a slumbering body before sneaking out of the house when they lived in the city. The girl was wily to her core.

His eyes went to her wardrobe, where a door was ajar. Her favorite party dress was noticeably absent.

A frustrated growl escaped him. She'd gone to the Fuenteses' fiesta.

"Dammit, Fernanda."

Finding Rancho Fuentes had been easier than he thought. He simply ran as fast as he could through the valley, entered the massive gates secured by sentries holding shotguns at the ready, and followed the trail of marigolds through the main street in el pueblo. Dozens of armed men sat on horseback donning extravagant sombreros and mustaches thick as Lalo's forearm. He eyed them with a sorry hint of jealousy. His mustache was thin but well-kept as was the style in the ciudad, but he quite liked the way the men curled the sides of theirs up like a smile.

"Focus," he spat. He shouldn't be musing over facial hair. Lalo marched through the smaller gates that opened to the rancho without any trouble. He had been invited to the fiesta, after all. Not that any of the guards milling about seemed to care. But Lalo did. Sedientos could not enter one's home until they were welcomed. This strange boundary was another one of Tecuani's weaknesses. Unlike other gods, he could only come to the Land of the Living when called upon.

Beautifully colored banners hung from the large manor to the trees and smaller buildings within the hacienda complex. Golden flames flickered from fat candles leading up to stone steps that opened to the entrance of the grand home.

He'd done some more digging in the history books Fernanda

had brought from the town library. The Fuentes family had laid claim to these lands well over two hundred years ago. This very home was the first building to rise from the dirt in the area. The valley had been a booming place only a few generations prior. But then tragedy struck, and half the town had perished. What that tragedy had been was noticeably left out of the texts. Lalo didn't need ledgers to piece together what that was—the death of Alma Rosario.

One article he found said her body was brought back to el pueblo to be buried. Lalo could only guess Alma had turned sometime after and ravished the town in her newborn bloodlust, exactly as he'd done in the cantina. She had been turned. And she was the first of her kind to ever be recorded in Abundancia. Which meant, in his mind, whatever had made her might have been the original sediento.

His soul hurt for Alma. For himself too. Life was hard enough. Trying to survive death and its aftermath was nearly impossible.

He held his breath as he thrust himself into the throng of partygoers. But he was still bombarded with a thousand scents and heartbeats. His mouth watered. And Lalo's stomach growled viciously, reminding him it wished to be satiated.

The music and merriment were so loud he could hardly think straight. He had detested raucousness before he was a vampiro, preferring calm, but now the sounds of stringed instruments and uncontrolled giggles were bouncing wildly around his skull.

He winced and turned away from the band. Lalo stilled. Fernanda stood just a few paces before him, smiling and speaking animatedly to a small group. A man, larger than the horses outside, was grinning. He had a gloriously robust mustache, his long black hair was tied back at the nape of his neck, and his sideburns were impressively thick. There was a woman, beautiful with soft eyes, her hand resting on top of her rounded stomach. A pretty girl who seemed familiar stood beside her. He caught her scent. His eye twitched. She was similar in size and smell to the masked person who had hit him with a pan. A young man smirked near Fernanda. He wore the latest fashions from the ciudad: a form-fitting cream suit with a frill of lace at the neck.

Lalo's stomach twisted when his gaze landed on the last person in the small assembly. Her back was to him, but there was no mistaking that figure. And that aroma of vanilla, lavender, and leather. The thirst inside him roared to life. It clawed up his throat, begging to be fed. Lalo's fangs sank into his bottom lip. He clamped his palm over his mouth and spun around.

He needed to get away.

He wasn't paying proper attention and ran straight into a table laden with an ice sculpture made to look like the bust of a man. The massive carving wobbled for a horrifying moment before rocking off balance. Lalo tried to catch it, but the slick ice slipped through his grasp and crashed onto the floor, breaking into a million pieces.

The mariachi stopped playing. The voices and laughter went silent. A man paused mid-drink.

Every eye turned to Lalo.

He gulped. Forced his fangs to retract. Forced his knees to stop quivering.

"The . . . um . . . the legs on this table might need to be tightened," he stuttered.

All focus then turned to the pregnant woman standing by Fernanda.

She offered a shaky grin. "I didn't care for that sculpture anyway. They got Don José Miguel's nose wrong. It was much longer in real life, no?"

This was met with boisterous laughter and calls for more drinks in the hostess's honor. The fiesta continued, but Lalo could not move. The young woman standing near his sister had slowly turned. Her eyes locked with his.

Lalo's very soul, if he still had one, fled his body.

This was the fiend from the woods who had tried to murder him. He'd know that velvety scent from anything. And those eyes. Infinitely brown and shielded by black lashes. Those very eyes had glared at him from behind her ridiculous mask.

Seeing her face, unmasked, startled him more than anything. Because—holy saints—she was the most stunning person he'd ever seen.

CHAPTER 8

Carolina

He came.

Carolina narrowed her eyes. The sediento was even more handsome than she first thought. Not that that mattered in the slightest. She should be concerned about getting out her stake, not about that little dimple in his chin.

Her adrenaline spiked.

Not only had the sediento entered her home as if he owned it, but he had decimated the ice sculpture of her abuelo. Was that some sort of declaration of war?

"Brother!" Fernanda swept past Carolina, slipped her arm around the young man's elbow, and tugged him forward. She beamed. "Señor and Señora Fuentes, allow me to introduce my very clumsy brother, Eduardo Montéz."

The boy gave an uneasy half grin. He looked so human. His irises were a beautiful shade of honey. His skin a warm brown.

Carolina still couldn't make sense of his appearance, which was neither ghastly nor monstrous.

"Call me Lalo," he said, offering his hand to Papá. "Eduardo was my father's name."

Carolina's eyes widened as her papá took it and gave it a hearty shake. Would he notice what this Lalo was? Would a great battle commence right in the middle of her foyer? He better not. Lalo was hers to kill.

Papá laughed. "A good handshake you have there, son. I often explain to my boys how one can tell the true nature of a man by the heartiness of his greeting. And you"—Papá clapped Lalo on the back—"have got one hell of a grip."

Lalo didn't even flinch when Papá smacked his shoulder. And everyone did. Papa's hands were like mallets. She pursed her lips. That was the exact spot she had stuck him through with her blade. He had healed then. As only a true vampiro could.

"This is my wife, Señora Fuentes. My niece, Antonina. Our family friend, Rafael. And my lovely daughter, Carolina."

"A pleasure," Lalo said.

His voice was so soft and deep. Carolina felt suddenly overheated. She shouldn't have left her fan back in her room.

Lalo's gaze flicked to Carolina, and her stomach clenched.

Mamá tilted her chin. "Do you two know each other, too?"

Whatever spell they'd both been under popped like a bubble. The sounds of the ballroom filled her ears. The laughter. The mariachi. The ruckus.

"No," Carolina and the sediento said in unison, which only added to her mamá's suspicion.

He chuckled shyly and, by the stars, her knees weakened. She locked them. She could not and would not have wayward thoughts about a sediento. The main reason she wanted him there was to prove to her papá that she could handle her own against one.

"Apologies, but I must take my leave," Lalo said.

"But you only just arrived. And Carolina took great pains to invite us as her special guests," Fernanda said, a polite smile plastered on her face.

Oh, she is good. Carolina knew exactly what Fernanda was doing. She was silently proclaiming that she too understood the ways of war. If Carolina meant to stake Lalo among all these people, then Fernanda would easily let slip what had transpired between Lalo and Carolina the night before in the woods.

"I only came to retrieve my sister," Lalo said. "We have . . . some business to attend to."

"So late at night?" Mamá questioned. "Surely it can wait until morning. Especially since you live so far outside the barricades."

His brows raised slightly. "What are the walls for? Pardon me if that's too forward a question."

"No, it is fine," Mamá said. "We . . ."

"May I answer, Amá?" Carolina interjected, batting her lashes sweetly.

Mamá smiled tightly. "By all means."

Carolina cleared her throat. "There are these bloodsucking devils that wreak havoc on our . . ."

"Carolina!" Mamá scorned.

Nena snorted, then covered it with a cough.

"What sort of business are you in, young man?" Papá interjected, always interested in the comings and goings of anyone within his pueblo.

Lalo rubbed a hand against his neck. "Oh, I . . . I'm doing research. I'm a scholar."

This was perfect. Let them remain distracted so she could get to work.

Carolina's fingers slipped over her skirts. She shouldn't have strapped the stake to her thigh. She should have had it ready. Her nanny had taken to sewing her pockets shut when she was a girl after she had filled them with toads at a garden party, but she could have slipped a weapon in her bodice at least. How was she to grab it without scandalizing the entire room? A bead of sweat eased down her spine. The sediento's attention snapped to her. Fernanda mouthed, "Don't even think about it." Carolina glared at them both.

"What sort of research?" Papá plucked two flutes of bubbling liquid from a passing server and handed one to Lalo.

Lalo observed the glass in his hand with distrust. "History and origins of lore that stem from small pueblos. I sell my findings to libraries and schoolhouses."

"Can one make a living wage from such studies?"

"Our parents left me and my brother a comfortable inheritance, and our father's luxury boot business is quite profitable," Fernanda said. "Lalo will take it over when . . ." Her brother gave an almost imperceptible shake of his head at her.

He turned to Carolina. "Those bloodsucking devils you spoke about, Señorita Fuentes. I should very much like to learn more."

"I'm certain you know plenty about them, being the *scholar* you are," she said.

Rafa cleared his throat. "Have we met before?"

Carolina noticed the way Rafa slowly placed his body in

front of hers, as if he were claiming her. She suddenly felt a deep longing to pop him straight in the mouth as she had done when they were young.

"I don't believe so, señor," Lalo said. But Carolina noticed his jaw muscles flex.

"Where are you from, Lalo?" Rafa asked. "Your fashions speak of people who hail from one of our great cities."

Good gods, Rafa was nosy. And none of this mattered. The sediento was here for one singular reason—blood. Del Oro was the perfect place to find his victims. The town was hard to travel to, far enough away from most of the larger ciudades to make it an inconvenience for people to wish to come to the valley on holiday. There was no army here, no officials to ensure the safety of the people. Only her father's guard and a few rangers. And Carolina, of course.

Now, how was she going to retrieve her weapons from under her skirts without anyone taking notice?

"Are you from the capital? I have recently taken up residence in Los Campos. Perhaps that is why you seem so familiar," Rafa said. "Your family owns a luxury boot business, you say?"

"We . . ." Lalo placed the full flute on the tray of a server passing by. The platter flipped out of the server's hand and the fizzy liquid inside splashed onto Lalo's chest and face.

Mamá's eyes went wide with horror. Papá hooted his larger-than-life laugh.

"My stars, boy. You must be the clumsiest person in Abundancia." He smacked Lalo's back, but again, Lalo didn't flinch.

Lalo wiped at his eyes. "It would appear so, señor. Tell me, where might I clean myself off?"

"Right through the corridor," Mamá said kindly, almost

sorrowfully. She always cringed when people made clowns of themselves.

He turned to his sister with a tight smile. "Won't you join me, Fernanda?"

Fernanda tilted her head and fluttered her lashes. "I'm sure you can manage on your own."

"I must insist," he said through his teeth.

"And I must decline."

His eyes narrowed at her, but then he gave a nervous laugh. "My sister, she ... she is good with stains."

"I bet she is, sanguijuela," Carolina whispered under her breath.

Nena elbowed Carolina in the ribs and gave her a warning that said, *shut up before you get yourself, and me, in trouble.*

Lalo excused himself and dashed away before she had a chance to attack. Her feet ached to pursue him. But she had to play this levelheadedly. She couldn't run after some handsome young stranger. What a scandal that would cause.

She surveyed the ballroom, searching for some explanation to step away from her parents, Rafa, Nena, and Lalo's sister. Then inspiration struck.

"Amá," she said. "I just saw Luisa walking into the gardens."

Mamá's jaw dropped. Luisa was one of their milk goats. The damn thing escaped every chance she got, heading straight for Mamá's flowers without fail.

"I'll get the stable hand," Mamá said.

"No! I'll get Luisa. She likes me," Carolina lied. She and Luisa hadn't seen eye to eye since Luisa ate Carolina's favorite slippers last year.

"Perdón," she said with a bow.

93

"But . . . ," Fernanda started before stopping herself.

There was nothing for her to say, nothing to do to keep Carolina away from her brother. Carolina nearly cackled in triumph.

"I'll be back in just a moment," she said.

She winked at Nena, who took the cue and brought up the topic of this year's prized calves. The bull steers were rumored to catch a high price, and that fact was a particularly favorite subject of Papá's to speak about.

Carolina slithered away, weaving through the crowd of party-goers to hunt after a goat that wasn't truly there. Ready to stick her stake into the heart of the sediento she'd invited.

From the journal of Jonathan Monroe of Santemala

June 1, 1709

I have done the unthinkable.

In my desperation to bring my daughter back from the dead, I made a deal with a trickster god and brought a curse upon my family. I sliced my palm and placed my blood on her grave.

I invoked Tecuani.

Now, day and night, my daughter screams because her belly won't fill. She cannot stand the sunlight. Boils form. She will not drink water from the parish's well to ease her soul. She suffers because of me.

I must seek out our priests to see what can be done.

CHAPTER 9

Lalo

WHY WAS FERNANDA SUCH A STUBBORN MULE? HE GAVE HER A perfect reason to pardon herself, unintentionally making the worst first impression in the process, and she still didn't take the bait. Now he was merely left with a stain on his best coat.

Lalo made his way toward the water closet, but his eyes caught on the silver moon through an arching window. It was so large tonight. One could see the craters that pocked its terrain. The moon and stars, the planets and galaxies, they'd always been something that fascinated Lalo. Far more than joining his father in their boot business.

Studying the universe was like gazing into the past, in a way; once one answered the questions they had about the how and why, even more questions began to pile up. He supposed that was why he enjoyed history so much; it gave his brain something to reach for, something to explore in a solitary fashion. There weren't often troves of people milling about the archives underneath libraries, and one could be alone on a roof somewhere and stare at the universe beyond.

Solitude. Quiet. Calm. Those were the three things Lalo loved most in the world. He currently had none of them. He was at a fiesta with a huntress for saints' sake!

But why? That was the question he should truly be asking. Why had Carolina personally invited him?

He studied the moon once more. Two days had passed since he came to Del Oro, and he wasn't much closer to finding the answers he needed. Though, to be fair to himself, he had spent one of those days hidden in a foxhole, recovering from Carolina Fuentes's assault. How was he going to save himself before his body gave out from lack of human blood? He could feel the cruel thirst creeping into his system with each passing moment. Being in the Fuentes residence might offer a clue as to what he should do next. There had to be some sort of text that might help him know more about el pueblo in Alma's time. That might give him a clue about who the original sediento could be. If only the walls could talk.

He continued down the corridor and stopped when a familiar scent hit him. Dust. Leather. Parchment. Lalo let his senses lead him toward two double doors painted in a hue of burnt orange. He chanced a look back from where he came—there was no one. The guests were too busy with their drinks and chatter in the ballroom and courtyard to notice his absence. Plus, his sister had enough flair to woo any crowd. She would keep all entertained while he snuck inside and peeked through their things.

Slipping through the doors without a sound, Lalo found himself in a library that could rival the one in Los Campos. Books filled glossy shelves that reached the ceiling. He stood there for a moment, breathing everything in, letting his eyes lap over the worn bindings. These books had been cared for. He wondered if that brute of a girl read them.

His heart gave a sudden and painful thump, sending the blood he'd stolen from the buck through his veins. He bent over as a sharp cramp sliced through his belly. His fingers grasped at the back of the leather chair before him.

"Saints," he groaned. The beast inside didn't call for the blood of a deer. It screamed for that of a human. "Curse you, Maricela."

He dug his nails deeper, clenching his jaw tight.

His eyes flicked about the room. The plaster walls were a creamy white. The massive desk near the back was stained a rich mahogany but had nicks and dents as if it were well used. Two glass doors opened onto a balcony. From the library, one could see the valley, the rambling pueblo, the forest, and the small, rather terrifying peak of Devil's Spine.

Lalo strode toward the books that were shut behind glass. As gently as he could, he twisted the key that was in the lock and opened the delicate door. He could smell the age on the ancient parchment. Carolina Victoria Fuentes's scent was there too.

A heartbeat thumping quickly sounded down the hall. He needed to hide. Gently, Lalo shut the glass door and tiptoed back. He turned, readying to make his escape, but froze when he felt the prick of a blade dig into his jugular.

"One word and you're dust, sanguijuela."

Though Lalo took offense to Carolina calling him a leech, he did not utter a word. He preferred to leave unscathed. Instead, he raised his hands in surrender.

CHAPTER 10

Carolina

"WHY ARE YOU HERE?" CAROLINA'S VOICE CUT THROUGH THE quiet like the dagger in her hand.

The sediento blinked but said nothing. The coward was too frightened to speak. *Good. He should fear her.*

She dug her blade deeper. "I asked you a question."

"You said if I spoke, you'd turn me to dust. I'd very much like to remain in this form, so I choose to stay silent."

She rolled her eyes. "You just spoke. And far too much."

"I apologize. I don't know what the proper protocol is for one holding a weapon to my throat."

"And yet, here you are, speaking so freely when, a second ago, you were clammed up."

"What do you want from me, señorita?"

Her eyes went to the door. It was still ajar from when she'd slipped in. She nudged it closed with her toe, waiting for the soft click of the latch.

"Tell me what you are doing here," she ordered.

The sediento's lips flattened. "You invited me, remember?"

She shook her head. "No, pendejo. I mean *here*, here. In Del Oro."

Carolina's neck ached from tilting her head up at him. She didn't like that he made her feel small. She was one of the shortest people in her entire family and had often been teased for it. Not that she cared. But she didn't want this leech to assume he had the upper hand *because* of her size. Carolina straightened her spine and pressed close enough to feel his warmth.

Her brow furrowed. *Warmth?* She thought the dead were as cold as the ice sculpture of Abuelo. Her hand went to the monster's chest. Heat radiated from him.

"How can this be?" she whispered to herself.

"Señorita," he said, his voice thick and raspy. The notch on his throat bobbed. His eyes glazed with hunger.

Carolina pulled her hand back like she'd been burned.

"Why are you warm to the touch? And your eyes are brown, not ghastly red. What are you?" she demanded.

"A great hunter should understand her prey, no?"

Irritation sizzled beneath her skin.

She should have stuck her blade into his heart the first chance she had.

"Enough of this."

She raised her dagger and brought it down.

The beast ducked out of the way, and her blade sank into a book of poetry behind him. She gasped. "That's my favorite anthology!"

He flinched. "I'm sorry, but . . ."

His words were cut off as she flung a second dagger at him. He dodged to the right, but it grazed his shoulder before smashing into her mamá's vase. The two halted, waiting for the fiesta to go quiet and for people to come running in. But the horns and laughter still resounded.

"You will pay for that," she growled.

"But you threw it!" He had his hands up in surrender as she stomped toward him.

She grabbed her skirts and lifted them up.

The sediento had the nerve to appear scandalized. "Señorita, please."

She pulled the reata from her thigh.

"Not this again." He tried to back away, but there was nowhere for him to go. "Can you not speak like a reasonable . . ."

Carolina snapped the lasso into the air, catching him around his wrist. She tried to jerk him forward, but he did not budge. He wrapped his fingers around the braided leather and pulled. Carolina's breath came out in a huff as she slammed into his torso. Her fingers splayed over his chest. She tried to push herself off, but he enclosed her in his arms.

"Let go of me," she ordered, squirming against his grasp.

Stars above, did he have to feel so . . . so . . . good? His hold was strong and the muscles beneath his shirt and coat were hard but not in the bulky way of the men in her family. He felt . . . right.

"I will not release you until you agree to talk to me like two reasonable humans should."

"You are not human, though. You're a monster."

"Ah sí. But which of us is trying to kill the other?"

She struck with her forehead, landing hard against his face. A single drop of black blood dripped from his nostril.

Shock fell over his features. "That hurt."

"Yes, well. That was the point." She dug the heel of her boot into his foot, and he hissed.

His eyes bulged as she swung her knee into his nether parts. He made a strangled sound and released her. She stumbled and tripped on the rug. Carolina yelped as the weight of her dress yanked her backward. Her head was inches from smacking into the heavy desk her father kept his ledgers on, when fingers dug into her arms. The sediento pulled her up so fast, her mind spun. They were nose to nose, her hands grasping at his chest. His arms held her tight against him. She panted, but he stood frozen in place as if making a single movement might break him.

She couldn't help but feel every single point where his skin or clothing touched hers. She knew she should be revolted. His ilk took her grandfather away. They'd murdered her favorite person in the entire world. And yet, she hadn't shoved him back.

"Are you okay?" he asked, his tone achingly gentle.

Her eyes searched his. "Why would you save me like that?"

She would have cracked her skull on the corner of the desk and been an easy meal for the beast.

"Because I am not what you think. At least, I am not trying to be."

"Explain," she said. "And fast."

Neither of them made any effort to move from their embrace. She understood why he didn't let her go. He didn't want to die. But why wasn't *she* pushing *him* away?

"I was turned just over a month ago," he said. "By my calculations,

I have a few weeks until my body gives in, either to a final death or to the thirst. I am surviving by feeding off animal blood. I refuse to harm another human. I'd rather die than truly become one of the monsters we *both* hate. I have traveled all this way because I think . . ." He gulped. "I *hope* I can find a way to reverse what has been done to me before it's too late."

"As soon as you've been turned, your humanity is gone. There is no cure." Her mind went back to the last night her abuelo was alive. She thought of the sediento to first attack her, too. He had once been her cousin. He had once been an ordinary seventeen-year-old boy she envied because his parents always supported him. When she faced him in the courtyard, he was nothing more than a monster lost in bloodlust. But what if there had been a way to cure him? Lorenzo might be with his family now. She hardened herself against the sorrow before her heart ached. "You may as well let me kill you. You are as good as dead already."

"I can't," he said simply. "My sister's life depends on me finding what I came here for. I'm not only searching for a remedy. I'm trying to rid the world of sedientos for good."

Carolina scoffed. "Like I would believe that."

His eyes darkened. "You sound like the policía."

"You are a sediento, señor. If we purge the world of your kind, that means you will be gone as well."

"I will worry over that once I know my theories are correct."

"What sort of theories do you have?" she asked.

His eyes lit with hope. "I can show you. There are a number of transcripts and journals at my home. I have learned almost everything there is to know about sedientos."

The fact that she was entertaining this was ridiculous. He was playing her. She wasn't sure how or why. But if he knew things about the monsters that plagued her pueblo, shouldn't she at least ascertain what they were before thrusting her dagger through his heart? There was so much the people of Del Oro didn't know about los vampiros. Like where they came from. Why they started coming. And why they continued to return.

"Do you know the origins of your kind?" she asked. Her eyes slipped to his lips. She didn't know why. She didn't ask them to.

"I think I do," he said somberly.

"Tell me."

"I will, if you promise to—"

The doors to the library opened. In walked her papá and Rafa deep in conversation. The two men froze. Carolina gasped in horror. She and the sediento were chest to chest, breathless as if they'd just been engaged in a lover's kiss.

She pushed him away. "Papá, this is not what you think."

She saw the reata sprawled near the sediento's foot. She took Lalo's arm, hiding the rope under the hem of her dress.

Papá glared at them. The muscles of his jaw flexed and un-flexed as did the fists at his sides. Rafa looked equally enraged. Standing tall and large beside her father, his handsome face was etched with possessive ire.

"You dare dishonor me in such a manner," Papá growled. "Stealing away to be alone with some man I do not know."

"I . . ." How could she explain this? How could she possibly articulate to him what was truly going on without telling him everything she'd been up to? If she did that, he'd stop her mission to prove how good of a hunter she truly was. Papá would kill Lalo on the spot, and she'd be even more of a disgrace than he thought her to be for bringing a sediento into their home and hesitating.

Her pulse rushed through her ears. Sweat coated her skin.

She blurted out the first idea that bubbled to her brain. "We are in love!"

"What?" all three men said in unison.

She spun to Lalo and narrowed her eyes at him while she was turned away from her father. "Tell them, mi amor," she said through her false grin.

He gaped at her, and she squeezed his arm.

He forced a smile.

"It is as it seems, Señor Fuentes." The sediento straightened his coat. "I apologize for being so rash, for disrespecting you in this way, but one look at Carolina and I knew she was meant to be mine forever."

"You what?" Rafa said, squaring his shoulders. "You've only been acquainted for a few moments."

"And what is a few moments when our souls have known each other since the beginning of time?" Lalo said. When the men's faces went slack, he stiffened. "It is a line from Don Pío Parra's sonnet. Have none of you read . . ?" His words trailed off when Rafa cracked his knuckles, the sound like cannon fire in the quiet room. "No, I don't suppose you have. Well, I for one believe when one finds the person who is their match in both wit and, um . . ?"

He turned to Carolina for help, but she offered him nothing. She was too stunned by him reciting that poem. She had read that very line too many times to count.

"Are you betrothed, then?" Rafa asked.

Papá chuckled, incredulous. "Of course they aren't. My daughter will only marry a man of my choosing."

Carolina's hackles raised. "I am fully capable of deciding my own fate, thank you very much."

"Your fate has been decided, hija," Papá said through his clenched jaw. He clapped Rafa's shoulder. "My godson has already made an offer for your hand. And I have accepted it."

"*An offer?* What am I, some prize hog to be bartered for? My answer is no, in case you're wondering." Carolina gripped Lalo's arm tighter. "Besides, Lalo has already asked for my hand, and *I* have accepted. Right, Lalo?"

She shot daggers at him with her gaze.

"Yes. Indeed. I . . . I'd like to . . ." He shoved out the last two words as if they pained him. "Marry Carolina."

Carolina hoped Papá was buying this charade, but Lalo's acting abilities were lackluster.

Papá glared at Lalo like a bull readying to charge. "You would ask for my daughter's hand without speaking to her family first? To her papá! What type of man are you?"

Lalo blinked rapidly. "I . . . I suppose I was thinking with my heart, not my head."

"Yet you are a scholar. And I find you here, in the arms of a betrothed young woman."

"I never said yes to Rafa's proposal. I haven't even *heard* his proposal." Typical of her parents to assume they knew what was best for her. To lie and deceive and make deals with her "best interests" in mind. As if she couldn't decide for herself. Why did no one believe in her? Her father so easily dismissed her dreams, and her mother went right along with him. Not even her brothers or uncles stood up for her. The only two people in the world to ever even consider what she wanted out of life were Abuelo and Nena.

She clenched her fingers around Lalo's forearm. "I will marry whomever I want. When I want. *If* I want."

Papá's face hardened. "You will do as I say."

"Perhaps I should leave you two to discuss this family matter in private?" Lalo suggested, now looking physically ill.

"Oh, Lalo," Carolina said, adding a little break in her voice. She was indeed a magnificent performer. She'd been shedding false tears most of her life to get herself out of chores or trouble. Similar tears filled her eyes now. "Do not let our affection for each other be tarnished by my papá and his antiquated ways."

She kicked the reata under her skirts beneath the desk before rushing forward and seizing her father's sleeve. "Please, Apá. You and Mamá were a love match and see how happy you are. Shouldn't I be able to choose who I desire?"

Papá's eyes softened. He placed his hand over hers. "Mija, I have already given my permission to Rafa. And he has promised to take you to Los Campos as soon as his father is well."

"Los Campos!" she screeched. "That's at least two weeks' ride away."

"It's actually four," Lalo muttered.

She glared at him before turning back to her papá. "That's too far from home. No, I won't do it. I won't go." She loved Del Oro. She loved the people and the gentle change in seasons. She loved walking through the pastures and plucking wildflowers with Nena to weave into each other's hair. She loved her life here. She would not be forced to leave. "Lalo adores me. He said he will do anything to have me as his bride. He will not stand for this."

Papá's nostrils flared. "Oh really?"

Lalo shook his head. "I think what Carolina meant was—"

"Enough." Rafa began to roll up his sleeves. "We will settle this like men."

107

From the journal of Jonathan Monroe of Santemala

June 6, 1709

    Bloodlust is a real and visceral thing.

    I watched my daughter break through the bindings the priests assured us would hold her. But the chains of iron were no match for her strength.

    Tecuani is not weakened by iron, I told them. Sunlight, obsidian, tree roots, water from a flowing source. Those were what we needed. The only thing that kept her from tearing into us all was a string of wooden beads carved from oak root.

    The priests say there is only one thing to be done. Pierce her heart to sever the ties between our world and Tecuani's. But I cannot sentence my little girl to a final death. What father could? I will remain hopeful. Surely, there must be a way to control her thirst.

CHAPTER 11

Lalo

LALO FOLLOWED BEHIND THE PROCESSION OF GUESTS, HIS BOOTS dragging in the dirt, a mix of horror and confusion twisting deep inside his gut. Carolina's father and that brutish man who *actually* wanted to call himself her fiancé were leading the charge. Hushed gossip from the crowd filled Lalo's ears. People were beginning to take bets. If he were a gambling man, which he most assuredly was not, he would say the odds weren't in his favor.

He eyed Carolina, who stomped up the path beside him. Beautiful as the moon above. Beautiful yet vicious as a lioness, more like.

"This is your fault," he grumbled.

She glowered at him with a vehemence so palpable, he could feel the sting of hatred on his cheeks. "If you would have let me kill you, we wouldn't be in this mess in the first place."

"Perhaps if you were better with a blade, we wouldn't even be having this conversation. Alas, here we are." He gestured toward the growing throng.

"Lower your voice, fiend."

"Why should I be the one to die because you deem it so?"

"You exist. That is reason enough. I know about your kind. Murderers, the lot of you."

He laughed bitterly. "Takes one to know one, I suppose."

"What are you talking about?"

"What happens to all the cattle I see in the valley? Hmm? Do you not take their lives? Is it not the very same concept as what I've done?"

They wove up a hill to a patch of earth that was flattened out and filled with sand. *A fútbol court?* How ridiculous. This was to be where he would defend his and the hunter's honor? He didn't even like sports.

"It is not the same," she whispered. "And you know it. Your kind devours souls. You need human blood to survive. You crave it. You won't be able to resist for long, and when you give in, you'll enjoy sucking people dry."

"How little you understand. A pity I won't be around to educate you on the finer details of what it is to be un vampiro. Facts you should probably know, seeing as you traipse around as some masked vigilante at night."

"Quiet," she snapped. Her papá glanced over his shoulder at them. Slipping her arm into the crook of Lalo's elbow, she gave her father a defiant grin. "He thinks he can rule my life," she said through her teeth. "He is wrong."

"What a selfish thing to worry over at this moment. *My* life is the one at stake here."

"You'll be fine. These bullets are made of lead. Even if one pierces your heart, you should survive."

He gulped.

"Have you never been in a duel before?" she asked.

"Señorita, I've never shot a gun in my life."

She glanced up at him, shining stars dancing in her eyes. He didn't think the greatest artist could paint a face as beautiful as hers. Even that small line between her brows was a work of wonder. Too bad her personality was that of a badger.

"You are jesting," she said.

"I never joke," he replied.

She sighed and bit her bottom lip. The gesture made his body suddenly feel even more on fire than it already was. He jerked his gaze away.

"Shooting isn't too hard," she said. "You point and pull back the hammer. Don't fight the kickback, let your muscles absorb the shock."

"Easy for you to say."

She rolled her eyes. "The goal isn't to kill the person."

"Tell that to your fiancé."

"He is not my fiancé," Carolina said. Her smile widened. "You are, remember? That is, if you win this duel. And you'd better, or else I'll have to slay you here in front of everyone and I'm sure that won't bode well for either one of us. My papá would most likely ship me off tonight for causing such a scene."

"I wouldn't mind that last part," Lalo mumbled.

Rafael was now standing at the very center of the ball court. He loosened his cravat, then cracked his neck and knuckles. Torches were lit around the edges. Flames flickered and flapped

111

in the sudden breeze that swept over the distant mountains and through the valley floor.

"He is enjoying this," Lalo said, voice pitched with alarm.

"Yes, that is Rafa. He's always been a show-off. I heard he had a duel with the capitán of the Northern Army *and* his second-in-command after a card game."

"At the same time?"

"Sí. He got off two shots before they took one," she said in all seriousness.

"I am a dead man," Lalo whimpered.

"You already are deceased, señor. Therefore, you have nothing to fear."

"I have plenty to be afraid of." He lowered his tone as they drew nearer to the crowd. "I still *feel* pain. Getting shot cannot be a pleasant experience."

They stopped before her papá. Carolina never left Lalo's side. He had to give it to the girl, she was beautifully stubborn. His mother would have loved that. Not that she would have ever met her, of course. Lalo would never have brought some assassin from the middle of nowhere to meet his posh mother. Though, it would have made for an interesting affair.

As Señor Fuentes inspected both revolvers, Lalo found his sister among the throng. Fernanda appeared to be as sick as Lalo felt.

"You will each take five steps," Señor Fuentes said, loud enough for every guest to hear. "On my word, you will turn and shoot. The man left standing will win my daughter's hand."

How had Lalo gotten himself into this? All he wanted was to get his sister out of la ciudad before Maricela discovered them and find a way to save himself from the unrelenting thirst.

Yet here he was, getting ready to take part in a ludicrous show of machismo.

He should let Rafael shoot him and be done with the entire fiasco. He'd heal and then move on. But where could he and Fernanda possibly go next? Del Oro was el pueblo where Alma Rosario had died. She was the first to be slain, the first to have been bled dry. The original vampiro had to have been here, and they were the key to extinguishing both Lalo's unrelenting thirst and any vampiro in Abundancia.

"Apá, please," Carolina said. "Can we not resolve this by some other means?"

Rafael answered, "A duel is the only way to mend such disrespect. It will be he or I who survives. That is final."

Lalo gaped. "This duel is to the death?"

"Whoever is left standing will be the victor," Señor Fuentes offered. "You may decide whatever that means."

Rafael took the revolver from the case and held it at his chest. "Grab your weapon, Don Juan, or forever show this pueblo what a coward you are."

Don Juan! Lalo had been nothing but a gentleman his entire life. He hardly ever spoke to women before he was turned. He was most certainly *not* a rake.

He gingerly plucked the revolver from the velvet-lined case.

"Backs to each other," Señor Fuentes called.

Lalo turned and faced east. Rafael, west.

Carolina ran to the center of the pit. She wrapped her arms around Lalo, pretending to be a lamenting lover. Her lips tickled his cheek as she whispered, "Rafa is fast, but you are faster. Use your abilities. He will turn right before my father counts to five. He is aiming to kill, Lalo. Do not forget that."

Lalo's whole being felt fuzzy and warm. He should be focusing on the task at hand, but she was so soft against him. And her scent made his toes curl.

"Take your shot and duck to the right. Remain standing no matter what."

Carolina released her hold around his neck, eyes questioning. Everything inside Lalo ached for her comfort. But why? Why would his body betray him when she was the one to put him in this mess? She was his enemy in every sense of the word.

"Ready!" Señor Fuentes called.

Lalo fumbled with the pistol.

"One!"

This was really happening. His eyes met Carolina's. She urged him on with a jerky tilt of her head. He took a step.

"Two!"

He took another step. Fernanda covered her face but splayed her fingers so she could still watch.

"Three!"

He gazed at the moon, at his beloved stars. One more step.

"Four!"

Lalo spun.

"Five!"

A shot went off. Followed by a second.

Lalo winced. Then the world around him went silent.

CHAPTER 12

Carolina

Time stood still. No one moved. No one dared breathe.

Another burst of gunfire exploded through the sky. The blast came from a shotgun, loud and reverberating, emanating from the rich farmlands to the west. A fourth boom rang out in the distance.

"Sedientos!" someone yelled.

Papá had guards stationed within el pueblo so guests of the fiesta would feel safe. Only a few of his men were handling the outer farmlands.

The alarm bells began to clang.

The crowd turned to chaos. Flurries of people spurred to action. Grandmothers clutched their grandchildren and carried them toward Carolina's home. Many ran for the stables as Papá called out orders, Rafael moving by his side. Señora Orozco tripped on her huaraches and tumbled to the dirt.

Carolina lifted her skirts and ran for the older woman.

"Here," she said, gently wrapping her fingers around la señora's soft arms. "Let me help you."

She eased the woman up.

Señora Orozco hissed. "I scraped my knees."

"We better get you inside quickly," Carolina said. She remembered the last time blood had been spilt in el pueblo at night. How could she forget? Her blood had dripped from the wounds on her arms and Abuelo lost his life because of it.

Carolina froze as the memories flooded through her. The monster latching on to his neck. Her catching him as he fell. She could still feel his last breath on her skin.

"I've got her," Señora Orozco's daughter said, running to meet them. She took her mother, and they limped away.

The throng cleared, and Carolina caught sight of Lalo. He stood chillingly still. Like a predator readying to strike. The steel pistol hung loosely from his grasp. His eyes glowed a vicious red. His nostrils flared. His lips peeled back, revealing two dagger-like fangs.

"Shit," Carolina whispered. Between her papá giving Rafa permission to marry her and then the commotion of the duel, she'd almost forgotten what Lalo was: a leech. Seeing him now, turning into one before her very eyes, Carolina was doused in the bitter cold river of reality. She tugged up her skirts and reached for the last weapon she had. Someone grabbed Carolina by the wrist.

"Please," Fernanda pleaded. "You must help my brother. He's losing control."

Lalo's pistol plopped into the dirt. He lowered into a crouch. His focus set on the injured Señora Orozco as she limped toward the casa.

"This ends now," Carolina whispered. She drew free the wooden stake that she'd strapped to her thigh.

"No!" Fernanda clinched Carolina's arm. "Please. *Please* don't take him from me. He's all I have left."

Carolina scoffed but then she saw the utter desperation in Fernanda's face.

"I beg of you. Help my brother. He knows things. He . . . he can help your pueblo. If you kill him now, you'll lose that!"

The girls stared at each other for a moment. Carolina wanted to hate Fernanda, to shame her for sticking by a sediento's side, but Carolina could not see past the anguish in Fernanda's eyes.

Lalo started to advance.

Carolina cursed and heaved up her skirts. "Come on. I'll help your brother, but for selfish reasons only."

Fernanda nodded. "Fine by me."

Carolina ran after Lalo, Fernanda close beside her.

Lalo was gaining speed. If they didn't get to him now, he would have poor Señora Orozco by the throat.

"Take this," Carolina said. She dug into her bodice and took out a vial of springwater. It was a fact that sedientos could not touch the stuff. They could not even cross a creek without their bowels twisting.

See, she wanted to yell at Lalo, *I do know things.* People were always counting her out. Even pinche vampiros, it seemed.

"When I have him pinned, pour that water on his skin," she said.

Fernanda nodded, pulling the stopper out with her teeth.

A guttural hum came from Lalo's throat. One of the older women started to turn, but Carolina lunged and tackled Lalo into the brush before anyone took notice of his eyes and teeth. The two tumbled through the brambles and into a small opening.

117

She could feel the strength in his body. The power. But she was well trained in grappling. She was even better at fighting dirty.

Carolina kneed Lalo in the groin then his stomach. Warm air wheezed out of his lungs.

He grabbed Carolina by the hair and twisted until she bucked and exposed her neck. Lalo's scarlet-colored eyes raked over her throat. He growled.

Carolina elbowed him in the jaw to silence him.

Lalo's fingers dug into her wrists, stopping her from doing it again. He pinned her to the ground, holding her arms above her head, straddling her with his entire weight.

"You will taste divine," he snarled.

He opened his mouth, revealing gleaming fangs.

Water trickled over Lalo's neck and into Carolina's eyes. He reared back. A shocked howl burst from his lips. Fernanda had doused him with the springwater, and not a moment too soon.

Where the liquid had touched, Lalo's skin began to blister and sizzle. The sound reminding her of bacon on a frying pan. Disgust rocked through her. As he cursed in agony, she grasped the stake in her hand tighter, feeling the wood bite into her palms.

Plunge it into his heart, she told herself. *Finish what you started before it gets even more out of hand. Show everyone what you can do.*

"Don't hurt him!" Fernanda fell beside them. "Please!"

Lalo's maddened eyes softened. His head swiveled toward his sister's. He blinked.

"Fernanda?" he rasped.

His attention moved to Carolina, who was still very much underneath his weight.

"Oh no," he whispered. He peered down at his palms, and

118

for the first time, Carolina noticed there was inky blood on his hands. Horror twisted his features. "Did I hurt anyone?"

"No," Carolina said softly. The gentleness coming from her own lips surprised her.

Lalo sighed in relief.

He winced. Shakily, he pulled back his coat. A dark spot stained the center of his chest. Lalo blinked. "I believe I've been shot."

His eyes rolled back, and he slumped, landing face-first in the dirt.

September 3, 1829

LOS CAMPOS SOCIALITES
By Doña Larissa Cordova

*Eduardo Villalobos the Second entered the police station
on Sacramento Avenue a little after dawn. He is the son of
the late well-known luxury boot tycoon, Eduardo Villalobos
the First. People at the station overheard the younger Eduardo
screaming about a beautiful woman eating his parents. Of all
the absurd things to say.*

*His younger sister, Fernanda Villalobos, has recently
joined polite society. Though Fernanda was the belle of every
debutante ball she attended, I suspect that behind closed doors,
she is as strange as her older brother, who has always been a
recluse. Will Señorita Villalobos find a proper male suitor?
Will the troubled son of Los Campos's favorite socialites ever
take a wife?*

CHAPTER 13

Lalo

From the window Lalo watched his parents step onto the cobbled road in front of their townhouse in Los Campos. They walked arm in arm, both dressed in their finest clothes for some charity ball. Someone in a cloak sauntered by. Mother's heel got stuck between two stones. Father knelt, laughing at the situation. He must have pulled too vigorously because Mother's shin popped him in the nose so hard, he bled. The person in the cloak halted. Pale and delicate hands pulled back the hood, and long red hair flowed freely in the breeze. Her eyes glowed like embers. Then she struck.

Lalo jerked awake. He gasped for air.

His fingers brushed over the bedsheets that had been thrown loosely over his legs and torso. Odd, seeing as he never slept without them tucked tightly around him. Someone had helped him to bed then. But who? Matter of fact: *How* had he made it into bed?

The smell of warm vanilla, lavender, and leather floated into his senses carrying with them the memories of last night's fiasco.

He stilled. Lalo was not in his room. In fact, this wasn't even his house. The walls surrounding him were painted an ugly yellow. Swords and placards were displayed like artwork. The furniture was sparse.

But the scent of that demon girl was everywhere.

Something cold nipped into his throat. A dagger. His eyes snapped to the young woman hidden within the shadows, to the girl who seemed to always have some sort of sharp object pointed at him.

"One wrong move and you are dead," she whispered.

"Yes. I know the drill well enough. You might want to consider changing up your strategy, though. Along with a good kick to the groin, holding me at knifepoint is getting rather old."

She shushed him. "Keep your voice down, sanguijuela. Do you want another scandal?"

"Saints, no." A chill kissed his skin. And he was suddenly all too aware that he was naked from the waist up. He grabbed the covers and shoved them against his bare chest. "Where is my shirt?"

"I had to discard it."

"You disrobed me?" he said, incredulity dripping from his every word. He checked under the covers. His jaw dropped. "I am in nothing but my underpants."

She rolled her eyes. "I have seven brothers, señor. I have seen worse."

"What if someone comes in?" He jolted. "Where am I?"

"You are in my abuelo's bedroom. I had to get you somewhere no one would go while you healed."

122

He gulped. "So you can finally have your way with me in private?"

"Behave yourself." She wiggled her brows.

Lalo balked. "Saints, woman, that isn't what I meant. I meant so you can kill me like the murderess you are." A terrifying thought occurred to him. "Fernanda, where—"

"Your sister is asleep in my bed, pretending to be me. I'm here to make sure you don't try anything in my own home."

"Where would I go without any clothes?!"

"Keep your voice down," she snapped.

Lalo took a calming breath. "May I have my shirt and breeches?"

"I threw them in the fire. You were shot. There was blood or whatever the hell is inside you seeping out of your wound for the entire world to see."

He hadn't even pulled the trigger before Rafael had fired his weapon. That cheater had turned at the count of four not five, just like she had warned. Meanwhile, Lalo had panicked and forgotten to shoot his own weapon. Then the world had turned to mayhem around him. And his thoughts and control had dissolved when he caught a whiff of spilled blood.

She leaned forward. "You wouldn't heal for a long while. I've not seen one of your kind act so weakly before."

"As I said, I do not partake in feasting on human blood."

She pursed her lips in disbelief. How many times would he have to explain that fact before she took him seriously?

"What happened?" he asked. "After the duel you forced me into. You're welcome, by the way."

She snorted, rather rudely. "It is you who should be thanking

123

me. I saved you from going after sweet Señora Orozco. That would have ultimately forced me to kill you once and for all."

"How did you stop me?" he asked.

She pulled her dagger back and held it on her lap. The blade sparked in the low candlelight. It was thin, with star lilies depicted on the handle, while a single ruby sat at the tip of the hilt. The piece appeared old and expensive. A peculiar bit of weaponry for a ruffian.

"I know there are things I do not understand about you and your kind, but there are some things I do." Her fingers toyed with the necklace around her throat. She had a beautiful neck. And the vein just there, beneath her brown skin, throbbed ever so enticingly. He gulped and turned away, disgusted by the thirst and desire burning through him.

"I know your kind cannot enter a home unless welcomed," she said. "Springwater weakens you. Wood through the heart kills. Obsidian too. And the sun scorches your skin, of course."

"Indeed?" He leaned forward, trying to take in Carolina Fuentes's features. Trying to determine if there was any part of her he could trust with his truth. He'd so often been dismissed in his life because of his prickly personality. There had been too many times to count that he watched the light go out in people's eyes when he told them about his day. He'd given up trying.

He was awkward and shy, and he didn't care for going to balls or enduring meaningless small talk about people's wealth and popularity. He hated how the upper crust of society thought they were somehow more valuable than others just because of what was in their pocketbooks. He was brushed off as a bore. And after so long, he decided he would rather be alone and figure things out by himself than try.

Until now.

Now he needed help. So far, he'd only gotten into more trouble than out. Though, to be fair to himself, Carolina was mostly to blame as of late.

"You and you sister are close," Carolina said.

His brow furrowed. "Is that a question or statement?"

"She begged me to save you when the bloodlust took over. She wanted to protect you so badly." Carolina huffed. "Ironic, isn't it? Considering you are the one who we need to protect people from." He opened his mouth to retort, but she held up a hand. "You said in the library that you were searching for a way to end vampiros."

Lalo's spine straightened. "You remember that?"

"Not something I'd easily forget." She shrugged. "I can see you and your sister love each other, and that you're terrified to lose one another. I understand that feeling. I've buried too many loved ones to count at this point."

"Why have you never left this land?" he asked gently.

"And go where? The Fuenteses built Del Oro from the ground up. This place is all we know. Being rancheros is in our blood. And if we aren't here to stop the sedientos who plague Boca de la Muerte, who will?"

"So you are trying to protect your family too. Like me."

"Yes. In that single sense, you and I are the same." She met his gaze, and his body nearly melted onto the floor. She pulled away first and stood. "What do we need to do to end them?"

His mouth went dry at the word *we*. He scooted up a bit more, forgetting the blanket concealing his bare chest. Her eyes darted to his torso then to the floor. Lalo wondered if he should have squeezed his abdomen a bit tighter, just so she could see the defined muscles there like the boys in school did during ball games.

He shook his head. What was he thinking?

Lalo cleared his throat and asked, "What do you know of Alma Rosario?"

CHAPTER 14

Carolina

She frowned. What did this stranger from the south know of Alma?

"Why?" she asked, her tone more accusing than she meant it to be. "How do you even know that name?"

"Alma Rosario is the reason I am here," he said.

Carolina's brow furrowed deeper. "Are you related to her?"

She prayed to every god that weren't so. Because whether she cared to admit it or not, she was attracted to Lalo Montéz. Not emotionally, of course. He was still a sediento. But physically? She couldn't deny the fact that he was beautiful. Even the way he tried to flex his muscles nonchalantly was endearing. She lived in a world with barrel-chested brutes, and it was rather refreshing to meet someone so . . . unassuming.

"I am not related to any Rosarios that I know of," he said.

"That's a relief."

His brows shot up. "How come?"

"Um." She shook her head. "No reason." *Except for the fact that I am torn between pining for you and wanting to kill you.* She winced at her own thoughts. Who used the word *pining* anyway? Nena's secret-romance manuscripts she insisted Carolina proofread must have been rubbing off on her.

"Anyway, you were asking what I knew of Alma. She was alive three or four generations back. One day, not long after her husband passed, she went missing. The people of el pueblo searched high and low for her but could never find her. After a month, they assumed she had taken her life."

"You know quite a bit about her."

"I do," Carolina said. "She was my great-great-great-grandmother." Hence, her satisfaction that they were not some long-lost distant cousins.

"She was a Fuentes?" he asked.

"Yes. Rosario was her maiden name. She was Alma Rosario Fuentes."

"I tried to find such facts in my research before, but there had been no census or marriage certificates conducted during that time. Or, at least, duplicates of the records had not made their way to the cities."

She watched as his eyes grew distant. Carolina could tell his mind was whirling inside.

"What are you thinking?" she asked.

"Promise to have an open mind?"

"You are alive, no? That should prove my mind is open enough."

"Point well taken." He cleared his throat. "Alma's husband had recently perished," he said. "Then she went missing in the woods. Eventually, her body was found, but it had been drained of blood."

She sat on the bed, her thigh accidently bumping into his own leg. "How did you know that?"

"A society page."

She giggled. She didn't mean to. The laughter simply bubbled right out of her.

He half grinned. "Amusing, yes. But there's more. Do you know much about the gods?"

"Amá has had me in religious classes since before I could walk. I can name all seventy-seven of the lesser dioses in alphabetical order if you'd like."

"Perhaps another time." His gaze flicked to her thigh. She was in a nightdress—there was no skin showing, but the silhouette of her knee could be seen. Carolina liked the way his chest started to rise just a bit faster while he looked upon her. It made her feel strangely powerful.

He scooted away stiffly. "What about Tecuani? What do you know of him?"

"Abuelito used to tell us stories about Tecuani when we wouldn't go to bed." She smiled. "He said the dios took on the form of a jaguar to hunt for misbehaving children."

"Why would he terrorize his grandchildren like that?"

She chuckled to herself. "We were rather naughty." Her heart suddenly felt as raw as the day she'd lost him. "My abuelo was killed by un vampiro a month ago."

Lalo winced. "I am sorry. My parents were taken from me last year."

"By sedientos?"

He nodded once. "No one believed me. We aren't so acquainted in the cities with the monsters like Del Oro is. They do not attack so openly in the ciudad. I watched my parents die. I saw this monster that seemed so human tear into them. I went to the authorities, but they laughed in my face and disregarded me. I knew what I saw. So I started researching anything and everything I could find about creatures who fed off human blood. I went to every clandestine meeting or university lecture I could find on the lore of devils and the like. By pure luck, I found an old journal written by a man from Santemala for sale. The author stated that, in desperation, he called upon Tecuani and begged the god to bring his only daughter's soul back to the realm of the living."

Carolina's eyes widened. "That's blasphemous."

"Maybe so. But we all have the ability to do terrible things when we feel like hope is lost."

"And do you think that excuses their sins?" she asked.

Lalo shrugged. "I am the last person to judge anyone for their sins." He suddenly appeared haunted. She wasn't sure she wanted to know what he'd done since turning into un sediento.

"According to the man's journal, Tecuani said he would bring the man's daughter back from the Land of the Dead, but at a cost."

"What was the price?" she asked.

"I don't know. From what I gathered, the man agreed. But his daughter was not the same little girl he cherished. She was different. *Una diabla*, he wrote. He said she killed her own mother and he himself had to strike her down in the end."

"Gods above." Carolina made the sign of protection.

Lalo wiped his palms against the sheets. "What if Alma went into the forest to pray to Tecuani? I found no evidence of

130

vampiros in Abundancia prior to her death. You said she'd lost her husband, might she have—"

"Are you insinuating *my* ancestor went against the laws of nature? You dare say a Fuentes summoned these monsters!"

"When one is grieving the love of their life, they might do unspeakable things."

"Not a Fuentes." Carolina stood suddenly and began to pace. She clutched the dagger she'd found among her abuelo's things tight in her hand. "There were bite marks on her neck. She was a victim, not the wrongdoer."

"But what if she did summon Tecuani? What if her husband's soul returned to his body, and he became a monster like the other countryman's daughter?"

"Enough. I refuse to listen to you slander my family's name." She started for the door. She needed a moment to gather her thoughts.

Lalo threw the covers back, moved near her, and grasped her arm. "One last question, please. What happened when the people of el pueblo brought Alma's body back from the forest?"

Carolina slowly turned toward him, and he released his hold. Her eyes flicked to his bare chest, to the wound that had almost completely healed.

"She burst from her grave and killed nearly everyone in her wake," Carolina whispered.

He nodded. "She was *made.* Like me. What if her husband was one of death's curses? He might have lost control and killed Alma. Remorseful, he could have fed her his own blood to revive her. The process takes days. Her family might have found her and taken her to be buried without knowing she'd been turned."

"That is a far-fetched tale, señor."

"Maybe so. Maybe not. If I am correct, I can assure you that when she woke, the thirst was insatiable. The need to kill is uncontrollable."

From what Carolina understood, some fifty people lost their lives that night. Thought to be possessed, Alma massacred everyone in her path until someone sliced off her head.

Carolina studied Lalo's soft brown skin, his silly mustache, his kind eyes. Was he a victim like her great-great-great-grandmother?

"How many lives have you taken?" she asked.

"Let's just say I am damned." He rested his hand over his heart. "So long as I am of sound mind and I can silence the thirst, I will fight to ensure no one else loses loved ones because of un vampiro."

"*You* will fight?" she teased.

"It's a figure of speech."

She smiled. "I see." Carolina liked how seriously he took everything. She wondered if he ever laughed.

"If I'm correct and your great-great-great-grandfather was the first vampiro in Abundancia, he very well could be the monster to end my misery. When I was turned, I saw scattered bits and pieces of my maker's memories. I saw a jagged mountain range just like Devil's Spine. She was here at some point in her life. She very well could have been turned by Alma's husband. If we kill him, the thread of power that links people like me to the god of death will be cut. The power inside us will be destroyed."

"You know this for certain?"

"I don't. But at this point, it's my best working theory, the only thing that makes sense."

"My family has fought for generations to keep this pueblo safe. And here you are telling me it was us who brought the devils to the entire country. Alma's death could have been a random attack. Why do you specifically believe it was my great-great-great-grandfather who turned her?"

"If the attack was random, the vampiro who turned her would have fled knowing the people of Del Oro were after it. Your pueblo is small but resilient. Finding shelter in one of the larger ciudades would have been much simpler. But when a soul is pulled from the Land of the Dead by Tecuani, that person cannot venture far from their resting place. That soul is basically trapped. I believe it may be why they make new vampiros in the first place: the original sediento would need others to do its bidding elsewhere."

"Why would Alma bring her lover back knowing he could never leave these lands?"

"The god is a trickster. She might not have known. Besides, would she have cared if it meant her husband was alive? But the killings continued after Alma was slain because *she* brought him back. It only makes sense that he is still somewhere in or around the valley. He cannot leave. Thus, your precious pueblo is in constant danger from sedientos. Los vampiros are likely here to catch their maker's next meal."

"How do you know such facts?"

"We can go to my home right now. I can show you proof."

She pursed her lips. "What would the writings of a desperate father do to change my mind?"

"If you aren't going to at least try to understand, why am I still here? Why not kill me like you clearly wish to do?"

"Because your sister begged me to spare you, and because I need you."

Lalo balked. "You do?"

133

"You and I are to be betrothed."

He reared back. "¿Qué? How? I was very clearly shot. I lost. Where is your true fiancé anyway? Don't you think he'll be angered to see you in here with a bare-chested man?"

"Rafa is dead."

His jaw dropped. "Sedientos?"

She shook her head.

"Rafa was pierced by a horn," she said, picking at her nails.

"A horn?"

"From a bull."

"A bull?"

"It was an angry bull."

He blinked, stunned by her confession. "My stars. I . . . I'm sorry."

She snorted. The way his face became so suddenly animated made her heart twist in strange knots.

"I am only teasing, Lalo. Rafa is fine. He did get stuck by a bull horn, but he'll recover."

Lalo let loose a breath. "So we aren't engaged then?"

"Not yet. We will be, though. My papá cannot deny you now."

"You said he's . . . I lost the duel."

"No, you didn't."

"I was there, señorita. I was shot."

She smirked. "But no one else knows that. You were seen as the last man to leave the field. Rafa ran away, granted it was for a good reason, but you stood your ground. You are the victor. And I am your prize."

They stared at each other for a moment. A current thrummed through her core. She had to force her eyes to stay put. To not flick down to his chest and abdomen. She may have seen other boys in el pueblo with their shirts off before, but none made her cheeks feel flushed.

She cleared her throat. "I will help you search for answers, and in exchange you will be my doting fiancé. Just until I can find a way to convince my parents I am more than capable of taking care of myself."

He had the nerve to appear perplexed. "Proper women cannot live without a husband."

"Who said I cared a lick about being proper? I am here, aren't I? Practically in the arms of my sworn enemy."

"What about your father?" he asked. "He'll never approve of our betrothal. I'm quite certain he hates me."

"You can leave that to me, my love." She reached up and tapped him on the nose.

La familia Fuentes is the pillar of Del Oro, Abundancia. You will not pass a shop or home in el pueblo that a Fuentes hasn't had a hand in helping.

History of Del Oro, California. (1803) [Excerpt]

CHAPTER 15

Lalo

LALO JOLTED AT HER TOUCH. HIS BODY FIZZLED WITH ENERGY. He was alone in a room with someone who would happily stake him, and yet he could only focus on the way her touch made him feel . . . and her mouth.

Even when she was scowling, which was often, the corners of her lips turned up as if they were in on a joke that she wasn't aware of.

"Why are you staring at me like that?" she snapped.

"Like what?"

She simpered. "You are gazing at me as if you wish to kiss."

He choked on his own saliva. "Of all the ridiculous notions. You are the one who keeps touching me! If I didn't know better, I'd think *you* wished to kiss. In fact, I should run out of this room just as I am and scream to the world that you are trying to seduce me."

"You wouldn't dare. A scandal like that would ruin your sister's reputation as well."

"You are despicable," he said.

"No, I am capable. Most men can't differentiate the two."

That was true. And he couldn't deny that he admired the fire that came from her tongue. Quick and ruthless, she would definitely be able to help him through this mess if she agreed to it.

"How about this?" he said. "I will pretend to adore you, even though that will be practically impossible. And in return, you help me figure out if your great-great-great-grandparents started un vampiro bloodline. If I am wrong and your precious Fuentes name remains untarnished, I'll get on my knees and beg for your forgiveness. Do we have a deal?"

"I do like the idea of that." A single, dark brow raised. "Still, shouldn't people avoid making deals with the devil?"

He shrugged. "I'll manage."

Carolina snorted. "Was that a jest? Coming from you?"

He hadn't meant it as a joke. Carolina frightened him more than any monster. She made his body react in devilish ways he'd never experienced before. The sensation was rather terrifying.

"We have a deal," she said. "But before we step a single foot outside this room, I must teach you a thing or two about basic combat."

He recoiled. "Why?"

"Because if we happen upon any of your kind, I will not hesitate to fight, and an unworthy partner will slow me down."

"I'm only wearing underpants." He gestured at his body. "Shall I strip down too so we are on even ground?"

"Saints, no. You are a heathen."

She laughed, rolling her eyes. She placed the ruby-embellished dagger in her clutches on the night table, faced him, and put up her fists. "I want you to try and hit me."

Lalo balked. "I beg your pardon?"

"Try and hit me," she commanded again.

"I don't want to hurt—" Lalo's face cracked to the left. His hand cupped his throbbing cheek. "You punched me!"

"That was hardly a punch. And for the millionth time, lower your voice. We wouldn't want anyone to barge in on us like this."

That would be a disaster. Her father would probably duel Lalo himself.

"Lesson one," she said, bouncing lightly on her bare feet. "The person to throw the first blow typically wins. You can knock your opponent off their balance and strike again easier. Now, put your fists up and see if you can stop me."

"I don't think—"

She swung again, smacking him hard against his temple with an open palm.

Irritation blazed within him. "You demon!"

Carolina batted her lashes. "Takes one to know one."

This time, when she lunged for him, he was ready. He held up his arms and blocked her advance. It still hurt, though. The girl hit with the strength of a ram.

"Very good," she said. "Now it's your turn to swing."

Lalo knew if he hesitated the little brat would take the first opportunity she had to assault him once more. And she'd enjoy it too.

He half-heartedly thrust his fist. Carolina did not offer an ounce of mercy. She grabbed his arm and twisted his wrist so hard that he thought it might snap. His knees buckled when she pinched a nerve, and he collapsed onto the floor.

"Lesson number two," she said, hovering over him like a

reaper. "Never let your opponent get you on the ground. You are a dead man if so." She mimicked stabbing him in the neck and chest with her fingers.

"Come." She pulled him to his feet. "Ready for lesson three?"

"I—"

The air rushed out of his lungs, and he wheezed. He bent over, gasping for breath. The little beast had struck him in the gut.

She angled her body, so they were nose to nose. "Never let your guard down."

"You are wicked," he rasped.

"Be grateful I didn't demonstrate lesson four."

He grimaced. "What is it? Kick your opponent's puppy?"

"Close," she said in all seriousness. "The fourth lesson is to do whatever it takes to survive. Bite, pull hair, hit their nether regions. Fighting dirty is sometimes the only way to win." She patted his back. "You did well for your first training."

Slowly, he straightened, rubbing his throbbing temple. "Did I?"

Carolina raised her fist as if she were going to punch him again. He blocked his body, shielding himself from her abuse.

She beamed. "See. You do learn fast. Or perhaps I am a great teacher?"

"Your humility knows no bounds."

"I agree." Carolina winked. "One last lesson."

He frowned.

"I will not hurt you. I promise."

Silently, she stepped to him and took his hand. Her calluses scraped against his skin as she closed his fingers into a fist. She tucked his thumb just under his knuckles. A shudder ran through him at the sudden intimacy of the gesture.

"When you throw a punch, lead with these two knuckles."

She brushed the pad of her thumb over his pointer and middle finger. Chills exploded over Lalo's skin. "Rotate your hand inward and make sure to keep your wrist perfectly straight."

She eased his arm up and demonstrated what she meant. Her hands slid over his bare skin until his form was just right. He could only pray she didn't notice the goose bumps there.

He tilted his chin to catch a glimpse of her face. He wished he hadn't because their gazes met, and his stomach did that dreadful flip he found so unpleasant.

"I think I've got it," he whispered.

She stepped away. "Good," she said. "Very good. Let's get you dressed."

CHAPTER 16

Carolina

CAROLINA SWEPT TO HER ABUELO'S ARMOIRE AND THRUST OPEN the doors. His scent still lingered within. Leather, tobacco, and mint. She breathed in deeply. She'd come up here every day since he was slain just to feel like he was nearby. That was how she'd found the beautiful dagger with the ruby hilt she used to threaten Lalo with. The piece had been stashed away at the very rear of the dresser, hidden behind layers of dusty cloth.

She reached for a shirt and breeches, flinging them at Lalo. "Put these on."

He blinked at her, holding her abuelo's large clothes against his thin frame. "These won't fit me."

"Oh, I'm sorry. I'll fetch the tailor. While I'm at it, I should grab the barber as well. You need a trim off the top."

Lalo's lips flattened. "Since we are working together, you might want to reel in that attitude of yours. Starry-eyed lovers are supposed to bat their lashes at each other and call each other cariño."

"Did you read that somewhere?"

"Well . . . yes."

She scoffed. "We will worry about terms of endearment and my attitude later. We need to get you out of here. I think we've pushed our chances for long enough."

"That would be best. Tell me, has anyone in your family mentioned your great-great-great-grandfather? I'd like to know what sort of man he was."

"His name was Vidal. He would never do anything to harm his family. That is all you need to know."

Lalo crossed his arms.

Her irritation spiked. "Most everything in el pueblo burned down after Alma was turned. If there *is* any documentation about him, it would be in a sacred location—the one building that will never burn because everyone will do whatever it takes to save it."

"The church? The library?"

She shook her head. "La cantina."

Lalo snickered but then recovered that uptight scowl he seemed to prefer. He stuffed his legs into the pants. He was around the same height as Abuelo, but the fit was wrong. The moment he buttoned his breeches, they slid off his hips and pooled at his feet. Carolina huffed. She dug into her abuelo's armoire and pulled out a belt. She swept forward, yanked up his pants, and shoved the tip through the loop.

Lalo had gone perfectly still, save for the notch on his throat that bobbed up and down.

"We should talk about boundaries," he rasped. "That is, if you don't want me to go feral."

She ignored the sudden quickening of her heart rate when he spoke so quietly. Her fingers cinched the belt tight. "Care to have another sparring session to test my skills against your ferociousness?"

"Lucky for you, I possess self-restraint."

Carolina laughed. Something she had done more in the past few minutes than she'd done in the last few weeks. She turned to shut the armoire. She peeked over her shoulder as he slipped the borrowed shirt over his head. She couldn't help but appreciate a final glimpse of his abdomen. Of those muscles taut beneath his brown skin.

"We should go before dawn breaks," she said, needing to set her mind back to rights. "The rain has started. You will be sheltered from the sun, but we should sneak away before everyone rises."

"Are we safe leaving the town walls?" he asked. "Do sedientos attack often?"

"*I* will be fine. I can't say for sure how you will fare."

Lalo gave her a deadpan glare.

"We should be perfectly safe with so many of father's guard milling about. Getting past them, undetected, worries me the most."

They snuck out of her abuelo's room, and Carolina shut the door with an almost imperceptible click. She halted when she heard signs of life. Her family was already beginning to wake. Even after a chaotic night, the house stirred to life before the roosters crowed. She shouldn't be surprised.

The sizzle and pop of breakfast cooking over the fire and

whispers of chisme already floated into her ears. She could hear her younger siblings arguing about who got their chilaquiles first and could smell the tortillas frying on the aged skillet. This warmth, the constant bickering, the gossip, the hushed staccato of her mamá's and papá's whispers, was all she ever wanted. She never wished to leave Del Oro for this very reason. She wanted the noise, the arguments, the messiness of her family always.

She gazed up at the vampiro and caught him watching her.

"What?" she whispered.

He shook his head. "Nothing. You just looked, I don't know, sweet for a moment there."

"I *am* sweet. Just not to monsters. Or most people." She shrugged. "I'm an acquired taste." Grabbing his hand, she tugged him forward. His skin was soft and warm. So unlike the tales of sedientos and el pueblo boys she grew up with. She wondered how his fingers might feel fluttering across her cheek.

Stop that, she scathed. *Stop thinking about his hands and his lips and his damn chest. You should be focusing on finding the true original sediento. On ending them so your family can live in peace, and you can prove to your family how wrong they were to count you out.*

"We can't go through the kitchens or the front of the house, but there is a side entrance most people won't use. Are you friendly with dogs?" she asked.

"Not particularly."

"Well, let's hope ours are partial to you. There are five of them. Big beastly things my papá uses for hunting sedientos."

Lalo blanched. "Gods, help me."

They had just landed on the first floor when she saw her mamá approaching.

"Shit!" Carolina turned and shoved Lalo into the room

beside them with brute force. He tripped over the rug and fell backward. Carolina slammed the door shut just as Mamá caught a glimpse of her.

Mamá's eyes went as wide as full moons.

"What are you doing up and about at this early hour?"

"I was . . ."

"Sneaking off into your abuelo's rooms," Mamá finished.

Horror overtook Carolina. She shook her head. "No . . . I . . ."

Mamá placed her hand on Carolina's cheek. "You do not need to be ashamed of hiding away among his things, mija. We all grieve in different ways."

Carolina's face burned with shame. Here she was, sneaking about and allying herself with a sediento. For what? A fool's errand? Revenge? To spite her father? The lines were starting to blur. Besides Abuelo and Nena, Lalo was the only other person who believed in her abilities. That meant something to her.

Mamá gave her a little pat before starting to walk away. "Time to get ready. I've sent Luz Elena to your room to help you dress."

"What? Why?" Carolina tried to sound calm but inside she was shaking. Luz Elena, her very nosy, very snobby nanny, was on her way to her room. To the place she'd stashed Fernanda last night after the duel.

Wanting to keep Lalo's injuries a secret, Carolina told anyone who asked about the Montézes' whereabouts that they'd gone home last night to check on their goats to ensure they were safe. Carolina was certain they had no such goats, but it was the cleverest story she could scramble up at the time. Luz Elena would surely spot Fernanda and tell Mamá there was someone else in Carolina's bed. And that would lead to questions about why Carolina had lied, which would only force her to lie more.

"I'll go to her now." Carolina gave her mamá a peck on the cheek. She skidded to a halt and asked, "Why am I getting dressed up?"

Mamá put her hands on her hips. "We are going to meet your suitor, the one who so elegantly disrupted our entire fiesta by breaking the ice sculpture of your abuelito. Surely you remember the boy you were seen tucked away with in a darkened library."

Something crashed in the room beside her. Lalo most likely tripped over a broom. But at least he knew what Mamá's plans were. He could run to his home and be ready for them long before they arrived.

Mamá's brow furrowed. She started toward the source of the noise.

"Yes, um, about last night," Carolina said, moving in front of the door concealing the sediento in question. "We didn't mean to cause such a commotion. We are just . . . we . . . we're so in love."

Carolina's stomach pinched at the mere mention of the word. She hadn't been in love before, but she imagined her impulsiveness would kick in. She was forever running headfirst into things. Being in love might make her recklessness worse.

Mamá smiled wistfully. "I was young once," she said. "I know what it is to lose all sense at the sight of an attractive boy. When I first saw your papá, I knew he was the one for me. He was tall and strapping, even at seventeen."

Carolina plastered on a fake smile. She didn't need to hear about her parents' love story. She had to get to her room before Luz Elena did.

"He rode west for seven weeks just to visit my hometown of Presidio with the intention of marrying Cecilia Ramírez. But he fell for me instead."

There were so many Fuenteses in Del Oro. It was nearly impossible to find someone who was unrelated to Carolina's family within el pueblo, so going to another to find a bride or groom was common.

"We were caught as well. Did you know that?" Mamá asked.

"You were?"

"My father wanted to kill Luis. Actually, he tried." Mamá giggled like a schoolgirl. "A fact that I reminded your padre of this morning. Do not let your head hang low, mija. You are young and beautiful and full of life. Why shouldn't you fall for a man who is the same?"

Lalo was as alive as Carolina's leather boot. But nevertheless, if being betrothed to him meant not having to endure the presence of Rafa or any other arranged match, she would gladly cling to this falsehood.

She eyed the door. He was surely listening. But she had to continue with the charade. "Lalo is so handsome."

"Indeed. Though, poor Rafael came all this way. We are so close with his family."

"A pity."

Del Oro's mission bells clanged. "Go get ready, Carolina. We have a few stops to make in town, but after that, we will call on your admirer. We've already sent over correspondence to Lalo's home to let him know that we'd like to have drinks together later today."

"So soon?" Carolina asked.

"Do not fret. If you love this boy, I'm sure we will too. But we must know if his intentions are pure before we speak about this engagement."

Carolina gave a quick bob of her head. "Thank you, Amá. I

will go to Luz Elena at once." She could only hope Lalo would find the means to sneak away.

She took off at a meandering pace, but as soon as her mother was out of sight, Carolina bolted. Her arms pumped as she raced down the corridor toward her room.

She sped forward. From the corner of her eyes, she saw Luz Elena shuffling through the corridor on the other side of the courtyard. Carolina stopped and tugged off one of her slippers. She chucked it as hard as she could just behind Luz Elena. When the woman went to investigate the noise, Carolina pushed ahead.

Finally, her hand grabbed the handle to her room. She pulled the lever and dashed in, trying her best not to slam the door behind her.

Her eyes widened when she noted her bed was empty. The sheets hadn't even been ruffled.

Two heads shot up from the blankets on Nena's mattress. Nena's and Fernanda's.

Nena's curls were a tangled nest. Fernanda's light brown hair jutted out from her chignon. The same shade of rosebud lip paint stained their faces.

"Happy for you!" Carolina whisper-yelled. "But also, hide!"

When the girls did little but blink with bewilderment, Carolina waved her arms frantically. "Fernanda, get under the bed!" There was nowhere else large enough to conceal a body. "Our nanny is coming. She cannot know you are here."

"Did you not tell them you were taking on guests?" Fernanda asked, confused.

Carolina shook her head. "I didn't want anyone thinking your brother left you here unattended. Nor would I tell a soul he was healing in my abuelo's room. How could I explain his condition?" Plus, that would mean others would learn he had, in fact, been shot and lost the duel.

The door handle wiggled. It opened slightly. Carolina pressed her entire weight against the wood and slammed it shut.

"Carolina?" Luz Elena called. "What's the meaning of this?" Luz Elena shoved against the door, jolting Carolina. *Saints, la vieja was strong.*

"One second, Luz. Nena isn't proper."

"I've been bathing and clothing you two girls since before you could walk," Luz Elena said, jiggling the handle.

"Hurry," Carolina snapped to Fernanda.

Fernanda scrambled out of the sheets in nothing but her undergarments and slid under the bed. Her head popped out, her hair fanning around her face. "This is the most fun I've had in ages."

Nena grinned. "Me too."

"Just hide and stay quiet," Carolina whispered.

"Carolina? What is happening in there?" Luz Elena pushed harder against the door. Carolina couldn't hold the woman back any longer. She was petite, but she was as mighty as the bull that struck Rafa.

Carolina tripped forward as the door burst open. Luz Elena surveyed the room. She was shrewd as ever. If Mamá knew the comings and goings of the hacienda, Luz was the one who'd whispered into her ear.

Her nanny pursed her lips. The wrinkles on her face tripling. "What is that?"

She jerked her chin toward a gown draped over Carolina's vanity bench. Fernanda's gown. She would throttle Nena for being so careless later.

"A dress," Carolina said, very thankful that Luz Elena could not attend last night's fiesta due to gout and therefore wouldn't recognize the elaborate gown. "I just bought it from a tailor in el pueblo."

Luz Elena's sharp eyes turned to Carolina. "Which tailor? We have two."

"Smith," Nena shouted. "He did a fine job, no?"

There were actually three tailors within el pueblo, but Luz Elena never went to Mr. Smith after they had a dispute over silk prices twenty years ago—a fact her cousin knew well. Perhaps she wouldn't be throttled, after all.

Luz Elena scoffed. "You went to that thief?"

"He's no thief," Carolina interjected.

"Have you seen what he charges his customers? Thievery, I tell you." Luz Elena sniffed. "Do you smell that?"

"No," the cousins said in unison. What could Luz Elena possibly smell? Aside from Carolina's lies?

"Neither of you wear perfume like this. This one is much more floral in nature." She sniffed again, rather dramatically. "You don't smell it?" She shuffled dangerously close to Nena's bed.

"Oh, that! My dear soon-to-be sister-in-law let me try her perfume," Carolina said, laughing and putting her arm around the nanny's shoulders. "I think it is time I get dressed, no? I need to look my very best if I want to impress my new fiancé."

Luz Elena harrumphed. "This is all very scandalous if you ask me. Sneaking away and speaking to a man without an escort. You're a lady, señorita. Next thing we know, you two will be slipping lovers into your rooms." She made a sign of protection over her chest.

"Dios forbid," Nena said.

Carolina cleared her throat. "Yes, well, now we will set it to rights." She swept over to her bureau and thrust open the doors. "What shall I wear? Something bright to accentuate my skin tone? Something modest?"

Luz Elena grabbed the dress on the bench. Her callused fingers brushed the fabric. She harrumphed once more, but with a tone that said she was not so unpleased.

"Mr. Smith made this?"

"I believe he sent for it from the ciudad."

A knowing smile appeared on Luz Elena's face. "That makes more sense. That old rat couldn't make something so lovely. I'd know." She lifted it up.

There was absolutely no way Carolina could fit into such a thing. That is, if she wanted to breathe.

Luz Elena smiled. "This will do just fine. The green will be lovely on you. I don't believe you have anything of this color." She placed it on the bed and tapped her lips. She snapped her fingers. "Your mother's emerald earrings. They will look exquisite with this." She turned around. "I'll be back in two minutes, señorita."

The door opened and shut. Carolina ran toward her cousin's bed. Together, she and Nena grasped Fernanda's hand and heaved her up.

Fernanda was disheveled but had humor in her eyes. "That was brilliant."

"Thank you." She grabbed Fernanda's gown and shoved it into the girl's chest. "Put this on and fast. We have a dilemma. My family and I are getting ready to head to your house."

Fernanda's jaw dropped. "My house?"

"Sí. My family will be making a visit there this afternoon. Your brother should know. He was in the room beside me when

152

I ran into my mamá. Today's storm will keep him protected from the sun, at least."

Fernanda slipped into her gown, making jokes while Nena tied the laces tight. They grinned and giggled at each other. The heat of their flirtation was palpable.

"You are so vastly different from you brother," Carolina blurted out.

"Because I'm fun and funny, and he is a stick in the mud?"

Precisely, but in an engaging sort of way that Carolina found she quite liked. She knew she should stop herself from liking anything about him. She shouldn't let whatever feelings stirred inside her take shape because their predicament would never end well. Even if they somehow reversed the vampiro's curse, they could never be together. They were so unalike. And she was certain he had no intention of continuing this charade of an engagement anyway.

"Can you climb?" Carolina asked, pointing toward the window.

Fernanda smirked. "I've been sneaking out of my home since I was fourteen."

Carolina was further impressed.

She walked toward the shutters and thrust them open, blinking against the rain smattering her face.

"You can scale down the trellises," she said. "The stables are not far off. The mare you came on is in the second stall to the right. There is a stable boy, Ramón. He will assist you. He's very discreet, I assure you. We will meet you and your brother at your home in a few hours."

Fernanda nodded, then pulled on one of Nena's riding cloaks.

153

She made to leave but stopped when Carolina asked, "Why have you stuck by his side? He's . . ."

"A sediento?" Fernanda glanced over her shoulder at Carolina. "What would you do if the only family you had left in the world came home one day cursed and absolutely destroyed?"

Carolina felt like she'd been pierced with a knife in the gut at the mere thought. Her gaze flicked to her cousin. Nena was so silly and wild. What would she do if she'd been turned like Lalo?

The door to Carolina's room flew open and in swept Luz Elena. "Here they are. They were in the vault, so I had to walk down all those blasted steps. But I was right, they will be lovely with this gown."

Carolina snuck a glance at the window, but Fernanda was gone.

"Señorita?" Luz Elena's white brows raised in question. "Where is the gown?"

"I noticed a tear in the seams," Nena interjected. "I took it to Yolanda to be mended, but it will not be ready in time." She clicked her tongue. "Such a pity, cousin."

"I'll wear one of my other dresses. I like them better anyway."

While Luz picked through her wardrobe, Carolina glared at the rain. Fernanda's question continued to play in her mind. She supposed she should've asked what *wouldn't* you do if the only family you had left in the world came home one day cursed and absolutely destroyed? Since Abuelo's death all she could think of was ensuring no one had to make such a decision again. And now, possibly, she'd be able to do that.

From the journal of Friar Alejandro Ibarra

Because love, or the desperation it induces, can cause a person to go against the laws of nature and invoke the gods, it is only natural that the power of Tecuani dwells within the hearts of these abominations. It is the physical heart, the organ itself, that vampiros access their superhuman prowess. But that heart only thumps because of Tecuani, and it will only continue to beat if it is fed what he covets most: life.

From my conferences with holy persons in Santemala, Sevilla, and Paso Grande, I have ascertained these sorrowful missteps have happened since the dawn of time. As long as there is hope, people will reach for it.

Unfortunately, there is a false hope that leads the beast to win in the end. A stake of wood or blade of obsidian through the heart seems to be the simplest way to kill Tecuani's children, to restore peace. Though, I suppose it wouldn't be simple in the slightest.

CHAPTER 17

Lalo

THE RUFFIAN HAD SHOVED HIM INTO A ROOM THAT SMELLED like feet. Lalo covered his nose and took in his surroundings. He was in a mudroom of sorts. Boots lined one wall. Full of muck.

Lalo's parents had always instilled in him the importance of cleanliness. His mother made sure their clothes were pressed, their shoes shined. People respected a man who cared for his appearance. And Lalo made certain he and his sister continued to live that way. His sister did not complete her finishing school courses with a hair out of place. Even though everything else in his life was crumbling, he took pride in his image.

Random tools and buckets hung from the walls. Dusty coats lay strewn on top of discarded saddles. A single arched window ahead opened to a gloomy scene. Rain poured out of the clouds with unrelenting force.

But there was a door leading out of the casa, and the clouds covered the sun, which meant he wouldn't be trapped in another tight space for hours. Perhaps his luck was shifting.

Slowly, Lalo pried open the door and stuck his head into the downpour. He breathed in deep, taking in the familiar scents of mud and fresh air. Wet stucco and crisp grass. Dog. He sniffed again, brought his eyes to the ground, and found a giant beast glaring at him. Its upper lip quivered over its lengthy teeth.

"Nice puppy," he said quietly.

If he made the wrong move, the dog might alert the world of his presence. But he couldn't just stand here, staring at some mutt who seemed to have mange.

Lalo smiled. He didn't know why. Maybe the dog would find him friendly.

"Easy boy," he said as sweetly as he knew how. "I just need to . . ." He took a step and both of the dog's ears went back. A low growl rumbled from its belly. Four more perros trotted through the rain. Their thick brown coats bristled at the hackles. Lalo reversed, reentering the mudroom. "Easy," he said. "I'm not an intruder. I was invited. I'm just trying to leave." Why was he talking to these hounds like they understood him?

"What are you doing?" a child's voice asked.

Lalo yelped and whirled around. A little boy stood in the hall doorway donning a pirate's cap and holding a cloth full of bones.

"Why are you in the garden room?" The boy, who couldn't be more than six, raised a single brow. Clearly, this was one of Carolina's brothers. He had that same irritatingly charming smirk.

"I . . . I came to see your sister, but I've been told she will be joining my sister and me for tea later today. I will just meet her there instead."

The boy observed him, unimpressed. He walked into the room, toward the monster dogs.

"Be careful," Lalo said, but regretted it the moment the words came from his mouth.

"Sit," the boy ordered.

The beasts obeyed.

"You have to show them you are in charge," the boy said over his shoulder.

Lalo narrowed his gaze. "I see."

The boy chucked the bones into the air. The dogs caught them, then chomped them to shreds in seconds.

"You're the man who Carolina was caught kissing?"

Lalo's eyes widened. "We were not . . ." He cleared his throat. They had a deal. She was going to help him so long as he helped her. "I am to be her fiancé." He stepped closer to the boy, and the dogs growled at him. Lalo held out his hand. "Eduardo Montéz."

"I'm Adrián." The boy put his sticky palm in Lalo's and gave a hearty shake. "My cousin says you're a dead man. My father is mad. And when he gets mad . . ." The boy whistled and shook his head. "Watch out."

Lalo chuckled, but quickly covered it up when he saw the anger in the boy's eyes. Lalo's heart softened a bit. He liked a person who stood up for his family.

"Let us hope, for my sake, your cousin is incorrect."

Adrián nodded somberly.

"I shall take my leave then," Lalo said.

The boy scrutinized Lalo. "Do you love her?"

"Erm . . . yes . . . I do."

"Then don't let Papá send her away. Rafa will take her to the ciudad, and we'll never see her again."

Lalo's stomach dropped to his knees. He also knew the love of a good sister.

"I will try my best" was what he offered as a reply.

Adrián nodded. "Tell the dogs *get back* and they won't mess with you. Remember, you've got to show them who is el patrón." He hit his chest, a show of dominance, Lalo presumed. Adrián backed out of the room. He started to walk away. Over his shoulder, he yelled, "Good luck with mi papá. You're gonna need it, señor."

Lalo straightened his shoulders. He thought of how confident Adrián was, of how powerful and intimidating his sister was too. Lalo had been frightened of people and messes and awkward situations for most of his existence. He'd let those fears win. He didn't want to feel helpless anymore. He wanted to be the one in command of his life for a change.

He stepped into the rain, and the dogs began to growl.

"Back," he ordered, flashing his fangs. And to his surprise, the beasts obeyed.

He found his way out of the hacienda and ran in the direction of his new home. The Fuentes rancho was on the completely opposite side of the valley, close to the town center. Lalo's was tucked in the piney woods, away from civilization. Kind of poetic really. Carolina Fuentes being this self-proclaimed protector of her people, him being some devious fiend. Opposites attracting.

With Tecuani's power in his marrow, the world was as sharp as ever. To the west were rolling hills, with well-kept orchards and tiny adobe homes dotted about. Even from such a great distance, he could see a chubby raccoon scavenging through the compost in front of someone's house. To the northeast loomed the edge of the forest and the small mountain range it surrounded.

A pulse of sharp pain shot through his belly.

He gritted his teeth. Normally, these cramps only lasted for moments, a quick nudge that he needed to feed. But this one would not let up. He staggered forward and forced his legs to move. He had to get home to drink the pig's blood Fernanda had purchased from the butcher.

He slowed his gait as he entered the main square. El pueblo was empty. The citizens of Del Oro were most likely asleep or shielding themselves from the rain. He trudged past a large church, its stuccoed walls gleaming in the downpour. The building beside it appeared to be the schoolhouse, with a strangely patterned fence made for keeping small children in and cute paintings hanging from the inside of the windowpanes. Upon further inspection, Lalo realized the fence appeared to be made from tree roots. A clever bit of woodworking if one were trying to keep away wayward vampiros. A barbershop sign swung from a squat building to his right. He had not stopped to notice before, but it seemed everything a person would need was there—a small apothecary, the butcher, a general store.

The cantina doors opened and shut as laughing people burst out and in, carrying with them the merry tune of the piano. By his estimations, the time was nearing seven o'clock in the morning. Either these people started early or had yet to finish their fun from last night.

Lalo paused, ignoring the rain thumping against his hair and shoulders. Memories flooded his mind from the last time he'd been in such a place. He had sunk his teeth into so many throats. The lives he'd stolen in Maricela's cantina still played inside his mind. Their memories, their dreams, their sorrows tortured him even now.

He'd slayed a person his age that night. As Lalo drank the boy's life force, he saw the young man's memories flash through his mind. Lalo saw his deepest secrets, his disgusting desires. The boy had killed before, too. For pleasure. Lalo had tasted the glee tainting his blood as the young man dug his blade into a person's stomach.

Lalo had tried to purge the foul aftertaste and memories from both his tongue and mind. But they remained. They remained still. Every devilish act that young man committed was singed into Lalo's memories like a brand. All the lives he'd taken that night had a foul bitterness to them. Their souls were vile and vicious.

Humans and sedientos weren't so unalike as Carolina wished to believe. They were all monsters in their own right. But that didn't mean Lalo wished to remain a killer.

He caught sight of someone standing frozen in the rain. His brow furrowed. It wasn't the way they stood that snagged his attention but the lack of sound from a beating heart.

"Hello, love." The voice was whisper soft, but Lalo heard it clear as day. Chills rippled down his skin. He knew it wasn't Maricela—the tone was wrong—but he had heard this person the night he was turned. She was one of Maricela's children. The woman who had grabbed him by the shirt when he was walking through the cantina. She'd run away when his bloodlust overtook him.

"We've been looking for you," she said in a singsong way.

"Shit." Lalo's pulse thundered in his chest. His adrenaline roared. "Shit. Shit. Shit."

The woman bent her knees and shot toward him. She landed with a thud near his feet, bits of mud smattering his pants. Lalo stumbled back as she straightened to her full height. Her dark hair clung to her face, and her gown was soaked to the bone. Her lips pulled back, exposing her fangs.

"Mother is angry," she hissed.

"M-Maricela?" Lalo stuttered. "Is here?" But how? How had she found him?

"You will come with me," the vampiro ordered.

If Maricela got her claws on Lalo, there was no telling what sort of tortures she'd inflict on him. Going with this wretch wasn't an option.

What would Carolina do?

He chuckled inwardly because the answer was clear.

Lalo struck. Full force, he slammed his fist, knuckles first, into the vampiro's nose. Her head knocked back at an impossible angle. But just as quickly, it popped up. Her lips stretched into a wicked smile. Black gore flooded out of her nostrils and stained her fangs.

"Good gods," he gasped.

She shrieked and lunged, trying to tackle Lalo, but he held his ground. Her mouth snapped open and shut as she went for his neck, but Lalo clamped his palm over her face just before she found her mark.

Fight dirty, Carolina had said. *Do whatever it takes to survive.*

Lalo scanned the desolate pueblo until inspiration struck. He shoved her back, and she tripped into an overflowing horse trough.

He ran for the schoolhouse with what strength he had left.

Just as he made it to the fence surrounding the school, claws scraped down his shoulders. Lalo gritted his teeth and flung out his arms. Something snapped, and he roared as he tumbled into the mud. Lalo rolled onto his back just as the vampiro pounced.

Her glowing eyes widened when she landed on top of him. Her pale face grew ashen. Shakily, she reached for her heart where a sizable splinter of wood had pierced it through. Lalo had broken it off the schoolhouse fence.

The vampiro coughed and black spittle ran down her chin.

"You will pay dearly for this," she whispered.

Lightning struck as she crumpled to the ground.

Lalo lay there for a moment, letting the rain wash over his skin. He wished the downpour could wipe away his sins. Could sweep away the dirt and grime covering his body and the wretched guilt that plagued his soul. He'd killed again. Even though she'd wanted to harm him, it felt terribly wrong. But what was he to do? It was her life or his. He had to fight back, didn't he? There was no way he'd simply back down when he and Carolina might be able to end the death curse.

The sound of a heartbeat snapped Lalo out of his musings. He shot up.

A bear of a man stood just outside the cantina doors with a shotgun clutched in his hands.

"Did you kill it?" he shouted.

Lalo eyed the corpse. "I think so."

"Are you hurt?"

Lalo shook his head as he dragged himself to his feet. He had a few scrapes, but they were already mending. His borrowed clothes were a lost cause though. Other than knowing Maricela might very well be somewhere nearby, he was fine.

"I'll send for the guard to come fetch the body," the man hollered. "Good job, kid."

"Thanks. I guess?"

"Care for a drink?" the man asked.

Lalo wiped the rain from his eyes. "It's only seven in the morning, señor."

The man laughed. "If you add a splash of juice inside the glass, it no longer counts as drinking."

Lalo's brow furrowed. That hardly made sense.

"I really should be on my way." He had his fake fiancé and her family to meet. And if she was going to be of any help to him, he had to keep up this charade.

But Carolina had mentioned la cantina held most of el pueblo's records. If there was anything new to learn about Vidal and Alma Fuentes, he'd find answers inside. Maricela was here, meaning the number of days he thought he had left were long gone. He had to find a way to reverse the curse before she hurt him or anyone else. And it was still early. Carolina's family wouldn't be arriving to his rented home just yet.

The man started for the door.

"Wait!" Lalo shouted. He jogged closer to the entrance. A cramp pinched at his side. He stopped and rested his hands on his knees. "I think I could use a drink," he panted.

Smiling, the man said, "You've come to the right place."

CHAPTER 18

Carolina

AT A QUARTER TO THREE IN THE AFTERNOON, WOODEN COACH wheels bumped up the road that led to the old Alicante estate. No one dared live so near to the woods since the Alicante family had been slain by sedientos twenty-some-odd years ago. A host of Papá's guards rode horseback now, flanking the mayor to thwart any sudden attacks.

Mamá drew a curtain back and peered through the window. "Why would the Montézes choose to stay here of all places?"

Papá looked up from his newspaper. The lead article was about a slew of people found dead in some bar in Los Campos. The date of the article was from just over a month ago, but it had only reached Del Oro today. And Papá thought shipping Carolina away to the capital city would be safer than staying in Del Oro. She rolled her eyes. No matter where she went, there would be villains, even if they were of the human variety.

The carriage came to a stop and the door swung open. Instead of the cochero, Fernanda Montéz appeared, holding an umbrella.

"Welcome," she said. Her makeup and hair looked impeccable. She smiled warmly, but there was tension behind her eyes. Where was Lalo? They'd taken the long route to get here. Papá wished to stop by some of the guard towers and check in on his men. Lalo had plenty of time to sneak away from her home and get himself ready for her family's call.

"Ah, Fernanda. How are you this fine day?" Papá said as he clambered out of the coach, his weight, or lack thereof, causing the carriage to sway.

"I am well. So happy to have company. It gets rather dull out here."

"Yes, about that." Papá helped Mamá disembark. "Why did you choose this casa to lease? I believe the Gonzálezes are renting out, and their home is so near to the center of town."

"Apá," Carolina groaned. "That is none of our business."

"Says who? These are our potential in-laws, no?" Papá rested his hands on his hips and took in the crumbling manor. Raindrops bounced off his coat. "Are you certain your brother has his finances in order?"

"Luis," Mamá chided. "One thing at a time."

Fernanda smiled kindly. "It is quite all right, Señora Fuentes. I don't mind. Lalo and I hold no secrets."

Carolina snorted. When her parents gave her a quizzical look, she pretended to fight off a sneeze.

"My brother is frugal and also likes his privacy. Scholars crave quiet."

"Surely you know what a risk it is to be so near to the forest?" Mamá inquired.

Fernanda's smile did not falter when she said, "We didn't when we arrived. But we do now."

All this talk of the forest was getting dangerously uncomfortable. One slip from Fernanda and her parents might catch on to Lalo's true nature. Carolina couldn't let that happen.

"I am famished," Carolina said. She patted her belly in the most uncouth way.

"Please, come in," Fernanda said. "I made my very first batch of jamoncillo this morning."

Carolina inwardly winced. Her papá hated sweet treats. And Mamá's stomach did not favor foods made with leche. She supposed she'd have to eat enough for the three of them. Which was fine by her since she hadn't eaten all day.

Fernanda led them up the steps and inside. They followed Fernanda into a quaint sitting room that smelled of lavender and rosemary. "Have a seat. I will get refreshments."

"Where is your brother?" Papá asked, still standing, his arms clasped behind his back.

"He had more early morning business to attend to in the next pueblo over. He should be home any moment."

"The nearest pueblo is a day's ride away. Will he make it back so soon?" Papá inquired.

"He . . . um . . . My brother is a skilled horseman, señor." She curtsied. "If you'll excuse me."

"I'll help you!" Carolina nearly shouted. "I mean . . . if you'd like the company."

"Of course," Fernanda said. "Would you like rose or mint tea,

Señora Fuentes? I went and picked some myself. I understand they are good for people with child."

Mamá blushed. "That is so thoughtful of you. Rose would be wonderful."

Fernanda gave an elegant bow. A sting of jealousy bit at Carolina. She hadn't ever dipped so gracefully, not naturally anyway. Oftentimes, that sort of grace had to be smacked into her.

"And for you, señor? We have some rather fine port."

Papá now stood before the windows, which were open a bit but covered in thick curtains. His brows were knit together. "Sounds lovely. Thank you."

Together, Carolina and Fernanda headed for the kitchens, their silk skirts swishing in unison.

"Where is he?" Carolina whispered.

"I haven't the slightest clue. I thought he'd be here by now."

The Montéz casa had been bare of decorations the first time Carolina came. Now there were quite a few paintings on the walls. Her feet slowed when her eyes landed on a small but intricate portrait. A much younger Lalo stood next to a tall and angular man. Fernanda, who couldn't have been more than eight or so, sat on a bench next to a lovely woman with the kindest green eyes.

"Our parents," Fernanda said.

"You both favor them."

Fernanda smiled sadly. "I think so too. My brother can't stand to see this painting, but I put it up anyway. I couldn't leave the piece behind. I feel like if I don't look upon their faces every day, I might somehow forget them."

"I'm so sorry," Carolina said.

"My brother saw how they were taken from us." Fernanda

gulped. "I know he's hurt people. He doesn't talk about the night he returned to our home after being made, but I can see the pain in his eyes. He has done terrible things to make sure I won't be abandoned in this world, and I am thankful for it." A tear slipped down Fernanda's cheek. "Does that make me a monster, too?"

Carolina gazed at the younger version of Lalo. She thought about this prim and proper boy and how his entire life must have been turned completely upside down. And yet, he still fought so hard to keep his life together, to keep his sister safe. Fernanda wasn't a monster because Lalo wasn't a monster either.

Frustration breathed within Carolina. She used to see the world in black and white. Right or wrong. Monster or human. Why did Lalo have to add color where it didn't belong?

From the journal of Jonathan Monroe of Santemala

June 10, 1709

I fear my dearest daughter is truly lost, for the monster lying in her bed is a stranger to me. Day and night she cries for human blood, and I know she must have it. In my fatherly compassion, I offered her my wrist and I let her drink. She would not stop. I felt my life force drain away. I thought myself doomed. Only by the grace of the saints did she release me, but I am still not recovered from the affair. And her thirst only grows.

My niece is in contact with a woman who practices brujería. She has told me I could heal my body if I ingested my daughter's blood. The power of the gods lives within it, after all. They are immortal. Their bodies never hurt or deteriorate. And therefore, those linked to Tecuani are nearly unbreakable. But how could I possibly do such a thing? How could I take from my little girl when she is already writhing in agony?

No. I will suffer as she suffers.

CHAPTER 19

Lalo

THE CANTINA WAS LARGE AND STRANGELY CLEAN. SO UNLIKE THE underground pit he had slinked into the night he learned of Maricela's whereabouts. The Den was what she had named her tiny cantina. But it was missing the rest of the title. The Den of Leeches was what it should have been called. Or The Den of Sin. No, The Den of Death. Really, any of those would suffice. People—human or made—frequented the place because there were rumors of dark and dangerous activities happening behind the closed doors, and they wanted in on the depravity.

But this cantina in Del Oro was more of a restaurant than anything. The wood-paneled walls were lined with pretty paintings of the landscape surrounding el pueblo. One depicted Basilio's Point and had the sun rising from behind the peak of Devil's Spine. The winding river that wove in from the forest and through the valley. There was even a likeness of the Fuentes hacienda.

"Drinks on me," said the man Lalo had just met to the person tending bar. Then, to him, "I'll just go on and fetch the nearest guard and alert them about the dead sediento outside."

A woman in a low-cut gown played a haunting melody on the piano. She sang a rather fitting song about death knocking at the door.

Lalo had never drunk more than a snifter of brandy. He didn't like the taste of alcohol. But mostly he found the idea of total inebriation uncomfortable. His parents were both wonderful people, but when wine took hold of them, it often wouldn't let go for days. He supposed that was the strange thing about parents—you could want to be like them in so many ways but also not.

He sat at the bar and grabbed the glass placed before him. The liquid was amber in color and didn't smell terribly pungent. Without a second thought, Lalo knocked it back like he'd seen people do time and time again. His throat burned, and he couldn't swallow. Panic coursed through him. He turned his head and spit out the liquid.

A beast of a man stood before him. He growled as he wiped alcohol from his face.

"Oh gods," Lalo said. "I am so sorry. I didn't see you there."

"You're dead." The man grabbed Lalo by the collar and dragged him off his seat. He held Lalo above the ground with one hand as if he were a rag doll. "Any last words?" he growled, and cocked back his fist.

What had Carolina's younger brother Adrián said in the mudroom? You must show them who is boss. Lalo had, and the dogs obeyed. Perhaps it might work for brutes as well.

He cleared the fear from his throat. "You do not want to do

this, señor. I don't mean to sound arrogant, but I have fought far greater foes this morning alone."

The man barked an incredulous laugh. "Do you not know who I am? I'm Roberto the Bull!"

Lalo thumped his hand over his chest. "And I'm el patrón."

Roberto balked. "¿Qué?"

"I controlled five vicious beasts purely by the command of my voice. I slayed un sediento with nothing but my hands and bit of wood. I am not a man to be messed with. I have been shot and stabbed and hit with a pan, and yet, here I am. But if you want to try me, put me down and fight me like a real man."

Roberto's jaw twitched. He huffed. Smiled and huffed again. He started to chuckle. Then the Bull tilted his head back and howled with laughter. The room, which had gone deathly silent, joined Roberto in the hilarity. Gingerly, he placed Lalo onto his feet. He smacked Lalo across the back as tears fell from his eyes.

"He's el patrón!" the Bull wheezed. "He says he killed un sediento with his bare hands!" He grabbed his belly and bent over, crying about whatever he thought was so funny.

After far too long, Roberto the Bull wiped the tears from his face and stood tall. "You've got huevos, kid. I'll give you that." He snapped his fingers. "Concha, get this boy another shot!"

"Actually, I think I've had enough."

This comment only seemed to make Roberto laugh again.

"My gods, no wonder Carolina likes you. You're hilarious."

"You know Carolina?"

"Of course. Luis and I are cousins." That made perfect sense. Roberto was about the same size as Señor Fuentes. He was as intimidating too.

"And yet you threatened to murder me?" Lalo asked.

173

"Part of the Fuentes charm. You'll get to know our tempers soon enough." Roberto grinned. "Can I get you anything else? My sister and I own this cantina. Whatever you wish for, it is yours," he proclaimed.

He was about to pummel Lalo in his own establishment. That wasn't very professional, but if he was granting wishes …

"Actually, I've been told the cantina keeps old records? I'm a scholar, you see, and I'm doing research on small towns. Might I look at your papers?"

Roberto shook his head. "You're a strange one."

Lalo's heart sank. This was usually when he'd be rejected. He prepared himself to gather all the hope that would be dashed onto the floor.

"There's a small trapdoor cut out in the center of the office down the hall. It's dank and dusty, but there are plenty of old records that might be of use to you."

"Really?" Lalo's heart felt suddenly light.

"Of course. Anything for el patrón."

CHAPTER 20

Carolina

THE CARRIAGE RIDE HOME HAD BEEN TENSE. CAROLINA DIDN'T even want to turn in her papá's direction, less she be burned by the irritation in his gaze. He hated time being wasted, and that was exactly what their afternoon at the Montéz abode had been. Lalo never showed up.

Carolina glared out the dark window. With the clouds still thick, she couldn't see the setting sun. She clenched her legs together to keep her knees from shaking. She'd been scolded enough times to know better than to fidget in front of her parents. Instead, she chewed on her lip discreetly. Gnawing away at it to calm her nerves.

Papá rubbed his finger and thumb down his thick mustache, something he did whenever he was getting ready to say something that was sure to make her furious.

"Eduardo Montéz is not the man for you, mija."

Her spine stiffened. "You didn't even get to speak to him."

"I do not need to. What can a scholar do for my daughter? You need a man of means, not of ideals."

"You've conveniently forgotten that his family owns a profitable business. You only wish for me to be with someone who will do and say whatever you wish. Someone who will take me far from Del Oro, like Rafa."

"Del Oro isn't safe," Mamá chimed in. "It never was. Rafael will protect you from such dangers and treat you as a queen."

"Bad things happen everywhere, Amá. Look at the newspaper." She gestured toward the article about people who'd died in the ciudad. "Besides, there are sedientos in the cities. Did you know that?"

Papá and Mamá shared a startled look.

"Who told you such nonsense?" Papá asked. "There have never been sightings so far south."

"Sending me away won't help anything but your wounded pride over your godson losing a duel you encouraged. Evil always finds a way in. If it isn't sedientos, it is people."

"Some distance will do you good. You've never listened to anything I have said or commanded. Perhaps you will listen to Rafael," Papá said.

"So that is what this is all about? Your control. But what about me? *You* have never listened to a thing I have said either. You have never believed in me and what I can do. I can fight, Apá. I can ride as hard and fast as any of my brothers. I am capable. Abuelo supported it, why can't you?"

If Lalo, a boy she had tried to kill, a boy who hardly knew her, could trust her, could believe in her abilities to help, why couldn't her own parents?

176

The carriage came to a sudden stop.

"Señor!" one of the cocheros yelled.

They had halted outside the gates to their hacienda. Everything was still. The lanterns that flickered at either side of their entrance were snuffed out, and the guards that were usually there were gone.

"Come quick!" el cochero hollered.

Papá moved at once. Carolina scooted after him.

"Stay here," he commanded.

"But . . ."

"I said stay put, Carolina." Papá dashed out of the carriage.

"Come," Mamá said, tugging Carolina next to her. She raised her arm and pulled a small pistol from the lining of the roof. She pointed it at the door.

"Should you be handling a gun in your state?" Carolina asked.

Mamá scoffed. "There is nothing stronger than a woman with children to protect."

Carolina wouldn't argue with that. She'd once been chased by an angry hen after disturbing her nest. The bantam had kicked Carolina in the ankles until she climbed up a tree.

The ladies waited in silence until they heard footfalls pounding through the tall grasses. Mamá held her weapon at the ready. The door swung open, and Papá's frame filled the space. Mamá sighed, but her relief was short-lived.

"Joaquín!" Papá yelled. "To the casa. Hurry!"

The reins snapped, and Papá jumped into the carriage just as they lurched to full speed.

"What is it, Luis?" Mamá asked, clutching Carolina's arm.

Papá ran a hand down his face. "The guards, they're . . . they're dead."

"Dead?" Mamá gasped. "How?"

Carolina's pulse raced. Icy dread clawed up her spine. Lalo was missing. Lalo had been left to roam. By her. *Please don't say a sediento. Please don't say a sediento. Please . . .*

"It was a . . ." He shook his head. "It was another sediento attack." His eyes flashed to Carolina. "This is exactly why I want you gone."

"But my brothers and uncles and cousins get to stay?"

"Yes," he growled. "Because they follow my orders. You do what you want, and because of that people get hurt. Or worse."

Carolina recoiled, the guilt over Abuelito resurfacing. She didn't have the energy to argue. Her muscles, her bones, her heart had frozen over in fear as a realization dawned on her.

Lalo had killed the guards.

Oh gods. Oh gods! Her brothers!

"Hurry, Joaquín!" she screamed. Hot tears burned her eyes.

Before the carriage stopped, Carolina and her father bolted out and up the steps toward their home, leaving Mamá with the drivers. *Please let them be all right. Please let them be all right.* They burst through the doors and skidded to a stop as soon as they entered the foyer.

Carolina let out a small cry and clamped a hand over her mouth. Her two youngest brothers, Adrián and Marcos, were there, sword fighting one another with wooden weapons.

The twins stiffened. Their handsome little faces motionless with shock. They weren't allowed to play such games inside the house. Normally Papá would reprimand them or send them out to the horse stalls to clean the dung. Instead, he scooped them up in his big arms and squeezed them so tight, they dropped their wooden weapons.

"You're safe," Papá said, breathlessly.

"Sí, señor," both boys replied.

Papá set them down gingerly. "Where's everyone?"

"Nena is getting us some sweets for being good," Marcos beamed. "Our uncles and brothers left in a rush." Carolina had three uncles and fifteen boy cousins who had all been allowed to join the guard. The twins were the only boys under the age of fifteen, so they stayed home with all the women in her family who hadn't been invited to any hunt.

Papá sprinted to the kitchens.

Now it was her turn to pull her brothers into a crushing hug. They squealed and complained. They smelled of dirt and sweat, but she didn't care. She nuzzled into their scents. Their warmth. Their squirming, vigorous bodies.

Her decisions could have led to their demise. The very thought had tears streaming from her eyes and falling into their black curls. How could Lalo do this? Why did he lose control again?

"Ay, Carolina," Marcos complained, shoving himself away. "Enough. What is wrong with everyone?"

"We just . . ." Carolina wiped at her face. "We missed you."

The twins rolled their eyes.

"Nothing strange happened while we were away?" Carolina's gaze darted around. From here she could see Luz Elena dozing off in a rocking chair. As she breathed, her belly pushed the baby blanket she was knitting up and down.

"Nope. Nothing," Adrián said. He snapped his fingers. "Oh. I remember. Your husband was here."

"My what?"

"The boy Papá caught you smooching." He wiggled his eyebrows and made a kissing face.

Her heart raced faster. "Did my *fiancé* say anything else before he left?" *Like he was readying to slay their guards.*

"I don't think so. He's kind of strange, no?"

"He's a dead man, that's what he is," she grumbled through her clenched jaw.

The boys' eyes widened.

"I warned him. Papá killed him, right?" Adrián asked.

"No." But she was going to.

This whole ruse was a terrible idea. What was she thinking? That was the problem. She wasn't. She'd been so caught up in trying to prove herself, in trying to keep her papá from offering her hand to someone she didn't love, that she'd proven Papá's point. Her selfish decisions hurt people. She'd begged Abuelo to teach her how to fight, and where was he now? She'd forced Lalo to pretend to be hers, and guards were killed because of it.

Papá's boots clicked on the tile. Sweat ran down his forehead. "Everything and everyone are accounted for."

Mamá and the cocheros entered the house, along with Carolina's five older brothers, her cousins, and her uncles. They spoke above one another, their voices competing over who got to tell their story first.

"A sediento was killed near the schoolhouse this morning," Domingo, the oldest of her uncles, said. "We had just finished burning the body when gunshots came from the gates."

"We ran to investigate and found our men dead. Their pistols were still hot in their hands," her brother Manuel said.

"Something dashed away from the gates of the hacienda," another brother—Sergio—added.

"Damn thing was faster than any creature I've seen," her uncle Vicente said.

180

"We raced after it, but couldn't keep up, even on our swiftest horses," her uncle Malaquías noted.

Carolina could scream. She had trusted un vampiro in her own home, allowed him to walk this earth, and look what he did.

The alarm bells sounded from the bell towers to the east, right where Lalo would have gone if he was running toward his home.

Carolina clenched her fists at her sides.

She was never going to let that beast of a boy slip away again.

"I will kill you, Lalo Montéz."

From the journal of Friar Alejandro Ibarra

If one's lands are overrun by vampiros, there is only one thing to be done. Find the poor creature Tecuani dragged from the Land of the Dead and destroy its heart with the tool used to beckon the god with. This tool is typically a blade of some fashion, used by the conjurer to summon the trickster god. If the original beast is slain, the vampiros it created will also fall.

"But how does one find the blade used in the first place?" I ask myself.

It must be an item that held value to the deceased when they were alive. The conjurer will use this special tool to slice into their own hand before placing their open palm on the grave of the departed. Blood is the essence of life. It summons the god as well as feeds the dead.

CHAPTER 21

Lalo

HE'D BEEN IN THE CELLAR UNDER LA CANTINA FOR AT LEAST A
few hours now. Lalo knew he needed to get home in order to
keep up with the charade of his betrothal, but how could he leave
all these journals and books behind? Maricela was lurking in the
valley. The answers to finding more about Vidal could be here.
He couldn't leave until he discovered them.

His eyes leafed through the pages, the words on them scrawled
so delicately across the parchment. People didn't write like this
anymore. They didn't take the time to get the perfect amount
of ink onto the quill and curve their letters like this author had.

Lalo was reading through a woman's diary written some two
hundred years ago. She was a terrible gossip. This person did
not take care of their gardens properly because they were too
busy drinking in the barn. That person was seen slipping out of
a certain padre's rooms late one night. Funny how so much had

changed in the world yet stayed the same. Humans would always be humans. Flawed. Judgmental. No matter the century.

Lalo remembered his father grumbling about how good things had been a generation or two back, perhaps for some. For the privileged, things were never so terribly bad. They had time to sit in their reading rooms or rocking chairs and write about basic human follies while others were simply trying their best to survive.

His eyes caught on a name in the journal. Alma.

> *El patrón's daughter Alma has sadly lost her husband, Vidal, today. And they have the sweetest baby boy. I told my dear Nacho it was such a pity. But Nacho said Vidal knew better than to go stag hunting so late at night. Poor man tumbled right down Devil's Spine.*

There was another entry just below.

> *Vidal was buried in the graveyard at Orilla del Río today. I couldn't go on account of my bad knees, and I am glad for it. Nacho said the funeral was dreadful. Alma was too beside herself with grief to talk, and it rained the entire time.*

The next entry was about the new roses blooming.

"That's it?" Lalo said to the spiders in their webs above.

But at least la chismosa del pueblo gave him a new clue. Vidal had been buried in a place called Orilla del Río.

Lalo gasped as a sudden thought hit him.

If Alma had prayed to the god of the dead, if she had begged

184

to bring Vidal back, his body would not be in the grave. He could prove to Carolina he was right. And if that were the case, Lalo would just need to find him, kill him with whatever Alma had used to call Tecuani, and the god's power coursing through his vampiros, Lalo included, would vanish.

When he listed it out like that, the task seemed impossible.

He rose quickly from the crate he sat on and stretched. Carolina was going to kill him for missing their tea. But she might find what he had learned to be enough to stave off her desire to put a stake through him for a bit longer. A sudden pain sliced through his skull. He clutched his head and groaned.

Perhaps he could sneak in through the back of the butcher shop and pilfer some blood?

You need a human life, a sick voice inside him said. *Resistance is pointless. You need to kill and devour someone's soul.*

Lalo furrowed his brow. "Never."

His body felt sluggish and empty as he pushed open the hatch, and the world around him screamed with chaos.

He pressed his palms over his ears and climbed the rest of the way out of the cellar. Alarm bells clanged. Slowly, he stumbled down the darkened corridor and entered the main room of the cantina. The windows were boarded up. The door sealed shut with a heavy post.

People sat tucked under tables, clutching chairs or holding their pistols.

Fear fluttered in Lalo's chest. Those bells had rung the night of the attack. He was in such a daze then, but he remembered them reverberating in the distance.

"Sedientos," he whispered. He sucked in a breath. "Fernanda!"

He started for the door, but someone clutched his arm. "You

185

can't go out there. Those bells mean vampiros are still on the loose."

Lalo's eyes snapped to the man's face. He had a nick on his upper cheek. The wound had only just begun to scab over. Saliva pooled in Lalo's mouth. Even over the bells, he could hear the thump of the man's pulse. His fangs dug into his lip. A low growl emanated from within.

The man let go of Lalo as if he were made of flame and stepped back.

"Suit yourself, amigo. But it's your death."

Lalo lifted the bar barricading them in and stepped into the night air. The rain had ended, but there wasn't a star or the moon in sight. An ominous mist had blanketed the sky.

The door shut quickly behind him as he stepped into the muddy road.

Maricela and her children might come upon him at any moment, but he couldn't just leave his sister to fend for herself in their home.

Horse hooves pounded down the road to his right. The mist separated as if it were afraid of the rider. And perhaps the mist's fear had been justified.

The rider's cloak billowed about them. Their face was covered in shadow. They raised a stake and pointed it directly at Lalo.

"You are dead!"

CHAPTER 22

Carolina

CAROLINA SNUCK OUT OF HER HOUSE AND RODE LIKE HELL ON horseback to Lalo's casa. *He* did this. *He* killed the guards. Could that be why he hadn't gone home? Had he lost his composure and given in to his unholy ways?

She flicked the reins, and her stallion galloped faster.

"I should have killed him."

This was her fault. Everything was her fault.

If she hadn't been so careless and allowed herself to be ambushed by the feral sediento that night, her abuelo would still be alive. If she had listened to her papá and not tried to be a hunter, if she agreed to marry Rafa, she would have never made that deal with the devil. But she had because she was stubborn and foolish. And now people were dead.

Her father and his men raced for Boca de la Muerte, but

Carolina knew exactly where her vampiro was. Or at least where she could find him when he returned, and riding directly through town was the fastest way to his home.

A lone figure stumbled out of the cantina.

Carolina recognized that thin silhouette instantly. Fury overtook her.

"You are dead!" she bellowed.

Lalo had hardly a moment to act before she flung herself off her stallion and slammed into him. They tumbled in a tangle of limbs and curses into the mud. Carolina punched out, landing a hard blow to his cheek.

They bumped into a horse trough. But she wasted no time. She clambered on top of him and raised the stake in her hand. "I should have done this the second I met you."

"All this because I was late for tea?!" he screeched.

His nonchalance infuriated her. She grabbed him by the collar and pulled him up so they would be face to face when she pierced his heart.

"You killed our men."

His jaw dropped. "I did not!"

"Liar!"

The tip of the stake dug into his skin.

Lalo hissed. "Please. Whatever you think I did, I can assure you it isn't true."

She searched his eyes; they did not glow blood-red like the sedientos she'd seen before. His skin was ashen. His lips were tinged blue around the corners. He was weak in her arms. Had he recently fed, he would have been stronger, healthier in complexion.

"Where were you?" She twisted her fingers deeper into his shirt. "Where have you been?"

"In la cantina," he said. "Ask Roberto. He'll tell you!"

Carolina narrowed her eyes.

"Honest! I was in the cellar underneath the cantina, researching. You said there was a trove of old books, did you not? So, truly, you are to blame for my absence."

Her nostrils flared.

"I found something," he said. "A clue. If you release me and apologize for pummeling me into the mud, I might share what I've learned."

"We have more pressing matters at the moment."

She pushed off him and stood. Lalo raised his hand as if he expected her to help him up. She swatted his palm away and stepped back.

Lalo flattened his lips as he staggered up.

A scream tore through the air. Carolina whirled in the direction from which it came and shuddered. Two monsters in fine-looking suits raced toward them.

"These must be the leeches who killed our guards."

Lalo staggered slightly. And his skin blanched the rest of its color as if he were seeing ghosts, as if he recognized these men.

Carolina dug her fingers into her boot. "Here," she said, offering him a tiny pistol.

His brows raised. "Do you not remember the duel on your ranch?"

"I told you I would fight any monster I came across. Ready yourself." She raised the stake and pulled a rapier from her belt, then ran to meet them.

Their glowing eyes were a shock against the fog rumbling in. They were nothing like Lalo. She couldn't see an ounce of humanity within them.

And they were going to die.

Carolina ducked low as the first sediento swiped its claws in the air. She slid through the mud and sank the blade deep into its thighs. The beast shrieked with fury as it fell to the ground on hands and knees.

"To your left!" Lalo yelled.

She somersaulted, dodging a fatal blow from the second vampiro. Carolina scrambled to her feet and pulled a throwing dagger forged with obsidian from the holster on her chest. She sent it flying right for the second vampiro. Just like Abuelo had taught her to do. The knife hit its mark, slipping through the tendons and bones and into its rotting heart. The beast screamed as its body began to convulse. The glowing red of its eyes dulled, and it fell flat into the muck.

"Kill it!" she ordered, pointing at the vampiro crawling straight for Lalo.

The pistol in his hand shook like a leaf on a tree. She stomped over and snatched the weapon from his grasp. Without looking, she aimed at the beast who she first felled and let the wooden bullet fly.

She and Lalo stood there, panting, staring hard into each other's eyes.

"Why did you hesitate?" she hissed.

"I'm sorry. I wanted to shoot, but it was like staring down at the hell that is to be my fate. It unnerved me."

His face went paler than it already was. He swayed for a moment before his knees gave out completely. Carolina caught him by the arms.

"What is happening to you?" she asked.

"Nothing. I'm fine."

"Lalo." Her tone was stern, like what her mother would use when she or her siblings crossed a line.

"I need to feed, that is all."

"Fine. The butcher . . ."

He shook his head. "Can wait. I need to ensure Fernanda is safe."

"Your sister will be fine. My papá and his men are hunting in the forest now. They will check for monsters near your home. But *you* won't be able to move at all if you don't feed soon."

He glared at the dead vampiros. "No time. We must go to Orilla del Río," he said.

"Why?"

"Take me to the cemetery, and I will explain."

Carolina blinked at such a peculiar request, but what wasn't strange in her world these days?

"I will take you there *after* we get you some blood."

She started for her horse but halted when he added, "We're going to need a couple of shovels as well."

I often mistake love and loss. They are twin sisters.
Holding hands and scampering past. Teasing
me with their wicked beauty. Both make me feel
like my world is large and small. They remind
me I should be grateful but also terrified.

—Pío Parra, Psalms of the
Heart Anthology 1:1

CHAPTER 23

Lalo

LALO STOOD BEFORE A SPRAWLING GRAVEYARD. MOSSY HEADSTONES carved from granite and marble spoke of age. The moon had finally sifted through the clouds, illuminating the dark forest to their north and the valley to their south. Orilla del Río had been situated due east of the river that flowed from the woods and through Del Oro. In the daylight, Lalo imagined the small falls to be quite beautiful. And centuries ago, the cemetery was probably a lovely resting place.

The alarms still rang in the distance. Was Maricela out there? Was she hunting for him now, or another one of her children? He was still unsure how they had found him.

He and Carolina had stolen a small basin of blood from the butcher, most likely kept cool underground to make sausages. Lalo drank and drank, but he couldn't quite satiate the thirst. His body didn't feel nearly as wretched, though.

He chanced a glance at Carolina and jolted. She was glaring hard in his direction.

"This must be a jest," she said, a shovel gripped like a weapon in her hands. "We can't desecrate my great-great-great-grandfather's grave."

"It is the only way to prove if Alma asked Tecuani to bring him back from the Land of the Dead."

Carolina's fingers dug into the wooden handle. "You made me bring you all this way so you can tarnish my family's good name?"

"No. I brought you out here to help confirm that Vidal is the original sediento. Contrary to what you might believe, not everything is about you or your family."

"We're literally standing before *my* family's burial ground."

She had a point, but this wasn't some personal vendetta against the Fuenteses.

"The Fuenteses have protected the people of Del Oro for centuries. So, yes, this is about us because you are trying to say the very people who swore to protect this valley are the ones to cause this curse in the first place."

Carolina's horse whinnied. They both quieted, waiting for someone to bound out of the shadows. But then the stallion began to munch on the shrubs with ease.

"Whatever the case," Lalo said. "We must find the original sediento. Destroying him is the only way to fix everything."

"Yes, you keep saying that."

He turned to her. Though her face was lit by the moon, he didn't need it to see how stunning she was. How her lips always curved in a smirk. How her skin looked soft. How her eyes glistened with ferocity. He was so damn drawn to her. Despite how frustratingly stubborn she was, he found himself aching to move closer. He stepped nearer, just to see how his body might react.

Her pulse quickened.

Did she feel that pull too?

Of course not, he reminded himself. She was a vampiro hunter. He was, unfortunately, very much a vampiro. And even if he weren't, she was Carolina Victoria Fuentes—strong, witty, and as beautiful as a sunrise. She was surrounded by an enormous, boisterous family that cared for her; there'd be no room for him. He was just a bookish boy with only his sister who loved him— more like tolerated him—on most days.

He cleared his throat and took a step back.

"I have read articles, journals, books, and scriptures about monsters like this from across the world." He nodded toward the headstone. The granite was worn smooth from wind and age, but Vidal's name was still there. "If Vidal's body is not inside this grave, Alma came out here in her great sorrow and made a deal with the god of death."

Carolina's brow furrowed as she looked upon the grass. "I don't know if I should pray Vidal is in there or not."

Surprise bloomed within him. She didn't argue. She didn't say he was mistaken and disregard him. Carolina would see his ideas through with him. Raw emotion clogged his throat. Besides Fernanda, he hadn't had an ally in so long.

"For my sake," Lalo said. "Let's hope he is not."

"And if it is him?"

Lalo let out a sigh. "Then I'll find the tool Alma used to call upon Tecuani, locate Vidal, and strike him down before I am lost to the thirst." Before Maricela found him would be good as well.

195

Carolina huffed a laugh, her breath fogging the air around her. "Is that all?"

"Should there be more?"

"I'm teasing, Lalo." She shook her head, a smile tugging at her lips, and dug her shovel into the soft earth.

Lalo took up the shovel lying near his feet and joined her.

"May I ask you something, Carolina?" A chill swept through him. He didn't think he'd ever said only her first name aloud before. It felt intimate, especially under the stars.

"Only if it won't irritate me," she said.

"I cannot guarantee that. You seem to live in a constant state of exasperation."

"My own curse to endure."

Lalo held back his smile. "I am curious how vampiros get past Del Oro's barriers. It should be quite impossible."

"Usually it's human error. A gate left open here. A guard falling asleep there. Sometimes the leeches get creative and break through the weaker structures in the outer edges. Now I wonder if there isn't a bit of their soul still inside them and they know all the hidden ways in. Perhaps they aren't completely lost to the bloodlust, and some are just trying to find their way home." She paused. "I used to think every sediento's soul was gone the moment they turned. That they were these things whose only purpose was to kill. But you have changed my mind on the matter. I mean, look at you. How do you do it?"

"I am not special, if that is what you're saying."

"I wasn't."

Lalo snorted. "Well, just in case you were, I'll tell you this. When I was first turned, I could think of nothing but feeding.

My body physically ached inside when I didn't. But the people in the cantina I was in had horrendous thoughts and memories, I felt more disgust than anything. Those memories still play in my mind. I imagine, though, if the people I drank from had been happy or pleasant, I might have never been awakened from that fever dream. I could see how it'd be overwhelmingly addictive if those lives were good."

"Interesting."

They worked in silence. Heaving the damp soil over their shoulders and grunting with exertion.

After a while, Carolina asked, "What was that quote you told my apá the night we were caught in his library?"

"What a fond memory to bring up while we're knee-deep in a grave site."

"May I remind you this was your idea?"

"It was from a sonnet." He cleared his throat. "*And what is a few moments when our souls have known each other since the beginning of time?* It was written by—"

"Pío Parra," she finished. "Yes, I know. But you got it wrong."

Lalo stopped shoveling. "I beg your pardon?"

"That isn't how the poem goes."

"And how would you know?"

Even if he wasn't facing her, he would be able to sense the rolling of her eyes. "I've read all his works," she said.

Lalo gaped. "All? But that's . . ."

"Fifty-seven booklets. Fifty-nine, counting his anthologies. I've read most of the greats. Reyes, Espinoza, Jiménez, Torres."

"That's . . . You're . . ?"

"Exaggerating?" she challenged.

"No, that wasn't what I was going to say in the slightest."

She paused her digging and faced him. "What were you going to say?"

"I was going to say that *you* are amazing."

"Oh." She smiled bashfully. "Thank you."

"Do you have a favorite?" he asked. He'd never met someone who was more read than him in such a manner. He felt elated, despite their circumstances.

"Truth be told, that very sonnet and that exact line is my favorite above everything else. I've read it at least a thousand times because I love it so." Carolina began to shovel again. "That is how I know you misrepresented it."

"Impossible," he said. "It *too* is my favorite line, and I *too* have read it a thousand times."

"Then you wouldn't know it isn't *And what is a few moments when our souls have* known *each other since the beginning of time*? But *And what is a few moments when our souls have* loved *each other since the beginning of time*? You ruined the best part."

Lalo's brain nibbled on those words. By the stars, she was right. How could he have made that mistake?

He snuck a glance at Carolina. Her hair had fallen from its braid. Her brown skin was covered in dirt. And yet, she appeared perfectly smug. He quite liked that smirk playing on her face. Her confidence was inexplicably as charming as it was irritating. A conundrum, to be certain.

Her eyes met his.

"What?" she whispered.

"You've got mud on your cheek," he said. He didn't know why. He panicked.

198

She raised a brow. "So do you."

He recoiled. "I do not."

Carolina reached forward and something cool pressed against his cheek.

"Now you do," she said.

Lalo gasped.

She giggled as she pulled back her soiled hand.

"Oh, you are a devil," he scorned. But he found himself smiling. He grabbed a glob of dirt and flung it her way. Carolina laughed and shielded herself with a raised hand.

Shaking his head, Lalo dug his shovel into the earth again. This time, the blade bumped into something hard. They both froze.

"Vidal's coffin," Carolina uttered. She made no motion to move.

"Indeed." He swallowed the lump in his throat. This was it. Lalo would learn if he was one step closer or back at square one.

"Ready?" Carolina asked.

"Not really."

"Want me to do it?" Her eyes searched his. And for a moment, he was stunned by how empathetic her gaze was.

"Together?" he asked.

She nodded and knelt. He did the same. He reached down, ready to dig into the grave dirt. Their fingers grazed, and a shock of warmth sizzled up his skin. Carolina drew back.

Recovering from the moment, they began to shove the dirt away.

Together, they dug toward the center.

Lalo's heart dipped at the first sight of splintered wood.

"Holy hells," Carolina whispered.

They dug harder and found nothing but bits of shattered fragments until his knuckles bumped into the bottom of the coffin.

"There's nothing here," Carolina said.

"Keep searching. We must be sure."

His fingers skimmed against something cold and hard. He jerked back.

"What is it?" Carolina asked.

"There's something there." *Please don't let it be a bone. Please don't let it be a bone.*

Carolina shoved her arm into the hole he created. She frowned, then slowly tugged something out.

Lalo's pulse quickened.

She held up something that width-wise fit in the palm of her hand. The length was no longer than his forearm.

Carolina dusted the caked-on mud until a rusted hilt with curled edges could be seen.

"A dagger," she whispered, and brushed off the remaining dirt.

Lalo sighed with relief, then slouched, his chin tucked into his chest.

"The grave is empty," he breathed. He looked up at Carolina, who stared at the broken shards underfoot.

"This can't be real," she whispered. "He's not here. Perhaps we are mistaken? What if we desecrated the wrong site? It could've been mismarked. Or maybe a grave robber came and . . ." She clung to the soiled dagger as if that would offer her some clue.

"If a thief pilfered this grave, wouldn't they have taken the very valuable blade too?" Lalo asked.

"A Fuentes would never . . . We are here to protect our people. Not do"—she waved her hand at their surroundings—"whatever happened here."

"Have you ever been in love, Carolina?"

Her brown eyes flashed in the dark. "Why would you ask such a thing?"

"I cannot say that I am an expert." He'd never even held a woman's hand besides his mother's and sister's until Carolina took his before the duel. "But you've read the same sonnets about love and heartbreak as I have. Surely you know the power true love contains."

She pointed at the empty coffin. "This is destruction. There is nothing powerful about going to the gods and asking them to tear a hole through the veil of this realm and the next. This is selfishness."

"Then I am selfish too," he admitted. "After my mother and father were slain, I begged for the gods to bring my parents back. But alas, Fernanda and I are alone in this world."

"You aren't alone," she said softly. Had his hearing not been heightened by the power of Tecuani, he might not have caught those three beautiful words. "I did the same thing when Abuelo was taken. I prayed to the gods every night for weeks. I thought that if I begged hard enough, I'd wake up and learn it was just a nightmare." Her chin quivered. "Is it because I didn't cry hard enough? Because I didn't love deep enough? Do the gods only listen if you offer them something in return like Alma? What kinds of gods are those?"

"I don't know," he admitted. "But I am sorry."

"I miss him so much." She clamped her hand over her mouth as if that was the first time she'd ever confessed such a thing. Tears fell into her fingers. And then she began to sob. This was no ordinary cry either. This was deep and ferocious.

Lalo understood this heartache. It arrived suddenly and

201

viciously. The sorrow, the anger, the pain. No matter how hard a person tried to tuck away the feeling, grief came and went whenever it wished.

He had wanted to be held while he wept for his parents. But he was the one who needed to be strong for his sister while her world imploded. He didn't mind. Fernanda had become his everything in less than a minute. He offered his sister whatever consolation he could. And if Carolina allowed it, he'd do the same for her.

Slowly, as if he were approaching a bear, he slid his arms around her shoulders and pressed her body against his.

"I'm sorry," he whispered into her hair. "I'm so very sorry."

"I miss him so desperately I want to scream."

She clasped the back of his shirt, holding on to him as if he were a lifeline.

"He was the only one besides Nena to believe in me. And now he's gone."

"I believe in you," Lalo said. He hoped he hadn't overstepped, or that she would snort and tell him she didn't care, but instead she whispered, "Thank you. I believe in you, too."

Lalo stilled as that statement settled into his core.

"I'm sorry about your parents, too," she said softly.

His vision blurred. He blinked, and a tear ran down his cheek. Lalo swiped it away. His eyes snagged on the inky moisture staining his fingers. His jaw dropped.

Blood. He'd cried blood.

Frantically, he rubbed away the gore. He couldn't let her see him like this. He couldn't be a reminder of the very beasts that had taken her beloved abuelo.

Carolina started to pull away, but he held her tightly to his chest.

"Lalo?" she mumbled into his shirt.

He didn't let go until he believed he'd cleaned off the mess. When she slipped from him, he immediately missed the feel of her.

She laughed shyly and brushed at the tears drying on her face. "I feel rather foolish."

"Don't," he said. "Never be embarrassed about anything when it comes to me."

Carolina smirked. "I'll remember that."

A rooster crowed from somewhere in the distance. Her gaze went to the skies.

"We should go," she said. "Dawn is coming, and the clouds have gone."

"I'll escort you home."

CHAPTER 24

Carolina

CAROLINA'S MIND REELED WITH MORE AND MORE QUESTIONS the entire ride back from Orilla del Río. What had Alma done? More importantly, what were the exact terms of the deal she had made with Tecuani?

Her mind scoured over what she knew of the day Alma's body was found. The Fuentes familia had been the ones to lead the charge into the forest. They found her on a trail they'd crossed a few days prior. Her skin was ghostly pale. Her eyes had rolled back in her head. She appeared emaciated.

They covered her in veils and flowers as was the tradition then. But on the second day of mourning, Alma awoke. Her eyes were blood-red, and she had fangs and claws. Un diablo had taken her place, or so they thought.

Lalo said Tecuani was a trickster. Perhaps bringing back her lover only to have him kill her had been the god's cruel joke.

"Shit," she said, shaking her head.

Her great-great-great-grandmother accidently created the first vampiro in Abundancia.

The sun was cresting over Basilio's Point. Carolina shouldn't have stayed near the grave for so long. But she and Lalo had to cover the empty coffin back up. She'd told him to run back to his home as soon as she thought they'd be safe to check on Fernanda.

Carolina pressed her legs into her horse's body, urging him to move faster. Her family would be too busy hunting sedientos to worry over her. But Luz Elena was always sneaking about.

She rounded the bend of granite that stood as a marker she was nearing home. She needed to get through the cattle grounds unseen and then she could slink in through the rear of the hacienda.

Something massive cut right in front of her. Guapo reared up so suddenly, Carolina had no time to correct herself. Her hold on the reins faltered, and she tumbled back through the air. She landed hard on her bottom, her palms scraping over dirt and pointy shrubs.

Ignoring the stinging nipping at her hands, Carolina unsheathed the first weapon she could reach, the blade from the grave, and clambered to her feet. But a sword was already waiting for her. The point of it landing on her shoulder.

"What. Are. You. Doing?"

Carolina's stomach dropped to her knees. The voice dripping with fury was her papá's. His face was red. His eyes were bloodshot and swollen.

"Where have you been? Where? Where, mija?"

"I . . ." She couldn't tell him the truth. Not all of it, at least. "I went to hunt for the sediento who killed our men."

205

"You thought you'd take on a beast who could suck the life out of you? Without a single person to assist?" Spittle flung from her father's mouth. "Give that to me." Papá gestured toward the rusted dagger in her hand.

She held it tight against her chest. "But . . ."

"Now!"

With shaking fingers, she thrust the handle toward him. He jerked it out of her grasp and shoved it into his belt.

"I thought you were dead." His voice cracked. Fresh tears filled his eyes. "I've been looking for you since we found the felled sedientos in town. I was so scared. I . . ." He pulled her into his massive form. He crushed her in his arms. "Never do that to me again."

Even now, he did not believe her capable of surviving on her own. She had been the one to kill the monsters, but he would never believe that. Or he'd use this as the last straw and truly send her away for good. Yes, she knew he loved her with his whole heart. But why could he not love her as she was? Why could he value her as a woman but not as a fighter?

The sound of hooves thundering came from behind the boulders. Papá spun, pulling Carolina behind him, and thrust out his sword. His tension eased when two guards rounded the bend on horseback.

"Señor!" one of them called. "We believe we found something. Tracks going into the woods toward la casa del Alicante."

"That's where Lalo is staying," Carolina blurted out.

"And you think they were inhuman?" Papá asked.

"We cannot say for certain, but the strides are longer. Lighter. Something incredibly fast ran through there. And not so long ago."

Could those tracks have been Lalo's?

"Do you believe it was a lone sediento?" she asked, ignoring her papa's glare.

"It looks like several."

She had cut down two vampiros last night. There could have easily been more. If they were traveling toward Lalo, he could be in danger.

Carolina grasped her papá's arm. "We must go there, Apá. Right now!"

"Show me," Papá ordered his men. He turned to Carolina. "Go home. I don't want to even think you are outside the gates. Do you understand?"

"But . . ."

Papa's eyes narrowed with another heaping of fury.

"I understand." She would not waste time fighting him, not if Lalo and Fernanda were in peril.

"Please, hurry," Carolina said.

He ran to his mount and climbed onto the saddle. Papá and his men set off, pounding in the direction from which she'd come.

Carolina sighed and let her shoulders slump. She rubbed her bottom, which was sore from falling off Guapo. She was tired from her misadventures. And she was thoroughly confused.

She clicked her tongue and her horse stopped munching on the dried grass underfoot. He trotted over and bumped his snout against Carolina's back.

"Don't try to apologize now," she grumbled. "You threw me on my ass."

Guapo sighed into Carolina's hair and nuzzled in closer. Grinning, she scratched his jaw and nose. "All right," she said. "You're forgiven. But my apá is not."

From the journal of Friar Alejandro Ibarra

Tecuani cannot leave the Forest of Souls unless summoned. And thus, those inflicted with his death curse cannot enter a residence without permission.

It is easy to imagine how quickly the world as we know it could fall if these abominations weren't weakened by the laws of the gods. I often wake up in the night in a cold sweat wondering what would happen if said laws didn't exist. What would I do if one stricken with the death curse burst through my door?

The answer is nothing. I could do nothing to fight something so powerful.

And that is why I am grateful the gods grant us these small mercies. I thank the saints that there is a barrier between us mere mortals—the hunted—and the hunter's wrath.

CHAPTER 25

Lalo

Lalo had just changed out of his soiled clothes when something crashed on the first floor. Voices hollered.

"What in the devil?" Lalo ran across the room.

"Lalo!" a gruff voice yelled. "Fernanda!"

Lalo opened the door to his room and peeked out to see—oddly enough—Señor Fuentes bolting up the steps. He seemed furious. His massive hands gripped the railing with bone-crushing force; a sword swung at his hip. Lalo jerked back. Did Señor Fuentes know about him? Was he here to slay the resident beast?

Lalo searched for a proper place to hide. But his brain had stopped functioning. He was going to die. Here. In some drafty home. Without a single chance to retreat. He braced himself for whatever was to come, squeezing his eyes shut as if that would shield him from his impending doom.

Señor Fuentes's heavy footsteps clomped into his room. "Lalo?"

Lalo opened a single eyelid. Confusion twisted Señor Fuentes's face, then something like relief relaxed his features. El señor let out a long sigh. "You're all right."

"Am I?" Lalo asked.

"*Aren't* you?" Señor Fuentes tilted his head, surveying Lalo as if he were one of his prized bulls.

Lalo's brain gave a painful jab, and he winced. He pinched the bridge of his nose. "If you count feeling like my head might explode and having someone break into my home all right, yes."

El señor's mustache twitched. "Apologies about your front door. We thought . . ." He paused. "We were concerned for your safety. There was an incident." He ground his teeth together. "My men were killed last night. We've found three dead sedientos, but we believe there might be more."

Lalo's heart thudded inside his chest. Did Señor Fuentes think it was him? The man was truly going to kill Lalo, just when he'd gotten Carolina on his side. They were going to fix this.

"Señor, about the attack . . ."

"I know, it is a tragedy indeed. Fear not, we will find every leech responsible and cut them down."

Lalo blinked hard. Did he hear that correctly? Señor Fuentes wasn't here to avenge the victims?

"If I may be so bold," Lalo dared to say. "Why are you here?"

"Come with me," Señor Fuentes ordered.

Lalo followed el señor down the steps and into the library, making sure to give a wide berth to the shafts of sunlight slipping through the windows and open door in the foyer. There wasn't much as far as food to offer the man, but there was some rather nice port his sister kept hidden behind a stack of romance magazines. And Señor Fuentes looked like he could use a relaxer.

"I know it is early, but care for a drink?" Lalo asked.

"That would be nice."

As Lalo moved toward the stack of books nuzzled against the large armchair his sister had claimed for herself, el señor's eyes scoured over every window within the study. They were covered with thick draperies. The place was a tomb at all times so Lalo could sit with his sister.

"Why are the curtains drawn so tight?" Señor Fuentes inquired.

"I am prone to headaches." This wasn't a lie. "Brighter days make them worse."

He handed Señor Fuentes a full tumbler. The man drank it down in a single gulp, his eyes burning into Lalo.

"Is there something else, señor?" Lalo queried.

Señor Fuentes placed the empty glass on the small table beside him. He sat on the leather couch and leaned back in his seat as if he owned the home. "We are used to random attacks by sedientos. My guard is always prepared, but the monsters have grown bolder as of late. Never in all my years have we had so many strikes against el pueblo within a week." His jaw muscle twitched.

Lalo braced himself for the accusation sure to come—*you brought them here and now you will die.*

"The men of this family have a duty to uphold. And that starts by ensuring the women we are bound to remain safe. How will you keep my Carolina protected if you are wedded?"

Lalo was not prepared for such a question, and he laughed at this absurdity. He tried to cover it with a cough when Señor Fuentes glared at him with fatherly indignation.

"Something humorous to you?"

"No, Señor Fuentes. It is only, from what I know of your

211

daughter, she would be boiling mad if she heard you say such a thing. She is more than capable of keeping herself safe, no? She killed the vampiros in el pueblo last night."

"She did what?!"

Shit. Perhaps this subject should be avoided at all costs. "One of the many reasons why I fell for Carolina is because she is a fierce champion for the people she loves. She would do anything to see her family protected."

"You think you understand my daughter better than I?" Señor Fuentes leaned forward, resting his elbows on his thighs.

"Of course not. But I believe in her more than you."

Señor Fuentes shot to his feet, his fists clenched at his sides. Lalo would not let this man, or anyone, intimidate him anymore.

"I see how strong and resilient and brave your daughter is." She had confronted him in the woods when she thought him only a devil, and she had not hesitated to try to take him down. She'd faced him again and again, and those vampiros in el pueblo as well. "Carolina is not afraid to fight, señor. And she is damn good at it, too."

"Yes, but she is brash and stubborn. She does not listen."

"I wonder if your father ever said the same thing about you."

Señor Fuentes glared at Lalo, but then his features softened. He huffed. "He said that often, actually."

"You are a good father, Señor Fuentes. I know you are frightened for her because this world is terrifying, but don't push her away. Don't hold her back from living out her dreams because of *your* own worries." Lalo knew he should be heeding his own advice. He'd been isolating himself his entire life.

Señor Fuentes's face grew somber. He gripped Lalo hard on the shoulder. "I can see why she likes you so much, mijo."

Mijo. *My son.* The word stung inside Lalo's chest. He hadn't heard that endearment spoken in his direction since his father died.

Fernanda rushed into the library in her night coat, her face noticeably pale at the sight of Señor Fuentes.

"Might someone tell me why the lock on our door is broken?" she asked, breathless.

"It appears some beasts have been on the prowl nearby," Lalo said. "Señor Fuentes came to see if we were safe."

She raised her brow. "What sort of beasts?"

"The very worst, I'm afraid," Señor Fuentes said. "My men found tracks littered about your property. We believe they belong to sedientos."

Fernanda's eyes flicked to Lalo's. He saw her fear. Her concern. He could hear her pulse quicken and the blood rushing through her veins. And she should be afraid. Maricela had found them.

"I would not venture outside of your home at night," Señor Fuentes said. "In fact, I wouldn't suggest you open the doors or windows once the sun begins to set. I'd like to leave some of my people here as a precaution."

"No." That single word came from Lalo in a whisper, but it was loud enough for everyone to hear. Lalo stepped close to el señor. "Those monsters already took out some of your men. What is to stop them from doing that again? And we are so far from town. Don't you think it would be safer if we . . ." *What was he doing? Why was he speaking?* Lalo knew why. To keep Fernanda protected. To be closer to Carolina. If they were under the same roof, they could have more time to plan their next move, to try to find Vidal and end this nightmare. "May we stay with you, Señor Fuentes?" He forced out the question.

El señor's thick brows quirked.

213

"Perhaps this is unconventional," Lalo said. Perhaps it was also cowardly. But if Maricela and her goons found him, he couldn't defend Fernanda and himself. "When the sun sets, who truly knows what those monsters might do?"

Sedientos couldn't enter his home, but that didn't mean they couldn't smoke him out. He and Fernanda would be sitting ducks. Better to be behind the adobe walls of the Fuentes hacienda. If Maricela had the chance to sink her fangs into him, she would see Lalo's memories. She would understand what he and Carolina were planning to do, and Carolina would be good as dead, too. He couldn't take that chance. She was a tyrant of a girl, but she was so smart and full of life and—

"What are you thinking?" Fernanda whispered, cutting into his thoughts.

The irony that Lalo would seek refuge in a home filled with people who would happily kill him was not lost on him. This idea was more than insane. He'd have to somehow keep himself from being exposed to the elements. And then there was the matter of getting blood.

Señor Fuentes toyed with his mustache. "We wouldn't want anything to happen to either of you. You *are* practically family now."

"We are?"

"Of course. You are Carolina's beloved and an intelligent, brave, and practical young man. You understand that you could never fend for yourself or your sister out here and have come to me for help."

In light of their heartfelt conversation, he'd receive that as a compliment.

"You two will stay with us," Señor Fuentes ordered. "At least until we hunt down the bastards that took my men. We will speak more of your engagement as well and where you might move after you wed."

Lalo's heart did a strange sort of flip inside his rib cage.

Señor Fuentes clapped his hands together, the sound like thunder rolling through Lalo's skull. "It is settled. Pack your things. This is my nephew Jorge, you met his sister, Antonina, the night we were first introduced. He will follow your carriage on horseback. I have some other matters to attend to, meanwhile."

With that, he marched out the door.

Jorge was a slender young man with dark brown skin and a knowing smirk. He chuckled. "I'm sorry for you, man."

"For me?" Lalo pointed to himself. "¿Por qué?"

"I'm used to my outrageous family. But you? You're marrying into it. You've got a lot to learn."

Lalo stood there, arms slack at his sides, as Jorge sauntered off. This hadn't been how he thought his day would go, but it was much better than dying at the hands of sedientos.

He eyed the doorway that el señor and Jorge had left through. He turned to his sister. "Does this mean I have his blessing?"

"I think you have bigger issues." She jerked her chin toward the golden sunlight streaming in from the front door.

Lalo grimaced. His skin would blister and boil in moments. "I hadn't thought of that."

Fernanda smirked. "Of course not, you were too busy trying to weasel your way into Carolina's house."

"I am doing this for you."

Fernanda rolled her eyes. "Come on, Don Juan," she said as she started to stroll away. "We need to figure something out. Fast."

CHAPTER 26

Carolina

A SINGLE RIDER POUNDED UP THE ROAD AS CAROLINA CLIMBED on top of the saddle. She could see his broad shoulders and smirk through the dust storm his horse's hooves created. Carolina groaned.

Rafa brought his horse to a halt.

"Thank the stars you are safe," Rafa panted.

"What are you doing out here? Didn't a bull horn stab you in the ass?"

His lips flattened. "The horn grazed my side. And I am fighting through the pain to search for you."

"I appreciate you joining in the effort. As you can see, I am alive and well."

Rafa pulled off his sombrero and wiped the sweat out of his eyes. "Why do you look as if you've been tumbling in the dirt? You weren't *with* someone, were you?" He raised a brow.

She gripped her reins harder. "I am engaged, Rafa. I may do whatever I please."

"Your father has given his approval then?"

"Lalo has my approval, and that's what you should care about."

"There's something peculiar about that man, if that's what one would even call him. He's more of a boy, with those scrawny arms of his." He flexed his own. "Do you know what I find strange?"

"I'm sure you're about to tell me."

"That you, of all people, could fall so deeply in love with someone so vastly different than yourself. You are so . . ."

She glared at Rafa, waiting for him to finish.

"You're so picky," he offered.

"It is fate, I suppose."

"You don't find it odd that he would swoop in and propose after mere minutes of knowing you? Or that he has managed to snake his way into your family's trust?"

"And what of you? You show up out of nowhere and make an offer for my hand, even though we haven't spoken in ages."

"*We* haven't spoken. But your father and I have. He is my godfather, after all. How selfish of you to go against him for a boy whose head is in books. Together, we could build an empire."

Her hands went to her hips. "Sounds like you need a business partner, not a wife."

He smirked. "Why can't I have both?"

"I'm certain you'll find one. Elsewhere. I will only marry someone I consider attractive and interesting. Someone I love."

He laughed haughtily. "I am thrice as attractive as that reed of a man."

"No, your ego is thrice the size." She clicked her tongue, urging her horse on.

Rafa reached out and grabbed Guapo's reins, holding the stallion in place. "Mark my words, Carolina, I don't trust him. And I will find out why. I have already sent a courier falcon to a friend in Puerto Blanco. And when I find out who Eduardo Montéz truly is, your engagement will be broken, and you will be mine. We will leave this pit of a pueblo, and we will never return."

When he didn't laugh maniacally like a madman from one of her gothic stories, she leaned forward, glaring at the boy who once ate cockroaches just to make the girls in town scream. "If the skies fell to earth and civilization hinged on my marrying you, I wouldn't do it. I'd let the world crumble." She jerked the straps out of his grasp. "I wish you good day, Rafael."

"I'd be a bit nicer to me, señorita. There are several hours between now and the fiesta tonight, and I'm certain I'll learn everything there is to know about this Eduardo Montéz."

Carolina's stomach clenched. She'd forgotten about the party. Traders from the Greater North were coming to purchase cattle. She winced. Her mamá was most likely already up, frantically readying the barn for their arrival. She flicked her hair over her shoulder and raised her chin. "I cannot wait."

She took off at a dangerous pace. She needed to ride. She wished for the wind to take away her troubles too.

Rafa was so irritating. He was going to ruin everything. He might expose who Lalo truly was. And then what? She'd have to explain to her family that she'd lured un vampiro into their home and instead of killing him, she'd forced him to be her fiancé. Worse still, she'd grown fond of his quirks! Her family simply couldn't find out what Lalo was. She couldn't lose him.

Especially not when she and Lalo were on a path to ridding the world of sedientos. In one fell swoop, she could protect her loved ones and assure her parents that she was safe in Del Oro.

She gritted her teeth against the warm morning sun. She took the shortest route home, cutting through the barren lands that had yet to be turned into orchards of citrus, like her father intended. As their hacienda came into view, she saw a black coach kicking up dust on the road. A few trunks were strapped to the top and rear. The curtains were drawn so she couldn't see who was inside.

"Faster, boy!" she ordered Guapo.

As soon as he was in his stall and given water and grain, Carolina snuck to the side of the casa, scaled the trellis leading to the second floor, and climbed through the window to her rooms.

Nena was draped across her bed. Her legs kicking merrily behind her as she flipped through an old fashion magazine. She didn't even spare a glance when Carolina silently hopped into their shared bedroom.

"Have a nice night?" Nena asked.

Carolina swept over to the broken floorboard and started storing her weapons away. "Why aren't you out searching for me like everyone else?"

Nena turned another page. "Because I know you can handle yourself."

"Aren't you going to ask where I've been?"

Nena grinned, finally eyeing Carolina's harried appearance. "Looks like you've been having fun."

"If you count desecrating a grave as a good time, then yes, it was a hoot."

"How scandalous." Nena shut the magazine and clambered off her bed. "What's it like to kiss a vampiro?"

"Get your mind out of the latrine, prima." Carolina slid the floorboard in place and stood. "I wasn't out kissing all night. I was *literally* desecrating graves."

"Oh." Nena had the audacity to appear disappointed.

Carolina threw off the dirt-covered garment and shoved herself into a respectable black gown and heeled slippers.

"What are you getting ready for? The whooping your mamá is sure to give you when she sees you?"

"Shit," Carolina whispered.

"Don't fret. I swapped her regular tea with valerian root. She slept like a baby most of the night. She hasn't a clue you were gone."

Carolina dabbed at the sweat dripping from her hairline. At least she didn't need to put on rouge, for her cheeks were a sun-kissed pink.

"I saw a carriage laden with trunks when I rode in. I think the traders have arrived early."

"I see." Nena stood behind Carolina and began re-braiding her hair into two plaits.

"That is all you have to say? You, who counts down the days until the traders come so you can flirt with them."

Nena shrugged. "People change, Carolina." She raised her chin. "Perhaps I am one of them."

"Could this be because of a certain green-eyed young woman with a certain vampiro brother?"

A smile pulled at Nena's face. "I don't know who you are talking about."

Carolina splashed on some of the perfume she'd been given on her eighteenth birthday. She grabbed Nena's hand.

"Come on. We should welcome our guests before my mamá gets mad."

She and Nena hustled through the casa. Her mamá and younger brothers were there, already speaking to—Carolina's eyes bulged—Lalo.

At least whatever Papá had tracked near his home left him alone.

He wore a large coat, gloves, scarf, and sombrero. An absolutely ridiculous outfit, seeing as the sky was bright blue. But it certainly shielded him from the sun's rays. He looked so uncomfortable. He kept pulling at the scarf wrapped too tightly around his neck. The smile on his face was strained.

Lalo's head tilted, and he met her gaze. Her heart thumped hard in her chest. Something warm pooled in her belly.

He had held her in his arms only hours ago. He had comforted her when no one else had been allowed to. Nena and Mamá had tried, but she simply couldn't let them—not when she had been the reason her abuelo was slain. He had been out there to give her a birthday gift, to train her in secret like she begged him to do. She had been caught off guard and her blood had lured in more monsters. Aside from her sediento, no one else understood that heavy burden of guilt.

Lalo knew how to wade through the unrelenting bog of sorrow.

He never told her everything was going to be all right. Or lied and said she was faultless. Lalo simply said he was sorry and let her cry into his shirt. That had been enough.

She tore her eyes away from him. Heat clawed up her neck. The first young man to ever hold her so intimately had been the very same sort of creature who killed her abuelo. Though, she'd come to see that, unlike her cousin Lorenzo, his humanity remained intact.

She glanced at Lalo again. Her belly dipped once more. It wasn't because he was in her home, nor because of the moment they'd shared under the stars. The tremor of surprise buzzing through her body came from the fact that Lalo Montéz, in that very moment, looked utterly adorable.

From the journal of Jonathan Monroe of Santemala

June 18, 1709

I tried to bring my precious daughter to a bruja in Sololá. I wrapped her in ropes made with wooden beads and covered our wagon to shield her from the sun. We traveled east for half the night until she began to shriek as if she were being sliced apart. I couldn't force the wagon any farther for fear she would be lost to me.

 I sent word to the bruja, and this was her reply: "You did not tell me you made a deal with a trickster god. There is nothing I can do. Nor can you bring that thing here. Those given new life by Tecuani cannot venture very far from their graves as part of their curse. I shall burn incense and pray to Xipil, goddess of understanding, for you, but I fear only a stake to the heart will end your child's suffering."

CHAPTER 27

Lalo

THE SCENT OF ROSEWATER HIT HIM FIRST. THEN CAME THE SOFT smells of vanilla, lavender, leather, and horsehair, a special sort of aroma that belonged only to her. He couldn't help but breathe deeper.

Antonina leaned into her and whispered into her ear. She covered her hand to conceal what she was saying, but Lalo heard her clearly.

"Looks like he's prepared for a winter storm," she said.

Carolina snorted. "The poor man's face is growing redder by the second."

The two giggled.

Stars, she was beautiful. He'd only ever truly seen her at night or when clouds covered the skies. But here, with the light of day highlighting her rosy cheeks, she was like a goddess walking among them.

"You're staring," Fernanda whispered.

Lalo's head snapped toward his sister. "I am not." He absolutely had been. But sometimes such things could not be helped. Carolina was like a solar eclipse.

Carolina descended the stairs and offered a quick bow. "Lalo, Fernanda, to what do we owe the pleasure?"

Carolina's mother was the one to answer. "The Montézes will be staying with us for the time being. It seems the beast who killed our men traveled too close to their home for anyone's liking."

"I see." Carolina nodded.

"Lalo?" Carolina's mother eyed his clothing. "Would you like Luz Elena to take your coat?" She gestured toward an older woman with pearly white braids.

Saints, yes, he would. He'd soon be drowning in his own sweat because of the many layers he bore, but he couldn't risk his skin coming in contact with any of the dozens of windows glaring down at him throughout the sprawling casa. Luckily, his perspiration seemed to be somewhat normal, unlike the inky tears he'd shed in the cemetery.

"Actually, I'm not feeling my best. My mother always told me to sweat out the sickness. Hence, this absurd outfit," he said, chuckling and gesturing to himself. "May I excuse myself to whatever room I will be staying in?"

"You poor thing." Señora Fuentes's hand went to the top of her chest, just under her collarbone. A tiny vein throbbed at the side of her neck. His mouth watered. His thirst dug into his intestines and twisted them in knots. Suddenly, all the scents in the room were becoming overwhelming. The heartbeats, the blood, their essences—they were practically begging to be devoured.

225

Señora Fuentes turned to the woman by her side. "Luz Elena, please escort Lalo to Tía Morena's old room at once."

"I'll do it!" Carolina blurted out.

Antonina snickered.

Señora Fuentes quirked an eyebrow. "Mija, I don't think that is appropriate."

"Papá went out of his way to ensure Lalo and Fernanda were safe, which means he must care about their safety. That also means he must approve of Lalo. And if that is the case, are we not practically betrothed?"

Señora Fuentes didn't seem convinced. Lalo wished she would be, and soon. His pulse thumped hard against his skull. He was so thirsty and hot. If he didn't get out of this coat and have some of the blood Fernanda packed in his bag, he might lose control.

Fernanda, ever astute, spoke up. "Señora Fuentes, I noticed a glorious painting in the ballroom the last time we were here. I've been dying to ask you about the piece ever since."

Señora Fuentes's light brown face lit from within. "Would you believe me if I said I painted it?"

Fernanda gasped. "You are kidding?"

"You must show her, tía," Antonina chimed in. "You really are so talented."

"This is why you are my favorite niece," Señora Fuentes said with a warm smile.

Antonina laughed as she took her tía's and Fernanda's arms. "Let's bring her to your art room."

"Yes, please do!" Fernanda said.

As the others left, trailing behind the chatting women, Carolina gestured toward the western wing of the casa. "This way, Lalo."

Luz Elena shuffled after them.

226

"It's okay, Luz," Carolina said in that impatient but loving way one has with their nanny. Not that he was an expert on such manners; they'd had a sitter for only six months growing up. She had quit, saying Lalo was too picky about his food and Fernanda was a terror. He couldn't blame the nanny on the latter point—Fernanda *had* been a little devil. Still was. Lalo, however, had been a perfectly pleasant child, so he didn't know why she had complained about him.

Luz Elena shook her head. "Being alone together isn't proper."

Carolina slithered her arm around Lalo's elbow. He jolted at her sudden touch. And his appetite tripled in its ravenousness. His free hand clenched into a fist.

Think of taxes, he said to himself. *Think of math equations. Of anything but Carolina touching you.*

"I may walk unaccompanied with my fiancé," Carolina said.

The vieja raised her chin. "The betrothal is not official."

Lalo tried to pull free—Carolina's nearness was too much—but she gripped him harder, tugging him even closer to her soft body. The scent of her made him want to do the most inappropriate things. Like run his fingers through her dark hair. Like sink his teeth into her.

What is wrong with you? he scorned himself. She was a sediento killer, one that would happily stake his heart at this very moment if she didn't need him.

"Our engagement is certainly happening," Carolina said to Luz Elena. "So I may escort my husband-to-be unaccompanied."

Carolina hauled Lalo, not so gently, forward before Luz Elena could argue further. They moved as one in silence, walking at a brisk pace up the long hallway filled with portraits of people he could only assume were relatives. The large Fuentes familia had the same stern yet arrogant air about them. There was no mistaking them to be part of the same bloodline.

Was Alma among the gallery? Vidal?

Carolina pressed tighter against Lalo and whispered, "Is she still watching?"

Lalo forced a glance over his shoulder. The nanny was clutching a beaded necklace and mouthing something, observing him intently. "She is. I believe she's praying."

Carolina snorted. "Probably for your soul. She's a pious one."

"I'd like that actually," he said quietly.

He meant it in jest, but the truth was, he could use someone to pray to the gods on his behalf. He had slayed those people at Maricela's seedy cantina in Los Campos. Regardless of their own sins, how could he ever expect to enter the gates of el Cielo after something like that? Was there mercy for someone whose hands were stained with blood? Did his remorse make up for any of it? Could his soul be saved by slaying one last person, Vidal?

Their eyes met again. She had the longest lashes and loveliest lips. How could an individual be so perfectly beautiful? And her scent was so enticing. It burrowed into his very core. His stomach rumbled ferociously.

"You're hungry," she said.

Lalo scowled at the tile beneath his boots. "I'm always hungry."

"How do you control it? The bloodlust?"

"I try to think of anything else in the world. Anything at all. Taxes. Ledgers. Books. But mostly I remember what it felt like to take a person's life."

She hadn't let go of him, despite moving through the hallway with no one but her ancestors watching them from above. What would they think of their great-granddaughter in the arms of a monster?

"That is why we must find Vidal," he said. "I can't live like this much longer—always thirsty, constantly trying to not give in—and I need to ensure my sister's safety."

Carolina squeezed his bicep and offered a kind smile. "You are a good brother, Lalo."

Hot emotion clogged his throat. He hadn't always been the most understanding or patient of siblings, but there wasn't a day that went by where he didn't have Fernanda's well-being in mind. He cared for his little sister deeply, and it was almost healing to hear that Carolina took notice. If things went south and he gave into the thirst, there would at least be one person to remind Fernanda that she was loved by her brother.

They walked in silence until they came to a door. Carolina slipped her fingers from his elbow. With her touch gone, Lalo let loose the breath he'd been holding. He couldn't decide if he liked this kind side of Carolina. It made him feel things. Confusing things. At least when she was trying to murder him, he knew where he stood with her. But now, when they touched, he swore it was like the world around him was expanding and crashing in all at once.

Her back was to him as she opened the door. He used that time to rub his gloved hands across his face.

"Wait here," she said.

She rushed into the room and drew the shutters hanging on either side of the windows shut. Even in the low light, Lalo could see that every square inch of the space was plastered in gaudy furnishings.

"Better?" she asked.

"Entirely."

"Good." She smiled. "Now you can take off that ridiculous outfit."

"You do not like my fashion choices?" He gestured toward himself. The scarf, the oversize coat, the hat.

She snorted. "Not in the slightest."

"It was the best I could do on such short notice."

She crossed her arms. "What did my papá say to get you here?"

"It was my idea. I thought it safer and . . ." *And you are here.* "It will make our search easier, don't you think?"

She nodded.

Carolina plopped onto the bed. The one he was going to be resting on at some point. But how could he with her scent now infused into the blankets?

He grabbed the wooden chair that was tucked into a desk and motioned to it. "Do you mind?"

Her brows raised. "Is there a problem?"

"I just . . . I don't need . . ."

"Am I making you uncomfortable, Lalo?"

"I don't like dirt on my things."

She huffed. "Has anyone ever told you you're a real stick in the mud?"

"Señorita, that phrase makes no sense to me, so I truly don't care."

"You've been told that too many times to count, huh?" She rolled her eyes but stood. He held his breath as she swept past him and sat like the elegant lady the mayor's daughter should be.

"Happy?" she asked.

"As one can be in this type of situation."

Carolina paused. "Were you ever happy, Lalo? I mean, truly happy. Dancing-and-laughing-under-the-stars happy?"

"Have I given you the impression that either of those things would bring me joy?"

A sly smile slid over her face.

"Why are you grinning like that?" he asked.

"I was thinking about the sort of dance partner you would be."

"That is something you will never see from me, señorita." But what would having her in his arms and moving as one feel like?

Stay focused, he thought, seething.

They needed to figure out where the original sediento might be, not speak about dancing and happiness.

"Is there a log that lists the attacks on el pueblo?" he asked.

"I believe my papá keeps a record. It would be in our library."

"We should go there," he said. "Perhaps we might be able to track Vidal's whereabouts that way. If we can somehow find a pattern to these attacks—"

"They're completely random. The lone commonality is that they happen within the forest and the valley. That is it."

"Not Devil's Spine?" he asked. His thoughts tumbled back to the day he had been forced to drink Maricela's blood. The southernmost peak of Basilio's Point was the one clear detail from her life he could glean from her memories. How could he not take notice of a rock formation with such strange ridges?

"Well, I'm sure they do, but how would we know? It is a few days' hard ride from here. If there was an attack, who would survive to tell us?"

"Do you know anyone who has ever ventured to the mountains?"

Carolina pursed her lips as she thought.

231

Lalo dragged his attention away. He did not need to think about her mouth at this moment. Kneeling, Lalo clicked his trunk open and reached for the flask hidden beneath his things.

He twisted the cap off the flask and brought it to his lips but paused when he saw her watching.

"Do you mind?" he said. "This isn't a pleasant experience for me, and I'd like some privacy."

With a sigh of exasperation, she shifted in her seat until her back was to him.

"What happens when we do find Vidal?" she asked over her shoulder. "Do you expect us to so easily go to his hidden lair and strike down a centuries-old vampiro?"

"Actually, yes . . . after we find the tool used to create him."

Lalo took a deep swig. The cold boar's blood slid in gelatinous chunks down his throat. He gagged, nearly spit everything up, then forced himself to swallow.

"You truly hate the taste of blood," she said.

"Unequivocally so."

The cramps plaguing his stomach eased at once, but he would never be as strong as he had been after that night in the cantina.

He took another long drink then closed the cap. She must have found him so disgusting at that moment. He exhaled and dropped his chin to his chest.

Hands that were both callused and soft brushed over his.

"Lalo," Carolina said gently. She was on the floor beside him. So close, her skirts brushed against him. "Lalo, look at me," Carolina ordered.

Slowly, painfully, he did. *Saints, why did this girl have to be so befuddling?*

"This partnership will not work if we aren't honest with one another," she said. "May I be honest with you now?"

His pulse raced as she eased closer to him.

He nodded.

Carolina smirked. "You look awful."

Lalo balked. "I beg your pardon?"

"And you may have learned to punch and fight, but you cannot wield a weapon for shit."

Lalo frowned but a smile tugged at his lips. "You mock me?"

She giggled. "I'm sorry. Perhaps that was rude. But I needed to pull you from whatever sorrowful place your mind was headed. There is no more time for wallowing. How can we face the ultimate evil if you aren't completely ready to defend yourself?"

"I . . ." Lalo's throat bobbed. "I hadn't exactly thought of that."

"Well, you must. I know your brain will get you the answers you need. But what about the rest? Vidal will not be easy to kill." A gasp escaped her. "A brilliant idea just came to me."

He chuckled. "You are humble as ever."

"You're right. I shouldn't undervalue myself. My idea is *beyond* brilliant." She beamed then lugged him up. "Come. If we are going to kill my great-great-great-grandfather, you are going to need to at least know the very basics of wielding a blade."

Carolina snatched the sombrero hanging on the bedpost and shoved it on top of his head.

"Should I be afraid?" he asked in earnest.

She patted his hand and tugged him toward the door. "Only slightly."

CHAPTER 28

Carolina

CAROLINA AND LALO FOUND THEIR WAY INTO THE EMPTY COACH house. Papá's men had used the entire fleet to search for the missing sedientos. This was the perfect place to train.

"Abuelito used to teach me in this very room on days when the rain wouldn't let up." Carolina's heart pinched at the thought. She hadn't had the stomach to enter the coach house since Abuelo's passing.

"See that?" She pointed to a dent in the wall. No one would notice it was there, but she knew. "Abuelito and I were practicing hand-to-hand combat. I dodged an oncoming blow, and he smacked his knuckles right into the wood."

Lalo stared at the small crack. "Was he aiming to hurt you?"

She smiled wistfully. "Of course."

She released Lalo's hand and ran for a board lying on the floor. The cocheros would lie on it while they worked on cracked axles. With a grunt, she lifted the wood and leaned it opposite-end-up against a beam.

A thousand slices marked the thick board. She ran her finger along one.

"I can't tell you how many times my abuelo made me practice throwing my blades into this thing." Her eyes pricked with tears. She sniffed. "He tormented me."

"And now you get to torment me," Lalo said.

A bark of a laugh burst from her lips. Her cheeks grew hot. She hated how easily he made her giggle. How easily he made her smile.

Controlling her features, Carolina walked toward the large toolbox her abuelo hid their throwing knives in. She opened the largest of the drawers and pulled out the false floor. Gleaming blades winked at her. Her heart swelled. She felt her abuelo there at that very moment, watching with a proud grin as he always did.

"I've missed you," she whispered as she reached in and took the daggers.

When she turned around, she caught Lalo staring.

"Shall we begin?" she asked, throwing the blade in the air and catching it with ease.

He shucked off his coat, took off his gloves, and rolled up his sleeves. Her stomach dipped when she flashed back to the night he'd been shot in the duel. She, Nena, and Fernanda had undressed him to get rid of the evidence. Carolina had tried her best not to ogle him then. She had tried not to appreciate the muscles underneath his slender build, but there was no helping it. And she couldn't help but wish to see them again now.

She took in a deep breath and let it out.

"First things first," she said. "We must ensure the area is clear of people. We wouldn't want to accidently stab anyone."

"There's no one around," Lalo said simply.

"How do you know for certain?"

He pointed to himself. "Vampiro, remember?"

"How silly of me to forget." She stepped beside him. "Now that we know we are in the clear, let's focus on your stance. Do you write with your left or right?"

"Right."

"Okay. You'll lead with your left leg."

Lalo moved his foot forward. But his body was too stiff. His hands too tense.

"Relax," she said.

"This *is* me relaxed."

Carolina smiled. She placed her hands on his shoulders. Lalo's eyes widened. Before he could say anything, she shook him hard.

"What in the . . ?"

She laughed. "I'm trying to loosen you up." She grasped his waist and twisted his hips. "You're as stiff as the target board." She wiggled him around until Lalo was smiling too. And, stars, what a smile it was.

"I think I am quite loose now," he said.

Feeling a bit smug, Carolina plopped the first dagger into his palm. These blades were forged from steel not obsidian, so he could handle them with ease. "Throw this at the center of the board."

Lalo sighed. "*I am not a man built for fighting but a man built for love.*"

Carolina scoffed. "That is the very worst line Pío Parra ever wrote."

His brows raised. "You think so?"

"I know so. To love is to fight. You must fight for love every day. Don't you agree?"

He pursed his lips. "I suppose you are right."

She cupped her ear. "Say that again."

Lalo huffed. "I don't think your ego needs the encouragement."

He raised the blade and chucked it at the board. The dagger thumped on the wood and bounced into the dirt.

"I can already see the problem." She placed another dagger into his hand. When he gripped it, she wrapped her fingers around his wrist and pressed her body against his. "When you get to about here . . ." She moved his arm parallel to his eye level. "You release the blade. Do not flick your wrist. Just open your hand and let the dagger do the rest."

"That seems easy enough."

"It isn't. But if you practice a million more times, you might actually hit your target."

He chuckled. "I'm not so sure we have that kind of time."

"Perhaps not. But you have the speed and strength of a god thrumming through you. Surely that gives you a bit of an advantage. Focus in on how your body feels. Use those unnatural instincts." Carolina released her hold on him and backed away. "Give it a try."

Lalo did as he was told, he let himself tune into the power that he tried to hold at bay. He released the dagger. It sank into the very top of the board. It wasn't a bullseye, but at least it held.

She clapped. "Well done. Now do it again."

"Carolina!" one of the twins yelled from a distance.

"Carolina, you need to come help with decorations!" the other added.

She puffed. "I have to go." She patted Lalo's arm. "Keep practicing. I will tell my mamá to excuse you from lunch on account of your feeling unwell. I'll return as soon as I can. There's much to discuss before the fiesta tonight."

He nodded numbly, then balked. "The what?"

From the diary of Señora Llanos (town gossip)

The Fuenteses are a pious and integrous lot. It would be
any mother's delight to see their child marry into the
family. Why, my dear niece expects an offer of marriage
any day now from Rufino's boy. They would make a
handsome couple indeed.

But I told my Nacho one day, I said, "Nacho, even
the best of families has secrets they wish would stay
buried."

CHAPTER 29

Lalo

HE PRACTICED DAGGER-THROWING UNTIL HE HEARD THE CLIP-CLOP of hooves and creaking of wooden spokes. Not wanting to leave the board and knives, Lalo quickly put them back in the same place he had seen Carolina find them. He grabbed his coat, swung it over his shoulders and moved toward the door farthest away from where he sensed the carriages were entering.

The sun had already begun its descent. But the sweet relief of not having to worry about being scorched alive would be short-lived. Soon he'd have to endure yet another social gathering. He sighed against the coming night.

People bustled about the hacienda grounds. Colorful papers cut to look like lace had been hung from the trees to the outer buildings. Men stood around un cazo, stirring something in a vat of bubbling oil. The barn doors were wide open, and people were busy sweeping the dirt floor and carrying in tables and chairs.

"Why in the saints would anyone have a party at a time like this?" Lalo wondered aloud. The idea was preposterous. Sure, Señor Fuentes's guards were out hunting, but what if a sediento slipped in through their watch? A sediento like Maricela.

Though, he supposed, with so much commotion, Lalo could sneak into the library unnoticed. He needed that ledger her father kept.

Lalo tucked his arms into his coat and slinked toward the main house. He entered through the mudroom. He had learned to control the enormous dogs that guarded the chicken pens nearby. The act had been rather simple, thanks to Adrián's advice. *You've got to show them who is el patrón,* the boy had told him. And Lalo had. "Sit," he commanded los perros in his most stern voice. And los perros, to his delight, had obeyed.

Slowly, he opened the door that led from the mudroom to the main corridor of the casa. He could hear people laughing and chatting merrily in the kitchen. Could smell onions and tangy nopales frying in pans. Had he any lingering longings for food, he knew his mouth would be watering at that precise moment.

Lalo quickly found his way to the library. He shut the door behind him and began searching through every text. It was amazing that una hacienda so far from the ciudad would have so many incredible books. Carolina's scent lingered in every inch of the room. She had touched every damn spine. A smile crept up his face at the thought of her sitting in the leather chair reading about love and loss near the window.

What a strange and brilliant young woman she was.

Lalo frowned. There was no point in thinking about her in any way. Even if they found Vidal, there was no guarantee Lalo was coming out of that altercation alive. Vidal was old, and surely hard to vanquish. And when the power of Tecuani was severed, Lalo's connection to this world could snap, killing him in the process. Dying a final death would be worth it, in the end, because Lalo would know his sister was safe from Maricela and the whole vampiro race. And Carolina too.

The scent of freshly dried ink tingled his nose. Lalo followed the smell. It could be nothing, but he wasn't getting anywhere just staring at well-loved books.

His nose led him to the large desk at the rear of the library. Papers were stacked on top in an organized manner. There were bill receipts and letters from nearby pueblos. But nothing of importance where Lalo was concerned.

He chanced a glance at the door. No one was coming. He didn't hear any heartbeats. And his thumped so faintly it hardly counted.

Lalo opened the first drawer. Just blank parchment and tools for writing. He opened the second and found banknotes and coins. Seeing so much money lying around made him think of his own father's business. He'd left a note to Father's solicitor before he and Fernanda had fled. Hopefully, he'd done as Lalo asked and hid their inheritances in an account under a new name.

He shut the drawer and went for the third. It was locked. He wiggled the handle, but it did not budge.

Breaking the mechanism wouldn't do. For one, it wasn't right to destroy someone's property. Secondly, the moment Señor Fuentes saw that it was damaged, he would ascertain someone had been in here.

Lalo opened the first drawer and grabbed a pair of scissors and a thin strip of metal used for stirring ink. Kneeling, he got to work trying to disengage the lock. He was no expert, but

Fernanda had sealed her keys inside her jewelry box a time or two before.

Footfalls came from the corridor beyond. The familiar thud of heartbeats sounded in his ears, followed by voices.

Lalo's eyes widened. Señor Fuentes was coming this way.

He dug the scissors into the bottom of the keyhole, then inserted the thin rod. He lightly pressed the thin strip onto the prongs that held the lock in place.

Señor Fuentes was nearing the library. Lalo's fingers started to shake. He dropped the pin and cursed. Picking it up from the floor, he started again.

"Ah sí," Señor Fuentes said. "Our heifers are the finest in Abundancia."

An accented voice questioned, "But are you willing to offer the best prices, señor?"

Señor Fuentes chuckled. "You will want to pay me double when you see the leathers we produce."

The two laughed heartily.

"Come on. Come on," Lalo whispered, trying his best to get the right technique.

With a soft click, the lock disengaged. Lalo turned the scissors, and the drawer slid open. The scent of fresh ink wafted into his senses. A thick ledger with tarnished edges sat by itself inside the drawer. An intricate crest with a bull skull and flowers had been painted on the leather.

Lalo grabbed the book just as the door handle to the library turned.

He closed the drawers as quietly and quickly as possible and tucked himself below the desk as deeply as he could go.

The door opened, and the two men stepped in.

"I have been thinking of that birria your wife cooked us last time we visited," the other man said. "I've not had anything so tasty in all my travels."

"Nor will you ever. But wait until you try the carnitas my men are making now."

Lalo clamped his eyes shut as Señor Fuentes drew closer. What would he say if he was caught?

I sleepwalk. And steal people's property during that time? No, that wouldn't do.

I came in here to read and saw this book on the floor. And—what? Tripped under the desk? Pathetic.

"Here it is," Señor Fuentes said. Lalo heard a paper snap. "The list of rates for our heifers and steers."

The room grew quiet. *They must be some rates.*

"How about we discuss this over some cervezas. Do you drink, Jocobo?" el señor asked.

"I may start after seeing this document."

A roar of laughter came from Señor Fuentes. "Come, I had some mezcal put on the ice you brought in."

The men's voices slowly grew muted as they walked away. Lalo let out a deep breath and slumped. That had been far too close. Slowly, he eased himself out from under the desk. He opened the book and a folded piece of parchment slipped to the ground. He knelt, grabbed it, and opened the paper, flattening it on top of the desk. His eyes grew wide. The Fuentes family tree had been drawn in black ink and seemed to go back four or five generations. But that wasn't what had snatched the air out of his lungs. It was the tiny *x*'s next to so many of their names.

CHAPTER 30

Carolina

SOMETHING LALO HAD SAID TO HER EARLIER NIBBLED AT HER thoughts as she swept the dusty barn clean in preparation for the party that evening.

He'd asked about Devil's Spine.

Her cousin Lorenzo had always been obsessed with the mountain peak. He wanted to be a healer when he grew up and had thought there might be some flowers and herbs within the woods there that might have beneficial properties. When she saw Lorenzo again the night Abuelo was killed, he had appeared emaciated. His legs and feet were shredded, as if he'd walked through brambles and harsh terrain. Could it have been he was trying to get home after being turned somewhere far off?

Carolina studied her mamá, who was sitting on a cushioned chair outside the barn doors, giving orders to anyone who didn't already have a task to complete. With so much commotion, surely Mamá wouldn't notice if Carolina slipped away for a moment or two. She swept the broom back and forth, taking slow steps toward the opposite end of the barn. And when Mamá turned her head to yell at the twins, Carolina made her escape.

Tía Sofia was Lorenzo's mother and Abuelo's youngest sister. She and her husband, Javier, lived in one of the casitas within the hacienda. Before Lorenzo disappeared, the home was always full of laughter and storytelling. Carolina hadn't had the heart to visit her aunt, not since she and her abuelo had been the ones to cut him down. But now she had no choice.

If Lorenzo had in fact headed toward Devil's Spine, it *could* mean he'd been turned in that area. Which *could* mean Vidal's lair was there. That idea was a long shot, but so was a desperate sediento traveling far north searching for a way to reverse an ancient curse and coming upon a horde of vampiro slayers.

Carolina froze when she spotted Tía Sofia sitting on a small bench near a bubbling fountain. Her aunt seemed so much smaller now. As if the sorrow of loss had drained away her very essence. She had a blanket around her shoulders even though the temperature was especially warm for autumn.

Gulping, Carolina forced herself forward.

"Tía Sofia," she said softly.

Her aunt's gray eyes met hers. Carolina's body tensed. Was her tía going to scream at her? Was she going to tell her Abuelo's death was her fault? Was she going to somehow blame her for Lorenzo's death too?

"Carolina," Tía Sofia whispered. She offered a sad smile and patted the bench beside her.

Gingerly, Carolina took a seat. She frowned. When had Tía's thick black hair gone silver?

"I am sorry I have not come to speak with you since that terrible night, mija," her tía said.

Carolina's brows raised in surprise. "You lost your brother and your son. It is I who should be sorry for not coming to you sooner."

"I suppose the sorrow was too raw for the both of us. I will never again judge a person for how they mourn their loved ones."

"Nor shall I," Carolina agreed. And that was true. Whatever one did to survive unbearable loss, at least during the first initial blow, was exactly what they needed to do.

"Up until my Lorenzo showed up to the hacienda as un vampiro, I held on to hope." Her tía wrapped the blanket tighter around her shoulders. "Hope is a strange thing, don't you think? It can pull you out of your darkest thoughts, but also leave you destroyed if that hope turns into nothing greater."

Carolina's eyes pricked with tears.

"That's when we must lean on the people who care for us the most," Tía Sofia said. "They hold us steady and do the hoping for us when we no longer can." She squeezed Carolina's hand.

They could also try to make certain no one felt this way again, Carolina thought. And she was more determined than ever to find Vidal. To end this wretched curse.

"Can you tell me about Lorenzo's last days? Do you know where he was going when he went missing?" she asked.

Tía Sofia rubbed at the frayed edge of her blanket. "This was Lorenzo's. He slept with this very cobija every night. My son, he was the sweetest boy, you know that."

"I do."

"He heard me complain about my aching bones. Javier and I had him so late in life, and I know he worried for us. He told me there are healing herbs that grow up the craggy rocks just before Devil's Spine."

Carolina's hold on her aunt's hand tightened. So her primo was going to Devil's Spine. *Holy hell.* Might he have come in contact with Vidal himself? She relaxed her grasp and controlled her features before Tía Sofia took notice.

Her aunt's chin quivered. "He went there for me."

"You must know his death wasn't your fault, Tía."

"I do. My son risked everything to ease my burdens, and *that* is what I will remember." Her aunt sighed. "Do not let a moment go by where you aren't loving the people you care for with all your might. Love ferociously, mija."

Tears slid down Carolina's cheeks. "I will, Tía."

Her aunt patted her knee. "Now, go on. Get ready for the evening. Dance with the boy who stole your heart."

Carolina chewed on the inside of her cheek as she thought of the conversation with her tía. Their meeting had left her feeling vulnerable and heartbroken all over again, but it had also given Carolina a new clue. Lorenzo had ventured to Devil's Spine.

Her eyes swept over the barn filling with people. Papá towered over a group of guests, speaking animatedly about a prized bull. The group surrounding him wore the thick, fur-lined tunics of the Greater North. They came twice a year to the western coast of Abundancia, and only once a year to Del Oro, to trade with the rancheros. When they did, Papá cleared out their largest barn and hosted an extravagant fiesta with a baile after. The dance usually lasted well into dawn.

She turned and started for the main house in search of her vampiro but halted just before she bumped into a woman in a plum-colored gown.

Carolina clutched at her chest and breathlessly apologized. "I'm so sorry," she said. "I didn't notice you there."

The woman brushed her long red hair over her shoulder. She wore a wide-brimmed hat that covered most of her face, but Carolina could see her beautiful smile. "No worries, love. I'm told I'm rather light on my feet." The woman's voice was soft and warm. Sultry might be a better term.

Something about her made the hairs on the back of Carolina's neck stand on end. But if she was one of the wives or sisters of the traders, she couldn't be rude.

"I am Carolina Fuentes." She gave a small bow of her head. "Welcome to our home."

"Why thank you, Carolina." The woman held out a single gloved hand. "I am Maricela."

Carolina wrapped her fingers around the black lace and shook Maricela's hand. "A pleasure to meet you."

"Believe me when I say the pleasure is mine." A slow grin curved her lips upward.

There was something about Maricela, something in the set of her jaw that seemed so familiar.

"Have we met before?" Carolina asked.

"No. Not face to face, at least. But I am certain you and I are going to become well acquainted soon enough."

"Oh?"

A small group of young ladies ran past. Fabiola, always the loudest of the bunch, was giggling about a handsome boy. Carolina's eyes followed them toward the entrance. The crowd parted, and at the center stood a tall young man wearing a wine-colored charro.

Her mouth fell open. She'd seen Lalo in his dark suits that were the fashion of the ciudad, but she'd never seen him in anything so perfectly fit to his build. He looked . . . He was . . . She gulped. Lalo was beyond attractive.

She remembered her manners and brought her attention back to Maricela, but the woman was gone.

"What an odd person."

Lalo was being swarmed by the young women from el pueblo. One of them brushed their hand over the delicate stitching in Lalo's coat. His throat bobbed up and down. His spine stiffened straight as a rod. There were so many scents surrounding him, he was probably dying inside.

Before she could sweep in and save him, Fernanda and Nena pulled him from the crowd. He chuckled at something Nena, always the flirt, was saying. She was probably telling Lalo an embarrassing tale about Carolina's childhood. Carolina could only imagine what. She'd done plenty of humiliating things. Like the time she tried to ride Rey, their old and grumpy billy goat, through the orchards. He bucked her off, and she tumbled face-first into the muck. There was the time she tried to climb over the barrier wall and got her dress snagged on some iron stakes. She had to run home with nothing but her bloomers on. It was a mystery how she'd avoided scandal.

Lalo laughed, and Carolina's stomach dipped in response. Surprise flooded her when she realized she was . . . jealous. *She* wanted to be the one to make him laugh.

Carolina's feet were moving before she even realized them to be. She walked so swiftly, her eyes zeroed in on trying to read

Nena's lips, that she didn't see Rafa step before her. Carolina's nose bumped hard into his chest.

"Whoa there," Rafa said. "You almost took me out."

Carolina rubbed her face. "I doubt that very much." She remembered her manners and offered a curtsy. "How are you, Rafael?"

"Better now." His smile was big and wide. "Would you like to know something?"

She huffed. "Not particularly."

"You will find this news quite fascinating."

Rolling her eyes, she tried to move around the young man. "I don't think whatever you have to say will interest me in the slightest."

"It is about that boy you insist on marrying."

Carolina took a calming breath, but her body buzzed with tension from her head to her toes.

"Lalo isn't who you think," Rafa said, smug.

Carolina faced Rafa directly. "I know everything I need to about him."

"No one has even heard the name Eduardo Montéz in Puerto Blanco. Not a single soul. Which made me wonder, whyever not?"

"Could it be the type of people you speak to don't run in the same social circles as him?"

He sneered. "Unlikely. Then I spoke to a business partner in the capital. He said an affluent brother and sister with the same given names as your new friends but with the surname of Villalobos had suddenly fled the ciudad, leaving their father's successful business behind."

"Stop this, Rafa."

"The news is all anyone can talk about. The siblings said

they were heading east, but they could have easily come here instead. Those two are running from something. I can feel it in my bones."

"Enough. You lost the duel. I know you aren't used to losing, but you must move on. You do not need to fabricate ridiculous rumors just because you didn't get what you wanted."

"Don't be played for a fool, Carolina."

Bristling, she said, "Lalo has bested you in every way. He is smarter than you, kinder than you, and far more handsome. So back off."

Carolina spun on her heel and stilled.

There, standing before her, was Lalo. Carolina's cheeks burned. Judging by the ferocity within his gaze, he'd listened in on the entire conversation.

"Is this man bothering you?" Lalo asked. "Has he not yet accepted that your heart lies with me?"

Carolina's knees went weak. She hadn't heard Lalo sound so assertive. She liked it. A lot.

"This is absurd," Rafa grumbled.

"What is absurd, señor," Lalo said, "is that you do not seem to understand when a woman is finished speaking with you. I suggest you turn away before you make a bigger embarrassment of yourself than you already have."

Carolina's jaw dropped. Had that stern tone just come from Lalo, the same Lalo who panicked when his pants were dirty?

Rafa's fists clenched at his sides, but he did as he was told. His shoulder bumped hard into Lalo's as he passed, though.

Carolina beamed. "That was brilliant."

Lalo rubbed the back of his neck. "I fear my newfound dagger-throwing skills have made me arrogant."

A snort of laughter bubbled from Carolina.

But as she searched Lalo's eyes, she had to remind herself that this, *all* of this, was just a partnership of convenience. He did not actually care for her.

So why did her heart suddenly feel a thousand times larger? Why did she want to take his hand and dance with him for the rest of the evening like Tía Sofia suggested?

"Carolina?" Lalo said, his voice soft as a summer rain.

Her stomach tightened, her body betraying her once more.

She cleared her throat. "Yes?"

"Dance with me?"

"I . . ." She gulped. Her armpits began to sweat. Her palms grew clammy. She tingled everywhere. It was the strangest she'd ever felt.

She shook her head. "I think I need air."

Carolina brushed past Lalo and ran out of the barn, ignoring everyone's eyes glued to her back. She spotted the woman in the wide-brimmed hat tucked in the shadows. Even from this distance Carolina could see that knowing grin Doña Maricela seemed to prefer.

Carolina's arms pumped harder. Bolting with no direction in mind, other than to give herself space from that boy.

When Carolina was far enough away, she stopped and rested her hands on her hips.

"What is wrong with me?" she panted.

"I was going to ask the same thing."

Carolina jolted. She whirled around, her back hitting an old wooden fence.

"Lalo," she wheezed.

He'd come after her.

"What happened in there?" he asked. "I thought we were putting on quite the show."

Her heart pinched. *A show.* Yes. Of course. That was all this was. There were greater things at play here. She and Lalo were going to end the vampiros. She would keep her loved ones safe *and* get to stay in Del Oro.

Her feelings for Lalo should not be an issue.

Stupid brain, she chided within her mind. *Stupid body.*

She pushed herself from the fence. "I'm sorry for running away. I felt ill suddenly. I thought I was going to retch."

His eyes widened. "Do you need anything?"

He took a step closer.

"No!" She lowered her voice. "I mean . . . I am fine. A good jog did me well."

"I see." He tilted his head back and sighed. "I prefer it out here anyway. All those people crammed together, dancing and sweating, was becoming overwhelming. Truth is, I never cared for gatherings of that nature, even before I was . . . you know."

"You?" she half smiled. "I would have never imagined."

"I know it's hard to believe I wasn't the crown jewel of high society, but it's true. I have never felt comfortable around people. And when I am, my mouth takes on a mind of its own. I cannot tell you how many times I left a party early because I embarrassed myself in conversation. I haven't . . ." He stopped. "Never mind . . . Are you feeling better?"

"You haven't what, Lalo?"

"Nothing. You will probably just tease me for it."

A smile pulled at her lips. "Now I must know."

He turned his head back toward the barn. Even from this distance, the sound of slow music playing could be heard.

Lalo gulped. "I haven't danced with anyone before."

She was readying to tease him, but the pure mortification on his face had her schooling her features. "Why not? I'm certain every young person at those parties wished for you to ask them."

"I guess I was afraid of coming off as silly or getting laughed at. But mostly because . . . I don't like people."

A wholehearted laugh escaped her. "You and I are much more alike than I originally thought."

He chuckled, and her body softened. She wondered what else she could say to lure that amusement out.

Stop that, she snapped. Their courtship was not real.

Carolina changed the subject. "What were you and Nena speaking about before I made a fool of myself?"

He toed the dirt with his boot. "She was reminding me how special you are. She told me any man would be lucky to have you, even if you are a torment at times."

"And what did you say?" Her eyes traced over Lalo. With the candlelight of the barn and the torches flickering in the breeze behind him, he looked like he was made from the night itself. She liked watching him in any light, but here, away from the crowd, with only the stars and the moon spectating, Carolina found Lalo to be the most beautiful person in all the world.

"I agreed with her," he said, slowly shifting his body closer to hers. "You are exceptional."

Carolina held his gaze. She was good at running from her emotions or things that made her feel vulnerable. But after speaking to Tía Sofía, after feeling raw in her spirit but powerful too, she realized she didn't want to hide herself from him.

"Lalo, you told me you've never asked anyone to dance, right?"

His brows quirked.

"Well, that isn't true. You *have* asked someone to dance." She gestured toward herself. "You asked me."

"Sí. But I don't recall receiving an answer."

Dance with your love. Dance until your knees ache and your bones are brittle. Until your hair grows white. And when you find your love in el Cielo, dance some more.

—Pío Parra, "Lamentations of the Heart"

CHAPTER 31

Lalo

"Yes," she said.

He gulped. "Yes?"

She rolled her eyes. Carolina swept forward and rested a hand on his chest. His body shuddered in response. "My answer is yes. I will dance with you."

"Here?" He gestured toward their surroundings. They were alone, save for the chickens sleeping on their perches in the coop nearest to them. And the dogs. Those blasted dogs always seemed to be nearby.

"Why not? We can still hear the music. And everyone believes we are in love."

Hell, he'd believe they were in love too, if he were an on-looker, simply by the way she smiled at him.

"We might as well act the part of lovers," Carolina said. "A dance together will be fun."

"Fun? On second thought . . ."

She grabbed his hands. "You will dance, Lalo, or else."

"You really are a torment."

She bowed. "Thank you."

Before he knew it, she had him moving to the music. It wasn't a slow, graceful song but fast and thumping. Their boots moved and slid over the dirt, kicking up dust that tickled his nose. She spun herself around, holding her skirts in a way that showed a lovely array of colors. She stomped and clapped and laughed. Lalo found himself doing the same thing. Not the pulling of skirts part, of course, but the laughing. He laughed with his full chest. He didn't know if he'd ever done such a thing before.

"You're a natural," she said between twirls.

"It is easy when I have you to learn from."

She put her hands on his shoulders, his went to her hips, and together, they swept through the wide-open space. The grin that beamed from her was as stunning as the night sky. It was vast and unending and full of mysteries he knew he could spend his entire life searching through. He dipped her low and felt his own lips quirk into a smile.

But then, the music slowed and eventually came to an end. And it was the most miserable occurrence. If he could, he'd force the mariachi to never stop.

They stood there for a moment, staring at each other, swaying at the phantom song still lingering in the air.

"What are you thinking?" she asked.

"I was just wondering why I have waited so long to dance." He had to be made a monster to really understand what he'd been missing out on. And that thing he was missing out on was his own life.

"Carolina!" Señora Fuentes called from the barn.

"One second, Amá!"

"Now, hija."

Carolina winced. "I might be in trouble for that scene with Rafa."

"Would you like me to accompany you? That was partially my fault."

"No." She smiled up at him. "But thank you."

She stood on her tiptoes and kissed him on the cheek.

A shock of pure fire roared through him. He was surprised he didn't combust then and there. His hand went to his face. To the spot where her lips had just left their scorching mark.

"What was that for?" he asked.

"For the dance." She peered over her shoulder as her mother called her name once more. "I will find you as soon as Mamá has finished reprimanding me."

And with that, she raced away. He watched her go. She laughed and swerved around a slender woman standing in the shadows, yelling out her apologies before disappearing into the barn.

Alone, confused, and for some unexplainable reason rather sad, Lalo headed toward his room. He needed to feed again to stave off the claws of thirst raking down his throat.

He had just made it into the casa when a voice boomed down the hallway.

"There you are!" Señor Fuentes called.

Lalo turned. Three men stood behind el señor. Lalo recognized Jorge from the journey over. There was an older man who had a hardened version of Jorge's face—his father, Lalo presumed. And then there was Rafa, eyeing Lalo with enough contempt to fill the valley.

Lalo gulped.

"Come," Señor Fuentes said. "If you wish to be a part of this great familia, you must learn what it is we do."

"Tend to cattle?" Lalo asked, praying to every saint that was what Señor Fuentes meant. But judging from the whole-chested laughter coming from the other men, Lalo knew that wasn't what he was speaking of.

"The cattle are important, of course," Señor Fuentes said, nodding. "But there are things more significant than making money." He stepped closer to Lalo, his dark eyes growing serious. "Like protecting the people we love. This pueblo and all who live within it."

"Can you even ride a horse?" Rafael asked, his chin tilted so high, he was sure to have a kink in his neck the next morning.

"I can." Lalo raised his chin as well, higher than Rafael's by at least a pin's width. "I've won many races in my day." He didn't know why he said that—he hated horses and races. But he found himself wanting to outdo Rafael at every turn.

"Can you shoot, Lalo?" Jorge asked, his hand resting on the pistol slung from the holster on his belt.

Rafa chortled. "We all know he cannot."

Lalo raised a brow. "Yet somehow I won our duel."

"What about hand-to-hand combat?" Jorge's father asked.

"Does brawling with Carolina count?" This brought on a riotous bout of laughter from Señor Fuentes and his family. If only they knew Lalo hadn't been joking.

"What exactly will we be doing?" Lalo asked Señor Fuentes.

Rafael grinned and nudged Jorge in the ribs with an elbow.

Please don't let this be about sedientos. Please don't let this be about sedientos. Please . . .

"Come along, mijo. Tonight will be an adventure you won't soon forget."

261

CHAPTER 32

Carolina

"They've taken him where?" Carolina stood frozen in the doorway to her parents' room.

After the tongue-lashing she received for causing a scene—multiple scenes, really—Carolina escorted her mamá inside so she could rest her feet. Her last birthing had been hard. The twins had been willful, even in the womb. It was the most frightening moment in Carolina's life. Well, before sedientos had struck down her abuelo.

Mamá eased onto her bed, and said, "It was Rafael's idea. Clever boy thought Lalo needed to understand our world a bit better."

Carolina's mind screamed at the idea of Lalo being left in the hands of Rafa and the men in her familia.

She spun on her heel. She needed to get to them before Rafa

said anything incriminating but stopped when her mamá's voice called out, "Do not even think about it, Carolina Fuentes."

"I don't know what you mean, Amá." She batted her lashes sweetly.

"Don't act innocent with me. I can see mischief in your eyes from a thousand paces away. You will stay here, in this casa, or so help me I will . . ." Mamá winced and clutched her belly.

Carolina was at her side in the span of a heartbeat. "What is it? Is the baby coming?"

Mamá shook her head, her face still twisted in pain. "Just a little kick." She took Carolina's hand and placed it on the side of her round stomach. "Feel that?"

Squinting, Carolina waited. And then . . . She gasped. "That's not just a little kick. My sibling is strong."

Mamá's eyes sparkled. "Sí, they are." She squeezed Carolina's hand. "Please, this once. Listen to me. Stay put. Tend to your little brothers. Read. Sleep. Go back into the barn and dance to your heart's content. Do whatever you wish. Just don't go beyond the hacienda walls."

Worry bloomed inside Carolina for Lalo. She searched her mamá's face for a clue that something was amiss.

"Will Lalo be safe?" she asked.

"Of course, Carolina. Lalo will be fine." Mamá brushed a wayward hair from Carolina's face. "It is you I worry about. You are as headstrong as your papá and I love that about you both, but it will be the ruin of me. I must sit here and fret over him every night. Every time he steps out of this room." She sniffed. "I'll have to fuss over your hermanos. And this baby. I cannot worry over you as well right now. It's simply too much. Do you hear me, mija?"

Carolina wiped her mamá's tears. She felt bad for making her mother uneasy and she understood the dread. She felt it whenever her papá, hermanos, and tíos left, too. But why should she have to be the one to stay back? Because she was born a woman?

Mamá rarely looked this tired. She was usually ready to battle Carolina into submission. Or simply pretend she didn't notice when Carolina was up to something. Like the time Mamá caught her sneaking a gopher snake into the house to nurse it back to health after a rooster kicked the poor creature. Mamá had held in a smile and turned away when Carolina scampered by. This felt different. There was no fighting or turning a blind eye. Mamá was asking her to listen for a change.

The baby kicked again, hard, and Mamá winced.

"I will do as you wish," Carolina said, rubbing Mamá's belly.

"Thank you, mijita."

An object on the side table caught Carolina's attention.

"What is that?" she asked.

Mamá's eyelids were already beginning to droop. "Hmm?"

Carolina reached over and plucked up the familiar dagger. The hilt was curved and had a single emerald stone forged into the tip.

"I found it in your papá's things. I cleaned it up for him. It's rather pretty, no?"

The blade gleamed in the candlelight. "Pretty indeed."

"I believe it's a lover's blade," Mamá said. "Usually, they come in pairs. The blades are given to a bride and groom for luck. Very rare to find one so intricate. Rarer still to find the set."

This had been the dagger inside Vidal's empty grave. Carolina had wondered where Papá put it when he took it from her. She squinted. Where had she seen a dagger like this before? She stilled.

"May I . . ." Carolina stopped. Her mamá's eyes had shut, and she was fast asleep.

Carolina silently eased off the bed. "I'm just going to borrow this blade," she whispered. "I hope you don't mind."

As soon as she shut the door to her parents' room, Carolina raced toward the last place she had seen a similar dagger. She took the steps leading to her abuelo's room in twos. Her chest was heaving, battling against the corset she'd been forced to wear.

She burst through the door to Abuelo's room and thrust open the armoire. Shoving aside her abuelo's things, Carolina reached deep into the recesses of the dresser and found the cloth bundle. Heart thundering, she placed the gleaming blade in her hands on her abuelo's bed, then unfurled the bundle.

A gasp escaped her. They were nearly identical. One blade was slightly larger. One had a ruby in the hilt while the other had an emerald. But aside from that, they were the same. The metal they were made from was so silver it almost appeared white, and star lilies had been etched into the spines of both blades. They were beautiful on their own, but together they seemed almost magical.

"Holy hells," she whispered. These must've been Vidal's and Alma's. Their lover's blades.

Carolina placed them on the bed beside each other and stared at them in the low light. Was this the tool Alma used to call upon the god of death? Lalo said the weapon used to appeal to Tecuani, to help create the first sediento, would be the only tool to break the curse.

There, lying on cotton sheets, might be the very thing that had brought destruction and death to Del Oro.

"Did you know what these were, Abuelito?" she wondered aloud.

Her brow furrowed.

The Fuenteses were nothing if not honorable. They were pillars of their small community. Beacons of integrity and pride. Her grandfather and father would not hold on to these blades knowing they could potentially destroy the monsters they were hell-bent on protecting the valley from. Would they?

She rushed toward Abuelito's armoire. Surely there had to be something else hidden inside. A clue about what he knew. About why he had the blade in his closet rather than in the storeroom with many of their other family heirlooms.

Her fingers traced over the wood lining the walls of the dresser. She pressed on the right and left, but nothing gave way like the hidden compartments where they stuffed their training weapons often did. Carolina placed her palm on the rear panel. She shoved. Her eyes widened when she felt it spring ever so slightly and open a small crack.

His clothing blocked the panel from opening fully. Frantically, Carolina pulled out his shirts and jackets in handfuls and threw them behind her.

When everything was clear, she stuck her fingers into the crack and pried the panel open the rest of the way. A stack of papers and canvases tumbled out. Shakily, Carolina plucked the tattered canvas first. She turned it around and clamped her hand over her mouth.

The young woman in the painting had Carolina's same round eyes, her same full lips and stubborn chin. Even their hair was a similar shade of black. If Carolina didn't know for certain it wasn't, she might have believed she was gazing at a portrait of herself. But it was what was lying on the woman's lap that had Carolina's focus. The ruby-embellished lover's blade.

"Alma," Carolina whispered.

She ran a finger over the painting.

Growing up, Carolina had been taught that Alma was the first victim, the pour soul doomed by some evil monster that happened upon their lands. But Alma had been the monster. She had rebuked el Cielo and made a deal that would unleash an unholiness upon Del Oro.

Carolina placed the portrait down and began sifting through the parchment covered in writing by her abuelo's hand. The blade, it would seem, was found by Alma's body. Along with a single note. Chills rippled over Carolina's skin.

Please forgive me for what I've done.

I took my blade and sliced a deep gash against my palm. As my blood dripped onto Vidal's grave, I called upon Tecuani. I was incensed! I didn't know what I was doing. I was so desperate. So empty and lost without my Vidal. Dead after hunting, of all things.

The god of souls heard my cries and appeared when the moon was at her fullest. He offered me a deal. He said if I accepted, he would bring my lover back.

I should have said no and run. I should have gone home to baby Inigo. But what was a life without my Vidal?

I took Tecuani's deal. Days later, Vidal rose from his grave, but he was changed. His skin was blanched of color. He was my love but not. Vidal said he must feed. He said the

267

only thing that would give him strength was the blood used to revive him. My blood.

I tried to quench his thirst for weeks by offering a few drops on the tongue here and there. His thirst only built.

If you are reading this, I fear, the monster inside him has finally won. And yet, even as I write this, I cannot find it in my soul to plunge my dagger into Vidal's heart. Even though he begs of me to end his torment.

I am selfish and greedy and so very sorry. My sins against nature have brought Death to our doorstep. I have unleashed darkness. I offered what was never mine to give, and I have ruined us all.

Take this blade and do what I could not. It is the only way to end the death curse.

The paper slipped from Carolina's grasp. It fluttered onto the bed, landing beside a slip of parchment with an entry written in her abuelo's hand. Heart hammering, she snatched the note up.

Vidal must have turned her. I cannot say whether it was on purpose or if he was purely trying to revive his wife after draining too much blood. Either way, a Fuentes was to blame for the creation of los sedientos.

Carolina's knees went weak, and she slumped onto the floor. Abuelo knew the truth. He had this information, but he'd kept it hidden away. Had he known he could end all vampiros by killing Vidal? Surely not or he would have slayed him. Or at least spent his every waking moment searching for the man. Wouldn't he?

She looked up at the portrait hanging in his room of him and her abuela.

For the first time in her life, Carolina wondered if she'd ever even truly known him.

"Why would you keep this a secret, Abuelito?" she whispered. She thought of his death, the guards, and the countless others she'd experienced in her short lifetime. "My ancestors' silence has made murderers of us all."

September 13, 1830

LOS CAMPOS SOCIALITES
By Doña Larissa Cordova

A seedy cantina understandably called The Den has gone up in flames. It took three fire brigades to keep the flames from jumping to the buildings flanking the structure. I am told by credible sources many victims were inside. Two of which were notable fixtures in high society.

I cannot name names, of course, but one might take note that a certain county treasurer and his secretary are no longer among us. The real question is, why were they in such a vile place? The owner of the establishment could not be found for questioning.

CHAPTER 33

Lalo

LALO HAD EXCUSED HIMSELF FROM THE MEN AND RUN BACK INTO his room to change and to secretly feed himself. The blood in the flask was disgustingly warm, but he guzzled down the rest of the contents, only gagging twice, before running to meet Señor Fuentes and his family in the stables. They were already gone, but Lalo was instructed where to go by a ranch hand.

He'd been given a pony. A *pony*, of all things. Lalo tried to brush it off. He tried to pretend that the jest was in good fun. But a damn pony! And the pint-size beast was rude as a demon. It nipped at him constantly. The creature tore the pants he wore with its flat little teeth.

Lalo squeezed the monster with his legs. It bucked but moved forward. Huffing and complaining the entire way up the hill to meet the other men who had gone ahead before Lalo even climbed onto the saddle.

Señor Fuentes blinked with confusion when he saw Lalo trot up the hill. Rafael—*the wretch*—laughed loud enough to frighten the coyotes in the far-off orchard.

"How do you like Rita?" Rafael hollered.

The pony pulled against the reins, fighting Lalo's control at every instant.

"She's great," he said as calmly as he could muster. "Rita and I are getting on just fine."

Señor Fuentes's eyes darkened. He turned to Rafael. "Did you give him that mount? We have dozens of horses, and you wasted our time by offering this one? We have a reasonable lead, I left the tradesmen before they have even signed their contracts, and you think to do this?"

The smile on Rafael's face wilted.

"My men were killed, Rafael. Taken from their familias, yet you play pranks?"

"I . . . It was only . . ."

"Switch horses," Señor Fuentes ordered.

"¿Qué?" Rafael questioned. "Pero . . ."

"You made a mockery of this hunt. Now I shall make one of you. Switch horses."

"Señor, it is fine," Lalo intervened. "I'm sure Rita and I can keep up."

"No, you won't. That pony was Carolina's when she was a child. It isn't meant for such things. Besides, my daughter would kill us if she learned we'd taken Rita out here." He glared at Rafael. "You knew that."

Slowly, the two men dismounted and traded reins. Lalo could smell the animosity steaming from Rafael's skin. He really and deeply loathed Lalo. He supposed he'd hate himself too, if the

272

roles were reversed. Carolina was a desirable woman. And she had clearly chosen Lalo over Rafael.

"I know who you are," Rafael whispered as they passed each other.

Lalo's footing faltered, but he forced himself forward.

"I will expose you this night. I'll tell señor your name isn't—"

"Take Rita back to the stables," Señor Fuentes ordered him. "If you wish to join us, we will be heading west. If not, I will not hold it against you."

"But, señor . . ."

"You made a poor judgment call, Rafa. You must make it right."

"But . . ."

"You've squandered enough time. I will tell your father of this. Go."

Rafael's chin fell to his chest. "Sí, señor."

"¡Ándale!" Señor Fuentes tightened his heels on his stallion, and the pair took off at a startling speed. Jorge and his father followed suit. Lalo was the last to urge his horse on, holding tight to the leather straps as he raced after the Fuenteses.

He fixed his eyes forward. The men in his company hadn't exactly laid out what they were off to do, but it didn't take much to put the pieces together. Señor Fuentes had gotten word there were fresh tracks. And now they were hunting for whoever had killed the guards.

A shiver ran up Lalo's spine. Carolina had taken out two vampiros in the town square. And he'd killed the sediento near the schoolhouse. He had hoped they'd found and ended the guilty party. But after discovering these new tracks, Lalo wasn't so sure. Maricela, or another one of her children, could be the beast they needed to slay.

A scream tore through the night. Roosting birds took flight from within the woods.

"¡Vámonos!" Señor Fuentes called, and they rode as if the devil were nipping at their heels.

The horses' hooves pounded over nettle and dirt. The smell of fear and spilled blood filled Lalo's senses. He gripped the reins harder, fighting against his unnatural urges. His fangs pierced through his bottom lip and his mouth watered, the hunger inside him surging. *Saints above,* he was starved for human blood, its essence. If he could have one taste. A single drop.

"There!" Jorge yelled. The three men riding ahead of Lalo pulled their pistols out in unison. He remembered Carolina saying in the duel not to worry because the bullets weren't made of wood. But the bullets in these pistols must be.

Lalo couldn't see past their bodies, but he didn't need to see to know what stood before them. He could taste it in the air. Flesh and death and blood. So much blood.

"It's Fabiola!" Jorge yelled.

Lalo had heard that name earlier. She was one of the young women batting her lashes at him when he entered the barn.

"You bastard!" Jorge roared. He took aim.

Lalo's horse shifted, and he could see the vile scene. Fabiola dangled limp in a large man's arms. Even in the moonlight, the ashen tone of her skin was clear. Blood oozed from bite marks on her neck and wrists. And what was left over—the blood the sediento could not drink—dripped at his feet.

A blast rang out as Jorge pulled the trigger. Smoke filled the air. In the second it took for it to clear, the sediento had disappeared, leaving the woman in a heap on the ground. Jorge and his horse plunged into the forest after him. His father, Vicente, and his steed right behind.

"Check on the girl!" Señor Fuentes ordered Lalo before crashing into the woods.

"What? No! I'll come too." But Lalo was already abandoned.

He managed to bring his mount to a halt. His eyes jerked from left to right, hunting for any signs of the sediento. Everything was quiet. Lalo threw his leg over the saddle and ran toward the poor young woman, holding a bandanna over his nose and mouth to keep the scent away. Even still, his stomach squeezed. His body thrummed with thirst.

If he could have one drop. One tiny taste.

He shook his head.

"Why did he put me in charge of this?" he mumbled through the cloth.

Lalo shouldn't even be there. He should have refused. He should have said he was still ill. *Anything.* But no. He wanted to match Rafael in machismo. Look where that got him.

He bent down, doing his best not to breathe. "Señorita?" He gulped. "Fabiola?"

With a single finger, he prodded her, so her face was angled to him. He reared back, falling on his ass. Her eyes were moon white. Her mouth open in shock. Multiple bite marks bruised her skin, but there was nothing there. Not a hint of life. Not a sliver of a soul.

"Damn you," Lalo cursed the foul monster who did this. "Damn you!"

"But we are already damned," a slithering voice whispered from behind.

Lalo jumped to his feet and spun around. He recognized that voice instantly. How could he ever forget it?

"Maricela," Lalo growled, clenching his fists at his sides.

"Don't you mean 'Mother'?" The beast haunting his nightmares smiled, revealing fangs stained red.

Faster than Lalo could even think, Maricela was on him, slamming him hard into a large oak. He grunted in pain.

"You killed your siblings, then tarnished my business," the sediento said, her breath tainted with memories of a life taken too soon. "For weeks I trailed only days behind you. My time was not wasted, though." One of her sharp nails dug into his cheek. "Every minute of my journey, I thought of the most excruciatingly delicious ways to end you."

"How did you find me?" he rasped.

"You aren't as clever as you think. I drank your memories. I know all. When I returned to my cantina the night after you slaughtered my children and their guests, I searched through every thought I had taken. I saw what you read in your little books and scribbles about this valley. I knew you'd never do the smart thing and run. Though your mind is rational, your heart is too pure. Too attached to the people you care for. I knew you'd do whatever was necessary to save your sister. I suppose I should thank you, for bringing me back."

"You have come upon a valley of hunters. They will not let you live, Maricela."

"And yet I have already walked among them. Spoken with them." The sediento laughed. "I believe I will find my new friend Carolina first. Then I will snatch your sister and rip out her throat. Purely for my own amusement."

Rage roared to life inside Lalo. He fought against Maricela, but she only dug him deeper into the bark. "Tell me—does Carolina taste as good as she smells?"

Lalo growled, low and predatorial. She had taken his parents from him, had ruined his entire life.

"You will not touch a hair on the head of anyone I love ever again."

"Love?" Maricela raised a brow. "This makes things much more entertaining."

Using what he'd learned from Carolina, Lalo kneed Maricela hard in the groin. A shocked gasp escaped her, and Lalo attacked. He pounced on the sediento. The two tumbled into the dirt. They both hissed and snapped and dragged their claws across each other's bodies. But she was far too strong. She had fed off human life; her body was thrumming with power from a bounty of essences. Maricela pinned Lalo to the ground and Lalo bellowed as claws ripped into his torso. He felt his flesh tear open. Felt his ribs crack. The sediento was going for his heart. And the agony was unbearable.

"Time to fix my mistake. Your lover and sister will die knowing the monster they care for suffered a wretched—"

Her words cut off mid-sentence. Her eyes went wide before flicking down to her chest. To the wooden stake protruding from it. The sediento clutched at the blood-soaked weapon, gasping like a fish out of the sea. Hands clasped her shoulders and threw her off of Lalo.

Rafael's face came into view. He glared at Lalo, his body shaking with indignation, as he took in Lalo's exposed chest. "You are one of them."

"Let me explain."

"You brought them here?"

277

"No ... yes ... wait."

Rafael pointed his pistol at Lalo's head.

"I knew there was something off about you. Carolina would never choose someone else over me. You charmed her. For what purpose?"

"I came to end sedientos. She intends to help me."

A bitter laugh came from Rafa. "You expect me to believe that, sanguijuela?"

A third sediento burst from the thicket and launched himself at Rafael. A shot went off. A spark of light flashed in the air. But Rafael had missed. The vampiro grabbed him and flung him like he was made of feathers. Rafael's body smacked into a tree and bounced on the ground. He didn't move. Didn't attempt to rise.

"No!" Lalo clambered up. Clutching his chest, he raced after Rafael, but the burly sediento was faster. He reached Rafael, lifting a clawed fist to give death's blow. Lalo saw the pistol on the ground, picked it up, and aimed.

"Saints, guide me."

The bullet discharged with a resounding boom. Everything else was silenced by the ringing in Lalo's ears. The smoke cleared.

The sediento clenched at the hole in his chest before slumping to the ground. Lalo dropped the pistol as if it were aflame and rushed toward Rafael. The man was out cold, but his pulse still thrummed. His head must have taken the brunt of the hit.

Branches rustled behind them. Lalo braced himself. He sighed in relief when Señor Fuentes appeared, followed by a limping Jorge being held up by Vicente.

"What happened?" Señor Fuentes said, breathless.

"We were attacked by a pair of—" Lalo jolted. His eyes snapped to where Maricela had been. She was gone.

"No," he whispered. Had she heard what he said to Rafael? Did she know what he and Carolina were planning to do? "No. No. No."

"What is it, mijo?"

"There were two sedientos. But only one is here."

"Shit." Señor Fuentes wiped a hand over his face. "I shouldn't have left you. Carolina would have murdered me if you were hurt."

"We need to go after the last vampiro," Lalo urged. "Right now." Carolina's and Fernanda's lives were on the line.

"We will have to wait until tomorrow."

"But what if she kills again?"

Señor Fuentes's eyes met his own, and inside them, Lalo saw fear.

"I don't know. But I can only control what is in front of me at this moment. And that is Rafa and my nephew. We get them home. And we will protect what is ours until we come up with a better plan. Daylight is coming. The sediento will have to hide away. We will be safe for a bit."

Lalo sought out the skies. They were still shrouded in darkness, but he knew the sun would soon be up. There was nothing to be done. He himself needed to hide away.

"You did well," Señor Fuentes said kindly. He grasped Lalo's shoulder. "Thank you for saving Rafa."

"It was nothing, señor."

Rafa knew what Lalo was now. The moment he woke, he'd alert everyone of what had happened, and then Lalo would be even more dead than he already was.

CHAPTER 34

Carolina

CHURCH BELLS RANG IN THE FAR-OFF DISTANCE. CAROLINA RAN to the windows, pulling loose the shutters. Dawn was breaking over the forest, and she hadn't heard word of Lalo yet.

She chewed on her lip and started to pace. Something must have happened to him. She should go, saddle her stallion, and track down her family. What would they do to him if they learned what he really was? Her father would be irate. Probably angrier that he had been made a fool by having un vampiro in his own home.

Carolina stopped dead in her tracks.

Had that been why the evidence of what Alma did was kept hidden? To save face? She was a Fuentes. They ruled the valley. If word got out that one of their own had done this, what would el pueblo do? Would their neighbors turn on them? Exile them?

Horse hooves pounded through the gates. Someone calling

for help echoed through the courtyard. Carolina picked up her skirts and bolted out of her abuelo's room. Her thighs flexed as she moved as quickly as she could down the hallway and steps.

The front door burst open just as she entered the foyer. Lalo jogged in, appearing as disheveled as she'd ever seen him before. His shirt was open wide, stained blood clung to his chest. His hands were caked with soot. He seemed haunted. Frightened.

Anguish twisted his features when his eyes met hers.

Carolina rushed to him. She grabbed his arms. "Is it my papá?"

"No." He shook his head. "He's fine. Your family is whole."

"Thank the stars." She couldn't help herself; the relief of seeing him, of knowing they'd come home safely, overwhelmed her. She knew she shouldn't, but she found her arms wrapping around his torso. Her cheek pressing against his bare chest even though it looked like it had been through a battle. She could see remnants of wounds healing.

"I wasn't sure if I'd ever see you again," she whispered.

Slowly, he enfolded her and pulled their bodies tight to one another. "I didn't know if I'd see you again either."

His chest rose and fell for a moment. Then everything began to quiver and shake.

She pulled away, only enough to view his face. Tears of blood slithered down his dirt-covered cheeks. Carolina gasped. She grabbed his hand and pulled him toward his room before anyone noticed.

When the door was shut behind them, she asked, "What the hell happened out there?"

The notch in his throat bobbed as he gulped. "My maker found me. She is here. She knows of you."

"Of me?"

He nodded. "She . . . She smelled you on me."

Heat rose up Carolina's throat.

"Where is your maker now?"

"Rafael staked her, but she got away." Lalo slumped. "I believe she might have overheard what he and I spoke of before she disappeared. Maricela knows what we plan to do."

Carolina jolted. "Maricela?"

His eyes shot up. "Do you know her?"

"She was here. At the barn last night." Carolina balked. "She was watching us. That fiend watched you and I dance under the stars. I nearly ran into her when Amá beckoned me."

He pinched the bridge of his nose. "I've put you and your family in grave danger," he whispered.

"You're wrong," she said.

Lalo blinked with confusion.

"*My* family is the reason sedientos even exist. If it wasn't for my ancestors, you would have never endured such heartbreak. The fact that my family ruined such an amazing man's life makes me want to scream."

"You think I'm amazing?"

"Now isn't the time to jest, Lalo."

A grin pulled at his lips. "I believe that is my line."

Carolina rolled her eyes. "This isn't funny."

"No," he said in earnest. "None of this is funny, like none of this is your fault. Sometimes we carry the weight of our ancestors' actions on our shoulders, and there is nothing to be done about it. But you and me, we can ease that burden. We can fix this. There isn't any more time though. We must find the blade that created Vidal. If Rafael wakes up . . ."

"If he what?"

"Rafael saved me, but he also saw what I am."

Carolina's eyes widened. "What did you do to him?"

"Nothing. Another sediento threw him into a tree, and he hit his head. I'm sure he'll be all right, but . . ."

"He knows everything," she said, finishing his sentence.

"Yes."

"He will kill you." She knew it in her marrow. Rafa had been waiting for some reason to get rid of Lalo. There it was, gifted to him on a sediento-shaped platter.

"I have no doubt," he said. "We should go to your father. Explain to him what we know and—"

"My father will strike you down the second we tell him what you are. He will execute you and ask questions later."

Lalo jolted. "But he knows me. He's spoken to me."

"So had I. And perhaps, if I had been a better hunter, I might have struck you down that first night."

His eyes widened.

She touched his arm. "But I'm glad I didn't. I am forever grateful that I got to know you, Lalo. Because you have shown me something I would have never seen on my own."

"What is that?"

"The truth. My family swept all knowledge of what Alma did under the rug probably because they were afraid her actions would tarnish their name. They likely didn't try to figure out how to end the monsters, how to find Vidal, how to save their own bloodline, because they were too prideful."

Pride had stirred her forward in life. Arrogance. The need to be the best in all things. It was why she pushed Abuelo to train her, why she went against everything her parents wanted so she could prove her point. She didn't regret her time with Abuelo, but she did regret the way she had gone about things. The way she never compromised. She simply barreled through life until she got what she wanted. Her pride had been a shield in many ways, but it had also held her back from letting others in. She didn't want to do things on her own anymore; she didn't want to be as all the Fuenteses thought they should be.

"I found the blade Alma used," she confessed. "I am not afraid to face Vidal, but I need your help tracking him down."

"You found Alma's blade?" Lalo rushed to his trunk. Pulling out a leather-bound book, he stepped to her side. He placed it on the desk and opened the ledger to the end.

"This is in my father's hand," she said.

"Yes. And I'm certain every person who logged entries inside are the patriarchs of your family. This book gives detailed accounts of the attacks in or around Del Oro. The dates go back hundreds of years." He pointed to the most recent victims' names and their locations of death. "There are no patterns within the slayings. Mostly, the bodies of the victims are left to rot. Occasionally, the victims disappear altogether. But one detail caught my eye—several witnesses stated that some of the victims were either dragged toward, or heard murmuring upon their deaths, Devil's Spine."

"Lorenzo was believed to have gone missing after venturing to the mountains."

"Then that is where Vidal must be. All the vampiros who come to Del Oro and take your people do so for their maker. To feed the beast."

Lalo grabbed another book, splayed it open, and pointed at a sketch of Basilio's Point. The mountain range as a whole was nondescript. It looked like any other formation, with the exception of five jagged spikes jutting from the ground around Devil's

Spine. The sight always made Carolina shiver. Not with fright but with a curiosity that felt deliciously dangerous.

"That is where we need to go," Lalo said. "Preferably before Maricela finds Vidal herself and alerts him of our plans. If he is her maker, she will do anything to stop us." He ran a hand through his tangled hair. "We should also go before Rafael wakes up and tries to murder me."

"With the surprise of attack, we would have the upper hand," Carolina said. She eyed the perilous topography detailed on the sketch. "This will not be simple. Devil's Spine is at least two days' hard ride from here. Through the woods, mind you. And the lands there are devious in their own right. There is boiling quicksand, poisonous brambles, and the like. Not to mention the sun has already risen. How can we possibly get you out of the hacienda without anyone noticing?"

"Can you steal a coach?" he asked.

"Los cocheros might find that suspicious, but I'll figure something out." She started for the door. Halted. "Stay here, clean yourself up, and write a letter to Fernanda."

His eyes widened. "Why?"

"You should say goodbye. We may never come back."

The light inside him dimmed.

He dropped his chin to his chest.

"I'm sorry," she said, and meant it with her entire soul. Someone so gentle and kind and smart shouldn't have to endure such wretched things. Why should he have to pay for her ancestors' sins? "If it makes you feel any better, I know my family will take her under their wing. But you are her brother, and she will need closure. If you want her to live a long, full life with no unanswered questions, this is how."

A single inky tear fell down his cheek.

When her own eyes started to burn, she cleared her throat. "I will go and get supplies before writing my own notes. Are you prepared for this? It won't be easy."

"I'm ready as any man walking toward his own grave."

"That's the spirit, fiancé." She put on her best smile. "I'll meet you here in twenty minutes."

Carolina pushed the door open, checked left and right to ensure no one was around, then slid out. There were things she needed for this journey if they were going to even survive the ride there. Weapons, food, blood, the daggers. The woods had always held monsters, but the closer they got to the mountain, the more hardships they would encounter. That is, if they even got that far.

Due to the hostile terrain surrounding and within Basilio's Point, not much is known about the small mountain range. The dense forest flanking the southern ridge of Devil's Spine is marred with thick bogs, spiky brambles, and broken land. Vast stretches of desert on the western slope make for impossible living conditions. Temperatures reaching above boiling points can be dangerous for humans.

Sanchez. 1825. *Alta California, Abundancia: Pueblos, Cities, & Topography*. First Edition.

CHAPTER 35

Lalo

LALO GRABBED SOME BLANK PARCHMENT AND A PENCIL AND SAT at the desk in the room of Carolina's tía Morena. He sighed, glaring down at the empty page. How was one supposed to write a letter saying goodbye?

Carolina was right. He most likely wasn't coming back from Devil's Spine. Once they severed the ties to Tecuani, the power inside him would fade. Lalo's soul would no longer be able to stay within the realm of the living because he had died. Maricela had killed him weeks ago.

Fernanda's face came into mind. She'd always been so annoying to him growing up. Fernanda lived. She laughed. She had fun. He hated her for it after their parents were slain. He could never understand her carefree behavior when bills needed to be paid, a business needed to be run. How did she find time for friends and lovers when she had finishing school?

But now, facing the end, he wished he possessed a speck of her luster. He should have laughed more. Danced more. Hells below, he'd never even kissed anyone. Instead of turning his nose up at his sister, he should have learned from her.

But it was too late for that.

He bent over and began to write.

I am proud of you, dear sister. Proud that you have never dulled your shine. I'm sorry if I ever tried to convince you to be anyone but yourself. Because you are perfect. Smart, witty, fun. By birth, I am the big brother, but I look up to you. Please, do not let whatever happens to me take away the glistening spirit inside you. Remember me, of course, with fondness rather than sadness. I may have realized too late that I have not lived life to the fullest. At least I could watch you live yours.

I love you, Fernanda. Know that everything I have done, it has been because of my love for you.

He wiped at the tears falling from his eyes. He'd never been the type to cry, but it seemed in death, it was hard to hold in.

Thanks to Carolina, Fernanda would understand the feelings he could not express aloud. Lalo couldn't help but smile whenever he thought of his "fiancée." Carolina was stubborn, and irritating, and brilliant, and funny. And the way she had felt in his arms, that peck on the cheek she'd given him after they danced, brought a lump into his throat. He could only pray she survived this journey because the world would be darker without her in it.

He slipped another piece of parchment onto the desk and started to write a second letter.

When his name was signed, he dropped the charcoal pencil and eyed all that he'd written, satisfied.

A noise came from the hallway. Lalo shoved the letters inside the desk drawer and jumped to his feet, prepared to hide. Then he caught her scent. Her heart was racing.

The door slammed open, and Carolina rushed in. "Hurry!" she panted. "Put on your coat and sombrero!"

Lalo did what he was told.

"Have you packed?" she asked.

"Yes." He pointed to a small satchel.

Carolina grabbed it and swung it over her shoulder.

"What's wrong?" he asked.

"Rafa has awakened. The messenger boy said he had to be restrained. My papá is dashing to the healers as we speak."

Lalo cursed.

She offered her hand. He took it, ignoring how her soft yet callused skin felt in his.

Lalo stopped. "The daggers!"

"I've got them. Vámonos."

CHAPTER 36

Carolina

Carolina tugged Lalo along the corridor as fast as she could without drawing suspicion. Her heels clicked loudly against the tile as if the soles of her boots had been replaced with horseshoes. Though Lalo was draped in many layers, as soon as they stepped into the open courtyard of the casa, Carolina could feel his body tense. The morning sun was particularly bright for an autumn day.

"Tuck your hands into your pockets," she said. She'd forgotten to bring him gloves.

He did as he was told in silence. Lalo didn't need to speak for her to understand his worries—if they didn't get away before Rafa told the truth, her family would kill Lalo before he and Carolina had a chance to escape to the mountains.

She slinked her arm into the crook of his elbow. They needed to resemble two lovers spending time together. They needed to appear as if nothing was amiss. But inside, there was a nest of nerves.

Lalo leaned in close, his sombrero shading her face. "Your heart is thundering."

"Just focus on the task ahead," she snapped. She didn't mean to sound so harsh, but her overwhelming emotions made her frantic. "The carriage is just out front. The driver believes he's taking us to check on Jorge, but I have other plans."

Mamá swept into the foyer from the gardens.

"Ah, there they are," Mamá said, her cheeks rosy from walking, her hands pressed to her back.

"Amá," Carolina said breathlessly. "You're supposed to be resting."

Mamá waved her off. "How can I rest with so much uproar. The only good news is that Rafa has awakened."

"Have you heard anything from the healer? How is he faring?" Carolina's words came out rushed. She needed to slow down, to take a breath, before Mamá grew suspicious.

"Nothing yet, but I expect word any moment."

Lalo stiffened in her grasp. Carolina gave him a little shove, but he didn't move. They were both failing miserably.

Mamá raised a brow. "Are you well, Lalo? I know it was a harrowing night."

Leave it to Mamá to be concerned. If Carolina didn't make it back, if she for some reason was cut down, her mamá would make sure everyone was okay, even though she would never be the same herself. She was good and pure in that way. Perhaps Carolina hadn't appreciated her enough. She should have loved her mamá harder. Better. She should have told her she was doing a fine job more often. Raising children must be challenging. Especially willful daughters like Carolina.

Her eyes blurred with hot tears.

"Ay, Carolina. Do not cry," Mamá said. "Lalo is fine. Perfectly handsome and odd as ever." She winked and pinched his cloak.

Lalo cleared his throat. "I want to thank you, Señora Fuentes, for raising the bravest woman I've ever known."

"Oh," Mamá whispered. "That is so sweet of you to say."

"I mean it. You and Señor Fuentes should be so proud."

Mamá's chin wobbled. "We are."

Carolina turned her head from her mamá and wiped her cheek. "We really should get going," she said before life got trickier than it already was. "We're going to bring tequila to Jorge. We might go for paletas after. So we won't be back for some time."

Pretending as if her world wasn't imploding was exhausting. What if she never saw her mamá's face again? Carolina tried her best to memorize every angle and freckle. Every laugh line at the corner of Mamá's eyes.

Mamá sighed. "To be young and in love again." She smiled, waving her hand at them. "Off you go."

Mamá kissed Carolina and shuffled by, taking Carolina's aching heart with her.

I love you, she wanted to say. *Even when I was cross, or getting in trouble, or having to do a million chores. There wasn't a moment I didn't love you, Amá.*

"How do we do this?" Lalo whispered. "How do we leave our loved ones behind?"

"I will not judge you if you stay here," Carolina said softly.

She was done judging. Here she was, hating Lalo with an

unrivaled fierceness because he was something she thought she despised. When all along he should hate her family for cursing him.

"I can go on without you. This is my family's debt to undo."

"You think my fighting skills are that poor?" He raised his brow.

"We did only manage one training session."

"Two, actually. Though that first lesson in your abuelo's room probably didn't count. You spent most of the time punching me into oblivion." He smiled. "Nonetheless, I will not leave your side."

This time, Lalo took charge. He tucked his head in as they left the foyer, walked outside, and the sun's rays washed over them.

Lalo opened the coach door. He held Carolina's hand and guided her in first, even though the sun must have been beating down upon his shoulders. When she was seated, he removed his sombrero and slipped into the coach, placing himself as far as possible from any leaks of sunlight.

"Here," Carolina said, shifting beside him to block most of the sun. "Is that better?"

Lalo gave a curt nod. "Much. Thank you."

The coach lurched forward, and they bumped down the cobbled road.

"Where are the supplies you gathered?" he asked.

"Under the carriage." She smirked. "And hidden in my skirts. We will stop at Jorge's home first. He lives with his wife just outside the main square. He has a shed in the back with ample weapons. No one will notice if I take a revolver or two."

Lalo's throat bobbed.

"Are you nervous?" She scooted closer. He grew tenser.

"Exceedingly so."

"When I am anxious, I like to learn how to do something." She reached down and tugged her skirts up, pulling out one of the lover's daggers, the very tool Alma had used to call Tecuani from the Land of the Dead. She took his hand and placed the hilt in his palm. "To end Vidal, you can either slash"—she moved his hand in a slicing motion—"or you can stab." She thrust his hand forward. "But here . . ." She took his hand and pressed the blade to her chest, to the small space just between the ribs where her heart was beating like the horses' hooves outside. "This is the kill spot for your kind. For mine too, I suppose."

Lalo was still. His eyes remained focused on where the blade touched the exposed skin just above her bodice.

"If I cannot complete the kill," she said, "you must aim for this very spot."

"And if I miss?" His voice was gruff, as if he'd never spoken a day in his life.

"You won't."

"How do you know?"

"Because your sister's life depends on it." She released her grip on his hand. He pulled back immediately, and the dagger clattered to the floor. Carolina bent to retrieve it at the same time the carriage hit a dip in the road. She landed against him, her palms splayed over his chest.

His lips were so close to hers. Her gaze flicked to Lalo's mouth then back to his eyes, which were wide and panicked.

She frowned. "Why do you look so terrified?"

"Because . . ." He gulped. "Because I desperately wish to kiss you."

Carolina's heart plunged to her belly.

"Why don't you?" she said breathlessly.

"I'm afraid," he said. "I've never . . . I haven't . . ." He shook his head. "I want to kiss you, Carolina. But I fear that if I do, I might never stop."

Dammit. Why was this boy so . . . perfect?

"Kiss me anyway," she said. And she meant it.

"Do you feel something between us, truly? No pretenses?" he asked, all the hope in the world pooling within his gaze.

"Kiss me, Lalo Montéz, and I will show you."

He grimaced. "My real name is actually Lalo Villalobos."

Carolina snickered. Rafa was right. "I want Lalo Villalobos to kiss me too, then."

His hands wrapped around her back, and he drew her in. He hesitated. "What if I lose control?"

She grinned. "I have daggers strapped to both thighs."

Carolina's fingers moved from his chest to the collar of his shirt. She gripped the fabric tight and eased herself close to him until their lips were nearly touching. Lalo closed his eyes, waiting. Carolina smiled at his innocence. Then she closed her eyes too.

Pure energy sizzled through her body when their lips met. The feeling was as if the world inside Carolina exploded into starlight. She jolted back—her lips, her body, her everything tingled.

"Wow," Lalo whispered.

She had been thinking the same thing.

And now she yearned for more.

Carolina kissed him again, but it wasn't enough. She crawled onto his lap. She wanted to feel every part of him against her. And when he pulled her closer to him, the world fizzled away. There was only the caress of his soft lips, his lithe form. The taste of him. The quiet moans he made when their tongues touched.

She dug her fingers into his hair. Pulled his head back so she might kiss the sensitive skin on his neck. Lalo groaned, gripping at her layers of skirts.

The cochero called out to the horses, and the carriage came to a sudden stop. Lalo flung Carolina to the other side of the seat. His face was flushed. His lips were pink. His eyes were wild and glossy.

"I . . . I'm sorry," Lalo rasped. And when he spoke, Carolina saw the tips of his fangs. He clamped a hand to his mouth. "I shouldn't have . . . ," he mumbled. "We shouldn't have . . ."

Hurt flared within her, then anger. She crossed her arms. "No one should look so horrified after a kiss like that."

Lalo's eyes bulged. "That kiss was a mistake."

The door opened and—Carolina's jaw dropped. Nena poked her head in. "Hello, lovebirds," she said merrily.

"What are you doing here?" Carolina asked.

The sudden brightness of the day filled the coach. She could only hope Lalo was too busy suffering from the sunlight to see how rosy her cheeks were.

"Checking in on Jorge. What else?" Nena's eyes flicked between the two of them. "Am I interrupting something?" She wiggled her brows.

"No!" Lalo said. Just as Carolina said, "Yes!"

She glared at Lalo, the miserable fool who thought he could regret her kisses, before starting for the door.

"We were stopping in to see how your brother is faring," she said.

Nena waved her hand. "Don't bother. Jorge is fine and resting. The sediento gave him a good swipe to the chest, but his wound will mend. Worse things have happened to him. Remember the time he threw a stone at that hornet's nest?"

"How could I forget. I was standing next to him. My eyes were swollen shut for a week from the pests' stings," Carolina said.

"Oh yes! It was the prettiest you ever looked," Nena teased.

"Hilarious." Carolina inched toward the door, but Nena didn't move. How was she going to sneak to the shed and snag extra weapons with nosy Nena to block her way? They were ten minutes into her plan of escape, and things were already going awry.

Fernanda's head popped into view next. She narrowed her eyes. "Is my brother boring you to death?"

"I think it's the opposite," Nena said.

Fernanda grinned. "How scandalous."

"Scoot over," Nena commanded.

"What?" Carolina's spine stiffened. "Why?"

"Because it's hot, and I'm tired and I want to go home."

Carolina didn't budge. If Nena placed her bottom on the seat, Carolina knew she'd never leave el pueblo. Nena understood all of Carolina's tells. She would notice something was amiss. The last time Carolina tried to hide a bag of sweets from Nena, she was onto her lies in seconds. Nena said she could tell by the way Carolina had acted. She was a bit *too* good-natured and supposedly batted her lashes twice as much as normal.

"We aren't headed home," Carolina confessed.

Fernanda's gaze kept flicking to her brother, who was hunched in the corner to stay away from the sun. He stared at nothing, rubbing the pads of his fingers over his lips.

"Is something wrong?" Fernanda asked. Clearly, she was aware of her brother's tells, too. Carolina had to get away from these clever women.

"Your brother and I just kissed," she admitted.

Both girls gasped.

Carolina let her chin quiver. "And now he feels as if it were a mistake."

They gasped again.

"Is it because he is a sediento?" Nena queried.

Carolina shook her head. She pretended to dab at her tear-filled eyes.

"Is it because he has never kissed anyone?" Fernanda asked.

Carolina paused her performance. "Really?"

"Sí. Perhaps kissing was simply too . . ."

"I am right here," Lalo deadpanned. "Please do not speak of me as if I do not exist."

"I think Lalo and I have some issues to work out. You two don't mind walking to the casa on your own so we can have some privacy, do you?"

"Of course not. Especially if it ends with passionate makeup kissing." Nena puckered her lips and batted her lashes.

"Gross," Fernanda said, but the corners of her lips curved into a smile.

"We'll see you later." Nena wiggled her fingers.

"Don't expect us home anytime soon," Carolina replied.

Fernanda and Nena squealed with glee. "Glad to see you finally living, brother." Fernanda winked and shut the door in her wake, leaving Carolina and Lalo alone again.

Carolina wilted. That might have been the last time she saw her cousin, and she'd ended it with titillating half-truths and fake tears.

She hit the sidewall and hollered, "To Señor Leaños's, Joaquín!" The coach lurched forward.

The small paletería dug into the ground was the closest building in Del Oro to the forest. Once Señor Leaños started adding other flavors into his creamy ice mixture of eggs, milk, and agave honey, everyone in Del Oro enjoyed their cool treats. His chili lime paleta was worth dying for.

"What is the plan?" Lalo asked.

She stuck her nose up. "I'd rather not speak to people who think kissing me is a mistake."

"Has it happened before?"

"I haven't had a complaint yet." Not that she'd kissed many boys. Only two, and one was an insufferably handsome sediento. Most in town were too afraid of Papá to even try.

The coach jostled, but this time she did not fall into his arms. They were nearing the paletería. That divot in the road two shops down from Señor Leaños's had been there for three years now.

They came to a slow stop. "Pretend you are ill," she ordered.

"I beg your pardon?"

"Act sickly."

The door swung open, and Joaquín's large frame blotted out the sun.

"Carolina, we are . . ."

Lalo groaned and grasped his stomach, slumped against the wall.

"Are you unwell, Lalo?" the cochero asked.

"All this movement has given my poor beau motion sickness. You have seen that he is prone to ailments."

She patted his thigh, trying to appear sympathetic.

"I'm certain he will be fine after he collects himself. Do you mind waiting in line for us, though? I know how long of a wait it can be."

"Of course." Joaquín snuck one last glance at Lalo before shutting the door.

Carolina counted to twenty, giving Joaquín time to disappear into the crowd of patrons.

She started for the door, but Lalo grabbed her wrist. "What are we doing?"

She jerked her hand free. "*We* are not doing anything. *I* am."

Hurt flashed across his face as if he wasn't the one who had rejected her. "If this is about the kiss, I . . ."

"You are sorry for it. I understand fully well. It is evident on your irritating face. And don't worry, it'll never happen again."

His mouth fell open.

Good, she thought. She hoped her words stung worse than nettle.

"Stay in here, and hold tight, because I'm hijacking this carriage."

I sliced into my flesh and lay upon the dirt, begging for Tecuani to hear my cries. He rose from the soil in a writhing mist. I could not see his face, but I heard his rumbling voice. The sound was that of thunder, of a jaguar ready to strike.

"Who disturbs my peace?" he snarled.

I raised my hands and pleaded, "Forgive me, Lord, but I need your help."

The great god of souls laughed. And my bones quivered from its resonance.

"I will assist you, my child, but my benevolence comes with a price."

—Xóchitl 18:9

CHAPTER 37

Lalo

THE COACH LURCHED FORWARD. LALO FELL BACK, BUMPING INTO the hard wood of the wall.

Again, he found himself pressing the pad of his finger to his lips.

He brushed his hair out of his eyes, locks Carolina had moments ago tugged out of place. "What are you doing?" he whispered to himself. "Now is not the time for this."

But if he was to face the original sediento soon and possibly die for real this time, shouldn't he be allowed to kiss the girl he was falling for?

"Bloody hell," he murmured. "You've fallen for Carolina Victoria Fuentes." His head dropped. "And you are going to lose her before she was ever even yours."

The clopping of the horses' hooves on dirt and the rattling of the wooden spokes filled the infinite quiet. He shouldn't have said their kiss was a mistake. He could never regret something that was so . . . He felt the heat rise to his cheeks. That kiss was perfect in every way.

He should tell her that.

"No," he said. Confessing his love would only be a distraction. He jolted. *He loved her?*

"Saints above," he groaned.

He sank into the bench. He wished he could speak to Fernanda at that moment. She was an expert at love. By his count, she'd fallen in and out of it at least a dozen times.

But what did it matter when Devil's Spine grew closer?

"We're entering the woods now," Carolina yelled. "I'm taking us on a hidden path. It's going to get bumpy."

An hour or so went past. He couldn't really tell. His rear was getting sore from being jostled about so wildly.

"Hang on to something!" Carolina yelled.

Before he could even attempt to stabilize himself, the entire right half of the coach dipped low. A miserable crack sounded from one of the axles before everything came to a crashing stop.

"Carolina?" he called. She said nothing. Panic tore through him. He started toward the exit. "Carolina!"

The door to the coach slowly opened and Carolina's face peered into the darkness.

"Are you hurt?" he asked, noting the paleness of her skin.

She shook her head. "I'm fine. Just . . . embarrassed. I crashed the carriage," she said. "I thought it was a small dip. I was wrong. The axle is busted."

She lifted her face toward the sun. Her hair blew in the breeze. "This isn't going to be easy."

His mouth ran dry. "Are there no trees to shelter us?"

"I took a path no one would dare use. If my papá comes after us, he'd never think I'd be foolish enough to come this way."

"Why is this path so dangerous?"

She chewed on her lip. He wished to kiss it.

"The road is basically impassable with a coach. And . . ."

"And what?"

"Wolves run rampant here."

"Why in el Cielo would you choose this way?"

"It's the fastest route to Devil's Spine. And with the winds so fierce, our tracks will disappear behind us in moments. No one would be able to track us."

"And now we are stuck," he said.

"The carriage certainly is." She looked around at what appeared to be a barren landscape. The few trees he could make out in the distance were spindly and freakishly large but had no leaves to speak of, as if even the leaves knew to stay away.

"What are our options?" he asked.

"We sit here and wait it out. The sun will go down in a few hours."

He shook his head. "Any sediento in the area will find us as soon as night falls."

"Then you will just have to trust me to see you to the other side of this valley." She gave a weak smile. "We'll cover up any of your exposed skin and ride like hell."

"I'm not very good on a horse," he admitted. *Or a pony*, he thought. He'd leave that fact out.

"You'll have me to guide you," she said. "You can trust me."

Their eyes linked. Heat spread through his body like he was already on fire. If he could, he'd forget everything and kiss her until the world slipped away.

He cared for her so very much. And he could see it in her eyes that she felt the same. It was in the sound of her heart. The softening of her body. Alas, he had to end whatever this was. He was already going to destroy his sister if he perished; he didn't want to hurt Carolina as well. Maybe it was cowardly but knowing he would pain her was too much to bear.

"Carolina." He cleared his throat. "About this kiss."

Her heart thumped faster.

Tell her the truth, his mind and body urged. *Forget playing it safe. Tell her you love her. That you want nothing more than to live and be with her.*

But he wouldn't. He couldn't. It was better for her to hate him than to spend the rest of her days thinking about what could have been.

"It was selfish of me to want something like that from you. Even if the circumstances were different, this would never work."

Carolina's skin was bleached of the last of its bronze color. "You are right. How foolish of me." He watched as she built a barrier between them. Brick by brick. She nodded once as if in agreement with herself. "I will ready the horses."

He moved to grab her, to pull her back into the cool shadows of the coach and tell her he lied, to tell her he didn't want to die, that he wanted to be with her always, but he stopped. And he let her go.

CHAPTER 38

Carolina

She freed the horses from the coach and tied all the supplies she knew they needed around their necks. She packed weapons. A bit of food for herself. Some boar's blood for the brat.

Carolina cinched a knot with a grunt. Lalo was lying to her. He may believe her to be the one to wear her emotions on her face, but he should study himself in the mirror sometime.

"The toad. The wretch. The—" She couldn't come up with anything else and growled in frustration.

He wanted to play the part of a gentleman. The part of poor martyr. Well, she wouldn't make it easy for him. No, señor. She knew what had to be done. She understood that traversing Devil's Spine and killing Vidal was going to be the hardest thing she'd ever completed, but that didn't mean they should lie to each other. Not when neither knew if they'd make it back.

"Coward," she spat. "Selfish pile of dung."

Dung or not, she had to find something to cover his face completely with. The sombrero would only do so much. She hadn't brought any extra clothing with her. Carolina hadn't thought it would be necessary. She should have known better.

Her fingers gripped the first layer of her skirts, and she ripped at the seams.

"What are you doing?" Lalo's voice was an octave too high.

"I have nothing else to cover you with. This will have to do."

"I ... can see your underthings."

She snorted while tearing more of her skirts. Nothing inappropriate was showing. She had on pantaloons. But the way Lalo's mouth opened and shut like a guppy, one would think she was wearing nothing but what she was born with.

She flung the torn fabric at him. "Cover your face and put your sombrero over it to keep it in place."

Lalo didn't move, his eyes were glued to her figure. She held in her smile. If their kiss was such a mistake, why was he looking at her with such feverish lust in his eyes?

"Lying dog," she whispered.

"Beg your pardon?"

"I said, are you ready?"

"Do I have any other choice?"

It wasn't going to be a simple journey to the trees. There was nothing to shield him from the sun for at least a mile.

"I've tied our horses together. I'll guide us to the woods. You simply need to keep out of the sunlight to the best of your abilities and not fall off."

"I can promise nothing."

He wrapped the scraps of her floral embroidered skirts around his neck and face. It was a pity to cover something so perfect, but it was better than watching him suffer as he blistered beyond recognition.

When every part of Lalo's skin was covered, Carolina reached into the coach and grabbed the lapel of his coat. "Time to go. Hold on to the back of my bodice," she ordered, then took one of his cloth-covered fists and brought it to her lower back. She wished she'd had time to make him a proper mask to see through, but she'd be his eyes. "I'll lead you to your mount and then we'll ride like pinche bandidos."

He said nothing.

"You aren't going to chide me for my foul language?" she asked.

"Perhaps later." His tone was tight edged. "If there is a later to have."

"Don't be so dramatic. I will get you across this valley." *She hoped.*

Carolina discarded that thought, stuffed it right behind her need to punish him for pushing her away. She'd make certain Lalo survived, just so she could make him regret what he had said after. Their kiss was anything but a mistake. Something that beautiful and breathtaking should be cherished. Should be done over and over and over again. *When* they made it through the valley, she'd make certain to set him straight.

"I'm taking you out of this carriage. Don't let go of me."

His fingers dug into the thick material. In a voice as quiet as mist, he said, "Never."

Chills rippled over her skin. Her heart fluttered painfully. Never was too hefty a promise.

Sighing, she led them out of the coach and into the blistering heat. The winds whipped about them. Pulling at her hair, at the clothing covering Lalo's body. He hissed.

"Do we need to go back?" she called over the gusts.

"No. I'm fine. I've never been better," he yelled back.

"Has anyone ever told you that you are a terrible liar?"

"Once or twice."

She smiled into the wind. "They were right."

Slowly, they made their way toward the horses. Fighting against gusts determined to claw off his defenses.

Carolina brought his hands to the gelding's back. "We have no saddles; can you ride without?"

"I haven't the slightest clue."

She snorted and helped him up. It was an awkward, embarrassing affair where he accidentally smacked her in the face with his boot, but he got up, nonetheless.

Quickly, she ran over to her mount, which was tethered to his, and clambered onto the beauty's back. "Hold on, Lalo."

Carolina clicked her tongue, and the horses began to move. Sluggishly at first, building speed when she knew he wouldn't fall. Before they gained ground, she needed to ensure his coverings would hold when they took off at full force.

They started to trot, and a corner of the cloth loosened, revealing the warm brown skin on his neck. He let out a shocked yell.

"Should we stop?" she hollered.

"No! Keep going. The faster we enter the woods, the better."

He held on to the horse's mane with one hand and shakily tried to conceal himself with the other, but the fabric loosened even more. He let out a string of curses. Words even Carolina had never used.

Her eyes went to the horizon, to the forest slowly edging closer to them.

"Do you smell that?" Lalo asked. "Is that sulfur?"

Carolina's eyes snapped to either side of them. A cloud of dust bloomed to her left where the canyon blocked them in. Rocks tumbled down the granite wall from high above. She searched the spot from which they had come. Her stomach pinched with horror, and she gasped.

"Shit." She flicked the reins. "We must go faster!" she called out. "Hang on!"

Carolina dug her heels into the horse's side, and they raced ahead. Her gaze kept flicking to the canyon walls, and her heart thundered inside her. At least six wolves clambered down the rocks. Six! But when she squinted, she could see there was something different about them. Something otherworldly. Monstrous.

And they were making quick work of descending the cliff face.

Lalo cursed again. His covering was truly coming undone. Even with the horses' hooves pounding over the dirt and the wind biting at their faces, she could hear the disturbing hiss of his flesh burning.

But they couldn't stop now. The wolves would easily pin them here. At least in the woods, she wouldn't have to worry about Lalo's skin melting away.

A sharp howl coming from one of the beasts broke through her thoughts. It was louder than any wolf she'd heard before and so deep she felt it in her bones.

She jerked her head back. The monsters were catching up. Her horses were going at a full sprint but couldn't outrun them.

"Come on," she urged her mount. "Just a little bit farther."

Lalo chanced a look back and gasped. "Chupasangres!"

"What in the hells are those?" she shouted.

She snapped the leads harder, praying the carriage horses could move faster.

"Whenever the veil between the Land of the Dead and the Land of the Living is breached, these creatures sneak through. This is great news!"

"Your idea of great news and mine are vastly different."

Lalo grunted in pain. "It means we are on the right track. Chupasangres hunt for whatever doesn't belong in this realm."

"Like a sediento?"

"Yes," he wheezed.

"Like you?"

He cursed.

The trees were ahead. They might make it. They had to.

Lalo's horse whinnied as a dark mass surged beside it. The creature's body was long and hunched. Where fur should have been lay thick black scales, like crocodile skin.

"Carolina!" Lalo let out a horrified yelp when the chupasangre swiped at him and his steed. "Help!"

She dug her hands into the bag she'd strapped to her horse and pulled out three gleaming obsidian daggers. She threw the first one. It bounced off the chupasangre's reptilian hide.

"Come on," she growled.

Taking a deep breath as her abuelo always taught her, she let the second dagger fly. It somersaulted into the air just as the monster shoved off its hindlegs and launched itself toward Lalo. The blade sank deep into the beast's exposed chest. The chupasangre crashed into the dirt and exploded into a plume of dark smoke.

"Carolina!" Lalo cried. Half his face was exposed. Boils were festering and popping on his cheeks and neck. "Behind you!"

She whirled around. Flung the dagger. Watched as the blade found its mark and another beast exploded into the ether. But there was no cause to celebrate, more monsters were coming.

"We'll never make it!" she screamed. "They're too fast."

"Stop the horses!" Lalo yelled.

"What? Have you lost all sense?"

"Stop the horses, now!"

From the journal of Friar Alejandro Ibarra

The gods' bloodhounds, also known as chupasangres in the west of Abundancia, serve one purpose: to hunt and destroy whatever may disrupt the balance between the realms of the living and the dead.

A human has nothing to fear of these elusive creatures. Unless they have broken into the Land of the Dead, of course. Or perhaps aren't so human at all.

CHAPTER 39

Lalo

His skin sizzled. He writhed in agony. The pain was like nothing he'd ever experienced before. He was living through a rampaging wildfire. He couldn't breathe. Couldn't think. The torment was too great. But he'd fight through hell and back to keep Carolina safe. She'd gotten them far enough for him to take over.

The covering flung back yet again as Carolina jerked at the reins and they came to a sudden stop. His full face and neck were exposed to the blazing sun. An explosion of heat seared through his entire being, cutting to the very wick of his soul. Bellowing, Lalo jumped off his horse. He dug his head into his shoulders and ran for Carolina who stood, readying to fight the chupasangres.

Lalo spared no time by explaining himself. He scooped her into his arms, held her tight against his body, and bolted for the trees.

"What are you doing?!" she shrieked.

"Is it not obvious?!" He gritted his teeth and kept his eyes locked on the spindly branches ahead. His thighs pumped as the power of Tecuani thrummed through his veins.

"Holy shit, you're fast!"

Her legs and arms wrapped around him, and she clung tight, making it easier for him to maneuver and shielding him from some of the sun's agonizing rays. One of his hands fisted the back of her bodice like a life raft while the other pumped as hard as it could. Everything hurt. His skin, his eyes, his scalp. The sun's rays were like badgers clawing away at his flesh.

"Almost there," she said softly into his ear. And the sound was like jumping into cool waters.

His muscles were tiring. The daylight was ravaging him. He would not make it much longer.

But then he smelled the pines and damp earth. The torture eased as his feet pounded through the mouth of the woods. Lalo didn't stop. He could hear the chupasangres still speeding toward them.

Something rattled in his chest. His lungs seized, and he gasped for air. His boot snagged on a fallen branch, and they tumbled forward. Carolina fell out of his grasp as they hit the forest floor. Lalo tried to push himself up, but the last of his energy depleted and the pain he'd been suppressing exploded within.

Carolina scrambled to his side. She gasped. His injuries must be extensive. They certainly felt like it.

"We've got to keep going, Lalo," she panted. "Those beasts are still coming, and most of my weapons were left with the horses. Can you stand?"

He could hardly open his mouth to reply.

A chupasangre howled dangerously close.

"Shit," Carolina spat. "Shit. Shit. Shit."

"Go," he wheezed. "Leave me."

"I'm not going anywhere without you."

Her confession tore through his heart.

She was quiet for a moment. "They are attracted to sedientos, right?"

Lalo whispered, "Yes. They cannot see, but their sense of smell is extraordinary. They can smell death on sedientos. They know we do not belong in this realm."

Another howl echoed through the trees. Loud and near.

"Then there's only one thing to do," she said.

She eased her body on top of his until every part of her touched every part of him.

Lalo's eyes bulged.

"Are you trying to get us both killed?"

"I'm hiding your scent from them." Her face hovered just above his. Her lips were dangerously close. Her *everything* was close.

A twig snapped.

"Do not move," she mouthed.

Slowly, she pulled one of the lover's daggers from its sheath and held it at the ready.

Three chupasangres burst through the brush. Lalo listened to Carolina's pulse racing as the beasts' heavy paws crunched over fallen branches and dead leaves. Her gaze held his. And for possibly the first time since meeting her, he saw true fear within her eyes.

Two of the chupasangres edged slowly toward them. One sniffed at the air; it let out a deep puff of breath, causing Carolina's dark hair to flutter over her face.

A low and hungry growl came from the chupasangre. Its haunches raised like spikes down its spine. The hound's lips pulled back, revealing its razor-sharp teeth. It bent low as if readying to pounce.

Carolina took the dagger and sliced into one of her arms and then the other. The chupasangre quirked its head as her blood seeped over Lalo's body. Its shoulders relaxed ever so slightly.

Lalo gritted his teeth and held his breath. Her blood was so warm. It smelled of Carolina. Of fire.

A howl sounded in the far-off distance, and the three chupasangres' heads snapped up. Two bounded into the brush straight away but one lingered. Its nostrils flared as it gave the air around Carolina and Lalo one more deep sniff. The beast took another step toward them but halted when a second howl came.

Its ears flicked toward the noise, and it huffed before turning west, disappearing behind the trees.

Carolina let loose a breath and slumped onto Lalo's chest. The sudden pain rocked through his core. The edges of his vision blurred.

"I'm going to faint," he wheezed.

CHAPTER 40

Carolina

CAROLINA SCRAMBLED OFF HIM. HIS FACE HAD SLOWLY STARTED to mend, but she hadn't had the time to check on anything else. Slowly, she peeled back the layers of cloth still wrapped around his neck. She gasped. Boiling blisters oozed and stretched over the raw skin.

"How are you even functioning?" she managed.

Lalo groaned something unintelligible.

"You aren't healing fast enough."

It dawned on her; he was probably half starved. He had only had a few sips of boar's blood before they left.

She cursed.

The satchel with all of Lalo's sustenance was gone with the horses. As were the bandages she'd packed for herself in case of injury.

She needed to get something to Lalo and fast. He looked dire and, besides that, they really should keep moving. This was the deepest she'd ever been within the forest. There might be more monsters creeping about. And if Maricela or Vidal found them now, they would have no chance to fight back.

He shifted and moaned. He truly was in the very worst way.

She chewed on her lip. Mulling over the thoughts running through her mind. There was only one option. She'd have to offer herself to him. Just a bit. Just enough to see him through. But that would mean some of the years of her life would be forfeit. She eyed Lalo, still sizzling in the grass. A few years of her own existence were a small sacrifice when she thought of everything Lalo had endured. Besides, there was no guarantee she was making it off Devil's Spine anyway.

Gently, she eased Lalo up. Ignoring the exclamations of pain, she brought him to a seated position against the trunk of a wide pine tree, making sure to keep his skin from scraping against the bark. She pulled one of the lover's daggers from its sheath, rested it upon the soft flesh just between her pointer finger and thumb.

"What are you doing?" Lalo's voice came out in a rasp.

"You aren't healing. I must get you back on your feet."

A single eye popped open, bloodshot and glossy. "You don't look so good yourself," he said.

She grinned. "Since when did you become such a jester?"

"Oh, I've always been funny." He winced as he shifted. "I've just kept that fact a secret."

She chuckled and scooted closer to him, and he shook his head. "No. I can't. I won't."

"You *can* and you *will.*"

"Drinking from your essence will shorten your life span."

"If we stay here, I will be dead anyway, so drink, dammit."

320

"Always a tyrant." He chuckled and hissed with pain.

Carolina sliced through her skin again, giving him a fresh trail of blood. The wound stung but felt like little more than a paper cut, especially when she examined Lalo's wounds.

"Here." She offered her hand to him, the blood already dripping down her palm.

He turned his head away. "It might only be days or weeks taken from you, but I won't do it."

"Careful, Lalo. Keep acting as if you care, and I might start thinking that kiss wasn't a mistake."

He gulped.

She moved nearer, feeling as drawn to him as ever. "Take it. If we don't start moving, we will both be dead."

Lalo's honey-colored eyes met hers. There was hunger there. Yet he made no move.

"Do not make me force you," she said.

He licked his cracked lips. "What if I lose control?"

"I can handle myself."

They held each other's stares as she brought her palm toward his mouth. His incisors grew. He sighed as if holding his fangs back had been a discomfort.

"What's it like?" she asked. "What do you feel?"

"Disgust. I am a creature who drains a person's soul for nourishment."

She opened and shut her palm, soaking her fingers in her own blood. What would he see within the fabric of her essence? What memories might he find within? Surprisingly, Carolina wasn't worried. Lalo might scoff at her or tease her, but he wouldn't judge her mistakes. She pressed her finger to his lips, watched as his saliva and her life force intertwined. "But what does it *really* feel like?"

Lalo's lashes fluttered. "Like the heavens have exploded and the stars are raining down upon me."

She snorted. "A poet even in agony."

Shakily, he took hold of her wrist. "Are you sure?"

Carolina nodded. There were still hours in the day, but the night would come soon enough. They had to get to Vidal before anything else got to them.

"Do it."

Lalo didn't hesitate this time. He brought his mouth down upon her flesh. His tongue swept over her cut, and the stinging sensation dissolved away. His other hand clenched into a fist on his lap. Her eyes widened as the blisters on his skin began to shrink away almost instantaneously.

"It's working," she said.

A groan of pleasure purred from Lalo's throat. The sound made her own body thrum. She wanted to hear that sound come from him again. And again. And again.

If you are ever lost, simply search into my heart and there you will be.

—Pío Parra, "Lamentations of
the Heart"

CHAPTER 41

Lalo

THERE WAS NO PROPER WAY TO EXPLAIN HOW LALO FELT AT THAT moment. He was on fire and plunging through a pool of ice simultaneously.

She tasted like life itself. Like the earth after the rain. Like summer mornings when the temperature was just right. She tasted like autumn and laughter. Like honey on the tongue.

Flashes of Carolina's life flitted through whatever magic he was trapped in. He saw Carolina and Nena giggling in a field of poppies. Saw her arguing with her papá over him not letting her saddle up like her brothers. Dancing with Luz Elena in her room and forcing the woman to move and laugh.

Lalo gripped her tighter, groaning in pure pleasure as he drank more of her.

Faintly, he thought he heard Carolina gasp.

But then other memories lured him into a brilliant haze.

Their first meeting in the dark. She had him pinned and saw his face. She thought him handsome. Strikingly so. He saw them in the empty grave, embracing. Them kissing in the coach. He could feel the desire thrumming through her. Could feel the yearning.

Gods, he wanted her so desperately.

He wrapped his arm around her body. He wanted her pressed against him. All of him.

"Lalo," he heard her say. She sounded distant. An echo in the very back of his mind. "Lalo, you're hurting me."

CHAPTER 42

Carolina

She tried to pull away, but his hand was like a padlock on her wrist.

His other hand went to her side, clamping around her waist, holding her there. "Lalo," she whispered. His nails dug into her flesh. "Lalo, you're hurting me."

Irritation flared within her, and she jerked her hand free.

"Dammit, Lalo," she said, panting.

She held her arm to her chest and glared at him, scowling at the young man she'd fallen for, but he was no longer there. Gone was the kind Lalo she'd come to hold dear to her heart. Gone was the Lalo who looked after his sister, even when his own world was falling asunder.

His eyes were overlarge and glowing red like the day of the duel. His lips were stained with her blood. An almost purring sort of sound came from his throat.

"Lalo Villalobos," she whispered, and reached up with her uninjured hand. She cupped his cheek, planted a light kiss on his stained lips. "Can you hear me?"

Slowly, his face softened, and the boy returned. His focus flicked to her hand. "I am so sorry."

Blood flowed from her palm and into her bodice. "For what? I am okay. Everything is all right."

He shook his head. "It isn't. Not in the slightest. I hurt you. I could have completely lost control."

She pulled the dagger from behind her back. "I would have been ready if you did. I trust you, Lalo, but not the beast inside."

This seemed to break him a little, but what else could she say? She'd seen the monster firsthand.

His head dropped.

"You did good, Lalo. I mean, you didn't even try to go for my throat."

"But I thought about it. Believe me, I wanted all of you in that moment."

Warmth pooled in her belly. "*All* of me?"

He met her gaze. "Yes." She felt his eyes travel down her neck and to her chest, then stop at her hand. "You're bleeding."

Who cared about that? She wanted to hear more about how much he wanted her.

"You need to be healed. Any sediento within this forest will smell you from a mile away."

She eyed the gashes marring her skin. "I suppose you have a point."

Now almost completely healed, he scrambled onto his knees. He looked abashed. "This is going to get rather strange."

"Why?"

"Sediento blood mends wounds but . . . only when ingested."

She balked. "You wish for me to drink your blood?"

"I fear I must insist on it."

Carolina merely blinked.

"There's more," he said.

A tiny, panicked laugh escaped her.

"I understand the sensation of healing to be rather painful." He cleared his throat. "But, as you know, our saliva has numbing properties. I will need to . . ."

"You must lick me?" Her words were laced with incredulity.

"It's the only way. Trust me, I'd know. I've researched everything there is about vampirism," he said. "But I really must insist before that festers."

And they still had a hard night's trek up the mountain.

Lalo bit into his wrist like an apple. He offered his arm to her. Gingerly, she wrapped her fingers around his skin and brought her lips to his gash. Her lashes fluttered. She saw into Lalo's world. Saw his townhouse near the center of the bustling ciudad of Los Campos. Saw him sitting at a charming desk, reading books. Saw him kill and weep and run. She saw him gazing at her with a desperate hope in his heart.

"That's enough," he whispered.

Carolina pulled back, breathless and woozy from all she had witnessed.

He loved her. She had seen it. He loved her, and it scared the life out of him. She loved him too, but that love didn't scare her. If anything, his love made her feel braver than ever before.

Because if he could see her, see the truest and most private parts of her, and love her still, then that love was something worth facing a thousand monsters for.

An icy heat began to prick her lips, then the inside of her throat, her stomach. The pain Lalo spoke of was starting. She straightened her spine, not meeting his eyes. "Do your worst."

He took her hand first and ran his tongue over her palm. Her mind went completely numb and the pain dulled at once. His soft fingers brushed her hair from her shoulder next. The sensation of his skin against hers was like a lightning bolt. Invisible sparks sizzled where his fingers touched her ever so gently. She couldn't help but sigh.

"Don't do that." His voice came out hard and tense.

"Don't breathe?" she asked.

"Yes. No." He shook his head. "I don't know. Just . . . stay as still as possible. Please."

She grinned. "Why is that, sediento?"

"Don't make me say it," he whispered.

"Tell me."

"You must know what you do to me," he said softly.

Before she could reply, he bent forward and ran his tongue over her cuts. She had to bite down on her lip to keep from gasping. Everything inside her came alive because of his touch. His tender magic. Her fingers reached out and clenched his shirt.

She wanted him. His kisses. His hands. She just wanted him. And before they set off on their final adventure, she would have him.

She dug her hands into his hair and pushed his face up, so they were nose to nose.

"Kiss me," she whispered.

"I already told you what would happen if I did. I said I might never want to stop."

"Then don't."

He closed his eyes as if her words pained him.

"We have this moment, Lalo. Let's pretend this is our forever."

He cupped her cheek. "You are so beautiful."

He kissed her, but there was no softness in this brushing of lips. No hesitation.

An explosion of need burned through her. She could not take the wanting anymore, she needed to explore him.

She tore open his shirt. Lalo's eyes widened in surprise.

"Was that too much?" she asked.

He chuckled. "Nothing you do to me will ever be too much."

The husky tenor in his voice drove her mad. Before she realized what she was doing, her fingers splayed over his warm chest and down to his abdomen.

He sucked in a breath.

"Is this okay?" she whispered.

He nodded.

She brought her hands farther downward. Her calluses scraped over every hard muscle.

"And this?"

He grasped her wrist, stopping her before she went too far. "What are you doing?" he panted.

"We are about to embark on a journey neither of us may come back from. I don't want to leave this realm not knowing what it feels like to be touched by the person I desire."

"And that person is me?"

She giggled. "I don't see anyone else here."

"What about precautions?" he asked.

"I have been taking herbs since I first started my monthlies."

He brushed a lock of hair from her face and gazed upon her. The way he studied her in that moment made her feel as if she were the most beautiful person alive.

"If I didn't know better, I would think this all a dream," he whispered.

Carolina nearly melted at his sweetness.

Slowly, Lalo bent down and kissed her. Their tongues met. Groaning, he wrapped his arms around her bottom and lifted her up. She squeaked into his mouth. Then she giggled as he gently laid her on the grass.

Carolina wrapped her legs around his torso and drew his body onto hers. The sensation of him so near rocked her entire body. Their kiss deepened and her need for Lalo unfurled into something that could no longer be contained. Slowly, softly, quietly, they became one. Carolina couldn't tell if her world was ending or just beginning, but she knew at that moment, she would never be the same.

Few explorers have ever returned from the small mountain range of Basilio's Point. Fewer still from its southernmost peak, Devil's Spine. Locals believe the harsh landscape to be cursed by angry deities. The reason for the supposed curse is unknown.

Juarez. I. (1766) *Compendium* **(Volume 3, p. 501)**

CHAPTER 43

Lalo

HE KEPT STEALING GLANCES AT CAROLINA, WHO WAS BUSY inspecting the horses. With her blood coursing through his veins, Lalo's senses were heightened to their full ability. He had smelled the geldings trapped in brambles from a distance.

Carolina had been ecstatic to find them because she'd strapped a satchel containing supplies over the larger horse's neck, but now her expression was serious. His heart twisted in his chest. He could hardly believe the last hour they'd shared together. They'd fought like hell to survive and after, for the first time perhaps ever, Lalo felt like he had truly lived. But now they were heading toward his ultimate demise.

Did she know he probably wasn't going to survive this night? What if she'd only been with him for pity's sake? No. He would not tarnish his first and possibly last time with such a thought.

He dragged his attention back to his task, which was to read over the papers she'd taken from her grandfather's room and stuffed into the satchel and make certain the path they were going was the one that would lead them to Vidal.

But his mind kept slipping back to her. His body still buzzed from drinking her blood. She tasted how he imagined fire would. Her life force burned as brilliant as any flame. But it was not something to be contained in a hearth. Carolina was a wildfire. One could only sit back and watch her burn.

And every part of Lalo's undead heart burned for her.

He had never longed for passion. His parents lived a perfectly unromantic marriage most days, and they had seemed content. Lalo thought it was safe to keep one's partner at arm's length. But with Carolina, he pictured an eternity of passion. Every emotion she had was big.

He thought of their kisses. How she pulled loose something he thought he never craved. Laughter. Joy. Friendship. Desire. What he wouldn't do to have more time with her. To ride into the valley just to watch the sun rise. To kiss her always. To hold her and watch as her hair turned gray.

When he drank in her life force, he'd seen the world through her eyes. It was so colorful. So exciting and beautiful.

A lump formed in his throat. Lalo wasn't sure what happened to a sediento when they passed to the Land of the Dead. What if his soul was damned? What if he never found her in el Cielo because he wouldn't be admitted?

He rubbed a hand over his face.

What did it matter? If Vidal was gone, and all sedientos died with him, the world would be a safer place. Fernanda and Carolina would be spared. He would not fail in his mission no matter the consequence to himself.

Carolina plopped beside him and cursed. "The speckled horse cannot carry any weight. One of his ankles is swollen."

"What shall we do?"

"We'll just have to ride together. I hope you don't mind."

Lalo shrugged. "I'll endure it if I must."

"You're such a saint," she replied. "Here." In her palms were two thick globs of clay that smelled like death.

"What do you expect me to do with that?" he asked.

"We need to cover our scents. I've already caked our horse with the stuff, though he should be fine anyway—animals are a natural part of the woods. But us? I think the chupasangres are proof enough that you stink."

Lalo chuckled. "I love it when you talk dirty." His nostrils flared at the rank odor. "Speaking of dirty, where did you find that mud?"

"In that bog over there. It's vile, no?"

"That's an understatement." His lip curled. "You really wish for me to put that on myself?"

A single brow shot up. "Now is not the time to act pompous."

His mouth dropped. "*Pompous?*"

"Yes. Snobbish. Superior. Whatever word you like. You will put this on or else."

"Or else what exactly?" he asked, wiggling his brows.

Carolina snorted and rolled her eyes.

"You are beautiful when irritated," he teased. "I remember when I first saw you, even as you snarled, I thought you were the most beautiful woman I'd ever seen."

"And did you think that still after all the times I tried to murder you?"

He grinned. "I didn't say I liked you very much, but yes."

And, oh, did he still. She was hardly wearing anything now. Her hair was a mess of tangles framing her face. He imagined this would be how she looked like in the morning when she woke. Save for the dirt on her face and clothes. What he wouldn't give to wake up next to her daily, to see the morning sun kiss her cheeks as they nuzzled close.

He leaned in to steal a kiss but froze when an owl flapped its wings in the distance, hooting as if it had been spooked.

Lalo snapped out of his trance and cleared his throat. "We should get going, shouldn't we?"

"Put this on first." She plopped a blob into his lap.

He gasped at the sudden throb of pain in his nether parts. "You are a terror," he wheezed.

"I know," she said while painting her skin with the brackish clay.

"For the love of el Cielo," he complained, but he slathered the wretched stuff over himself.

When they were both covered and green with moldy-smelling mud, Carolina jumped up, offering her hand. "Time for the fun to begin," she said.

He rose and wrapped his arms around her. "I think I'd rather stay here and enjoy your kisses instead."

The owl hooted again. Her eyes flicked to the thick woods beyond. "We will have to wait, I fear. Best hurry."

He handed her the papers, and she slid them into the satchel tied to their horse. She climbed up and patted the horse's rear. "Get on."

Lalo did so, not so uncouthly as other times, but no less embarrassingly. When he shuffled in behind her, he had to bite down on his cheeks. How in the world was he going to handle this now that their relationship had entered uncharted territory?

"Hold on to my waist," she said.

Stars above.

He placed a light palm upon the soft curve of her side.

She scoffed. "Are you trying to get thrown off this horse?" She grabbed one of his hands and brought it around her, pulling him right against her backside.

Taxes. Chupasangres. Maricela. Trees with eyes. He was trying to keep his mind clear, but dammit—Carolina fit so perfectly between him. His everything ached for her. It wasn't right that one person could completely unravel another from the inside out.

Something rustled in the far-off distance. Lalo could hear a host of wings flapping as birds suddenly took flight.

"Carolina," he said.

He felt her nod and sensed her pulse starting to beat at a frightening pace. "I heard them too."

Lalo squeezed his arms around her and whispered, "Go."

CHAPTER 44

Carolina

FAST AND STEADY, THEY PACED THROUGH THE WOODS. EVERY sound had her on edge. They were not alone. She could feel it in her bones.

"When we get to the summit . . . ," Lalo started, but she hushed him.

"Lean in closer to me if you have something to say," she whispered. Hearing him speak, feeling his body vibrate against her, eased her mind.

Lalo pressed against her. They were almost cheek to cheek. "Like this?" he asked softly.

An explosion of goose pimples rippled over her skin. The hairs on her arms and neck stood on end.

"That'll do," she said, leaning into his warmth.

"When we get to the summit, the first thing we'll need to do is build a protection ring. Vampiros cannot cross a line of obsidian. We'll build the ring and use your blood to lure him out. Then I'll take the lover's blade that belonged to Vidal and strike him through. While he is caught off guard, you use Alma's blade to finish him."

"I'll be ready."

"I've no doubt, but know my main concern is to protect you at all costs."

The pit in her stomach grew. She shook her head. "Here I was judging you for being a monster when it was my family who started this whole mess."

"But it will be you to fix that."

"No, *we* will fix it."

When she was younger, she only cared about being the best hunter in Del Oro to prove her papá wrong. To show she was worthy, that he was mistaken for not believing in her. She didn't really care about helping anything but her own pride. It wasn't until Abuelo was slain that she truly understood the desperate hopelessness of loss. But even then, she'd only wanted to kill sedientos to make herself feel better, safer, and to establish herself as a fighter. Perhaps Papá had been right in holding her back. She wasn't ready to join the guard because she was selfish. And arrogant. And stubborn. How could she protect anyone when her heart was in the wrong place?

Abuelo had tried to tell her when he'd given her the reata for her birthday. He wished to remind her to be humble. She didn't want to hear it then. But Lalo had stumbled into her life and showed her what true goodness was, what true selflessness was. Since the very first day they met, he'd been trying to reverse the curse so his sister wouldn't live in fear from that wretch of a woman Maricela. Now Carolina knew he was doing it for her and her family, too.

And she loved him for it.

The horse followed her lead up a craggy path. From the map she'd stolen from her papá's office, this was the way to the tip of Devil's Spine.

A strange, sizzling sound came from ahead. She narrowed her eyes and peered into the darkness. Their horse whinnied and suddenly reared back.

"Hold on!" Carolina yelled. But Lalo's arms didn't squeeze around her tight enough and he tumbled off the back of the gelding. Carolina struggled to regain control but caught a glimpse at what had startled her horse. The dirt trail they were on was moving just a few steps ahead. Undulating and lapping like a small lake. Something fizzled to the top and a bubble burst with a hiss.

"What in the saints?" Lalo asked while dusting off his bottom.

"Lago del fuego," she said. "Boiling-hot quicksand."

"Of course it is!" His voice had raised in pitch. "What else shall we come across? Evil mushrooms? Snakes with three heads?!"

"Lalo, lower your voice," she warned.

"Or what?" He raised his hands. "What else can possibly go wrong? If we move in the wrong direction this way, we will be drowned in burning sand. But we cannot go back because wolves the size of wagons wish to devour me. Oh, and then there's Maricela too. And Vidal. And . . ." He stopped short as his voice broke.

"What? And what, Lalo?"

His chin wobbled. "I've been fighting for air since the moment my parents were murdered. And every time I get close to the surface, every time I think I might finally break through, something even more terrible comes. I have been turned into the very thing I hate most. I was hunted and stabbed and shot. I killed! Day and night, I dream of the lives I took. I have nightmares about leaving my baby sister to fend for herself. And now there's you, too." He shook his head. "I can't do it. I can't take another step. It's too much. I can't lose you, Carolina. Not when we've only just found each other."

Carolina inhaled deeply. "We won't lose each other, Lalo. We will make it through this."

"You don't understand. I won't be going back with you."

"What?" The horse shifted under her as she tensed. "What are you talking about?"

His face twisted with anguish. "When we sever the ties between Vidal and Tecuani, it won't only kill Vidal and undo the curse. Any sediento born of his blood will fall, too. Without him, there will be nothing to bind us to this realm anymore."

Dear Gods, she had asked him about this when he first told her his plan, but he seemed so unconcerned, she just assumed it was because he wasn't worried about anything happening to him.

"How long have you known?" she asked.

"I've always hoped it wouldn't be so, but every journal or book I've read about those given new life because of Tecuani leads to the same conclusion. Kill the original sediento, and the rest will fall."

"And yet you still fought so hard to find Vidal and the daggers that would kill him? Why? Why come all this way just to die?"

"Because I want Fernanda to be safe. I killed Maricela's children. Journeying here was the only way I could ensure Fernanda would never have to look over her shoulder again."

341

"Then continue for her. And for me. But do not give up, Lalo. Do not forfeit your life. Because I . . ." She palmed her chest as the scope of his heartbreak befell her. He had endured endless tortures for his sister's sake. But he wouldn't anymore. At least, not alone. "I love you, Lalo. And I need you here. Your sister and I need you here. Do you understand? There must be a way for you to survive this. I will find a way, and you will not give up because I cannot face this world without you."

"Lina," he whispered.

A sob escaped her. Abuelo had been the only other one to call her that, but it sounded so effortless from Lalo's lips.

"Maybe it is selfish of me to beg for you to not give up when you've been through so much," she said. "But life isn't something one just eases through. Life is a constant battle. Every moment of peace, every smile, every kiss that is worth a damn must be earned. So fight with me, Lalo. And if you are too weary from everything you've already been through, then I'll raise my fists and fight for us both."

Lalo held her gaze as black tears slid down his cheeks. He quickly wiped them away. "I pity anyone who stands against you."

Carolina laughed through her sorrows. "Me too."

"And I pity myself for having to spend the last five minutes listening to you two," a sultry voice taunted.

Lalo's eyes widened before his body jerked back and disappeared into the shadows. Shock filled every morsel of Carolina's flesh. She dug her heels into the horse and pounded after her love.

"Lalo!" she screamed.

She could hear his curses. Could hear the panic in his voice.

"Hold on!" Carolina bellowed.

Something slammed hard into Carolina's body. Her hands

tore away from the reins, and she tumbled off her horse and onto the hard earth. The air in her lungs whooshed out of her body. Her back skidded against rock and thistle, and she gritted her teeth to hold in a shriek.

A sediento with long red hair and gleaming eyes climbed over her body. Maricela, the woman from the tradesmen party. Lalo's maker. She grabbed Carolina's wrists and slammed them over her head and into the ground.

"So nice to see you again, Carolina." Maricela grinned.

Carolina tried to free herself, but the woman's grip was bone-crushingly strong. "I'd say it is nice to see you too, but it isn't. In fact, I may as well tell you exactly how I feel about you, you coldhearted, ugly beast."

Maricela clicked her tongue. "Don't be ridiculous, amor. I am far from ugly." Her gaze flicked to somewhere just beyond Carolina's line of sight. "I really should thank you for bringing me back to Del Oro, Eduardo. It has been a long time since I have been home, and I nearly forgot how delicious it truly is."

Home? What was Maricela talking about?

"Let her go, Maricela," Lalo shouted. "Your quarrel is with me. I killed your children in the cantina. Me. This has nothing to do with Carolina."

"That is where you are wrong." Her gaze snapped to Carolina. "She has pure and sacred Fuentes blood, that of our mother and father." She grinned and turned her head toward Lalo. "It is probably why you think you've fallen so hard for her. But it isn't Carolina you want. The life force thrumming inside her veins calls to you."

"You know nothing of love," Lalo spat.

"Love is a curse. Just look at what has happened to the Fuenteses because of it." She squeezed her claws deeper into Carolina's

343

wrists. "Alma's love cursed an entire bloodline. Everyone is damned. She gave Tecuani the souls of her descendants as payment for her beloved. The golden gates to el Cielo will not open for a Fuentes. They are confined to the Forest of Souls, doing Tecuani's bidding forevermore. It is only by Vidal's grace and affection that a Fuentes may live on. He turns those that are worthy. He keeps their souls in this realm."

Did that mean Abuelo's soul hadn't found peace? He was trapped in Tecuani's forest, serving the hunter of hearts instead of finding Abuela in el Cielo.

"Now." Maricela's eyes suddenly blazed like embers. "Let's see how la niña tastes. I am so very thirsty."

Carolina squirmed underneath Maricela. She kicked out her legs and thrust her shoulders, but the vampiro's hold was unyielding.

"You won't best me, Carolina Fuentes. I know your tricks. I've been watching you since I arrived. Waiting for my chance to strike."

"Get on with it then," Carolina growled.

Maricela chuckled. "You certainly have the Fuentes arrogance." The sediento revealed razor-sharp fangs.

"No!" Lalo roared. "Do not harm her. Please! Please!"

"Shut him up!" Maricela snapped to the sediento holding Lalo at bay.

Lalo's muffled cries echoed through the night. Carolina fought to free herself, but she couldn't break away. A small gasp escaped her lips as Maricela sank her teeth into Carolina's throat.

Terror coursed through her. She tried to scream but everything from her head to her toes had gone numb. Gritting her teeth, she ordered her limbs to move, to do anything, but they would not listen.

This couldn't be how her life ended. She could not get so close to ridding the world of these bastards only to be taken down by the monster who turned Lalo. It wasn't fair. He'd already watched his parents get slaughtered. She wouldn't let him see her die too.

Something sizzled to her right. She dragged her attention to the ground. The writhing sand was only inches away. If she could just get the sediento off her. If she could just . . .

A chupasangre howled in the distance, rumbling through the night. The vampiro jerked up. Her glowing eyes scanned the forest. Carolina took her chance. She forced her body to move.

She shoved her numb feet under herself and used her leg muscles to lift up the sediento. The momentum flung Maricela forward. She released her hold on Carolina's wrist to catch herself. With her arms free, Carolina clamped them around the vampiro's waist and used her strength to scoot her bottom up. With a better position, she dug her elbow into Maricela's arm. Maricela buckled and Carolina sent them rolling toward el lago del fuego.

A bubbling hiss fizzled up and then a fiery burst exploded from the quicksand. Maricela screamed when her foot sank into the burning sinkhole. She attempted to yank out her leg, but el lago del fuego only pulled her in deeper.

Carolina attempted to scramble away, but Maricela snatched her by the ankle. She kicked out, slamming her boot into Maricela's face, but the two women kept inching deeper into el lago. Carolina could already feel the scorching heat emanating from it. She reached out and grabbed on to anything she could. Her fingers scraped over dirt and stone and fallen leaves until they snagged on an exposed root.

"Lalo!" she screamed.

"I'm coming!" he roared. He clashed with the vampiro holding him captive. Lalo's claws slashed through the air. His fangs dug into flesh. But the vampiro he faced was thrice his size.

Maricela shrieked. Half her torso was now inside the quicksand. Carolina's fingers slipped from the root, and she skidded back.

"Lalo!"

The sediento Lalo battled thumped to the dirt. Lalo yanked one of the lover's daggers from the dead sediento's chest and stalked forward, hatred glowing in his eyes. He raised his arm and threw the dagger. The blade pierced Maricela's neck.

Maricela's head fell back, and her hold on Carolina's ankle released. With a cry of relief, Carolina crawled away.

Lalo ran past her toward el lago del fuego.

"What are you doing?" Carolina yelled.

He skidded to a stop at the very rim of the quicksand and reached out. His fingers wrapped around the hilt of the dagger and he jerked it free. Lalo stumbled back and landed hard on his bottom beside Carolina just as Maricela's head and red hair were devoured.

"Holy shit," he panted. He turned to Carolina. "I killed her. The beast who murdered my parents is gone."

Carolina reached out and grasped his hand, ignoring the aches screaming through her body.

He shook his head. "I . . . I thought I'd feel relieved. But my mother and father are still gone. Her death doesn't change that."

"No," Carolina said. "But now there is one less vampiro trying to end us before we reach Vidal. Two, if you count the oaf you also killed. Besides, Maricela was a real bitch."

Lalo chuckled. "Truer words have never been spoken."

A deep howl rumbled through the air. Birds that had been roosting in the trees above took flight.

"The chupasangres are coming," she said.

Lalo nodded. "And who knows what other sedientos might be heading this way?"

Slowly, they stood. She started forward but her knees gave out. Lalo's hand caught her.

"What is it? Is it your ankle?"

She shook her head. "The bite," she gritted her teeth. "It burns."

"Saints," he whispered. His thumb grazed over the wound.

Carolina hissed. The sensation felt like a thousand knives digging into her skin.

Lalo bent down and licked her burning flesh. His warm tongue slipped over her. But no relief came.

"It's not working," he cried.

He tried again.

"You aren't healing."

Her veins felt as if they were on fire. "What is happening to me?"

Lalo sucked in a breath. "You drank my blood."

She gripped his arms as hard as she could, but it was barely a pinch. "What are you saying?"

"You . . ." His eyes met hers, so full of sorrow. "You're turning."

"What? No. That can't be." Her chest, shoulder, and arm burned as if the bite was lava seeping down her body. She gritted her teeth. "How long until I become a sediento?"

"Depends on the person. It's faster when the body is already dead, but the power of Tecuani unleashed with her bite will stop your heart eventually. The process could take a week. Could be days." He paled. "Could be hours."

A howl sounded again. This time terribly close.

"We must go," she whispered. "I see a path through the lago del fuego just ahead."

Carolina tried to get up, but pain exploded through her body.

"Here." Lalo gently put his arms around her and eased her up, holding her against him.

She cried out in agony.

"I know," he whispered. "I'm sorry."

Bushes rustled in the distance. A voice roared with fury. "Carolina!"

They both gasped. Papá had found them.

From the diary of Maria Rosario
(Alma Rosario Fuentes's mother)

We draped her body in her favorite flowers, star lilies. My dearest daughter was as beautiful as the pearl-white flowers she adored, but now she is gone. When she was first brought back to Del Oro, I could hardly recognize her. Her skin was so pale. And she looked like a hollow husk of herself. The men who carried her body to the church said there had been blood on her lips and puncture marks on her throat. We do not know what happened in the forest or why she went out there at all. I can only pray my Alma did not suffer long. My only solace is that she will be with her beloved Vidal in el Cielo soon.

CHAPTER 45

Lalo

THEY BARRELED UP THE MOUNTAIN AS FAST AS THE HORSE COULD go with two riders clinging on to his back and tree roots growing thicker underfoot like angry spiderwebs. The trunks and branches of the great oaks twisted and stretched at odd angles, making a clear path impossible to find.

Lalo urged on the horse, cutting left and right. He held on to Carolina with all his might, watching in horror as she writhed in torment.

"How much farther?" she asked through her clenched jaw.

He wasn't sure. Lalo knew they needed to reach the peak of Devil's Spine, but that was all the information he had.

A tiny clump of pink and white flowers caught his gaze, a shock against the deep green moss and black trunks. "Star lily."

His mind scoured over everything he had read. Alma's body

had been found in a field of star lilies. And the lover's daggers both had engravings with star lilies on the blades.

Was it a coincidence? Fate? A small ache thrummed in Lalo's chest. Had Vidal planted fresh flowers here? Might the original sediento still have some of his humanity left?

A shadow bolted through the trees. Then another.

"We have company," Lalo said.

"Here." Carolina pulled her revolver from its holster. "I haven't wanted to use this because I didn't want to alert anyone of our location, but I think we are past that now."

Lalo took it.

"Remember to—"

"I know, Carolina," he said. "I've done this before."

"Don't get cocky now."

Hope filled his chest. If she could tease him, it meant she wasn't completely lost to the poison eating away at her life force.

"Can you hold on to the horse's mane yourself?" he asked.

Her hands reached forward, and she clasped the coarse hair.

A chupasangre bounded onto the path behind them. Its glowing eyes focused. Its snout frothed. When it drew closer, the beast leapt forward. Lalo pointed at the monster's chest and fired. The chupasangre exploded in smoke.

"There's a fork within the trees ahead!" Carolina yelled.

Lalo's attention snapped forward. Left seemed less ominous by far. He could see a bit of moonlight filtering in from the canopy. The vegetation was sparser and less inclined to tear them apart. The right of the fork was darker and a much tighter squeeze. Bare branches stretched like witches' fingers, ready to pick them apart.

There was no way they could bring the horse in. But the star lilies sprouted at the mouth of the right fork.

"We go right!" he hollered. "We have to dismount and run for it!"

"Carolina!" Señor Fuentes's voice reverberated around them.

What would he do if he saw his daughter had been bitten? Would he cut her down on the spot?

Something blasted from behind them. A bullet whizzed right past Lalo's ear.

"They're trying to shoot us!" he yelled.

"It's a warning," she said. "If they were trying to hit us, we would have holes in us already."

The horse skidded to a stop just before the path split into two. Lalo hopped off the back and helped her down. He eased her against a tree and set to work loosening the knots that held the satchel with their supplies in place.

Another bullet screamed through the air. This time, it sank deep into Lalo's shoulder.

He gasped at the sudden shock of fire eating away at his muscle.

"No!" Carolina screamed. She shoved off the trunk and limped toward him, grabbing him by the shoulder.

He howled.

"Bloody hell, Carolina!"

"I'm sorry!" She pressed her hands over his body, searching for the wound. "I thought you'd been hit in the heart."

"My shoulder. It's just my shoulder."

She breathed a sigh of relief. "Thank the gods."

"Thank the gods?" he cried, his tone incredulous. "I've been shot! Again!"

"And I've just been bitten by a damn vampiro. We will both survive, remember? You and I, we keep on fighting."

He opened his mouth to rebut but jerked his attention toward the woods behind them. Voices tumbled through the thicket. More gun blasts rocketed.

Lalo and Carolina ducked. But the bullets weren't aimed in their direction.

"They must be shooting at the chupasangres trying to get to me," he panted.

"Now's our best chance to run," Carolina said. "Can you move?"

"Yes," he rasped. The blood he'd drank from her earlier was still working its magic on him. He could feel the wound sealing itself at that very moment. But the bullet was lodged into his bone and the wooden fragments kept the power within him from working to its full potency.

He draped Carolina's arm over his uninjured shoulder. Together, they hobbled toward the dark woods that resembled a nightmare come to life.

CHAPTER 46

Carolina

As THEY SCRAMBLED FARTHER UP THE PATH, THE ROOTS UNDERFOOT disappeared. Her boots crunched on something that shifted under her weight. She couldn't see a thing with no moonlight to guide her.

"What are we stepping on?" she asked.

"You don't want to know."

Chills crawled up her spine like tiny spiders. "Tell me, Lalo."

"They're bones, Carolina. We are stepping on human bones."

She gulped. "There must be hundreds of remains here."

"He's been a sediento for generations."

"Because of my family. *We* are the true monsters."

"All of us are monsters in one form or another," Lalo said. "Perhaps the vampiros are a physical representation of that, but humans can be just as ugly on the inside. Your ancestors weren't evil for acting on love."

"But Alma . . ?"

"Alma was just a woman who was grieving."

"She ruined generations of lives, Lalo."

"I suppose. But I don't think I can judge her because, now that I have loved romantically, I don't know what I'd do if I lost you."

Tears pricked her eyes.

Carolina wished she could kiss Lalo at that moment. She wished she could hold him so tight the world would slip away, taking with it their sorrows too. But her gaze caught on blue light filtering in from the moon ahead. "We're almost to a clearing."

"With all the ruckus we've caused, Vidal must know we are coming by now," Lalo said. "He might be waiting for us at the end of this tunnel."

"Then we'll be ready for him." With shaking fingers, she held up the ruby-embellished dagger that belonged to Alma.

Lalo raised the blade that they'd found in Vidal's grave.

They'd meet the original vampiro and end this misery for good. But what of Lalo? Carolina hadn't had time to think of ways to save him and now it was too late.

She stopped moving.

"What is it?" he whispered.

"Blood is a powerful thing, no?" she said.

"I think we've already established that."

She rolled her eyes. "Give me your palm."

"What?"

"Just do it."

Carolina reached out in the dark until she found his hand. She took the dagger and sliced into his skin.

Lalo hissed. "Have I not experienced enough abuse already today?"

"Hush." She offered her hand to him. "Now you do it to me."

"Carolina . . . really . . ?"

"There is power in blood and vows," she said. "We make a promise here and now that we will find each other again. No matter what happens, you will return to me. We have believed in each other enough to get us this far, let's not stop now."

Without another word spoken, Lalo sliced into her palm.

Carolina took his hand in hers. "We are meant to be, Lalo Villalobos."

"Forever."

She smiled and intertwined their fingers. "I like the sound of that."

"Though, we should really talk about your bossiness."

"Me? Bossy?"

They started for the clearing. They were beat up and tired but at least they had hope.

Lalo started to speak. "When we reach—"

The ground beneath them shifted suddenly. Lalo shoved Carolina back before plunging into a massive pit below.

She scrambled from her ass to her hands and knees and screamed his name. Her voice reverberated into the expanse. She leaned forward waiting for him to call out for her, but only an echo of her voice came back.

"Lalo!" she screamed again. "Lalo!"

She heard nothing.

Glowing torchlight bounced off the brambles behind her. Carolina spun around and gasped. Her father and his men had finally caught up.

From the journal of Jonathan Monroe of Santemala

A fully fed vampiro is a terrible thing to behold.

CHAPTER 47

Lalo

BONES AND ROCKS CRUMBLED ON TOP OF HIS BODY AS HE crashed into hard earth, sealing him in a dusty tomb.

"Carolina," he rasped, the sound less than a whisper.

She'd never hear him. Not from underneath so much rubble.

Lalo shoved at the stones crushing him. He pushed and dug and clawed his way out. As he thrust the last rock off his chest, he assessed the scene before him.

He was in a massive cavern. Limestone walls curved upward, revealing various pockets like the one he'd fallen through. Moonlight trickled in from above. If his body weren't screaming with pain, he'd be able to scale up the stones.

"No!" he heard Carolina cry. "Leave me be!"

Her father's shouts of anger echoed off the walls.

"Don't touch me!" Carolina shrieked.

Gritting his teeth, Lalo tried to get up. He had to get to her.

He had to explain to her father what was going on. If he could explain to Señor Fuentes what he was, could show him there was a way to end vampiros for good, then surely he'd see the amazing feats his daughter had made to save them all and he'd want to help her instead of controlling her.

He opened his mouth, ready to call after Señor Fuentes and his family when a gravelly voice cut through the darkness.

"What do we have here?"

Lalo froze.

Glowing eyes broke through the darkness. A slender figure slinked into view. He wore breeches and a simple shirt but nothing more. His black hair was pulled back and tied at the nape of his neck. If it weren't for the blood-red irises, he might look like nothing more than a young man not much older than Lalo himself.

The vampiro knelt beside Lalo. He sniffed. "Why has one of Maricela's children come to my lair?"

Shock tore through Lalo. "You know my maker?"

The sediento chuckled. "I am her sire. Yours too, my boy."

So this was Vidal. In Lalo's mind, he'd always pictured some beastly fiend with a snarling maw. But this man appeared as human as Maricela did. He was evidently well fed. Lalo couldn't even fathom the number of souls he'd taken and discarded over the centuries.

He needed to die.

Lalo reached into his pocket. His stomach plummeted when he realized he'd lost the lover's dagger. It must have slipped from his grasp during the fall.

Voices raised from above, but they were growing fainter.

Vidal's head snapped skyward. His fangs glistened in the

darkness. "You have brought me offerings, I see. Maricela is often charitable with her gifts. She has always been a dear child to me."

An almost gleeful purr rumbled from his throat. Vidal slowly rose, his nails expanding into claws. He was going to hunt Carolina and her family. Lalo couldn't let that happen. Not without warning.

"Wait!" he yelled.

Vidal stopped. "You dare speak to your maker with such insolence? I am hundreds of years old, boy. I can snap your neck in the time it takes your pitiful heart to beat once."

"I do not fear you, Vidal," Lalo said. And, to his surprise, he meant every word. He was not afraid of some monster. Or what that monster could do to him. What truly terrified Lalo, above all else, was leaving this beautiful world worse off than when he'd entered it, was leaving Carolina and her family without a chance to fight back. If he was going to die tonight, he would at least help the girl he loved first.

"I will end you like I ended Maricela," Lalo said.

A growl came from the original sediento. "What did you say?"

"I killed your child. I sank my blade deep into her throat."

Vidal turned his full body to Lalo.

Gone was any hint of humanity. Only a vampiro stood before Lalo now. A vicious killer ready to tear into its prey. *Good*, Lalo thought, *let him keep his focus here and not on Carolina*. Perhaps she'd have a chance to prepare her family for what was coming.

"Maricela deserved it," Lalo taunted, seeing the fiery wrath in Vidal's eyes. "And you will meet a similar fate."

Viper fast, Vidal struck. He sank his fangs into Lalo's shoulder and drank him in. Lalo clenched his jaw, dug his claws into Vidal, but the sediento didn't budge. Vidal searched for Maricela in his memories. He would not have to go back far.

Vidal ripped his fangs from Lalo's flesh.

"You killed her!" he hissed, his mouth dripping with saliva and Lalo's blood.

"And I would do it again!" Lalo spat.

Vidal threw up his arms and roared. Lalo's skull felt like it might cave in.

Come, he heard in the recesses of his mind. *Come, my children. They killed your sister.*

Vidal was calling his sedientos to him.

Lalo had to cut off his maker's summons before every blasted sediento in Abundancia heard his command. He sank his claws and fangs into the vampiro. As the two sedientos collided with rage, three words tore from Lalo's lips, "Vidal is here!"

CHAPTER 48

Carolina

"Let go of me!" Carolina screamed to her papá's back as his men dragged her from the path and toward their horses. "I said, let me go, you traitor!"

Papá whirled around, ferocious fury shaking his face. "How dare you!"

"How dare *I*?" Carolina bellowed.

"Yes!" Papá roared. "I had to learn from Rafael that you brought a devil into my home! You welcomed him in, with your little brothers, with your expecting mamá, your tías and tíos who could not defend themselves. You put our family in danger. You pretended to be his lover. For what? For what, mija?! To hurt me?"

She shook her head "No! I wanted to keep our pueblo safe from sedientos. I wanted to prove myself as a hunter but so many things got in the way."

Carolina couldn't deny how selfish she had been, but he had been selfish too. All the Fuenteses had been.

"I was wrong to go behind your back, Apá. And I'm sorry for that. But I am glad I did because I learned the truth."

Her father blinked with confusion.

"The sedientos aren't the only enemy here. They aren't the only monsters we face."

"What are you talking about, Carolina?" Papá asked.

"Alma Rosario Fuentes, *our* ancestor, is responsible for the vampiros plaguing our lands. She called the god of souls to this realm and begged him for her husband, your great-great-grandfather, back. She went against the laws of nature and struck a deal with Tecuani. He brought Vidal from the Land of Souls, but Vidal was no longer the man she loved. No longer a Fuentes. He was a monster."

Her uncle Domingo's brow furrowed with confusion. "Gods do not intervene in the ways of humans."

"But they will if that human offers them something in return."

Tío Domingo turned toward her father. "What is she talking about?"

Anger laced through Carolina. Why look to Papá when she was right here, explaining everything? Would they never believe in her?

"Vidal was created with Tecuani's power and Alma's blood," she explained. "Why do you think attacks are more rampant here than anywhere else in Abundancia? Because *she* damned us, out of desperation. She promised Tecuani her descendants' souls. We are either made into vampiros or stuck in purgatory, never allowed out of Tecuani's forest. Abuelo is not in el Cielo. He is trapped in the Forest of Souls."

"Carolina, stop!" Papá ordered, but she continued.

Fiery pain shot from her head to her toes. The wound on her neck throbbed. But she couldn't let the agony distract her from what needed to be said. "Our forefathers knew what she did but kept her secret hidden. All this time we could have sought a way to end these monsters but failed to because our forefathers would rather let people die than expose our family's dirty sins."

"It isn't as simple as you think, mija, we did not know what we were facing."

Her eyes widened. "So you knew?"

"What I knew is that I had to protect my people."

"Yet so many still died. You didn't see what befell primo Lorenzo. His humanity had been stripped as un vampiro. Lalo and I have come here to end what the other Fuenteses could not." Her mouth had gone dry. Her throat desperate for drink. "We must end this, Apá." She shoved her braid back, revealing the raw bite marks on her skin. "Or I am dead, too."

Carolina would never forget the absolute devastation twisting her papá's features.

"No," he whispered. "Please, saints, no." Tears welled in his eyes. "Not you. Not my baby girl."

"Lalo and I can fix this. If you would just help me get to him, we can explain everything. We can—"

A roar echoed from where Lalo had fallen into the cavern below. Carolina gasped.

"Lalo!"

She shoved the men holding her and started to run back toward the fork in the forest but was caught by her papá.

Tears raced down his cheeks. His chin quivered.

"Mija, I . . ." His eyes roamed over her face. "I can't lose you."

"Apá, we must help him."

Faintly, she thought she heard Lalo scream.

"Let me go, Apá! Please!"

A thunderous crash came from deep in the woods. Trees snapped. Branches fell like boulders to the ground. The horses whinnied and reared back in fright.

"Arms ready!" Papá ordered. He released her and stepped back, pulling out his prized double-barrel shotgun. "Get behind me, Carolina."

Her family drew their swords.

"Let me fight with you, Apá."

"I said, get behind me!"

She wanted to argue but now wasn't the time. And why should she anyway? Carolina knew what she could do. She didn't have to prove her worth to him anymore.

The reata Abuelo gave her had been lost at some point during their flight from the chupasangres, but the rope was just an item, some *thing;* she had a lifetime of memories with him to last her through. But she remembered what he had said to her just before she lost him. *"The kind of weapon doesn't bring us triumph, Lina. The ferocity of the person who wields it does. Believing in yourself and what you are capable of is sometimes enough on its own."*

He had been right.

She was a fighter. And she would not fail. Regardless of what her papá thought.

Carolina still had Alma's dagger in her grasp. She held it before her, even though her neck and shoulder screamed with fire.

A dozen figures burst through the brush. Vampiros dressed in clothing from bygone times charged toward Carolina and her family with their fangs and claws bared. The sound of their snarling hisses filled her ears and chilled her to the bone.

"This is for Maricela!" one of them roared.

The obsidian blades crafted by the Fuentes family clashed with the monsters who thirsted for their blood. They sliced and fought and kicked, killing and cutting down anything that stood before them. Bullets rang out. Screams ripped through the skies.

One of the sedientos raced for Carolina's papá, who was too busy fighting off two other vampiros to notice. She bolted forward, pumping her arms with all her might. She didn't dare throw the lover's blade; she didn't want to risk losing it. So she dove after the beast and tackled it at the knees.

Claws raked over her skin. She screamed, but she didn't dare let go.

A gun went off, and the vampiro's body slackened.

Papá's face came into view. His skin was drained of its color, sweat dripped down his temples. "You saved me," he said, his voice hardly audible over the chaos.

"Of course I did. You're my father."

He reached down, pulled her up.

He stared at the body. "If you hadn't been there, this beast would have taken me to the ground." His eyes flicked to her. "I . . . I am sorry, mija. I . . ."

Carolina shook her head. She didn't need her papá's apologies. What she deserved was his respect.

"More are coming!" Tío Vicente yelled.

"We fight together," she said. Papá blinked, then nodded. He unsheathed his short sword and offered it to her. Carolina grasped it with a smile.

She and Papá turned back-to-back. They held their weapons ready, protecting one another in battle for the first time. This had been the very thing she'd always wanted but she'd never expected it to be like this. She'd never expected to be so afraid, so tired, so damn worried for the soul of the boy she loved.

An angry snarl reverberated through the trees. One of her cousins bellowed before his voice cut off altogether.

"Martín!" her tío Malaquías roared.

Another cousin cried out on the opposite side of her. He fell to his knees, holding his stomach.

"What is it?" Papá yelled. "Do you see anything?"

"No." Whatever it was, it wove in and out of the forest with inhuman speed.

Dread took hold of Carolina.

Only one sediento was so powerful it could move in the blink of an eye. They had found Vidal.

Or perhaps he had found them.

"¡Ayúdame!" Tío Domingo cried out as more sedientos broke through the woods.

Something landed at the very center of the battle. A large body crouching low and predatorial like a jaguar. Like the god who had created him.

"Vidal," she whispered.

When he stood to his full height, he towered over Papá.

Papá raised his gun and pulled the trigger. But the sediento was far too quick. He was gone in an instant, the bullet smashing into a nearby tree. The next moment, the vampiro stood before

Carolina's father. His veiny hands grabbed her papá by the throat and lifted him over his head.

"No!" Carolina shrieked.

She raised her arm and smashed the lover's dagger into Vidal's back. The blade cut through muscle and tissue, but she had missed his heart. She tore the dagger out. Vidal screeched. His hold on Papá faltered. He threw his arm behind him, smacking his backhand hard against Carolina's cheek and flicking her away like a bug.

Carolina rolled through the dirt. The wails of her dying loved ones burned into her ears.

She shoved herself up and cried out as her father and her family fought for their lives against their ancestor and his unnatural bloodline.

Hands grabbed her shoulders. She spun. Her dagger was ready.

"It's me!"

A sob escaped Carolina. Lalo's clothing was ripped and torn to bits. But he was alive.

She wrapped her arms around him. "Where have you been?"

"Fighting like hell to get back to you." Lalo squeezed once, then eased her back. "I lost this when I plummeted down the sinkhole." He raised the emerald-adorned dagger. "But I have it now. It's time."

Papá stumbled, falling hard on his rear, his rapier swiping through the air to defend himself against Vidal. Blood trickled down the side of Papá's face. Deep gashes cut through his cheek and chin. Her uncle had been felled beside him. Meanwhile, the monsters seemed to multiply by the minute.

"We're heavily outnumbered," she said. "What if we all fall here and now?"

Lalo's gaze found hers. "I won't let anyone hurt you again."

Papá grunted in pain. A low growl escaped Lalo. Claws elongated from his nail beds. "Let us end this beast for good." He lunged forward.

Lalo jumped and climbed onto Vidal's back just before the wretch could land a killing blow to Papá. From behind, he dug into Vidal's face. Vidal reached up and gripped Lalo by his collar. He flung him hard over his head, slamming Lalo into the dirt beside Carolina's father.

Vidal glared at Papá. "My Fuentes bloodline has come to smite me." His voice was gargled, as if he drank down acid. His heated gaze flicked to Lalo. "I shall wipe you traitors out of existence for this. My one question is, which of you dies first?"

Lalo tried to rise, but a bone was jutting out of his arm. Vidal set his sights on him.

He launched for Lalo.

"No!" Carolina screamed. She dove between them. She would not let Vidal take her love.

Her back slammed into the dirt. Something hard and unyielding dug into her belly as Vidal's body crashed into hers. She wheezed, her lungs expelling the last of their air.

Vidal's teeth glistened with blood. But his glowing eyes were the only things she could focus on.

At that very moment, Carolina felt as if she could break apart entire worlds to save Lalo. She would tear this realm to shreds to have him nearby.

That kind of love was dangerous, all-consuming. If sedientos were monsters, it was only because Alma's love for Vidal was more monstrous than anything on earth. There was no definitive right or wrong. There was only love and the aftermath that came.

"I understand," she whispered. It was all she could manage, the tiniest of sighs. "I'm sorry for what you and Alma lost."

Vidal blinked. Something like surprise flickered over his features.

"You and Alma loved each other so fiercely, but your love story was cut short. I am sorry that time was stolen from you."

And she meant it. Time was the most powerful and frightening force because it could not be controlled. Alma was asking for more time. Carolina could no longer blame her for that because she wanted that with Lalo, too.

"She loved you ferociously."

The devastation etched on his face nearly brought tears to Carolina's eyes.

Movement pulled her attention to just behind Vidal. She held her features steady as Lalo raised a gleaming blade above Vidal's back.

"Time to find your love once again," she whispered.

As Lalo brought one of the lover's blades down, Carolina used the last of her strength to lodge the other dagger deep into Vidal's heart. She did not miss.

Her ancestor sucked in a breath. The light in his glowing eyes burned so bright, Carolina flinched. But just as fast as the light shone, it fizzled away, leaving only the bottomless brown of his irises. He let out a deep sigh before slumping on top of Carolina.

Burning heat rushed through Carolina as she felt the power of Tecuani inside her blood start to dissolve. She gritted her teeth to seal in her cries but couldn't hold them back. She screamed until her throat could no longer bear it. But she was whole. She was alive. Maricela's bite had not fully taken hold of her, and she'd not yet succumbed to the thirst.

Shrieks split open the skies. The sedientos surrounding them were falling one by one. They were dying. The vampiros were dying!

Carolina jolted.

Where was Lalo?

With a sob, she shoved Vidal's dead body to the side. She scrambled to her hands and knees and crawled toward the boy she loved. He squirmed and howled.

Shakily, she grabbed him and pulled his body against hers.

"Carolina," he managed. "It hurts."

Papá edged to her side. "What's happening? Why are they dying?"

"The lover's blades. It was the only way to destroy Vidal, but with the power of Tecuani leaving their bodies, they're all dying too." She sobbed. "Stay with me, Lalo. Please. Remember our promise."

He grimaced. His body writhed within her grasp.

"I love you," he whispered.

And she knew this might be the final moment they saw each other in this life.

She gripped him tighter. Only a month ago she'd lost her abuelo. She held him just so. And now her Lalo was leaving her too.

She brushed a thumb over his beautiful cheek. "Find me when I move to the other side."

Tears slithered down his temples. "I won't rest until I do."

She is the sun.

—Pío Parra, *Una Canción Para Mi Amor*

CHAPTER 49

Lalo

"Kiss me before I go," he whispered.

"No," Carolina sobbed. "You can't leave me."

His heart was breaking. Smashing into a million pieces because of everything he had lost. But Lalo couldn't help but feel relieved too. He would no longer have to take someone's life in order to feed his. He would no longer have to devour and kill just to survive.

And everyone would be safe. Everyone would be all right.

He held on to that fact. He clung to it with everything he had.

Lalo leaned into her, ignoring the fire rushing through his veins. He sealed her cries within his own mouth.

As their bodies pressed against each other, he felt his heartbeat come to an end.

An explosion of light and energy surged between them. He

could have sworn it was the sun even though it was the middle of the night. How he missed the feel of it on his skin like this. Warm and not the cause of blistering agony. He opened his eyes and smiled as the heat of it slammed into him. Then everything went dark.

CHAPTER 50

Carolina

THE WORLD EXPLODED WITH SCORCHING LIGHT. A THOUSAND shrieks tore through the air, piercing her ears in the worst of ways. She screamed at the sheer force of their cries. At the utter torment of Lalo's blood still warm on her hands, but she would not let him go.

Just as fast as the brilliant light came, it disappeared, leaving the world around her blanketed in silent darkness.

Lalo's body went slack in her arms. She held him tight against her chest and howled with sorrow.

They'd done it. Lalo's wish of saving his sister, of ridding the world of his kind, her dream of wanting to keep her pueblo safe, had come true. But now his beautiful soul was gone.

A part of her wished to tear at the dirt. To claw her way into the underworld and find the boy who stole her heart. She could do it. She could use her blood and the lover's blade to bring him back to her. She could call Tecuani to her and make another deal. Lalo would never be like Vidal. But no, he wouldn't want that. And she'd never want him to suffer again.

Papá's arm wrapped around her shoulders, and she wept into his embrace. "Why did it have to be him? Why Lalo?"

A torch was struck. She saw her papá's face. There was no resentment in his eyes as she had expected, only sorrow. Her family limped toward her, clutching each other. But there were no sedientos alive to attack. They had all fallen. Their eyes had gone white. Their skin had been bleached of color. Their bodies had practically withered away.

She peered down at Lalo and cupped his cheek. "We did it."

She jolted. "He's still warm and his skin is still brown. What does this mean?" she asked her papá.

"I do not know," Papá admitted. He'd never not had an answer for her before.

Was there still a chance? Perhaps he hadn't been a sediento long enough? She'd been bitten and was still there. Perhaps he hadn't stolen enough human lives?

She clutched him tighter. "Lalo," she whispered. "Come back to me."

Anger surged within her. She could not be offered this spark of hope only to be devastated again.

"Come back, do you hear me? Come back, or I will never forgive you."

A PRAYER FOR THE DEPARTED

Be kind, Tecuani.
Grant us passage through the Forest of Souls.
Be gentle, Atzin.
Grant us safe travels through the River of Sorrows.
Be merciful, Itzmin.
Grant us sure-footedness through the Valley of
*   Remembrances.*
Be gracious, Tlali.
Grant us steadfastness to move through the Desert of
*   Iniquities.*
Be caring, Chipahua.
Grant us strength to climb the Mountain of
*   Retributions.*
Be understanding, Xipil.
Grant us permission to enter the gates to el Cielo.

CHAPTER 51

Lalo

DEATH WAS NOT WHAT HE EXPECTED. THERE WAS NO SCREAMING of tortured souls. There was no infinite doom. The world around him was quiet, peaceful, and smelled quite a bit like dog.

He was lying flat on his back. Grasses tickled his arms. Something sniffed loudly at his side. A warm snout nudged his shoulder. When Lalo opened his eyes, he shuddered. A chupasangre was hovering over his body.

Lalo scrambled to his feet. The beast simply tilted its head like a common pup. They stood in the center of a dense forest, one so similar to the one he'd gone through with Carolina only hours ago.

"The chupasangre know you do not belong here," a voice called from within the trees.

Lalo spun around but saw no one. "Here?" he yelled. "Where is here?"

"You are in Tecuani's territory now. The hounds protect the

Land of the Dead from the living. It is their duty to ensure only the truly departed may enter."

"But I *am* dead," he said.

"Her blood thrums inside you. Her love will not let you go."

"Carolina's?" Lalo gulped. "Does this mean . . ."

A man and woman holding hands stepped from behind the stretching branches. He recognized them at once. Alma Rosario Fuentes, a nearly identical match to her great-great-great-granddaughter, and Vidal Fuentes, more human than Lalo thought possible. Golden light haloed the lovers' bodies.

A cool breeze whispered about Lalo's skin as dozens of men and women slipped from behind the trees. He had seen many of these faces in the portraits hanging within the Fuentes casa. He was among Carolina's ancestors.

Chills rippled over his skin when a woman with red hair stepped through the throng. She was in a simple garment of black linen, something he would have seen people in el pueblo wearing decades ago.

"M-Maricela? What are you doing here?"

"I lost my way. There were so many voices, so many thoughts running through my mind from the lives I stole, I had all but forgotten who I was. Who my family was. I am sorry, Lalo. I . . ." She shook her head.

"You are a Fuentes," he whispered as he noticed the likeness among the relatives.

She looked at her hands and nodded.

He gazed at the faces surrounding him and saw so much of Carolina within them. His heart ached for his vampiro hunter.

He folded his arms against himself. "What does this mean?"

"That is up to you," Alma said. "You may cut the ties that bind you to Carolina. Your heart will stop, and the chupasangre will bring you to Tecuani's throne. He will decide if you may enter the Land of the Dead, where you will ultimately discover the gates to el Cielo. There, you will find nothing but peace and comfort."

He shifted his weight. His parents would be there. He would find the quiet and serenity that he always wanted. But that had been before he met Carolina Victoria Fuentes.

"Or," Vidal said, "you can climb through the veil and truly live."

Lalo stared at the ground. The crack between this world and that of the living was little more than a glistening vein in the soil.

"You must hurry," Alma urged. "Make your choice before Tecuani knows you have come, and it is too late. Stay here and find the harmony you once longed for or go back and experience a life full of dangers and joy."

A distant voice echoed through the forest. "Lalo. Come back to me."

Lalo's pulse thumped hard against his chest. He pressed his hand over his ribs.

"Come back, do you hear me? Come back, or I will never forgive you. I will wreak havoc on you in the afterlife. If you don't wake up, so help me, I will spit on your prized books."

He laughed and faced Alma and Vidal. "I think I know the answer."

The lovers smiled in unison.

"What will happen to you when Tecuani finds you?" Lalo asked. He had to know if their souls would find peace even after what they had done.

"I have been here for a long while now, waiting in the silent forest with my kin, doing whatever Tecuani asked, until someone was able to set us free," Alma said. "There are countless sins to be atoned for. Terrible hurts I caused. But the death curse has been broken. Thanks to you and my great-great-great-granddaughter, the souls of my descendants and all they've turned can finally move on."

Vidal looked down at his wife, at the woman who tore worlds apart just to be with him. "We are together now. We'll face whatever comes as one."

Alma smiled sadly, pressing deeper into her lover's body.

"Now go," Vidal said. "Live a full life for us."

Lalo nodded.

"Wait!" A large man with gray hair and a thick mustache jogged toward Lalo. He resembled Señor Fuentes so much so that Lalo knew this could only be one person.

"Abuelo?" he asked, almost feeling shy about using such a title.

The man smiled. "Sí. And you are the boy who captured mi nieta's heart."

Lalo chuckled. "I suppose I am. Though, I don't think she'd let anyone capture it. More like, I was offered it and threatened bodily harm if I let it go."

Abuelo laughed heartily. "That is my Lina." He wiped a single tear from his eye. "You tell Lina her abuelito is fine. Tell her I will be with her abuelita soon. Thanks to her stubbornness, and yours too, of course, I can now enter the gates to el Cielo. Tell her that she was always my special girl and to continue giving the world hell."

Lalo smirked. "I will, señor."

"Best hurry before she gets angrier."

"I will, señor."

Lalo dropped to his knees and began to claw at the dirt. He would get to her. He would find the girl he loved.

Brilliant light exploded behind the hoods of Lalo's eyes. He let out a groan and moved his arm to shield himself from the intense rays.

Something squeaked and tumbled to a hard floor. Hands grabbed him.

"Lalo?"

He tried to pry his lashes apart, but they were heavy, and everything was so damn bright.

"Lalo!"

A hand slapped across his cheek. It hurt. It hurt like the devil, really.

"Wake up, you damn fool!"

This had Lalo's eyes finally working. He blinked rapidly.

"The sun," he croaked. "Shut the curtains, Fernanda, or it will kill me."

"No, it won't, but I sure as hell feel like murdering you."

What was happening? Last thing he remembered was kissing Carolina goodbye and then . . . He shot up. His head spun in circles. Black dots flashed in his vision. But then everything cleared. There, beside him, in Tía Morena's gaudy room, sat Fernanda.

Her hand went to her chest. "Oh, thank the stars."

She smacked him hard in the shoulder.

"Ouch." Lalo rubbed his arm. "That hurt." He stopped. Grinned. "That *hurt*."

His fingers went to his jugular, feeling for a pulse. It was there. As strong and resilient as ever.

He smiled so hard his cheeks burned. "I'm alive!"

"I ought to slaughter you here and now for putting me through this." Fernanda was fuming red. Her hands were readying to smack him once more. "What were you thinking?"

"I didn't want to live out the rest of my days as a sediento. I wanted to protect you."

"So you decided to put yourself in grave danger?" She hit him again. And he gladly let her.

"Saints, that feels wonderful." He laughed with the whole of his chest and dodged another blow.

"How are you human again?" Fernanda asked. "None of this makes any sense."

Nothing did, truly. But that was the world he lived in. It was weird and mysterious and confusing. Messy and loud. And he would enjoy that always. Because he was alive. And he was in love.

Lalo threw the blankets off his body and jumped out of bed.

"Where is she?" he asked his sister.

Fernanda gasped and covered her eyes. "You can't go out without any pants on."

He was wearing nothing but a long nightdress with bears on it. A bit humiliating, but who cared?

"The hell I can't. Don't you know when to live a little?" He kissed his sister on the forehead. "Where is she?"

Fernanda's smile was as big and as cheerful as he'd seen it in months.

"She's in the garden."

"Thank you."

And with that, Lalo was gone.

He raced down the hallway. His heart thumped hard against his chest. Dozens of portraits whizzed by. The Fuentes ancestors could stare at his bare *human* ass all they wanted, but he had a feeling they were too busy making their way toward el Cielo.

Lalo turned toward the staircase that would lead him to Carolina. He took a deep, utterly human breath, then he smiled. "Time to find my love."

CHAPTER 52

Carolina

HE WAS GOING TO BE ALL RIGHT. SHE JUST KNEW IT. SHE AND HER family rode like the wind on their way back as soon as she felt a single thump of his pulse. Gone were the chupasangres and any hint of sedientos in the woods. She had nothing to do but to speak to him the entire journey home.

"You better come back to me, Lalo, or I will wreak havoc on you in the afterlife. If you don't wake up, so help me, I will spit on your prized books."

She didn't know how to speak sweetly, and she had a feeling he wouldn't recognize it was her if she did. So she kept threatening him until they laid him down to rest in his bed.

For a day and night, she and Fernanda had taken turns staying by his side. She read that ridiculous note he had left behind in the desk.

Carolina, I think I might like to kiss you, it said.

No. I really want to kiss you. Do not laugh at me for it. I find you utterly enchanting in every way possible. Had we more time together, I believe you would have come to love me as much as I fear I love you.

I know it is sudden but . . . "what is a few moments when our souls have known each other since the beginning of time?"

She grinned. He still quoted the sonnet wrong.

Carolina had laughed and cried over the note. She held it now as she paced in the garden.

Her energy was building, her irritation too. What if he didn't come back to her?

No, she wouldn't even let that thought grow in her mind. She would continue to hope.

She needed to focus on something else. She opened and closed her fist. It still ached from the night before. Rafa had slipped into Lalo's room while Carolina sat by his side. One look at Rafa's face and her annoyance bloomed. She stomped over to him and popped him in the nose.

"That is for trying to give Lalo my pony to ride," she'd said.

Carolina punched him again.

"That is for being a torment to the man I love," she'd added.

Rafa clamped a hand over his face. He held his other hand up in surrender. "Apologies!" he said through his fingers. "I came here to offer my apologies!"

A tiny bit of her vitriol had eased. "Why?"

"I was a selfish prick. I thought I could bully my way into being your husband, and it wasn't right. I am sorry, Carolina. Honest." His eyes flitted to Lalo's prone form. "I heard about how you two risked everything on the mountain. I . . . I came here to commend you for being braver than any of us ever could be."

When Rafa left, Carolina had cried some more. Lalo had been the brave one. He was best of them all.

She kicked a rock now, then watched it soar.

"Careful. Wouldn't want to stub your toe. I've heard it's rather painful."

Carolina froze. That voice. That was *his* voice.

She spun and gasped.

There, standing in nothing but a long child's shirt, was *her* Lalo.

"Are you real?" she whispered.

He grinned. And oh, what a beautiful grin it was.

"Why don't you come and see for yourself?"

Carolina let out a sound that was part scream, part cry and bolted for him. She jumped, wrapping her arms around his neck. His skinny legs buckled, and they tumbled into the grass.

He groaned, taking the brunt of her weight and force.

"Trying to kill me again, I see," he moaned, still grinning.

"You're . . . you . . ."

"I'm here. And I am very much alive. Thanks to you."

A sob escaped her. "You kept your promise! You came back to me!"

"I was too frightened not to."

"Very smart of you."

"Indeed."

She realized they were lying on the grass for anyone to see. But she didn't give a single damn about propriety.

"I'm going to kiss you, Lalo Villalobos."

"On one condition," he said.

"Anything. Anything at all."

"You marry me. Here, in the sun, with the ones we love and the ones we lost watching over us."

"Marry you?"

"Yes. I have pretended to court you for long enough. I want it to be real."

"You are a glutton for punishment."

"When it comes to you, I suppose so. Say yes. And then we will do whatever it is you wish. I'll even learn to properly ride a horse."

She narrowed her eyes. "You have become bossy now that you are human again."

"And you are still a tyrant."

"You have some nerve to speak to me in such a way after what you just put me through." She tilted her head up. "You know what? I don't think I need that kiss anymore." Smirking, she began to pull away.

Lalo's mouth opened in surprise. "But—"

His words were cut off as she brought her lips upon his.

He wrapped his arms tight around her, sealing their love in the warmest of embraces.

Slowly, she eased back. She wanted to see him up close, wanted to note the sun shimmering in his honey-colored eyes.

Lalo smiled. "What are you thinking at this very moment?"

"I'm thinking how wonderful it is to be alive."

He chuckled. "Me too."

Stars above, she loved this man.

"So? Will you marry me?" he asked, hope shimmering in his gaze. "Will you experience whatever the world has to offer with me, Carolina Victoria Fuentes? Will you dance with me always? Now, and when we're old and gray, and thereafter, when we find ourselves in el Cielo?"

She brushed her lips against his warm cheek as butterflies

twirled inside her stomach. "There's nothing I want more," she said. "My answer is a wholehearted yes."

Carolina brought her lips back to his.

It was a perfect kiss.

One that would last for a lifetime.

And into the next.

ACKNOWLEDGMENTS

I REMEMBER SOBBING WHILE WRITING THE ACKNOWLEDGMENTS for my debut novel, *Sinner's Isle*. I couldn't contain my emotions when I thought about how many people rallied around me and helped turn my dreams into a reality. Finding people who truly believe in you is a beautiful and life-changing thing. It's certainly sob-worthy.

Working on the acknowledgments for *A Cruel Thirst*, my sophomore book, has been a totally different experience. I'm still grateful and humbled, of course. But now, instead of tears, I'm all smiles. I'm jumping and dancing and forever proud.

Writing one book was hard. Writing a second book felt impossible most days.

But I did it.

With the support of my publishers, editor, agent, family, friends, and writing community, I did it.

And that's a cause for celebration.

A Cruel Thirst would not be the book it is today without my editor, Bria Ragin. Bria, I love how fierce you are. If I'm confident in my words, it's only because I know you've read them and approve. You are competitive and passionate and honest, and I love you for that. The sky isn't even the limit for you because there is no limit.

Nicola and David Yoon. Thank you for trusting me to write a second book! Your ideas and input are always spot on. Not only are you geniuses, but you have hearts of gold, too. I also love that I get to brag to everyone that I know you.

None of this would have been possible without my amazing agent, Larissa Melo Pienkowski. Larissa, I adore you. I value your passion for books and your undying loyalty to your clients. I couldn't ask for a better champion.

To the Random House team who helped bring the book to life—Wendy Loggia, Beverly Horowitz, Ken Crossland, Colleen Fellingham, Tracy Heydweiller, Tamar Schwartz—thank you.

I'd also like to thank my cover designer, Trisha Previte—you are a true visionary. And to my cover artist, Eevien Tan, you are an absolute talent!

I can't go any further without thanking my family. Armando, Alicia, and Adrián, I love you. Thank you for leaving me alone so I could work. I'm only partially joking. Thank you for believing in me and always cheering me on. And for only slightly cringing when you see my social media posts. I'd like to take a moment to offer my highest praise to Joseph Montoya and Steven Montoya. I didn't mention my brothers by name last time I wrote acknowledgments, and they both cried because of it. But seriously, I am forever proud of my big brothers and all they have accomplished in life. My sisters, Tara, Kelsey, and Sophia, are pretty awesome too, though, if I'm honest. And so are all of their significant others. As well as my four nieces and two nephews. To the rest of my family, the Montoyas, De Leons, Sevillas, y los Millers, thank you for being some of the very best humans on the planet.

I've got to say thank you to my girl Melanie Schmubert, who

not only gave me the idea to write about a vampire boy who really sucked at being a vampire but also forced me to write the story by battling me in a "draft race." I won, by the way, but I have a feeling that was her plan all along. Thanks for making this roller coaster fun and therapeutic. Thank you for joining me every week on our podcast and reminding me there is still magic in this world.

Speaking of the podcast, I'd like to offer a special shout-out to all the listeners of *Of the Publishing Persuasion*. You are the best and have great taste in podcasts. To the friends in the Pub Persuasion group chat, thanks for helping me come up with titles for this book! You are all so creative.

Thank you to all my friends who read *A Cruel Thirst* when it was messy and made no sense. Thank you for humoring me and helping me scratch through the dirt to find gold, Megan LaCroix, Marlee Bonnette, Jenny Marie, Sandra Proudman, Marve Michael Anson, Melanie Schubert, Kelsie Gonzalez, Megan Curtis, Rachel Lesiw, Alyssia Vasquez, Alexis Maragni, Syd Burciaga, Mevia Mastropietro, Kim Chance, Jackie Morera, Tara Miller, Louise Rowe, Monique Marsten, Aleera Anaya Ceres, Kate Martin, Dahlia De La Vega, and Carolina Gómez. Fun fact: Carolina Gómez was such a champion of *Sinner's Isle* that she inspired the main character's name. If there is anyone I missed who read for me, please know it is because your critiques were so amazing that I'm still stunned by them and have no words.

Much love to Jessica Parra, Courtney Kae, Davona Mapp, Inés Lozano, Kate Martin, Katya de Becerra, and Jill Tew for always screaming for me in the DMs. Thanks to my idols, J. Elle, Rebecca Ross, Zoraida Córdova, Amparo Ortiz, and Isabel Ibañez.

You inspire me every day. To Margie Fuston, I'm sure you know how much I worship you. Gabriel Torres, I hope the entire world listens to your amazing podcast, *Try Reading*.

Thanks to Las Musas for always boosting and supporting. Thank you to Latinx Kidlit Book Festival for sharing so many amazing stories. To the Latine BookTokers, Booktubers, Instagrammers, and bookish influencers, I see you and I appreciate you. Keep fighting the good fight. And to every author who has reached out to me just to offer encouragement or exchange memes, thank you.

Lastly (but only because I was avoiding this part because I didn't want to cry), I want to thank anyone who has read *Sinner's Isle* and/or *A Cruel Thirst*. I know time is a valuable commodity, and I do not take that lightly. For you to take any bit of your day to read my words is an absolute honor.

If you have ever DM'd or emailed me with your kind words or excitement about my books, THANK YOU. Your support means the world to me. You have made me feel like I've found my calling. You have made me feel like I found my "why."

Thank you.

ABOUT THE AUTHOR

ANGELA MONTOYA HAS BEEN OBSESSED WITH THE MAGIC OF storytelling since she was a little girl. She hasn't seen a day without a book in her hand, a show tune in her mind, or a movie quote on her lips. Her debut novel, *Sinner's Isle*, received starred reviews from *Kirkus* and *Publishers Weekly*. When she isn't lost in the world of words, Angela can be found hiding away on her small farm in Northern California, where she's busy bossing around her partner and their two children, as well as a whole host of animals.

angelamontoyawrites.com

THE JOURNEY STARTS HERE

As a Young Adult and New Adult imprint, Ink Road is passionate about publishing fiction with a contemporary and forward-looking focus. We love working with authors who share our commitment to bold and brilliant stories – and we're always on the lookout for fresh new voices and the readers who enjoy them.

@inkroadbooks